D0466698

CHILDREN'S CLASSICS
EVERYMAN'S LIBRARY

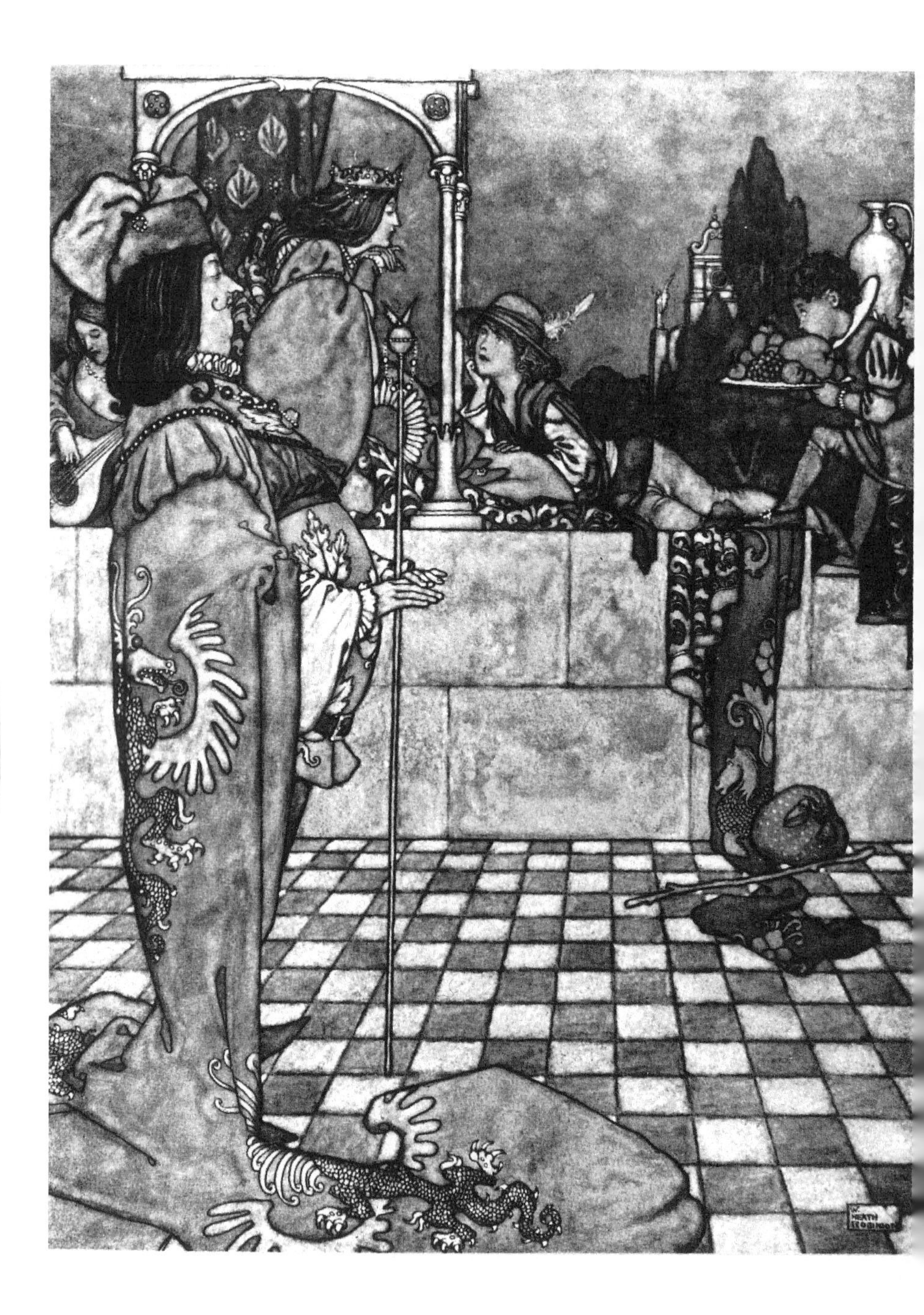

Hans Christian Andersen

Fairy Tales

Translated by
Reginald Spink
With Illustrations
by W. Heath Robinson

EVERYMAN'S LIBRARY
CHILDREN'S CLASSICS
Alfred A. Knopf New York London Toronto

THIS IS A BORZOI BOOK
PUBLISHED BY ALFRED A. KNOPF

First included in Everyman's Library 1906
This translation first published in Everyman's Library 1960
and first included in Everyman's Children's Classics 1992

Book design by Barbara de Wilde, Carol Devine Carson
and Peter B. Willberg

Fourteenth printing (US)

Five of Ernest H. Shepard's illustrations from *Dream Days* by
Kenneth Grahame are reprinted on the endpapers by permission
of The Bodley Head, London. The sixth illustration is by S. C. Hulme Beaman.

 Published in the United States by Alfred A. Knopf, a division of
Random House, Inc., New York, and in Canada by Random House of Canada Limited,
Toronto. Distributed by Random House, Inc., New York. Published in the United
Kingdom by Everyman's Library, Northburgh House, 10 Northburgh Street,
London EC1V 0AT, and distributed by Random House (UK) Ltd.

US website: www.randomhouse.com/everymans

ISBN 978-0-679-41791-0 (US)
978-1-85715-901-1 (UK)

A CIP catalogue record for this book is available from the British Library

Library of Congress Cataloging-in-Publication Data
Andersen, H. C. (Hans Christian), 1805–1875.
[Tales. English Selections]
Fairy tales / Hans Christian Andersen.
p. cm.—(Everyman's library children's classics)
Translated from the Danish.
Summary: Presents a collection of Andersen's fairy tales.
ISBN 978-0-679-41791-0
1. Fairy tales—Denmark. 2. Children's stories. Danish—Translations into English.
[1. Fairy tales]. I. Title. II. Series.
PZ8.2. A54 1992 92-53178
[Fic]—dc20 CIP
AC

Printed and bound in Germany by GGP Media GmbH, Pössneck

CONTENTS

THE TINDER-BOX

A SOLDIER was marching along the high road: Left, right! Left, right! He had his knapsack on his back and a sword at his side, for he had been to the wars and was going home. And on the way he met an old witch. Oh, she was horrid: her bottom lip came right down to her chest.

'Hello, soldier!' she said. 'What a nice sword you've got, and what a big knapsack! You're a *proper* soldier! Now you shall have all the money you want!'

'Thank you, you old witch!' said the soldier.

'Do you see that big tree?' said the witch, pointing to a tree which grew by the roadside. 'It's quite hollow inside. Climb to the top of it and you'll see a hole; and if you slip through that, it'll take you right down into the tree. I'll tie a rope round your waist, and then I can pull you up again when you give me a shout.'

'What am I to do inside the tree?' asked the soldier.

'Get money!' said the witch. 'Now listen to me. When you come to the bottom of the tree you'll find yourself in a big passage. It will be perfectly light, as there are over a hundred lamps burning there. Then you'll see three doors, which you'll be able to open as the keys are in the locks. Now, if you go into the first room, you'll see, in the middle of the floor, a big chest and, sitting on top of it, a dog. He's got eyes as big as breakfast cups! But never mind that! I'll give you my blue-checked apron, which you can spread out on the floor. Then walk quickly up to the dog, put him on my apron, open the chest, and help yourself to as much money as you like. It will all be copper. If you'd rather have silver, you'll have to go into the next room. There sits a dog with eyes as big as mill-wheels! But never mind that! Put him on my apron, and help yourself to the money. And if you want gold, you can have that as well—as much as you can carry—if you go into the third room. But the dog that sits on the money-chest in there has eyes as big as the Round Tower in Copenhagen. There's a proper dog for you! But never mind that! Just put him on my apron, and he won't harm you. Then help yourself to as much gold as you like.'

'This doesn't sound so bad!' said the soldier. 'But what do you want from me, you old witch? Because you'll be wanting something, I expect!'

'No,' said the witch, 'I won't take a ha'penny. All you have to do is to bring me an old tinder-box that my grandmother forgot the last time she was down there.'

'All right, then! Put the rope round my waist,' said the soldier.

'Here it is,' said the witch. 'And here's my blue-checked apron.'

And so the soldier climbed up the tree, dropped down through the hole, and found himself, exactly as the witch had said, in the great passage where hundreds of lamps were burning.

Then he opened the first door. Ugh! There sat the dog with eyes as big as breakfast cups, glaring away at him.

'You're a fine fellow!' said the soldier, putting him on the witch's apron and helping himself to as many coppers as his pocket would hold. Then, shutting the chest, he put the dog back again and went into the second room. Dear me, there sat the dog with eyes as big as mill-wheels!

'You shouldn't stare at me so,' said the soldier; 'you might strain your eyes!' And with that he put the dog on the witch's apron. But when he saw all the silver money in the chest, he threw away his coppers and filled his pocket and his knapsack full of silver. Then he went into the third room. Really though, it was horrid! The dog in there actually did have eyes as big as the Round Tower, and they were going round and round in its head like wheels!

'Good evening!' said the soldier, touching his cap, for he'd never seen a dog like this before. Still, after looking at him for a bit, he thought: 'That will do!' and, lifting him down on the floor, he opened the chest. Goodness gracious, what a lot of gold there was! He could buy all Copenhagen with it, along with the cake-woman's sugar-pigs and all the tin soldiers and whips and rocking-horses in the world! Yes, it was a lot of money! So the soldier threw away all the silver money he had filled his pockets and his knapsack with and helped himself to gold instead; in fact, he filled his pockets, his knapsack, his cap, and his boots so full that he could scarcely walk. Now he did have some money. Putting the dog back on the chest, he shut the door and called up through the tree: 'Pull me up again, old witch!'

'Have you got the tinder-box?' asked the witch.

'Why, no!' said the soldier; 'I'd clean forgotten that!' And he went back and got it. The witch pulled him up, and back he was on the road again, with his pockets, boots, cap, and knapsack full of money. 'What do you want with this tinder-box?' said the soldier.

'That's nothing to do with you!' said the witch. 'You've got your money! Now give me my tinder-box.'

'Fiddle-faddle!' said the soldier. 'Tell me straight away what you want it for—or I'll draw my sword and cut your head off!'

'Shan't!' cried the witch.

So the soldier cut her head off. So much for her! Then he bundled his money up in her apron, slung it over his shoulder, put the tinder-box in his pocket, and made for the town.

It was a grand town, and he put up at the grandest inn, where he ordered the best rooms and all his favourite dishes—for now he was a rich man, with all that money.

The servant who cleaned his boots thought, to be sure, that they were funny old boots for a rich gentleman like this to be wearing, but then he hadn't bought any new ones yet. The next day he got himself boots and clothes that were really smart. Now the soldier had become a fine gentleman, and they told him of all the sights to be seen in their town, and about their king, and what a pretty princess his daughter was.

'Where is she to be seen?' asked the soldier.

'She isn't to be seen,' they all said. 'She lives in a big copper castle with lots of walls and towers round it. Nobody but the king is allowed to go in, because it's been foretold that she will marry a common soldier, and the king doesn't like that.'

'I'd love to see her!' thought the soldier. But of course he wasn't allowed to.

From now on he lived a gay life: going to the theatre, driving in the park, and giving away lots of money to the poor. Now, this was very good of him, but then, you see, he remembered how hard it was to be penniless. He was rich and well-dressed now and he had lots of friends, who all said he was a fine fellow and a perfect gentleman—and the soldier loved hearing that! But as he was spending money every day and never getting any again, he found himself in the end with only two ha'pennies left. And so he had to move out of the grand rooms he had been living in and go into a tiny little attic under the roof, where he had to clean his own boots and do his own mending with a darning-needle. And none of his friends came to see him, because there were so many stairs to climb.

Now, one evening, when it was quite dark and he couldn't

even buy himself a candle, he suddenly remembercd that there was a candle-end in the tinder-box he had fetched from the hollow tree that the witch had helped him up into. He got out the tinder-box and the bit of candle; but the moment he struck a light, and the sparks flew from the flint, the door sprang open and there before him stood the dog with eyes as big as breakfast cups that he had seen underneath the tree, and said: 'What are my lord's commands?'

'Why, whatever's this?' cried the soldier. 'It's a funny sort of tinder-box, if I can get what I like with it! Bring me some money,' he said to the dog. And whip, it was gone, and whip, it was back again with a big bagful of coppers in its mouth.

Now the soldier knew what a fine tinder-box it was. If he struck once, the dog that sat on the chest of coppers appeared; if he struck twice, the one that had the silver money; and if he struck three times, the one with the gold. So the soldier changed back into the grand rooms and the handsome clothes; and all his friends knew him at once and were very, very fond of him.

Now, one day he thought to himself: 'This is a funny idea, nobody being allowed to see the princess. She's supposed to be so lovely—they all say so! But what's the good of that, when all the time she's kept shut up inside that copper castle with all those towers? Is there no way of getting to see her? Where's my tinder-box?' And he struck a light, and whip, there stood the dog with eyes as big as breakfast cups.

'I know very well it's the middle of the night,' said the soldier, 'but I should so love to see the princess—just for a minute!'

The dog was out of the door at once, and before the soldier had time to think was back again with the princess. There she sat, fast asleep on the dog's back, and she was so lovely it was plain to see she was a real princess. The soldier just couldn't help it, he had to kiss her—he was a proper soldier.

Then the dog ran back again with the princess. But in the morning, when the king and queen were having their breakfast, the princess said she had had such a curious dream in the night, all about a dog and a soldier. She had been riding on the dog's back, and the soldier had kissed her.

'That's a pretty tale, I must say!' said the queen.

And so one of the ladies-in-waiting had to sit up by the princess's bedside the next night to see if it was really a dream or not.

The soldier wanted ever so much to see the lovely princess again; and so along came the dog in the night and took her and ran off with her as fast as his legs would carry him. But the old lady-in-waiting put her waders on and ran just as fast after them; and seeing them disappear into a big house, she thought: 'Now I know where it is!'—and she chalked a big cross on the gate. Then she went home to bed, and the dog came running back with the princess. But seeing a cross chalked on the gate where the soldier lived, he took a piece of chalk himself and made a cross on every gate in the town. This was clever of him, because now, of course, the lady-in-waiting couldn't find the right gate, when there were crosses on all of them.

Early the next morning the king and queen, the old lady-in-waiting, and all the Court officials went to see where it was the princess had been.

'There it is!' cried the king, catching sight of the first door with a cross on it.

'No, it's there, my love!' said the queen, seeing another door with a cross on it.

'Oh, but there's one; and there's one!' they all cried.

Whichever way they looked, there were crosses on the gates. So it was plain to see that it was no use looking any further.

But the queen, you know, was a very clever woman, who could do more than ride about in a coach. She took her big golden scissors, cut up a large piece of silk, and made a nice little bag out of it. Filling this with the finest buckwheat grain, she fastened it on to the princess's back, and then she snipped a little hole in the bag, so that the grain would trickle out and leave a trail wherever the princess went.

That night along came the dog again, and putting the princess on his back, ran off with her to the soldier, who loved her so much and wished he were a prince so he could marry her.

The dog never noticed the grain trickling out all the way from the castle to the soldier's window, where he ran up the wall with the princess. And so in the morning it was perfectly plain to the king and queen where their daughter had been going; and they took the soldier and clapped him in jail.

There he sat. Ugh, how dark and dreary it was! And they said to him: 'Tomorrow you're to be hanged!' This was no joke—and what's more, he'd left his tinder-box at his lodgings. In the morning, between the iron bars of his little window, he could see people hurrying out of town to see him hanged. He heard the sound of drums and he saw marching soldiers. Everybody was running. Among the crowd was a cobbler's boy in leather apron and slippers; and he scampered along so fast that one of his slippers flew off, landing up by the wall where the soldier sat, looking out between the iron bars.

'Hi, cobbler boy!' cried the soldier. 'There's no need to be in such a hurry! There'll be nothing doing till I get there! But look here: if you run round to my lodgings and get me my tinder-box, I'll give you something for yourself! But you'd better make haste!' The cobbler's boy was glad of a copper or two; so off he dashed for the tinder-box and gave it to the soldier, and—well now, we're coming to that!

Outside the town a big gallows had been put up, and round it stood soldiers and hundreds of thousands of people. The king and queen sat on a beautiful throne opposite the judges and the whole Council.

The soldier was already at the top of the ladder; but they were just going to put the rope round his neck when he said that a criminal before punishment was always granted some harmless wish. He would love to smoke a pipe of tobacco; after all, it would be the last he would get here on earth.

Now, the king didn't want to say 'No' to this; and so the soldier took his tinder-box and struck it once, twice, three times! And there stood all the dogs: the one with eyes as big as breakfast cups, the one with eyes like mill-wheels, and the one with eyes as large as the Round Tower.

'Now save me from being hanged!' cried the soldier. And the dogs flew at the judges and all the councillors, and seizing some by the leg and others by the nose, tossed them high up into the air, so they all fell down and were dashed to pieces.

'I'm not going!' cried the king. But the biggest dog seized both him and the queen and tossed them after all the others. At this the soldiers got frightened, and the people all shouted: 'Good soldier, you shall be our king, and marry the lovely princess!'

So they put the soldier in the king's coach; and all three dogs went dancing along in front shouting 'Hurrah!' and the boys whistled through their fingers and the soldiers presented arms. The princess came out of the copper castle and was made queen, and that was just what she liked! The wedding feast lasted a week, and the dogs sat at table with the rest and were all eyes.

LITTLE CLAUS AND BIG CLAUS

THERE lived in one village two men who both had the selfsame name: both were called Claus. But one owned four horses and the other had only one; and so, to tell them from each other, they called the man who had four horses Big Claus and the man who had only one horse Little Claus. Well now, let's hear how they both got on; for this is a proper story.

All through the week Little Claus had to plough for Big Claus and lend him his only horse; and in return Big Claus helped him with all four of his, but only once a week and that on Sundays. Hurrah! How Little Claus used to crack his whip over all five horses! For, you see, they were as good as his on that one day. The sun would be shining beautifully, and all the bells in the church tower would ring for church. People would pass by in their Sunday best with their hymn-books under their arms, going to hear the vicar preach; and they would look at Little Claus ploughing with five horses, and he'd be so delighted that he'd crack away with his whip and cry: 'Gee-up, all my horses!'

'You're not to say that,' said Big Claus. 'Only one of the horses is yours!'

But when anybody again went by on the way to church, Little Claus would forget that he wasn't to say this, and would cry out: 'Gee-up, all my horses!'

'Now will you please stop it!' said Big Claus. 'If you say it again, I'll whack your horse over the forehead and kill him on the spot; and that'll be the end of him.'

'I promise not to say it again!' said Little Claus.

But when people went by and nodded 'Good day!' he would be so delighted, thinking how grand it must look having five horses to plough his field, that he would crack his whip and cry out: 'Gee-up, all my horses!'

'I'll gee-up your horses!' said Big Claus; and he took a mallet and hit Little Claus's only horse on the forehead, so that it fell down quite dead.

'Oh dear! Now I haven't got a horse left' said Little Claus; and he started to cry. Later, he skinned the horse and left the hide to get well dried in the wind; then putting it into a bag which he slung over his shoulder, he set off to sell his horse-hide in the town.

He had such a long way to go, and it took him through a big, dark wood; and all at once a dreadful storm came on. He quite lost his way, and before he could find it again it was evening, and much too far to get to the town or back home before night-fall.

Standing by the roadside was a large farmhouse; the shutters had been put up outside but the light was shining through at the top. 'I expect they'll put me up for the night,' thought Little Claus; and he went and knocked at the door.

The farmer's wife opened it; but, on hearing what he wanted, she told him to be off: her husband wasn't at home and she didn't take in strangers.

'In that case I shall have to sleep outside,' said Little Claus; and the farmer's wife shut the door on him.

Nearby stood a big haystack, and between this and the house a small shed had been built, with a flat thatched roof.

'I can sleep up there!' said Little Claus, catching sight of the roof. 'It should make a lovely bed; and I don't suppose the stork'll fly down and peck at my legs.' (For standing on the roof was a real live stork, which had its nest there.)

And so Little Claus climbed up on the shed, where he snuggled down and made himself nice and comfortable. The shutters of the windows didn't fit properly at the top, and so he could see right into the room.

A big table was set out with wine and roast meat and a most delicious fish. Sitting at the table were the farmer's wife and the parish clerk, all by themselves; and she was filling up his glass, while he was digging into the fish, for he was very fond of it.

'I could just do with some of that!' said Little Claus, craning his neck in the direction of the window. My word, what a lovely cake he could see in there. This was a feast, if you like!

All at once he heard somebody riding along the road towards the house; it was the woman's husband, coming home.

He was such a very good husband, only he had one failing: he couldn't bear the sight of parish clerks. If a parish clerk showed his face he used to get quite furious. That was why the clerk had called on the woman when he knew that her husband was away, and why the good wife had put before him all her nicest food. Now, when they heard the husband coming they got very, very frightened, and the woman told the parish clerk to get into a big empty chest which stood in the corner. And so he did, knowing very well that the poor husband couldn't stand the sight of parish clerks. The woman quickly hid away all the delicious food and wine in her oven; for if her husband had seen them he would have been sure to ask what it was all about.

'Oh dear!' sighed Little Claus, on top of the shed, seeing all the food disappear.

'Is there somebody there?' asked the farmer, looking up at Little Claus. 'What are you up there for? Come along into the house!'

Little Claus then told him how he had lost his way, and asked if he might stay the night.

'Why, of course,' said the farmer. 'But first let's have a bite of supper!'

The woman welcomed them both very warmly, and. laying a long table, served a large bowl of porridge for them. The farmer was hungry and ate heartily; but Little Claus couldn't take his mind off the lovely roast, fish, and cake he knew to be inside the oven.

Under the table, at his feet, he had put the sack containing his horse's hide; for, as we know, he had left home with that, meaning to sell it in town. He just couldn't fancy the porridge; and so he trod on his bag, and the dry hide inside gave out a rather loud squeak.

'Sh!' said Little Claus to his sack, treading on it again as he did so and making it squeak much louder than before. 'Why, what's that you've got in your bag?' asked the farmer.

'Oh, that's a magician!' said Little Claus. 'He says that we shouldn't eat porridge; he's conjured the whole oven full of roast meat and fish and cake.'

'What!' said the farmer; and opening the oven in a twinkling, he saw all the delicious food which his wife had hidden, but which he thought that the magician in the bag had conjured up for them. His wife daren't say anything, but put the food straight on the table, and they helped themselves to the fish, the roast, and the cake. Presently, Little Claus again trod on his bag, making the hide squeak.

'What's he say now?' asked the farmer.

'He says,' replied Little Claus, 'that he's conjured up three bottles of wine for us as well; they're in the oven, too.' So now the woman had to bring out the wine she had hidden; and the farmer drank and was soon merry. A magician like the one in

Little Claus's bag was just what he could do with, he said.

'Can he conjure up the Devil as well?' he asked. 'I'd love to have a look at him, while I'm in merry mood!'

'Why, yes,' said Little Claus, 'my magician can do anything I care to ask him. Can't you, old fellow?' he asked, treading on the bag and making it squeak. 'Did you hear him say Yes? But the Devil's so ugly to look at; it wouldn't do to see him.'

'Oh, I'm not afraid! I wonder what he really looks like?'

'Why, he'll be the very image of a parish clerk!'

'Ugh!' said the farmer. 'How ugly! You know, I can't bear the sight of parish clerks! However, I shall know it's the Devil, and so I dare say I can face it. I feel brave now. Only don't let him come too near me!'

'I'll ask my magician, then,' said Little Claus, treading on the bag and putting his ear to it.

'What's he say?'

'He says you can go and open that chest in the corner there, and you'll see the Devil crouching inside it. But you must hold on to the lid, so he doesn't slip out.'

'Will you help me to hold on to it?' said the farmer, going over to the chest in which his wife had hidden the real parish clerk, who sat there in a fright.

Raising the lid a little, the farmer looked inside. 'Ugh!' he shrieked, jumping back. 'Well, now I've seen him, and he looked exactly like our parish clerk. I say, how awful!'

They had to have a drink after that; and they went on drinking till well into the night.

'You must sell me that magician,' said the farmer. 'Ask what you like for him. Why, I'll give you a whole bushel of money straight away!'

'No, I can't do that.' said Little Claus. 'Think what a lot of good that magician can do me!'

'Oh, but I'd give anything to have him!' said the farmer, pleading with him.

'Well then,' said Little Claus in the end; 'as you've been good enough to give me a night's lodging, we won't argue. The magician's yours for a bushel of money, but I shall want full measure.'

'You shall have it,' said the farmer. 'But see you take that chest away with you, because I won't have it in the house an hour longer. Who's to know that he isn't still inside!'

Little Claus gave the farmer his sack with the dry hide inside it, and was given a whole bushel of money, full measure, in exchange. The farmer even made him a present of a large wheelbarrow to wheel the money and the chest away in.

'Goodbye!' said Little Claus; and off he went with his money and the big chest with the parish clerk still inside.

On the other side of the wood there was a deep river, which flowed so fast that you could hardly swim up it. A big new bridge had been built across it; and, stopping in the middle of it, Little Claus said, in a rather loud voice for the parish clerk inside to hear it:

'Now, what am I to do with this silly old chest? It's so heavy, you'd think it was full of stones! I'm sick to death of wheeling it. I think I'll pitch it into the river. If it comes floating home to me, all well and good; and if it doesn't, then it's all the same to me.'

And so, taking hold of the chest with one hand, he lifted it up a bit as if about to drop it into the water.

'No, stop!' cried the parish clerk from inside the chest. 'Let me get out!'

'Ugh!' said Little Claus, pretending to be frightened. 'He's still inside. I'd better drop it straight in the river and drown him!'

'Oh no! Oh no!' cried the parish clerk. 'I'll give you a whole bushel of money if you don't!'

'Ah, that's another story!' said Little Claus, opening the chest. The parish clerk scrambled out, and, pushing the empty chest into the water, went home and gave Little Claus a whole bushel of money. As he'd already been given one by the farmer, he now had his wheelbarrow quite full of money.

'It seems that I got a pretty good price for that horse,' he said to himself, when he got home to his own house and tipped all the money out in a big heap in the middle of the floor. 'Big Claus will be annoyed when he finds out how rich I've grown out of my one horse! But I'm not going to tell him so.'

Presently, he sent a boy to Big Claus's to borrow a bushel measure.

'I wonder what he wants that for?' thought Big Claus. And he smeared some tar on the bottom, so that a little of whatever was measured would stick to it. And sure enough that's just what happened; for, when he got the measure back, there were three new silver florins sticking to it.

'What's this?' said Big Claus; and running straight over to Little Claus, he asked: 'Where did you get all this money from?'

'Oh, I got that for my horse's hide. I sold it last night.'

'A pretty good price, too!' said Big Claus; and running home he took an axe, hit all four of his horses over the forehead and skinned them, and then drove to town with the hides.

'Hides! Hides! Who'll buy my hides?' he went shouting through the streets.

All the cobblers and tanners came running out to ask what he wanted for them.

'A bushel of money apiece!' said Big Claus.

'Are you mad?' they all said. 'Do you think we have money by the bushel?'

'Hides! Hides! Who'll buy my hides ?' he shouted again. But to everyone who asked him the price of the hides he replied: 'A bushel of money.'

'He's trying to make fools of us,' they all said; and so the cobblers took their straps and the tanners their leather aprons and began to beat Big Claus.

'Hides! Hides!' they jeered at him. 'We'll tan your hide for you! Out of the town with him!' they cried. And Big Claus had to run for his life; he'd never had such a beating.

'Right!' he said, when he got home. 'Little Claus shall pay for this; I'll knock the life out of him!'

Now, over at Little Claus's his old grandmother had died. It's true she'd been very peevish and cross with him, but he was rather sorry; and so he took the dead woman and laid her in his warm bed to see if that would revive her. He thought he would leave her there all night, while he would sleep sitting in a chair in the corner, as he had done before.

He was sitting there during the night when the door opened, and in came Big Claus with his axe. He knew where Little Claus's bed was, and, making straight for it, he hit the dead old grandmother on the forehead, thinking it was Little Claus.

'Take that!' he said. 'You won't come fooling me any more!' And off he went home again.

'What a naughty, wicked man!' said Little Claus. 'He really meant to kill me. It's as well for old Granny she was dead already, or he'd have knocked the life out of her!'

He then dressed his old grandmother in her Sunday best, and, borrowing a horse from a neighbour, he harnessed it to the cart and propped his old grandmother up in the back seat so she wouldn't fall out when he got up speed; and off they started through the woods. By sunrise they had come to a large inn, and here Little Claus stopped and went inside to get something to eat.

The innkeeper had lots and lots of money, and besides was a very nice man, though hot-tempered, as if there'd been pepper and snuff in him.

'Good morning!' he said to Little Claus. 'You've got your Sunday best on in good time today.'

'Yes,' said Little Claus, 'I'm going to town with my old grandmother. She's sitting outside in the cart, and I can't get her to come in. Would you take her a glass of mead? Only you'll have to speak up, as she's hard of hearing.'

'Why, yes!' said the innkeeper; and pouring out a large glass of mead, he took it out to the dead old grandmother, who sat there propped up in the cart.

'Here's a glass of mead from your son, ma'am,' said the innkeeper. But the dead woman said never a word, and never moved.

'Don't you hear?' shouted the innkeeper at the top of his voice. 'Here's a glass of mead from your son!

He shouted the same again, and yet again; but when she never budged, he lost his temper and threw the glass straight in her face, so the mead ran down her nose and she fell backwards out of the cart, for she had only been propped up instead of being tied fast.

'There now!' cried Little Claus, springing out of the door and seizing the innkeeper by the throat. 'You've gone and killed my grandmother! Just look at this big gash in her forehead!'

'Oh, what an accident!' cried the innkeeper, wringing his hands. 'It all comes of my hot temper! Good Little Claus, I'll give you a whole bushel of money and have your grandmother buried as though she were my own, if only you won't tell; because if you do, they'll cut my head off, and that's so awful!'

And so Little Claus got a whole bushel of money, and the innkeeper buried the old grandmother as if she had been his.

Now, when Little Claus got home again with all his money, he sent his boy straight over to Big Claus to ask if he could borrow a bushel measure.

'What's this?' said Big Claus. 'Didn't I kill him? I'll have to look into this.' And so he went over to Little Claus with the measure.

'Why, where did you get all that money from?' he said, opening his eyes wide at the sight of all this fresh money.

'It was my grandmother and not me you killed!' said Little Claus. 'And now I've sold her for a bushel of money.'

'A pretty good price you got, too!' said Big Claus; and, hurrying off home, he took an axe and straight away killed his old grandmother. Then putting her in the cart, he drove into town to the chemist's and asked if he would buy a dead body.

'Whose is it, and where did you get it?' asked the chemist.

'It's my grandmother,' said Big Claus. 'I've killed her for a bushel of money!'

'Good gracious!' said the chemist. 'You've taken leave of your senses! Don't come saying things like that, or you may lose your head!' And he told him straight out what a dreadfully wicked thing he had done and what a bad man he was, and that he ought to be punished. At this Big Claus got so frightened that he jumped straight out of the chemist's shop into the cart, whipped up his horses, and made for home, the chemist and everybody else thinking him mad and letting him drive off where he wanted.

'You'll pay for this!' said Big Claus, once he was out on the road. 'Yes, you'll pay for this, Little Claus!' And so as soon as he got home he took the biggest sack he could find, went across to Little Claus, and said: 'Now you've fooled me again! First I killed my horses, and then my old grandmother. It's all your fault, but you'll never fool me any more!' And seizing

Little Claus round the waist, he put him into his sack and threw him over his shoulder, shouting: 'I'm going off to drown you now!'

He had a long way to go before reaching the river, and Little Claus wasn't so easy to carry. The road passed by the church, and the organ was playing and people were singing away beautifully inside. So Big Claus put down the sack with Little Claus in it at the church door, thinking it would be rather nice to go inside and hear a hymn before going on his way; Little Claus wouldn't be able to get out, and everybody else was in church. So in he went.

'Oh dear! Oh dear!' sighed Little Claus, inside the sack. And he twisted and he turned, but all to no use, for he couldn't undo the cord. Just then along came an old cattle drover with snow-white hair and a big stick in his hand. He was driving a herd of cows and bullocks, and they stumbled against the sack with Little Claus inside and knocked it over.

'Oh dear!' sighed Little Claus. 'I'm so young, and going to heaven already!'

'And I, poor fellow,' said the cattle drover; 'I'm so old and can't get there yet.'

'Open the sack!' cried Little Claus. 'Get in in place of me, and you'll go to heaven straight away.'

'I'll be only too delighted to!' said the drover, undoing the sack for Little Claus, who at once sprang out.

'Will you look after the cattle?' said the old man, getting into the bag. And tying it up, Little Claus went off on his way with all the cows and the bullocks.

Soon Big Claus came out of church and threw the sack over his shoulder again, thinking as he did so how very light it had grown, the old drover being no more than half the weight of Little Claus. 'Why, hasn't he grown light! I dare say it's the hymn I've been listening to.' And going off to the river, which was deep and wide, he threw the sack with the old drover inside it into the water, as he shouted after him (thinking, of course, that it was Little Claus): 'Take that! You'll not fool me any more!'

He then turned for home; but on coming to the cross-roads, whom should he meet but Little Claus, driving off with all his cattle.

'What's this?' said Big Claus. 'Didn't I drown you?'

'Why, yes!' said Little Claus. 'You threw me into the river, nearly half an hour ago.'

'Then where have you got all those fine cattle from?' asked Big Claus.

'It's sea-cattle!' said Little Claus. 'I'll tell you the whole story; and thank you, by the way, for drowning me. I'm getting along swimmingly now, and believe me, I'm really rich. Oh, but I was frightened when I lay inside the sack; and how the wind whistled in my ears when you threw me down from the bridge into the cold water! I sank straight to the bottom; only I didn't hurt myself, because down there grows the loveliest soft grass. I fell on that, and the bag was opened straight away and the loveliest girl in a snow-white dress with a green garland round her wet hair took me by the hand and said: "Is that you, Little Claus? First of all, there's some cattle for you! A mile farther up the road there's another drove which I'll give to you!" I saw then that the river was a big road for the sea-people. At the bottom, they walked and drove straight from the sea and right up into the country where the river ends. It was lovely there, all flowers and the freshest of green grass; and fishes swimming in the water went darting past my ears just like birds in the air above. What nice people there were, and the cattle there were walking about on the dikes and the ditches!'

'But whatever made you come up here again?' asked Big Claus. 'I wouldn't have, when it was so nice down there.'

'Ah!' said Little Claus. 'Now, that's where I'm cunning. You heard me tell you how the sea-maiden said that a mile farther up the road—and of course by "road" she meant "river", because that's the only place she can go—there would be another drove of cattle for me. But I know how the river winds about, first this way and then that: it's a long way round, you know. Well, to anyone who can come up on land it's a short cut to go straight across the bends! In that way I shall save nearly half a mile and get to my sea-cattle in double-quick time.'

'Oh, aren't you a lucky man!' said Big Claus. 'Do you think I'll get some sea-cattle if I go down to the bottom of the river?'

'Why, yes, I should think so,' said Little Claus. 'But I can't carry you to the river in a sack; you're too heavy for me. If you'll walk there and then get into the bag, I'll throw you in with the greatest of pleasure.'

'Thanks very much,' said Big Claus. 'But if I don't get any sea-cattle down at the bottom I'll give you a hiding; just you see if I don't!'

'Oh no, don't be hard on me!' said Little Claus. And so off they went to the river. Being thirsty, the cattle when they saw the water ran down to it as fast as their legs would carry them to get a drink.

'Look what a hurry they're in!' said Little Claus. 'They're longing to get down to the bottom again.'

'Yes, but help me first,' said Big Claus, 'or you'll get a hiding!' And he got into the big sack, which had lain across the back of one of the bullocks. 'Put a stone in, or I'm afraid I shan't sink,' said Big Claus.

'You'll sink!' said Little Claus; but he put a big stone in the sack, and, tying the cord tight, gave it a push. Plomp! There was Big Claus in the river, and he went straight to the bottom.

'I'm afraid he won't find the cattle!' said Little Claus, driving home what he had got.

THE PRINCESS AND THE PEA

ONCE upon a time there was a prince and he wanted to marry a princess, only she had to be a *real* princess. So he went all over the world looking for one. But every time there was something the matter: princesses there were in plenty, but whether they were real princesses or not, he could never really make out, there was always something not quite real about them. So he came home again and was so very sad, because he did so want a real princess.

Now, one night there was a terrible storm. It thundered and lightened and the rain poured down—it was frightful! All at once there was a knock at the city gate, and the old king went out to open it.

There, standing outside, was a princess. But dear me, what a sight she looked, in the wind and the rain. The water was running down her hair and her clothes, and it was running in at the toes of her shoes and out again at the heels. And then she said she was a real princess.

'We'll see about that!' thought the old queen. But she didn't say anything; she went into the bedroom, took off all the bedclothes, and put a pea in the bottom of the bed. Then she took twenty mattresses and put them on top of the pea, and then again twenty feather-beds on top of the mattresses.

That was to be the princess's bed for the night.

In the morning they asked her how she had slept.

'Dreadfully!' said the princess. 'I hardly got a wink of sleep all night. Goodness knows what can have been in the bed!

There was something hard in it, and now I'm just black and blue all over. It's really dreadful!'

So now they were able to see that she was a real princess, because she had felt the pea right through the twenty mattresses and the twenty feather-beds. Only a real princess could be so tender as that.

So the prince took her for his wife, now he knew he had a real princess. And the pea was placed in the museum, where it may still be seen—if nobody has taken it.

There, now that was a real story!

LITTLE IDA'S FLOWERS

'MY POOR flowers are quite dead!' said little Ida. 'They were so pretty last night, and now the petals are all withered! Why?' she asked the student who sat on the sofa. She was really very fond of this student, for he could tell the loveliest of stories and cut out such amusing pictures: hearts with little ladies in them that danced; flowers; and big palaces with doors that you could open. He was a really jolly student! 'Why are the flowers looking so poorly today?' she asked again, showing him a whole bunch that were quite withered.

'Shall I tell you what's wrong with them?' said the student. 'The flowers were at a ball last night, and that's why they are drooping.'

'Oh, but flowers can't dance!' said little Ida.

'Oh yes,' said the student; 'when it grows dark and we are all asleep, they skip around to their hearts' delight. They have a ball nearly every night of the week.'

'Are children ever allowed at their ball?'

'Why, yes,' said the student. 'Baby daisies and lilies of the valley.'

'Where do the nicest flowers dance?' asked little Ida.

'You must often have been out by the gate of the big palace where the king lives in summer, where there's a lovely garden full of flowers. Surely you've seen the swans that come swimming towards you when you go to feed them with breadcrumbs? That's the place for a ball, all right!'

'I was in that garden yesterday, with my mother,' said Ida. 'But all the trees were bare and there wasn't a flower left. Where are they? In the summer I saw so many!'

'They're in the palace,' said the student. 'You know, as soon as the king and all his courtiers move into town, the flowers run straight into the palace from the garden and have a gay time. You should just see them! The two most beautiful roses seat themselves on the throne and are king and queen. The scarlet cockscombs all line up alongside and stand and bow: they are the gentlemen-in-waiting. Then along come all the prettiest flowers and there's a grand ball. The blue violets are little naval cadets and dance with hyacinths and crocuses, calling them young ladies! The tulips and the large yellow lilies are old ladies; they see to it that everyone dances nicely and that everything goes off properly.'

'But,' asked little Ida, 'does nobody ever say anything to the flowers for dancing in the king's palace?'

'Nobody really knows anything about it,' said the student. 'Sometimes during the night the old caretaker who has to look after the palace may come along, carrying his big bunch of keys. But the moment the flowers hear the keys jingle they are perfectly still, hiding behind the curtains and poking their heads out. "I can smell flowers in here!" the old caretaker will say. But he can't see them.'

'How jolly!' cried little Ida, clapping her hands. 'And can't I see the flowers, either?'

'Why, yes,' said the student. 'Next time you go there just remember to look in at the window; then you'll see them. I did today, and there, lying full length on the sofa, was a tall yellow daffodil, pretending to be a lady-in-waiting!'

'Can the flowers in the botanical gardens go there as well? Can they go all that long way?'

'Why, of course!' said the student. 'When they want to they can fly. Surely you've seen those pretty butterflies, the red and yellow and white ones? They look almost like flowers, and in fact that's what they've been. Jumping off their stalks high into the air, they flapped their petals like little wings and flew away. Having got off to a good start, they were allowed to fly about all day too, without having to go home again and sit still on their stalks. And so in the end their petals turned into real wings. Well now, you've seen that yourself! But perhaps the flowers in the botanical gardens have never been to the king's palace, and don't know that it's so gay there at night. I'll tell you something that will surprise the old professor of botany who lives next door; you know him, I'm sure! When you go into his garden, tell one of the flowers that there's a grand ball taking place at the palace. It will pass on the news to all the others and they'll fly off. Then, when the professor goes into his garden, there won't be a single flower there, and he won't be able to make out where they've all gone.'

'But how can the flower tell the others? Flowers can't speak, can they?'

'No, of course they can't!' replied the student. 'But they can make signs. Surely you've seen, when a breeze is blowing, how the flowers nod and move all their green leaves, just as plainly as though they were talking?'

'Can the professor understand sign language?' asked Ida.

'Yes, to be sure he can! Going into his garden one morning, he saw a big stinging-nettle making signs with its leaves to a lovely red carnation. It was saying: "You are so pretty, and I love you so very much!" Well now, the professor doesn't like that sort of thing, and he at once rapped it over the leaves, for those are the nettle's knuckles. But of course he got stung, and from that day he has never dared to touch a stinging-nettle.'

'What fun!' cried little Ida, laughing.

'What nonsense is this to stuff into the child's head?' said the tiresome old councillor, who was on a visit and was sitting on the sofa. He didn't like the student and always used to grumble when he saw him cutting those comical pictures: now a man hanging from a gibbet and holding a heart in his hand, because he was a stealer of hearts; now an old witch riding a broomstick and carrying her husband on her nose. The councillor didn't like it, and so he would say as he said now: 'What nonsense is this to stuff into the child's head? What a lot of silly rubbish!'

But little Ida thought that what the student told her about her flowers was great fun, and she kept on thinking about it. The flowers were drooping because they were tired after dancing all night; they were certainly ill. And so she took them to where all her other playthings were, standing on a nice little table, the drawer of which was full of things. Lying asleep in her cot was her doll, Sophie. But little Ida said to her: 'You'll really have to get up, Sophie, and make do with a bed in the drawer tonight. The poor flowers are ill and will have to lie in your bed. Perhaps then they'll get well!' And with that she picked the doll up; only it looked so grumpy and never said a word, because it was annoyed at having to leave its bed.

Then, putting the flowers in the cot and drawing the little blanket right over them, Ida told them to be nice and quiet and then she would make them some tea, so that they might get better and be up the next day. And she drew the curtains close around the little cot, so the sun wouldn't shine in their eyes.

All that evening she couldn't take her mind off what the student had told her; and when her own bedtime came round, she first had to go behind the curtains which hung in front of the windows where her mother's lovely flowers stood—hyacinths and tulips. And there, very softly, she whispered: 'I know that you're going to a ball tonight!' The flowers behaved as though they didn't understand a thing and never stirred a petal; but little Ida knew differently.

She got into bed and lay there a long while, thinking how nice it would be to see the lovely flowers dance, out there at the king's palace. 'I wonder if my flowers really have been there?' she thought. But then she fell asleep. Late at night she woke up again. She had dreamt about the flowers, and about the student whom the councillor had scolded and said was stuffing her head with nonsense. In the bedroom where Ida lay it was perfectly still. The night-light was burning on the table, and her father and mother were asleep.

'Now, I wonder if my flowers are in Sophie's bed?' she said to herself. 'How I'd just love to know!' Sitting up in bed, she looked towards the door, which was half open. Through there lay all her flowers and toys. She listened; and then all at once she seemed to hear a piano being played in the room, but very softly and more beautifully than she had ever heard before.

'I dare say all the flowers in there are dancing now!' she said. 'I say, but I would love to see it!' Only she didn't dare to get up, as she would have woken her father and mother. 'If only they would come in here,' she said. But the flowers never came. And the music went on playing so beautifully that she just couldn't help herself—it was too lovely for words! Creeping out of her little bed, she went ever so softly to the door and peeped into the sitting-room. And then, my word, what a jolly sight she saw!

There wasn't a night-light in there, and yet it was perfectly light. The moon shone through the window on to the middle of the floor; it might almost have been broad daylight. The tulips and hyacinths all stood in two long rows on the floor; there were no more in the window, only empty pots. Down on the floor the flowers were all dancing very prettily round one another, forming a grand chain and holding one another by their long green leaves as they swung round. Sitting at the piano was a big yellow lily which little Ida was certain she had seen that summer, for she distinctly remembered the student saying: 'Goodness, isn't it like Miss Lena?' Then they had all laughed at him. But now Ida really did think that the yellow flower was like the young lady, and it was behaving in exactly the same way while playing: now laying its oblong yellow face to one side and now to the other, and nodding in time to the lovely music. Nobody took any notice of little Ida. And then all at once she saw a big blue crocus jump right up on to the table where the toys were, and, going straight to the doll's bed, pull aside the curtains. There lay the sick flowers, but they at once got up and nodded to the rest to say that they, too, wanted to join the dance. An old pipe-smoker, whose bottom lip was broken off, stood up and bowed to the pretty flowers. They didn't look a bit ill, but jumped down among the others and were ever so delighted.

All at once there was a sound of something falling off the table, and on looking across Ida saw that her streamer had jumped down; it seemed to think itself one of the flowers. It was a very pretty one too; and at the top there was a little wax doll wearing exactly the same sort of broad-brimmed hat as the councillor. Hopping on its three red wooden legs in among the flowers, the streamer stamped about rather heavily, dancing a mazurka. This was a dance which the flowers couldn't do, because they were so very light and weren't able to stamp.

And then all at once the wax doll grew big and long; and, whirling round above the paper ribbons, it cried out in a loud voice: 'What nonsense is this to stuff into the child's head? What a lot of silly rubbish!' And at that moment it was the very image of the councillor in the broad-brimmed hat, and looked just as grey and grumpy. But the paper ribbons beat him about his lanky legs and he shrank and became a tiny little wax doll again. This was such fun to see! Little Ida couldn't help but laugh. The streamer kept on dancing, and the councillor had to dance with it. It wasn't a bit of use trying to make himself big and long, or turning himself into the yellow doll with the big black hat. But then the flowers pleaded for him, especially the ones which had lain in the doll's bed, and so the streamer stopped. Just then there was a rather loud knock from inside the drawer, where Ida's doll, Sophie, lay together with all the other toys. Running to the edge of the table and lying full length on his stomach, the pipe-smoker managed to pull the drawer open a little. And then Sophie got up and looked around full of surprise. 'A ball, I see!' she said. 'And why was I never told?'

'Will you dance with me?' asked the pipe-smoker.

'You're a nice fellow to dance, aren't you?' she said, turning her back on him. And with that she sat down on the drawer, thinking that one of the flowers would surely come and engage her. But none of them did, and so she coughed: 'Ahem! ahem! ahem!' And still nobody came. The pipe-smoker then danced all by himself, and that wasn't so bad.

Now, as none of the flowers seemed to notice her, Sophie dropped from the drawer straight on to the floor, causing quite a stir. All the flowers came crowding round her, asking her if she had hurt herself. And they were all so nice to her, especially the flowers which had lain in her cot. But she hadn't hurt herself a bit. And all Ida's flowers thanked her for the lovely bed, and made such a fuss of her, taking her into the middle of the room where it was moonlight and dancing with her. And all thc other flowers formed a circle round them. Now Sophie was delighted, and she told them they might keep her bed. She didn't mind sleeping in the drawer at all, she said.

But the flowers said: 'Thank you very much, but we can't live for very long! Tomorrow we shall be quite dead. Only tell little Ida to bury us in the garden where the canary lies; and then we'll grow up again next summer and be prettier than ever.'

'Oh, but you mustn't die!' said Sophie, as she kissed the flowers. At that very moment the door opened and a whole crowd of lovely flowers came dancing into the room. Ida couldn't make out where they had all come from; they must surely have been the flowers from the king's palace. Leading the way were two lovely roses, wearing little gold crowns; they were a king and a queen. Then came the prettiest of stocks and pinks, bowing all around them. They brought music with them. Big poppies and peonies were blowing pea-pods till they made themselves red in the face. Bluebells and little white snowdrops were tinkling as if they had real bells on. It was the gayest of music. And then came many other flowers, all of them dancing: blue violets and red daisies, mayweeds, and lilies of the valley. And all the flowers kissed one another in a way that was delightful to see!

At last the flowers wished each other good-night, and then little Ida, too, crept back to bed, where she dreamt of all that she had seen.

When she got up next morning she went straight over to the little table to see if the flowers were still there. She drew aside the curtain from the little bed, and—why, yes, there they all lay. Only they were quite withered; much more than the day before. Sophie lay in the drawer where she had put her, and looked rather sleepy.

'Can you remember what you had to tell me?' said little Ida. But Sophie looked utterly stupid and said never a word.

'You're a really naughty girl!' said Ida. 'And yet they all danced with you.' Then, taking a small cardboard box on which were drawn some pretty little birds, she opened it and laid the dead flowers inside. 'This shall be your pretty little coffin,' she said. 'And when my Norwegian cousins arrive, they shall help me to bury you in the garden, so that next summer you will be able to grow up and be prettier than ever!'

Her Norwegian cousins were two smart boys called Jonas and Adolph. Their father had given them new bows and arrows, and they had brought them to show to Ida. She told them about the poor flowers that were dead, and then they were allowed to bury them. The two boys walked in front carrying their bows over their shoulders, and little Ida followed with the dead flowers in the pretty box. In the garden they dug a small grave. Kissing the flowers first, Ida laid them in the ground with the box; and Adolph and Jonas shot their arrows over the grave, having neither shot-guns nor cannon to fire.

THUMBELINA

ONCE upon a time there was a woman who dearly wanted a baby child, only she had no idea where she was to get one from. So, going to an old witch, she said to her: 'I'd love to have a baby child! Do tell me where to get one.'

'Why, that's easily arranged,' said the witch. 'Do you see this barleycorn? It's different from the ones that grow in the farmer's field, or that the poultry are fed on. Now, put that in a plant-pot, and see what happens!'

'Thank you!' said the woman. And after giving the witch a shilling, she went home and planted the barleycorn, and soon there grew up a lovely big flower. It looked exactly like a tulip, only the petals were shut up tight, as though it was still in bud.

'There's a pretty flower!' said the woman, and she kissed its beautiful red and yellow petals. But the moment she kissed it it gave a loud pop and opened. It was a real tulip; you could see that. But sitting on the green pistil in the centre of the flower was a tiny girl—such a pretty little thing! She wasn't any bigger than your thumb; and so they called her Thumbelina.

A nicely varnished walnut shell made a cradle for her, blue violet petals were her mattresses, and her counterpane was a rose petal. This was where she slept at night, but during the day she played on the table where the woman had put a plate with a ring of flowers arranged round it, their stalks all sticking into the water. A big tulip petal floated on the top, and on this Thumbelina would go sailing from one side of the plate to the other, rowing with two white horsehairs. It looked really lovely! And, what's more, she could sing—sweeter and more prettily than anyone had ever heard before . . .

She lay in her pretty little bed one night when there came jumping in at the window, through a broken pane, an ugly toad. It was such a horrid toad—big and wet—and it jumped right on to the table where Thumbelina lay fast asleep beneath the red rose petal.

'She'd make my son a lovely wife!' said the toad. And, picking up the walnut shell with Thumbelina asleep inside it, she hopped away through the window and into the garden.

A big, wide stream flowed through the garden. The edge of this was all swampy and muddy, and here lived the toad with her son. Ugh, he too was ugly, just like his mother! 'Ko-ax, ko-ax, brek-ek-ek-ex!' was all he could say when he saw the pretty little girl in the walnut shell.

'Don't talk so loud, or she'll wake up!' said the old toad. 'She'll run away from us yet, she's as light as swan's-down. We'll put her out on the stream, on one of those broad water-lily leaves; light and tiny as she is it'll make an island for her. She won't be able to run away from there, and meanwhile we'll get ready the front room under the mud, where you'll be making your home!'

Growing in the middle of the stream were many water-lilies, with those broad green leaves which seem to float on the water. The leaf farthest out happened also to be the biggest, and swimming out to this the old toad placed the walnut shell with Thumbelina on it, and left her there.

The poor little thing woke up very early the next morning, and seeing where she was she cried her little eyes out. All round the big green leaf there was nothing but water, and to get ashore was quite impossible.

Down below the mud the old toad decorated her room with rushes and yellow water-lily buds, so as to make it really smart for her daughter-in-law, and when she had finished she swam with her horrid son to the leaf where they had left Thumbelina; they had come for her pretty little bed, to set it up in the bridal chamber before she arrived herself. Curtsying low in the water before her, the old toad said: 'Here's my son. He's going to be your husband, and you'll have a lovely home under the mud!'

'Ko-ax, ko-ax! Brek-ek-ek-ex!' was all her son could say.

And then they took the pretty little bed and swam away with it, leaving Thumbelina crying on the green leaf, all by herself. She didn't want to live with the nasty toad, or marry her ugly son. The little fishes that were swimming about in the water must have seen the toad and heard what she said, because they popped up their heads to have a look at the little girl. They thought when they saw her how charming she was, and were very sorry that she had to go below and live with the nasty toad. No, that would never do! And so, crowding round the green stalk that held the leaf on which she stood, they nibbled at it with their teeth, and the leaf floated off downstream, carrying Thumbelina far away, right out of the toad's reach.

Thumbelina went sailing on past all sorts of places, and the little birds sitting in the bushes would sing as they saw her: 'What a dear little child!' Her leaf floated farther and farther away, and so it came about that Thumbelina went abroad.

Fluttering round about her was a lovely little white butterfly, and in the end it settled on her leaf, as it had taken a liking to her. And Thumbelina was so happy, now that she was out of the toad's reach, and it was so lovely where she was sailing; the sun shone down on the water, and it sparkled like gold. Taking her sash, she tied one end to the butterfly and the other to the leaf, and the leaf floated along faster than ever, she standing on it and floating with it.

All of a sudden a big cockchafer flew up and, catching sight of her, at once fastened its claw round her slender waist and flew off with her into a tree, while the green leaf floated away downstream, the butterfly flying with it because, being tied to the leaf, it couldn't get loose.

Oh dear, how frightened Thumbelina was when the cockchafer flew up into the tree with her! But most of all she was sorry for the beautiful white butterfly that she had fastened to the leaf for unless it could get loose it would starve to death. But the cockchafer never gave that a thought. Settling with her on the biggest green leaf in the tree, it fed her on the honey of flowers and said how pretty she was, though not at all like a cockchafer. Before long all the other cockchafers that lived in the tree called round to see them. They looked at Thumbelina, and then, shrugging their feelers, the young lady cockchafers said: 'Why, she's only got two legs; doesn't she look a fright!' And they said: 'She hasn't got any feelers! Isn't she thin round the waist! Ugh, she looks almost human! Isn't she ugly!' And all the time Thumbelina was so pretty! So, too, thought the cockchafer who had carried her off; but when all the others said she was ugly, he came round to the same idea and would have nothing more to do with her, saying she could go if she liked. And so, flying down from the tree with her, they left her on a daisy, crying to herself because she was so ugly that the cockchafers wouldn't have her, while all the time she was the loveliest little thing that ever there was, as gentle and as delicate as the prettiest rose petal.

All that summer Thumbelina lived by herself in the big wood. She wove herself a bed from blades of grass that she hung up under a big burdock leaf, which kept off the rain. She gathered the honey of flowers for food, and drank the dew which every morning she found on the petals. And so summer and autumn passed by, and were followed by winter—the long, cold winter. All the birds that had sung for her so pleasantly flew away, the trees and the flowers withered, the big burdock leaf which she had been living under shrivelled up into only a dead yellow stalk, while she herself felt dreadfully cold. All her clothes were torn, and she—poor Thumbelina!—was so tiny and delicate that it seemed as if she would freeze to death. Then it began to snow, and every snowflake that fell on her was like a whole scoopful on us, for we are big and she was no bigger than your thumb. She wrapped herself in a dead leaf, but it didn't warm her: she was shivering cold.

Just outside the big wood where she'd been taken there was a large cornfield, but the corn had long since gone and only the bare, dry stubble stood up from the frozen ground. To her, walking through this was like walking through a forest. Oh, how she shivered with cold! In time she had reached the door of the field-mouse. It was a little hole under the stubble. There the field-mouse lived snug and warm with a room full of corn and a lovely kitchen and larder. Poor Thumbelina stood in the doorway like a poor beggar-girl and asked for a little bit of barleycorn, as for two days she hadn't had a bite to eat.

'You poor little thing!' said the field-mouse—for she was really a kind old field-mouse. 'Come into my warm parlour and have a meal with me!'

Later on, as she had taken a liking to Thumbelina, she said: 'If you wish, you can stay with me for the winter, if you'll keep my parlour nice and clean and tell me stories—I'm so fond of stories!' So Thumbelina did as the good old field-mouse asked her to, and felt very much at home.

'We'll be having a visitor before long,' said the field-mouse. 'My neighbour calls on me every weekday. He's even better off than I am; he has big halls to live in and wears the loveliest black coat. Now, if you could marry him, you'd be well provided for, though he can't see. You'll have to tell him all your very nicest stories!'

But Thumbelina didn't care for the idea; she didn't want to marry the neighbour, as he was a mole. He came round in his black velvet coat. He was so very rich and such a good scholar, said the field-mouse; and sure enough, his house was over twenty times as big as the field-mouse's and there was no doubt about his being a scholar. But the sun and the beautiful flowers meant nothing to him at all, and never having seen them he would get spiteful about them. Thumbelina had to sing, and she sang both 'Ladybird, ladybird, fly away home!' and 'Ring-a-ring-o'-roses!' till the mole fell in love with her for her beautiful voice. But he never said a word, he was such a thinking man . . .

He had lately dug himself a long passage under the ground leading from his house to theirs, and here the field-mouse and Thumbelina were allowed to walk whenever they liked. He told them not to be afraid of the dead bird which lay there in the passage. This still had its beak and all its feathers, and had very likely died just recently with the coming of winter, and been buried where he had happened to make his passage.

Taking in his mouth a piece of touchwood (which in the darkness glows like fire), the mole went on in front to light their way in the long, dark passage; and when they got to the place where the dead bird was he put his broad nose to the roof, and pushing the soil up made a big hole for the light to shine through. There on the floor lay a dead swallow, its beautiful wings pressed tightly to its sides and its legs and head drawn up under its feathers; the poor bird must surely have died of cold. Thumbelina felt so very sorry for it, for she was so fond of all the little birds and they had sung and twittered so beautifully for her all through the summer. But the mole only kicked it with his stubby legs, and said: 'That'll chirp no more. How miserable it must be to be born a little bird! Thank goodness, none of my children ever will be! Why, a bird like that hasn't a thing but its twitter, and it can't help but starve in the winter.'

'A man of sense like you may well say that,' said the field-mouse. 'What has a bird to show for its twittering when winter comes? It's bound to starve to death! But then that's all very grand, I suppose.'

Thumbelina kept quiet; but when the others had turned their backs on the bird she stooped down, brushed the feathers from its head, and kissed its closed eyes. 'Perhaps this is the one which sang so sweetly for me last summer,' she thought. 'What pleasure it gave me—the dear, sweet bird!'

The mole stopped up the hole through which the daylight had shone, and then saw the ladies home. But that night Thumbelina just couldn't sleep, and getting out of bed, she took some hay and wove from it a fine big blanket which she spread over the dead bird, putting soft cotton-wool that she had found in the field-mouse's parlour along its sides to keep it warm in the cold ground.

'Goodbye, you pretty little bird!' she said. 'Goodbye; and thank you for your lovely singing last summer when all the trees were green and the sun shone so warmly down on us!' Putting her head to the bird's breast as she said this, she got such a start, for inside it something seemed to be throbbing. It was the bird's heart. It wasn't dead: it had been in a swoon, and being warmed up had revived.

In the autumn, all the swallows fly away to the warm countries; but if one should happen to be late it gets so frozen that it drops down as if dead and, lying where it falls, is covered up by the cold snow.

Thumbelina trembled all over, she was so frightened; for the bird was so very, very big alongside her, who was no taller than your thumb. But plucking up courage, she tucked the cotton-wool round the poor swallow, and fetching a mint leaf she had been using as a counterpane laid it over the bird's head.

She crept down to it the next night; and there it was, quite alive, only so faint that it could just open its eyes for a moment and see Thumbelina as she stood there with a piece of touchwood in her hand, the only lantern she had.

'Thank you, you pretty little child!' the sick swallow said to her. 'I've been so nicely warmed up. I shall soon get back my strength, and then I'll be able to fly again, away into the warm sunshine.'

'Oh!' she said. 'It's so cold outside; it's snowing and freezing. Stay in your warm bed, and I'll take care of you.'

And she brought the swallow some water in a petal, and it drank it and told her how it had torn its wing on a bramble and been unable to keep up with the other swallows, which had flown off far away to the warm countries. In the end it had fallen to the ground, but could remember nothing more and had no idea how it had got there.

Now all through the winter it stayed down below, and Thumbelina was kind to it and very, very fond of it. Neither the mole nor the field-mouse was told anything at all about this, for of course they didn't like the poor little swallow.

As soon as spring came round, and the sun had warmed up the earth, the swallow said goodbye to Thumbelina, and she opened up the hole in the roof, the way the mole had done. The sun shone beautifully in to them, and the swallow asked her if she wouldn't like to come too: she could sit on his back and they would fly far away into the green wood. But Thumbelina knew that the old field-mouse would be sorry if she left her like that.

'No, I can't come!' said Thumbelina. 'Goodbye, goodbye, you darling little girl!' said the swallow; and off it flew into the sunshine. Thumbelina watched it go; and tears came into her eyes, she was so very fond of the poor swallow.

'Tweet! Tweet!' sang the bird, as it flew off into the green wood . . .

Thumbelina was so sad. She was never allowed out into the warm sunshine. The corn that had been sown in the field over the field-mouse's house was growing quite tall now, and it was like a dense forest to the poor little girl who was no taller than your thumb.

'Now, during the summer, you must begin making your trousseau!' the field-mouse said to her; for now her neighbour, the tiresome mole in the black velvet coat, had proposed to her. 'You'll want both woollens and linens. You'll need things to sit on and things to lie on, when you marry the mole.'

Thumbelina had to work at a spindle, and the field-mouse hired four spiders to spin and weave night and day. The mole called round every evening, and would keep on saying that when the summer was over it wouldn't be half as hot (for just then it was baking the earth as hard as bricks). Yes, when the summer was over, his wedding with Thumbelina would take place. But she wasn't the least bit happy, for she didn't like the tiresome old mole at all. Every morning when the sun rose, and every evening when it set, she would steal out through the door; and whenever the wind parted the tops of the corn and she could see the blue sky, she would think how bright and beautiful it was out there, and would long to see her dear swallow once again. But it never came back any more, and must have flown far away into the beautiful green wood.

Now, when autumn came round, Thumbelina had quite finished her trousseau.

'Four weeks from now it will be your wedding day!' the field-mouse said to her. But Thumbelina only cried, and said that she wouldn't have the tiresome mole.

'Fiddlesticks!' said the field-mouse. 'Now don't you be stubborn, or I'll bite you with my white tooth. You're getting a nice husband there. And as for his black velvet coat—why, the queen herself hasn't got one like it. He's on velvet, and no mistake. You should think yourself lucky!'

And so the wedding day came round. The mole had already come to fetch Thumbelina; for she was to live with him deep down under the earth and never come out into the warm sunshine, as that was nothing in his line. The poor child was so sad at having to say goodbye to the beautiful sunshine, which at the field-mouse's she had at least been allowed to look at in the doorway.

'Goodbye, bright sunshine!' she said, stretching her arms up into the air and stepping just a little bit outside the field-mouse's door; for now the corn had been harvested and there was only the dry stubble left. 'Goodbye! Goodbye!' she said, flinging her tiny arms round a little red flower that was growing there. 'Give my love to the dear swallow, if you should see him!'

'Tweet! Tweet!' sounded from above her head as she spoke. She looked up, and there, just passing by, was the swallow. It was so very delighted when it saw Thumbelina. And she told it how much she hated the idea of having the horrid mole for a husband, and living deep down under the earth where the sun never shone. The very thought of it made her cry.

'The cold winter is coming on now,' said the swallow. 'I shall be flying far away to the warm countries. Will you come with me? You can sit on my back! Just tie yourself by your sash, then we'll fly away from the horrid mole and his dark parlour; far away over the mountains to the warm countries where the sun shines more beautifully than here, where there's always summer and lovely flowers. Fly off with me, dear sweet little Thumbelina who saved my life when I lay freezing cold in the dark under the ground!'

'Very well, I'll come with you,' said Thumbelina; and sitting up on the bird's back with her feet on its outstretched wings, she tied her belt fast to one of the strongest feathers. And then the swallow flew high into the air, over wood and over sea; high up over the great mountains where the snow always lies. And Thumbelina shivered in the cold air, but then snuggled under the bird's warm feathers, just putting out her little head to see all the loveliness that lay beneath.

And so they came to the warm countries. The sun there shone much more brightly than here; the sky was twice as high, and on terraces and trellises grew the loveliest of green and black grapes. In the orchards hung oranges and lemons; sweetly scented myrtles and mints grew there; and the loveliest of children were playing on the road with big, prettily coloured butterflies. But the swallow flew even farther away, and it got more and more beautiful. Under the splendid green trees by the blue lake a gleaming white marble palace had stood from olden times, and grape-vines were twining up its lofty pillars. There, at the very top, were a lot of swallows' nests, and in one of these lived the swallow that carried Thumbelina.

'Here is my house,' said the swallow. 'But if you will choose for yourself one of the most beautiful of the flowers growing down there, I'll put you off on it, and you'll be as happy as ever you could wish for!'

'Why, how lovely!' she cried, clapping her little hands.

Lying on the ground was a big, white marble pillar, which had fallen down and broken into three pieces, and between these grew the prettiest big, white flowers. The swallow flew down with Thumbelina and put her off on to one of the broad petals; and what a surprise she got then! Sitting in the middle of the flower was a little man, as white and transparent as though he'd been made of glass. On his head was the prettiest golden crown, and on his shoulders the loveliest clear wings; he himself was no bigger than Thumbelina. He was the flower's angel. A little man or woman like him lived in every flower, but this one was king over them all.

'I say, isn't he handsome!' Thumbelina whispered to the swallow. The little prince was quite frightened of the swallow; for, of course, it was a real giant of a bird compared to him, who was so tiny and small. But when he saw Thumbelina he was so glad; she was the very prettiest girl he had ever seen. And so he took his gold crown off his head, and, putting it on hers, asked her her name and if she would be his wife, when she would be queen of all the flowers! Well, here was a husband indeed; a very different one from the toad's son, and the mole with the black velvet coat. So she said yes to the lovely prince. And from every flower came a lady or a gentleman: so charming it was delightful to see. Each brought Thumbelina a present; but the best of them all was a pair of pretty wings from a big white insect. They were fastened to Thumbelina's back, and then she

too could fly from flower to flower. There was such rejoicing, and the swallow sat up in its nest and sang to them for all it was worth; though sad at heart, because it was so fond of Thumbelina and would never have parted from her.

'You shan't be called Thumbelina any more!' said the flower's angel to her. 'It's an ugly name, and you are so pretty. We'll call you Maia!'

'Goodbye! Goodbye!' said the swallow; and off it flew from the warm countries, far away back to Denmark. There it had a little nest over the window of the man who can tell fairy tales; to him it sang 'T-weet! T-weet!' and it's from there that we have the whole story.

THE NAUGHTY BOY

THERE was once an old poet—such a nice, kindly old poet. He was sitting at home one evening when a dreadful storm broke out; the rain came pouring down. But the old poet sat snug and warm by his fireside, where the flames were leaping and the roasting apples were hissing.

'They won't have a dry stitch left, the poor things that are out in this weather,' he said; for he was such a kindly poet.

'Please let me in! I'm so cold and wet!' cried a little child outside. And he stood weeping and knocking at the door, while the rain came pouring down and the wind rattled every window.

'Poor little fellow!' said the old poet, going to open the door. Standing outside was a little boy; he was all naked, and water was streaming from his long, golden hair. He was shivering with cold; if he hadn't been let in he must certainly have died in that dreadful storm.

'Poor little fellow!' said the old poet, taking him by the hand. 'Come along to me, and I'll soon have you warm. You shall have some wine and an apple, you're such a lovely boy!'

And he was indeed. His eyes were like two bright stars; and though water was running down his golden hair, it had such beautiful curls. He looked like a little angel, but was pale with cold and shivering in every limb. In his hand he had a lovely bow, but the rain had quite spoilt it, and all the colours of its pretty arrows had run in the wet.

Sitting down by the fire, the old poet took the little boy on his knee, wrung his hair dry, warmed his hands in his own, and

heated some sweet wine for him. Soon he was better; he had rosy cheeks, and jumped on to the floor and skipped and danced around the old poet.

'You're a jolly boy!' said the old poet. 'What do they call you?'

'They call me Cupid,' he replied. 'Don't you know me? Look, there's my bow! I can shoot with that, you know. Look, the weather's clearing up now! The moon's come out!'

'But your bow's spoilt!' said the old poet.

'What a pity!' said the little boy, picking it up and looking at it. 'Why, it's already dry and none the worse. The string's perfectly tight. I'll try it!' And drawing his bow he put an arrow in, took aim, and shot the kindly old poet right through the heart. 'There, you see, my bow wasn't spoilt!' he said, and with a loud laugh he ran off. The naughty boy, to shoot the old poet who had taken him into his warm room and been so good to him and given him the lovely wine and his best apple!

The kindly poet lay on the floor crying. He really had been shot through the heart; and he said: 'For shame! What a naughty boy that Cupid is! I'm going to tell this to all the good children I know, so they can beware of him and never play with him, or he'll do them harm.'

All the good children, the girls and the boys, to whom he told the story took good care to avoid the wicked Cupid, but he deceived them all the same, he's such a cunning one! When students are leaving their lectures he'll run alongside them, carrying a book under his arm and wearing a black gown. They never know him, and so they take him by the arm, thinking that he's another student. Then he shoots his arrow into their hearts. When the young women leave their confirmation classes, and when they're in church being confirmed, he's on the look-out for them too. Why, he's on the look-out for people all the time. He'll sit up in the big chandelier at the theatre, burning brightly to make people think he's a lamp: only later they learn better. He runs about the park and on the promenade. Why, he once shot your father and mother through the heart! Just you ask them and see what they say. Oh, he's a bad boy, this Cupid! Don't you ever have anything to do with him. He's after everybody! Just fancy, he even shot an arrow into your old grandmother, only it's a long time ago and she's got over it. But it isn't the sort of thing she'll ever forget. Shame on him, that wicked Cupid! But now you know him, and what a naughty boy he is!

THE TRAVELLING COMPANION

Poor John was so sad, for his father was very ill and would not live. There was no one else in the little room but these two; the lamp on the table was burning out, and the evening had grown late.

'You've been a good son, John!' said the sick father. 'Our Lord will help you on in the world!' And gazing at him with grave and gentle eyes, he drew a deep breath and died; it was as though he had fallen asleep. And John cried, for now he had no one in the whole world, neither father nor mother, sister nor brother. Poor John! He knelt down by the bedside, and kissing his dead father's hand wept so very bitterly. But in the end his eyes closed and he fell asleep, with his head on the hard bed-post.

He then had a curious dream; he saw the sun and the moon bowing down before him, and he saw his father well and strong again and heard him laugh as he used to laugh when he was really happy. A lovely young woman with a golden crown over her beautiful long hair held out her hand to John, and his father said: 'Do you see what a bride you've got! She's the loveliest in all the world.' Then he woke up, and all the beautiful things were gone; his father lay dead and cold on the bed and they were all alone. Poor John!

The week after, the dead man was buried. John walked just behind the coffin, and now could no longer see his good father who had loved him so dearly. He heard them throw earth on to the coffin, and saw the last corner of it, but at the next spadeful of soil that too was gone; and then it was as though his heart would break, he was so sad. Round about they were singing a hymn. It sounded so beautiful that the tears came into John's eyes; he cried and it brought relief to his sorrow. The sun shone brightly on the green trees, as if to say: 'Don't be so sad, John! Do you see what a beautiful blue sky there is? Your father is up there now, praying to the dear Lord that all will go well with you!'

'I'll always be good,' said John. 'Then I'll go to join my father in heaven, and what a joy it will be when we see each other again! What a lot I shall be able to tell him; and he'll show me so many things again and teach me so much about the loveliness of heaven as he used to do here on earth. Oh, what a joy it will be!'

John imagined it all so clearly that it made him smile while the tears were still rolling down his cheeks. The little birds sat up in the chestnut-trees, twittering 'Tweet! Tweet!' They were so pleased, even though they were at a funeral. But then they knew that the dead man was now in heaven, and had wings much bigger and more beautiful than theirs, and was so happy now because he had been good here on earth; and they were so pleased at this. John watched them fly away from the green trees out into the world, and had a strong mind to go with them. But first he carved a large wooden cross to put on his father's grave; and when he took it there in the evening he found that the grave had been covered with sand and decorated with flowers. Some strangers had done this, for everyone had been so fond of the dear father who was now dead.

Early next morning John packed up his little bundle and put the whole of his inheritance (which was twenty-five shillings and a few pence) into his belt, meaning to go off into the world with it. But first he went to his father's grave in the churchyard, repeated the Lord's Prayer, and said: 'Farewell, my dear father! I'll always be a good man, and then you can pray to the good Lord that all may go well with me.'

In the field where John walked all the flowers stood fresh and lovely in the warm sunshine, nodding in the breeze as if to say: 'Welcome to the country! Isn't it nice here?' Then, turning once more to see the old church where he had been christened as a baby and where every Sunday he had gone to service and sung hymns with his father, he saw there the church brownie, standing in his little pointed red bonnet high up in one of the loopholes in the tower, shading his face with his crooked arm to keep the sun from dazzling his eyes. John nodded goodbye to him; and the little brownie waved his red bonnet, laid his hand on his heart, and blew lots of kisses as a sign that he wished him good luck and a very happy journey.

John thought of all the beautiful things he would now be seeing in the great big world, and so walked on and on, further than he had ever been before. He no longer knew the towns he passed through or the people whom he met; he was far away now among strangers.

The first night he had to lie down to sleep in a haystack in a field; it was the only bed there was. But then it was very nice, he thought; a king's bed could be no better. The open field with the stream, the haystack, and the blue sky up above made the finest of bedrooms. The green grass and little red and white flowers were a carpet, the elder bushes and the wild-rose hedges were bunches of flowers, and for a wash-basin he had the whole stream with the clear, fresh water, where the rushes nodded 'Good evening' as well as 'Good morning.' The moon was a great big night-light right up under the blue ceiling, and never set fire to the curtains. John was able to sleep quite peacefully, and that was what he did, waking only when the sun rose and all the little birds round about sang: 'Good morning! Good morning! Aren't you up?'

The bells rang for church. It was Sunday; people were going to hear the clergyman, and John went with them, sang a hymn, and listened to the word of God. And it seemed like being in his own church, where he had been christened and had sung hymns with his father.

In the churchyard there were a lot of graves, and on some of them long grass grew. It reminded John of his father's grave, which too would come to look like these, now he could no longer weed and trim it. And he sat down and plucked off the grass, raised up the wooden crosses that had fallen down, and put back the wreaths which the wind had blown away from the graves, thinking: 'Someone may do the same to my father's grave, now that I can't!'

Standing outside the churchyard gate, leaning on his crutch, was an old beggar. Giving him what coppers he had, John walked on, pleased and happy, into the wide world.

Towards evening a terrible storm came on. John hurried on to find shelter, but it was soon pitch-dark. At long last he came to a little church which stood all by itself on the top of a hill; luckily the door was open and he slipped inside, meaning to stay there till the storm dropped.

'I'll sit in a corner here,' he said. 'I'm tired out and could do with a little rest.' And so he sat down and, folding his hands and saying his evening prayers, before he realized it was fast asleep and dreaming, while outside it thundered and lightened.

When he woke up again it was the middle of the night, but the storm had passed over and the moon was shining in at him through the windows. Standing in the middle of the church there was an open coffin with a dead man inside it, one who had not been buried yet. John was not afraid, for he had a clear conscience and knew that the dead never do anyone any harm; it is living bad people who do harm. Two such living, wicked people stood close to the dead man, who had been brought into the church before being buried. They were bent on doing harm to him, by not leaving him to lie in his coffin but throwing him out of the church door, the poor dead man.

'What are you going to do that for?' asked John. 'It's a bad and wicked thing to do; in the name of Jesus let him sleep!'

'Stuff and nonsense!' said the two wicked men. 'He cheated us. He owed us money and couldn't pay it, and now he's dead into the bargain, and we shan't get a ha'penny. So we mean to have our revenge; he'll lie like a dog outside the church door!'

'I've only twenty-five shillings,' said John. 'It's my whole inheritance. But I'll gladly give it to you if you'll faithfully promise to leave the poor dead man in peace. I'll get on all right without the money; I've strong and healthy limbs, and the Lord will always help me.'

'All right,' said the horrible men, 'if you'll pay his debts we'll leave him alone. You can take our word for it!' And taking the money John offered them, they gave a loud laugh at his goodness and went their way. Replacing the body in the coffin, John folded the hands, said goodbye, and went off contentedly through the forest.

Round about him, where the moon shone in through the trees, he saw the most charming fairies, playing merrily together. They went on undisturbed, well knowing that he was a good and innocent person; and it's only wicked people who never can see the fairies. Some of them were no bigger than a finger and had their long yellow hair fastened up with golden combs. They were seesawing two and two on the big dew-drops which lay on the leaves and the tall grass. From time to time the drop would roll over and they would fall down among the long blades of grass, and then the other little folk would laugh like anything. It was ever such fun! They were singing, and John clearly recognized all the beautiful songs he had learnt as a little boy. Large, brightly coloured spiders wearing silver crowns on their heads had been set to work, spinning from hedge to hedge long suspension-bridges and palaces, which when the delicate dew fell would look like sparkling glass in the clear moonlight. And so it went on till sunrise. Then the little fairies crept into their flower-buds and the wind seized their bridges and palaces, making them fly into the air as big cobwebs.

John had left the forest behind when a man called after him in a loud voice: 'Hi there, friend! Where are you bound for?'

'The wide world!' said John. 'I have neither father nor mother, and am just a poor lad, but the Lord will be sure to help me.'

'I'm bound for the wide world as well,' said the strange man. 'Let's keep one another company!'

'All right!' said John; and so off they walked together. They soon grew to like one another, for they were both good people. But John could tell that the stranger was much cleverer than he was; he had been nearly round the world and could tell of all manner of things in it.

The sun was already well up when they sat down to have breakfast under a big tree; and just then an old woman came along. She was such an old woman and she was quite bent, supporting herself as she walked on a crutch and having on her back a bundle of firewood which she had gathered in the forest. Her apron was pinned up, and sticking out from it John saw three large faggots of bracken and willow twigs. She was quite near to them when suddenly her foot slipped and she fell down, giving a loud cry, for she had broken her leg, the poor old woman.

John wanted them to carry her straight home to where she lived, but opening his bag the stranger took out a jar, saying that he had in it an ointment which would make her leg strong and well again at once, so that she would be able to walk home, just as though she had never broken her leg. But for this he wanted her to give him the three faggots she had in her apron.

'It's good payment!' said the old woman, giving a rather strange nod of her head. She had no great mind to part with her faggots, but then it wasn't very nice to lie there with a broken leg. So she gave him the faggots; and no sooner had he rubbed the ointment on the leg than the old woman got up and walked a good deal better than before. The ointment did that. Only you couldn't have got it at a chemist's.

'What do you want the faggots for?' John then asked his travelling companion.

'They make three nice nosegays,' he said. 'They're the sort of thing I like, for I'm a queer fellow!'

They then walked on for another good stretch.

'I say, there's a storm brewing.' said John, pointing ahead. 'Those are awfully heavy clouds.'

'Oh no,' said the travelling companion; 'they aren't clouds, they're mountains. The lovely big mountains where you get right up above the clouds into the fresh air. It's grand, I can tell you! Tomorrow, I should say, we shall be far out in the world.'

It wasn't so near as it looked; it would take them a whole day to reach the mountains, where the black forests grew right into the sky and where there were rocks as big as towns. It was going to be a hard climb to get right up there; and so John and the travelling companion stopped at an inn to get a good rest and gather their strength for tomorrow's tramp.

In the tap-room a crowd of people were gathered, as there was a man giving a puppet-show. He had just set up his little theatre and people were sitting round ready to watch his play, the seat right at the front, the best of them all, having been taken by a fat old butcher. His big bulldog—ugh! such a fierce one it looked—sat beside him, wide-eyed like all the rest.

And then the play began. It was a nice comedy, with a king and queen in it; and they sat on a velvet throne and had gold crowns on their heads and long trains to their robes, for these they could afford. The prettiest little wooden puppets with glass eyes and big moustaches stood at all the doors, opening and shutting them to let in the fresh air. It was a most lovely play, and not a bit sad; but just as the queen got up and walked across the floor—goodness knows what was in the big bulldog's head, but the fat butcher wasn't holding him, and in a bound he was right on the stage and was seizing the queen round her slender waist and making her say 'Click-clack!' It was really dreadful.

The poor man who was giving the play got such a fright and was so upset about his queen; this had been the nicest of all his puppets, and now the nasty bulldog had bitten her head off. But later on, when everyone had left, the stranger—the man who had come with John—said that he would mend her; and taking out his jar he rubbed the puppet with the ointment he had used to help the poor old woman when she had broken her leg. The moment the puppet had been rubbed it was well again, and could even move all its limbs of its own accord, so there was no need to pull the string; the puppet was like a living person, apart from the fact that it couldn't speak. The man who owned the little puppet theatre was so pleased; now he had no need to hold the puppet—it could dance all on its own. None of the others was able to.

Now, late that night when everyone at the inn had gone to bed, somebody began to sigh: such dreadfully deep sighs, which went on for so long that everybody got up to see who it could be. The man who had given the play went straight to his little theatre; for the sighing was in there. The puppets were lying all over the place, the king among all his men; and it was they who were heaving the pitiful sighs, while they stared with their big glass eyes, for they wanted to be rubbed like the queen, so that they too could move of their own accord. The queen fell on her knees and held her lovely gold crown in the air as she pleaded: 'Take this, only rub my husband and my courtiers!' At this the poor man who owned the theatre and all the puppets couldn't help crying, he was so very sorry for them; and he promised the travelling companion all the money he would get for his play the next evening if only he would rub four or five of his nicest puppets. But the travelling companion said that all he wanted was the big sword he wore at his side; and having got that he rubbed six dolls, who at once began to dance, and so prettily that all the young women who saw it—the live, human young women—joined in. The coachman and the cook danced too, and the manservant and the maidservant, and all the visitors, and the ash-pan and the tongs; only these two fell over, just as they made their first leap. Oh yes, it was a jolly night!

Next morning John and his travelling companion took leave of them all and went up the high mountains and through the big pine forests. They climbed so high up that in the end the church towers far below them were like little red berries among the greenery, and they were able to see a long way off—many, many miles away where they had never been. Never before had John seen so much beauty in this lovely world at once; and the sun shone so warmly from the fresh blue air, and he heard the huntsmen blow their horns between the mountains so beautifully and marvellously, that tears of joy came into his eyes and he couldn't help saying: 'Our dear Lord, I could kiss you for being so good to us all, and for giving us all this world's loveliness!'

The travelling companion also stood with folded hands, looking out across the forest and the towns in the warm sunshine. All at once they heard a sound, wonderfully lovely, above their heads, and looking up they saw gliding through the air a big white swan; it was so beautiful, and it sang as they had never heard any bird sing before. But it grew more and more faint, and bending its head it sank, very slowly, down at their feet, where—beautiful bird!—it lay dead.

'Two such lovely wings,' said the travelling companion, 'as white and as large as this bird's, are worth something. I'll have them! Now you can see what a good thing it was I got a sword!' And so at one blow he cut off both the swan's wings, meaning to keep them.

And then they travelled on for many, many miles across the mountains, till in time they found themselves before a big city with over a hundred towers which shone in the sunshine like silver. In the middle of the town was a splendid marble palace, roofed with the purest gold, and here lived the king.

John and the travelling companion resolved not to go straight into the town, but to stay at the inn outside it to smarten themselves up, as they wanted to look nice when walking through the streets. The innkeeper told them what a good man the king was, who never did anyone any harm at all, but said that his daughter—well, she now was a bad princess! She was lovely enough in looks, and nobody could be prettier or more charming. But what good was that when she was a wicked bad witch, who had been the death of so many handsome princes? She would let anyone propose to her. Anyone could come: a prince or a beggar, it was all the same to her. All he had to do was to guess the answers to three questions; if he could, she would marry him and he would be king of the whole country when her father died. But if he couldn't guess the three answers she would have him hanged or beheaded: so wicked was she, this lovely princess. The old king her father was so very sad about this, but he could do nothing to stop her from being so wicked, as he had once said that he would have nothing at all to do with her sweethearts, she could do exactly as she pleased. Whenever a prince came and tried guessing the answers so as to win the princess, he would never succeed, and would be hanged or beheaded; of course, they had warned him in time and there was no need for him to propose. So sad was the old king at all this grief and misery that for a whole day every year he would kneel down along with all his soldiers and pray that the princess would be good; but she never was.

'The horrible princess!' said John. 'What she wants is a thrashing; it would do her good. If I were the old king I'd give her it.'

Suddenly there was a sound of cheering outside. The princess was passing by; and she was so very lovely that everyone forgot how wicked she was and began to cheer. Twelve lovely maidens, all dressed in white silk robes and carrying a golden tulip in their hands, rode beside her on jet-black horses. The princess herself had a milk-white horse which was decorated with diamonds and rubies; her riding-habit was of the purest gold and the whip which she bore in her hand shone like a sunbeam; the gold crown on her head twinkled like stars in the sky; and her cloak was made from the lovely wings of over a thousand butterflies. She herself was more beautiful by far than all her robes.

On seeing her, John went as red as fire and could scarcely get out a word; the princess looked exactly like the lovely girl with the golden crown whom he had dreamt about on the night his father had died. She seemed so very beautiful to him, he couldn't help loving her. Surely, he said, it couldn't be true that she was a wicked witch who had people hanged or beheaded when they couldn't guess the answers to her questions. 'Anyone may propose to her, even the poorest beggar; and so I'm off to the palace! I can't help it.'

Everyone told him not to go, saying he would be sure to meet with the same fate as all the rest. The travelling companion warned him not to go too. But John thought that he would be all right; and so he brushed his shoes and coat, washed his hands and face, combed his yellow hair, and went, all by himself, into the town and to the palace.

'Come in!' said the old king, when John knocked at the door. John went in, and the old king, in his dressing-gown and embroidered slippers, came forward to meet him. The gold crown was on his head, the sceptre in one hand, the orb in the other. 'Stop a minute!' he said; and he pushed the orb under his arm so that he was free to shake hands with John. But the moment he heard that he had come to propose, he broke into such a fit of crying that both the sceptre and the orb fell on the floor and he had to dry his eyes on his dressing-gown. Poor old king!

'Don't!' he said. 'You'll come to grief like all the rest. Just look here!' And he took John into the princess's pleasure garden. What a dreadful sight it was! Hanging from every tree were three or four princes who had proposed to the princess and had been unable to answer her questions. Every puff of the wind would set their bones rattling, frightening the little birds and making them afraid to come into the garden. All the flowers were tied up with human bones, and skulls were grinning from all the plant-pots. This was a garden for a princess, indeed!

'There now!' said the old king. 'You'll come to grief just like all the others here, so don't do it! You make me really unhappy, as I take it so very much to heart.

John kissed the good old king's hand, saying that it would be all right because he was so very much in love with the princess.

Just then the princess herself came riding into the palace yard with all her ladies, and they went out and said 'Good morning' to her. She was indeed lovely, and she shook hands with John; and he loved her more than ever. Surely she couldn't be such a bad and wicked witch as everybody said that she was, he thought. Then off they all went into the palace hall, where the little pages served them with sweets and ginger-nuts, though the old king was so upset that he couldn't eat anything—besides which the ginger-nuts were too hard for him.

It was then agreed that John was to come back to the palace the next morning, when the judges and the full council would be assembled to hear how he got on with the guessing. If he got on well, he was to come twice more; only nobody had ever yet guessed right the first time, and so they had lost their lives.

John wasn't a bit upset about how he would get on, but was perfectly happy, thinking only of the lovely princess and trusting, indeed, that the good Lord would help him; though how he had no idea, nor would he think of it. He went skipping along the road back to the inn, where the travelling companion was waiting for him.

John just couldn't stop telling about how nice the princess had been to him, and how lovely she was. He was already longing for the next day, when he was to go to the palace and try his luck at guessing.

But the travelling companion shook his head and was quite down-hearted. 'I'm so fond of you!' he said. 'We could have been together so much longer yet, and now I'm going to lose you already. Poor, dear John, I could cry; but I won't spoil your pleasure on what may be our last evening together. We'll be merry, really merry; and tomorrow, when you are gone, I can cry if I want.'

Everybody in the town had heard at once that a new suitor had come to propose to the princess, and so there was great sorrow. The theatre was closed, all the sweet-sellers tied black crape round their sugar pigs, and the king and the clergymen knelt down in church. There was so much sorrow; for John would never get on any better than all the other suitors had done. That night the travelling companion made a big bowl of punch, saying to John that now they would be really merry and drink the princess's health. But John, when he had drunk two glasses, grew so sleepy that he simply couldn't keep his eyes open and fell asleep. Lifting him very gently from the chair, the travelling companion put him to bed, and then, as soon as it grew dark, took the two big wings he had cut off the swan, fastened them tightly on to his shoulders, put the biggest of the faggots he had got from the old woman who had fallen and broken her leg into his pocket, and, opening the window, flew out across the city to the palace, where he came to rest in a corner under the window of the princess's bedroom.

The whole town was perfectly still; but then all of a sudden the clock struck a quarter to twelve, the window opened, and the princess, wearing a big white cloak and long black wings, flew out across the city to a large mountain. But the travelling companion, making himself invisible so the princess could not see him, flew after her, lashing her with his faggot as he did so and drawing blood where he hit her. Oh, what a speed they went at! The wind blew under her cloak, making it spread out on all sides like a big ship's sail, and the moon shone through it.

'It's hailing! It's hailing!' cried the princess at each stroke of the faggot, which served her right. Reaching the mountain at long last, she gave a knock at it. With a roll of thunder the mountain-side opened itself and the princess went inside, followed by the travelling companion, whom no one could see because he was invisible. They passed through a big long passage where the walls had a wonderful sparkle; it came from thousands of gleaming spiders, which ran up and down the wall, glowing like fire. And then they came to a large hall built of silver and gold; flowers the size of sunflowers, red ones and blue ones, glowed from the walls, though no one could pick these flowers, for their stalks were horrid poisonous snakes and the flowers were flames rising from their mouths. The whole ceiling was studded with sparkling glow-worms and sky-blue bats flapping their slender wings; it was all so weird. In the middle of the floor was a throne borne by the skeletons of four horses, which had harnesses formed by crimson fire-spiders. The throne itself was of milk-white glass, and the cushions for sitting on were little black mice biting one another in the tail. Up above this was a roof of rose-coloured cobwebs, studded with the prettiest little green flies that shone like jewels. Sitting on the throne was an old sorcerer, with a crown on his ugly head and a sceptre in his hand. He kissed the princess on her forehead and made room for her beside him on the gorgeous throne, and then the music started up. Big black grasshoppers played Jews' harps and the owl beat its own stomach, as it hadn't got a drum. It was a queer concert. Tiny little goblins with jack-o'-lanterns on their caps danced round the hall. Nobody was able to see the travelling companion; he had placed himself right behind the throne and heard and saw everything. The courtiers, who now came in as well, were so grand and genteel; though to anyone with any eyes it was plain to see what they were. They were no more than broomsticks with cabbages for heads, which the sorcerer had brought to life and dressed in embroidered clothes. But then that made no difference; they were only for show.

Now when they had had some dancing the princess told the sorcerer that she'd got a new suitor, and wondered what she should think of asking him the next morning when he came to the palace.

'Listen!' said the sorcerer. 'I'll tell you what. You choose something very easy and he won't have the slightest idea. Think of one of your own shoes. He'll never guess that. Then have his head cut off; only remember when you come again tomorrow night to bring me his eyes, as I want those to eat!'

The princess made a deep curtsy and promised not to forget the eyes. Then the sorcerer opened the mountainside and she flew back home again; but the travelling companion followed her, lashing her so hard with the faggot as he did so that, giving a deep sigh because of the heavy hail, she made off as fast as she could so as to reach her window and get into her bedroom. The travelling companion then flew back to the inn where John was still asleep, and, unfastening his wings, also lay down to sleep; for he was tired, and no wonder.

John woke up very early in the morning. Getting up too, the travelling companion told him that during the night he had had a very strange dream about the princess and one of her shoes, and said he was to be sure and ask her if she was thinking of one of her shoes. This, of course, was what he had heard the sorcerer say in the mountainside; but he didn't want to tell John about this and so only told him to ask if it was one of her shoes she had in mind.

'I can just as well ask one question as another,' said John. 'It may be perfectly true what you have dreamt; because I think our Lord will always be sure to help me. Still, I'll say goodbye to you;

because if I guess wrong I shall never set eyes on you again.'

And so they kissed one another; and John made his way into the city and up to the palace. The hall was packed out with people; and the judges sat in their armchairs with their heads on eiderdown cushions, as they had so much to think about. The old king stood up and dried his eyes on a white handkerchief. And then the princess came in. She was even lovelier than on the day before and greeted them all most kindly; only to John she held out her hand, saying: 'Good morning, my dear!'

And now it was for him to guess what she was thinking of. Really, how kindly she looked at him! But the moment she heard him say 'One of your shoes' she went as white as a sheet and trembled all over. But that didn't help her; for he had guessed right.

Dear me, how glad the old king was! He turned a somersault such as you never saw; and everybody clapped their hands both for him and for John, who had now guessed right the first time.

The travelling companion beamed with delight when he was told how well it had turned out; and John clasped his hands and thanked the good Lord, who would surely help him again on the two other days. The next guess was to be the day after.

The evening passed like the one before. When John fell asleep, the travelling companion flew out to the mountain after the princess, lashing her even harder than he had done the first time, for now he had brought two faggots. Nobody caught sight of him and he heard everything. The princess was to think of her glove, and he told this to John as though it had been a dream. And so John was able to guess right; and there was great rejoicing at the palace. The whole Court turned somersaults, the way they had seen the king the first time. But the princess lay on the sofa and wouldn't say a word. And now all depended on whether John could guess right the third time. If all went well he was to have the lovely princess and inherit the whole kingdom when the old king died; if he guessed wrong, he would lose his life and the sorcerer would eat his handsome blue eyes.

Going early to bed in the evening, John said his prayers and fell into a sound sleep; while the travelling companion fastened his wings to his back, fixed the sword at his side, and, taking with him all three faggots, flew off to the palace.

It was a pitch-black night, and it was blowing so hard that the tiles were flying off the roof-tops and in the garden where the skeletons hung the trees were swaying in the wind like rushes. From time to time it would lighten; and the thunder would roll like a single peal that was lasting all night. Then all at once the window sprang open and out flew the princess. She was as pale as death; and yet she laughed at the storm, seeming to think that it wasn't fierce enough. Her white cloak whirled about in the air like the sails of a big ship. And then the travelling companion gave her such a lashing with his three faggots that her blood fell dripping down to the ground and in the end she could scarcely fly any further. And so at long last she arrived at the mountain.

'It's hailing and storming,' she said. 'I was never out in such a storm.'

'It's true that you can have too much of a good thing,' said the sorcerer. And then she told him that John had also guessed right the second time; if he did the same again the next day, then he would have won and she would never more be able to visit him in the mountain and never more perform her old magic. And so she was very miserable.

'He shan't guess right,' said the sorcerer. 'I'll find something he's never thought of. Or else he's a bigger sorcerer than I am. But now let us be merry!' So saying, he took thc princess in both hands and they danced about with all the little goblins and jack-o'-lanterns in the room, while the crimson spiders jumped just as merrily up and down the wall and the fire-flowers seemed to be throwing sparks. The owl beat its drum, the crickets chirped, and the black grasshoppers blew their Jews' harps. What a merry dance it was!

Now when they had danced long enough it was time for the princess to go home, or they might have missed her at the palace. The sorcerer said he would take her there, so that they might be together for a little while yet.

So off they flew into the storm, as the travelling companion wore out his faggots on their backs; never in his life had the sorcerer been out in such a lashing storm. Taking leave of the princess outside the palace, he whispered to her: 'Think of my head.' But the travelling companion had heard it all right; and just as the princess slipped through the window into her bedroom and the sorcerer was about to turn back, he seized him by his long black beard and cut off his ugly head from its shoulders with his sword—too quickly for the sorcerer himself to see it. The body he threw to the fishes in the lake; but the head he only dipped in the water and, after tying it up in his silk handkerchief, took it home to the inn, where he lay down to sleep.

Giving the handkerchief to John the next morning, he said that he was not to undo it until the princess asked what she was thinking of.

There were so many people in the big hall of the palace that they were as tightly packed as radishes in a bunch. The judges sat in their chairs with the soft cushions and the old king was wearing new clothes; the gold crown and sceptre had been polished, and made a splendid show. But the princess was very pale and wore a jet-black dress, as though she were going to a funeral.

'What have I thought of?' she said to John; and with that he undid the handkerchief and got quite a shock himself at the sight of the ugly sorcerer's head. Everybody shuddered, it was so dreadful to look at. Only the princess sat like a statue, unable to say a word. In the end she got up and held out her hand to John; for of course he had guessed right. Looking neither at one person nor at another she gave a deep sigh and said: 'Now you are my master! We'll be married tonight.'

'That's what I like!' said the old king. 'That's the way we want it!'

Then everybody cheered, the royal guard made music in the streets, the bells rang out, and the sweet-women took the black crape off their sugar pigs; for now everyone was glad. Three roasted oxen, stuffed with ducks and chickens, were set up in the market square, where anybody could cut himself a piece; the fountains gushed delicious wine; and anyone who bought a pennyworth of biscuits at the baker's got six big buns thrown in, and they were buns with currants in.

That evening the whole city was illuminated and the soldiers let off their cannon and the boys their 'bombshells'; and up at the palace there was eating and drinking and clinking and jigging: all the grand gentlemen and lovely ladies danced with one another and could be heard from a long way off, singing:

'What a lot of pretty girls there are,
All pining for a dance:
So play up the pipes and tambourines,
And, maidens all, advance:
Sing along, swing along,
Fal-la-la-la!'

But of course the princess was still a witch and she didn't love John a bit. Remembering this, the travelling companion gave John three feathers from the swan's wings and a little bottle in which were some drops of liquid, telling him as he did so that he was to place a large bath full of water beside the marriage bed; and when the princess was getting out of bed he was to give her a little push and make her fall into the water, where he was to duck her three times, after first throwing in the feathers and the drops. She would then be freed from her spell and would grow to love him.

John did everything that the travelling companion had told him. When he ducked her under the water the princess gave a loud scream and squirmed in his hands in the form of a big, jet-black swan with glittering eyes. When she came up from the water for the second time she was a white swan, except for a single black ring round her neck. Praying earnestly to our Lord, John splashed the water over the bird for the third time; and in a twinkling she was changed into the loveliest princess. She was more beautiful than ever, and thanked him with tears in her eyes for having broken her spell.

Next morning the old king came along with all his household, and the congratulations went on till well into the day. Last of all came the travelling companion, with his stick in his hand and his knapsack on his back. John showered him with kisses and said that he was not to go yet but should stay with him, as he owed all his happiness to him. But the travelling companion shook his head and said gently and kindly: 'No, my time's up. I have done no more than pay my debt. Do you remember the dead man whom the wicked fellows meant to harm? You gave everything you had that he might rest in his grave in peace. I am the dead man!'

And with that he was gone . . .

And the wedding lasted for a week. John and the princess loved each other dearly; and the old king lived for many a happy day and would allow their little children to ride a-cock-horse on his knee and play with his sceptre. But John was king of the whole country.

THE LITTLE MERMAID

THE LITTLE MERMAID

FAR OUT to sea the water's as blue as the petals of the loveliest cornflower, and as clear as the purest glass; but it's very deep, deeper than any anchor will go. Many church towers would have to be placed one on top of the other to reach from the bottom above the surface. Down there live the mermen.

Now, we mustn't think that there's only bare white sand at the bottom: no, the most wonderful trees and plants grow there, with stalks and leaves which bend so easily that they move at the slightest stir of the water, as though they were alive. All the fishes, big ones and little ones, dart about among the branches like birds in the air up here. At the very deepest point stands the palace of the merman king. The walls are of coral and the long, pointed windows of the very clearest amber, while the roof is of cockle-shells which open and shut with the flowing water. It looks lovely; for in every one there are sparkling pearls, each of which would make a show in a queen's crown.

The king of the mermen had for many years been a widower, but his old mother kept house for him. She was a clever woman, though proud of her noble birth, for which she wore twelve oysters on her tail: other persons of rank were only allowed six. Apart from this she deserved much praise, especially because she was so fond of the little mermaid princesses, her granddaughters. They were six lovely children, the youngest being the prettiest of them all. Her skin was as clear and pure as a rose petal, her eyes as blue as the deepest lake. But, like all the others, she had no feet: her body ended in a fish's tail.

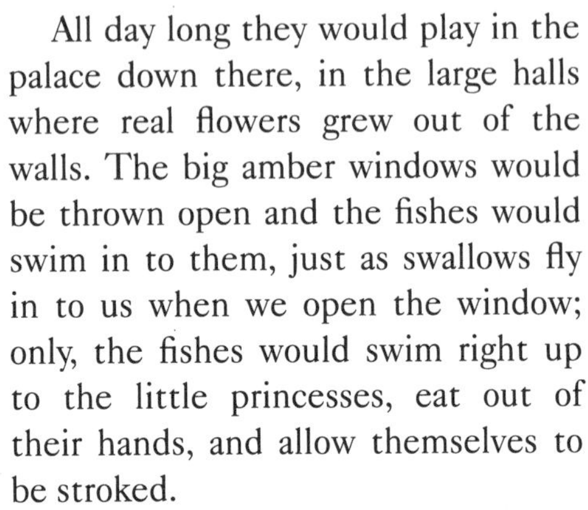

All day long they would play in the palace down there, in the large halls where real flowers grew out of the walls. The big amber windows would be thrown open and the fishes would swim in to them, just as swallows fly in to us when we open the window; only, the fishes would swim right up to the little princesses, eat out of their hands, and allow themselves to be stroked.

Outside the palace was a big garden where there were bright-red and dark-blue trees. The fruit flashed like gold and the flowers like a blazing fire, as they were always moving their stalks and leaves. The ground itself was of the finest sand, but as blue as sulphur flames. Everything down there shone with a strange blue light; you would really have thought that you were standing high up in the air, seeing only sky above and beneath you, instead of being at the bottom of the sea. In perfect calm you could make out the sun, which seemed like a purple flower, with all the light pouring from its cup.

Each of the small princesses had her own little plot in the garden, where she could dig and plant to her heart's content.

One would make her flower-bed the shape of a whale, another liked hers to resemble a little mermaid, while the youngest made hers perfectly round like the sun and grew only flowers which glowed red like it. She was a strange child, quiet and thoughtful; and while the other sisters decorated their gardens with the most wonderful things which they had got from wrecked ships, all she would have, besides the rose-red flowers which resembled the sun far above, was a pretty marble statue, a lovely boy carved out of the clear white stone, which had fallen to the bottom from a wreck. Beside the statue she planted a rose-red weeping willow, and it grew splendidly, its fresh branches overhanging the statue and reaching down to the blue sandy bottom, where the shadow shone violet and stirred like the branches. It looked as though top and roots were playing at kissing each other.

Nothing pleased her more than hearing about the world of people above them. Her old grandmother had to tell her all she knew about ships and towns, human beings and animals; and she thought it especially lovely that up on earth the flowers were scented (they weren't on the bottom of the sea), and that the woods were green and the fishes to be seen among the branches there could sing so loudly and beautifully that it was a delight to hear them. (They were the little birds which their grandmother called fishes, for otherwise they would never have understood her, never having seen a bird.)

'When you're fifteen,' said their grandmother, 'you may rise to the surface, and sit on the rocks in the moonlight and watch the big ships sail by! You shall see woods and towns!'

The following year one of the sisters was fifteen, while the others—well, each was a year younger than the next, so that the youngest of them had five whole years to wait before she was allowed to come up from the bottom and see what it looked like here. But each promised to tell the rest what she had seen and thought loveliest on the first day; for their grandmother never told them enough, and there was so much they wanted to know about.

None was so full of longing as the youngest; the very one who had longest to wait, and who was so quiet and thoughtful. Many a night she would stand at the open window, looking up through the dark-blue water where the fishes flicked their fins and tails. She would see the moon and the stars, shining rather palely indeed, but looking much bigger seen through the water than they do to us; if what seemed like a black cloud floated beneath them she knew that it was either a whale swimming over her, or a ship full of people. They can never have imagined that a lovely little mermaid stood below, stretching her white hands up towards the keel.

By this time the eldest princess was fifteen and was allowed to rise to the surface.

She had a hundred things to tell about when she returned; but the loveliest of all, she said, was to lie in the moonlight on a sand-bank in the calm sea, watching from close inshore the big city where the lights twinkled like a hundred stars, listening to the music and the sounds and noises of carriages and people, seeing all the church towers and spires and hearing the ringing of the bells. For the very reason that she couldn't go there, this was what she most longed for.

Oh, how the youngest sister used to listen! And afterwards, when she stood at the open window in the evening, looking up through the dark-blue water, she would think of the big city with all its noise and bustle, and then she would fancy she heard the church bells ringing down to her.

The year after, the second sister was allowed to rise up through the water and swim wherever she liked. She came up just as the sun was setting, and this was the sight she thought was the loveliest. The whole sky had looked like gold, she said; and as for the clouds—well, she had never done describing their loveliness! Red and violet they had been as they sailed over her. But far swifter than they, like a long white veil, a flock of wild swans had flown across the water against the sun. She had swum towards it; but it had sunk, and the rosy glow of the sea and the clouds had gone out.

The year after that the third sister came up. She was the boldest of them all, and swam up a wide river which flowed into the sea. There she saw lovely green hills with vines growing on them, and castles and manors peeping out from between splendid woods. She heard all the birds singing; and the sun was so hot that she had often to dive under the water to cool her burning face. At a small bend she met a whole crowd of little human children; they were running about splashing the water, quite naked, and she wanted to play with them. But they were frightened and ran away, and a little black animal came up (it was a dog, but she had never seen a dog before), and it barked at her so dreadfully that she was scared and made for the open sea. But never could she forget the splendid woods, the green hills, and the pretty children who could swim in the water though they had no fish's tail.

The fourth sister wasn't so bold; she stayed in the middle of the wild ocean, and said that that was the loveliest: you could see for miles around you, and the sky above was like a big glass bell. She had seen ships, but far off, looking like seagulls. The funny dolphins had turned somersaults and the big whales had spurted water from their nostrils, so there had seemed to be a hundred waterfalls round them.

The turn now came for the fifth sister. Her birthday happened to be in winter; and so she saw what the others had not seen the first time. The sea looked quite green and big icebergs were floating about; each like a pearl, she said, though much bigger than the church steeples which people built. They appeared in the most wonderful shapes, and sparkled like diamonds. She had sat on one of the biggest of them, and all the sailors had been frightened, and had steered clear of her as she sat with her hair streaming in the wind. Late that evening the sky had become cloudy and it had thundered and lightened, while the black sea had lifted the big blocks of ice into the air, gleaming in the flashes of lightning. All the ships had taken in their sails and their crews had been filled with fear and dread, but she had sat calmly on her floating iceberg, watching the blue lightning zigzag into the glistening sea.

When one of the sisters rose above the surface for the first time she would be delighted by all the new and beautiful things she saw; but as they grew up and were allowed to go whenever they liked they no longer cared for it and became homesick, saying, after a month had gone by, that the most beautiful place after all was down below, and that there one felt so nicely at home.

Many an evening the five sisters would take one another by the arm and rise above the surface in a row. They had lovely voices, more beautiful than any human being's; and when a storm arose, and they thought that ships might be wrecked, they would swim in front of them, singing so beautifully about how grand it was at the bottom of the sea and telling the sailors not to be afraid to come down. But the sailors would never understand the words; they would think it was the storm, and would never see the loveliness down there either; for when the ship sank, the people were drowned, and were dead when they reached the merman king's palace.

On these evenings when, arm in arm, the sisters rose right up to the surface, the little one would stay behind all by herself, gazing after them and looking as though she was going to cry; only, a mermaid hasn't any tears, and so suffers all the more.

'Oh, if only I were fifteen!' she would say. 'I feel sure I shall love the world and the people who live and work in it.'

And at long last she was fifteen.

'There, now we're getting you off our hands!' said her grandmother, the old queen mother. 'Now come along and let me smarten you up like your sisters.' And so on her head she placed a wreath of white lilies, every petal of which was half a pearl. Then the old lady got eight big oysters to nip themselves fast to the princess's tail to show her rank.

'It does hurt!' said the little mermaid.

'Well, you can't have good looks without paying for them,' said the old lady.

Oh, how she would have liked to shake off all this finery and give up the heavy wreath! The red flowers in her garden suited her much better; but she didn't dare to change. 'Goodbye!' she said; and as lightly and delicately as a bubble she floated up through the water.

The sun had just set when she raised her head above the surface, but all the clouds were shimmering like roses and gold, and in the middle of the pink sky the evening star shone out brightly and beautifully; the air was soft and mild, and the sea dead calm. A big ship lay there, with three masts, and only one sail up, for not a wind was stirring; and sailors were sitting in the rigging and on the yard-arms. There was sound of music and singing; and as the evening drew on, a hundred coloured lanterns were lit: it looked as though the flags of every nation were waving in the air. The little mermaid swam right up to the cabin window; and each time the waves lifted her up she could see in through the crystal-clear panes to where many well-dressed people were standing. The handsomest among them

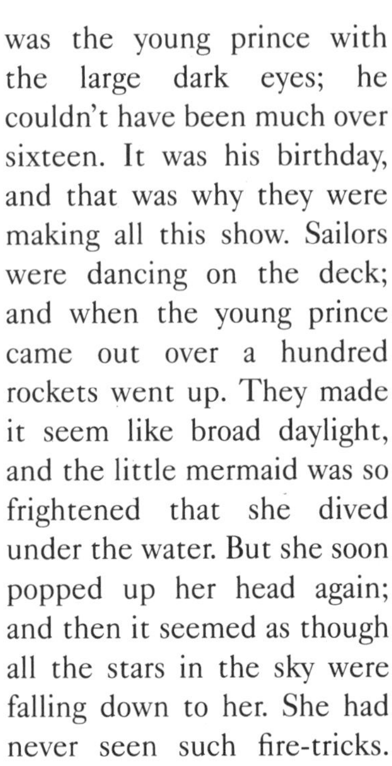

was the young prince with the large dark eyes; he couldn't have been much over sixteen. It was his birthday, and that was why they were making all this show. Sailors were dancing on the deck; and when the young prince came out over a hundred rockets went up. They made it seem like broad daylight, and the little mermaid was so frightened that she dived under the water. But she soon popped up her head again; and then it seemed as though all the stars in the sky were falling down to her. She had never seen such fire-tricks. Catherine-wheel suns went spinning round, gorgeous firework fishes soared into the air; and everything was reflected in the clear, calm sea. It was so light on the ship itself that you could see every little rope, the people easily. What a handsome young prince he was! And he stood there shaking hands with people, and laughing and smiling; while the music rang out in the glorious night.

It grew late, but the little mermaid couldn't take her eyes off the ship, and off the lovely prince. The coloured lanterns were put out, the rockets stopped going up, and there was no more gun-firing; but deep down in the sea there was a rumbling and a mumbling. All this time she sat on the waves, rocking up and down, so that she could see into the cabin. But the ship began to move faster, one sail unfurling after the other; the waves were growing stronger now, big clouds were gathering, and it was thundering and lightening in the distance. A dreadful storm was coming on! And so the sailors took in the sails. The ship was pitching and racing along on the fierce sea, the waves rising like big black mountains which seemed as though they would roll over the mast; but, dipping like a swan between the crests, the ship was lifted up again on the mountainous waves. To the little mermaid this speed seemed great fun, but the sailors didn't think so. The ship creaked and groaned; the thick planks bulged under the heavy buffeting given them by the sea; the mast broke in two like a reed; and the ship rolled over on its side, the water pouring into its holds. The little mermaid saw now that they were in danger; she had to look out for herself, because of planks and pieces of the ship that were floating on the water. At one moment it would be so pitch-dark that she could make out nothing at all; but when it lightened it became so clear again that she could make out everyone on the ship. They were all managing as best they could; it was the young prince she looked for most of all, and she saw him, as the ship split in two, sink down into the deep sea. At first she was very pleased, for now he would be coming down to her; but then she remembered that human beings can't live in water, and that he would never be able to come down to her father's palace, unless he was dead. No, he mustn't die; and so she swam to him between beams and planks that were drifting on the surface, quite forgetting that they might have crushed her. Diving deep into the water, she rose up again between the waves, and so at last reached the young prince, who could scarcely swim any farther in the raging sea. His arms and legs were growing tired, his handsome eyes were closed, and he must have died if the little mermaid hadn't come to him. Holding his head above the water, she allowed the waves to carry them wherever they would.

By the morning the storm was over; of the ship there wasn't a scrap to be seen. The sun rose red and bright above the sea, and it seemed to bring life into the prince's cheeks, though his eyes were still closed. The mermaid kissed his deep, handsome forehead and brushed back his wet hair; thinking that he resembled the marble statue down in her little garden, she kissed him again and wished that he might live.

And now before her she saw dry land: lofty blue mountains the tops of which shone white with snow, as though swans nestled there. Down by the shore were lovely green woods, and in front of them stood a church or a convent: which, she couldn't tell, but a building of that sort. Lemon- and orange-trees were growing in the garden, and tall palm-trees stood in front of the gateway. The sea here formed a small bay, which was perfectly calm but very deep right up to the cliff, where fine white sand had been washed in. Swimming to this with the handsome prince, she laid him on the sand, taking care to keep his head well up in the warm sunshine.

The bells in the big white building now began to ring, and many young women came walking through the garden. At this the little mermaid swam farther out and, getting behind some big rocks which jutted above the surface, she covered her hair and breast with sea-foam, so that no one would see her little face, and kept watch to see who came to the poor prince.

It was not long before a young woman came down. She seemed quite frightened, but only for a moment; then she brought several persons, and the mermaid saw the prince revive and smile to those who stood around him. He never smiled to her; but then, of course, he didn't know that she had saved him. She felt so very sad; and when he was led into the large building, she dived sorrowfully into the sea and made for home in her father's palace.

She who had always been quiet and thoughtful now became much more so. Her sisters asked her what she had seen on her first visit; but she told them nothing.

Many an evening and many a morning she floated up to where she had left the prince. She saw the garden fruits ripen and be picked; she saw the snow melt on the lofty mountains. But she never saw the prince, and so always she returned home sadder than ever. Her one consolation was to sit in the little garden and put her arms round the handsome marble statue which was so like the prince. But she never tended her flowers; they grew like a wilderness, spreading over the paths and twining their long stalks and leaves in the tree branches, so that it was quite dark.

In the end she couldn't bear it any longer, but told one of her sisters; and then all the rest heard of it at once, though no more than they and a few other mermaids, who only told their best friends. One of them knew who the prince was; she, too, had seen the party on the ship. She knew where he was from and where his kingdom lay.

'Come, little sister!' said the other princesses; and with their arms round one another's shoulder, they floated in a long row to the surface, coming up in front of the prince's palace.

This was built of shiny bright-yellow stone with large marble steps, one flight leading straight down to the sea. Gorgeous gilt domes towered above the roof, and between the pillars that surrounded the whole building stood marble figures which looked alive. Through the clear glass in the tall windows could be seen splendid halls hung with rich silk curtains and carpets, and all the walls were decorated with large paintings delightful to look at. In the middle of the biggest hall a large fountain was playing, the jets reaching up to the glass dome in the roof, through which the sun shone down on the water, and on the lovely plants growing in the big pool.

Now she knew where he lived, and she came to the surface there many an evening and night, swimming much nearer land than any of the others had dared, often indeed right up along the narrow canal under the splendid marble balustrade which cast its long shadow across the water. Here she would sit watching the young prince, who would think himself quite alone in the bright moonlight.

Many an evening she would see him sailing to music in his splendid boat, with flags flying. She would peep out from between green rushes; and if the wind caught her long, silvery veil and anyone chanced to see it, they would think it was a swan raising its wings.

On many a night she would hear the fishermen, lying with fires lit on the sea, tell such good things about the prince; and she was glad that she had saved his life when he had drifted half dead on the waves, and would remember how firmly his head had rested on her breast and how warmly she had kissed him. He knew nothing of all this: could never even dream of her.

She grew more and more fond of human beings, wishing more and more that she could go up among them. Their world seemed much greater than hers. They could speed across the sea in ships, climb lofty mountains high up above the clouds; and the countries they owned stretched, as forests and fields, farther than she could see. There was so much she wondered about; but her sisters didn't know the answers to all her questions, and so she asked her old grandmother. She knew all about the upper world, as she very properly called the lands above the sea.

'When human beings don't drown,' asked the little mermaid, 'can they live for ever? Don't they die, like us down here below?'

'Oh yes!' said the old lady. 'They too have to die, and their life is even shorter than ours. We can grow to be three hundred years old; but when our life here comes to an end, we become nothing but foam on the water and never even have a grave down among our loved ones. We have no immortal soul; we never have another life. We are like the green rush; once it is cut, it can never grow green again! Human beings, however, have a soul which lives for ever, lives after the body has turned to dust. It soars up into the bright sky, up to all the shining stars! As we rise to the surface to see human countries, they rise to lovely unknown places, places we shall never see.'

'Why weren't we given an immortal soul?' asked the little mermaid sadly. 'I'd give all my hundreds of years just to be a human being for one day and then get a place in this heavenly world!'

'You mustn't go thinking such things!' said the old lady. 'We are much happier and much better off than the human beings up there.'

'And so I am to die and float like foam on the sea, never hearing the music of the waves, or seeing the lovely flowers and the red sun! Is there nothing I can do to win an eternal soul?'

'No!' said the old lady. 'Only if a human being were to love you so dearly that you were more to him than father and mother; if he were to cling to you, with all his thoughts and affections, letting the clergyman place his right hand in yours and promising to be true to you here and for ever; then his soul would flow into your body and you, too, would receive a share of human happiness. He would give you a soul and yet keep his own. But that can never be! The very thing that is so lovely here in the sea, your fish's tail, they think ugly up there on earth. They know no better; there you have to have two clumsy props called legs in order to be good-looking!'

At this the little mermaid sighed and looked sadly down at her fish's tail.

'Let us be content,' said the old lady, 'to leap and plunge in the three hundred years which we have to live; I'm sure it's a long enough time. Afterwards we can rest all the happier in our graves. Tonight we're having a Court ball!'

This, too, was a splendid sight such as we never see on earth. Walls and ceiling in the great ball-room were of thick but clear glass. Several hundred enormous cockle-shells, rose-red and grass-green, were arranged in rows on either side, with a flaming blue fire which lit up the entire hall and shone out through the windows, making the sea outside quite light; you could see countless numbers of fishes, big and little ones, swimming towards the glass wall, some with scales glowing purple, others seeming to be silver and gold.

Flowing through the middle of the hall was a wide stream of water, and on it danced mermen and mermaids to their own lovely singing. No human beings have such pretty voices. The little mermaid sang the most beautifully of all; and they clapped her, so that for a moment she felt glad in her heart, knowing that she had the most beautiful voice of anyone on earth or in the sea. But soon her thoughts again turned to the world above her; she couldn't forget the handsome prince and her grief at not having, like him, an immortal soul. And so she slipped out of her father's palace, and while all within was singing and merrymaking, she sat sorrowfully in her little garden. There, coming through the water, she heard the sound of a horn, and she thought: 'I expect he's sailing in his ship up there! He whom I love more than father and mother; he to whom my thoughts cling, and in whose hand I would lay my life's happiness. I will venture everything to win him and an immortal soul! While my sisters are dancing in my father's palace, I'll go to the sea-witch, the one I've always been so afraid of; she may give me some help and advice.'

And so the little mermaid set off from her garden for the roaring whirlpools where the witch lived. She had never gone that way before. No flowers and no sea-grass grew there; there was only the bare grey sand stretching over towards the whirlpools, which churned round like roaring mill-wheels, dragging everything they caught hold of down into the deep. She had to pass right through these swirling waters to reach the sea-witch's country, and for a long stretch the only way was over hot bubbling mud, which the witch called her peat-bog. Behind it was her house, standing in the middle of a weird wood. All the trees and bushes in it were polyps: half animal and half plant. They looked like hundred-headed snakes growing out of the ground; all the branches were long, slimy arms with fingers like wriggling worms, moving joint by joint from the root to the tip. They twisted themselves tightly round everything they could catch hold of, and never let go again. The little mermaid was terrified as she stood there outside; her heart was pounding with fear, and she almost turned back. But then she thought of the prince and of the human soul, and plucked up courage. Tying her long flowing hair firmly about her head, so that the polyps shouldn't seize her by it, and laying her two hands together across her breast, she flew along as a fish speeds through water, in between the ugly polyps which stretched their waving arms and fingers after her. She saw how each of them held something it had seized, holding it with hundreds of little arms in a grip of iron. Human beings who had died at sea and sunk to the bottom were sticking out from the polyps' arms as white skeletons. Ships' rudders and chests had been grasped, together with skeletons of land animals and a little mermaid they had caught and choked: this, she felt, was the most dreadful of all.

Soon she came to a big, slimy clearing in the forest, where big fat sea-snakes frisked about, showing their ugly whitish-yellow stomachs. Standing in the middle of the clearing was a house built out of the bones of shipwrecked people; and here sat the sea-witch, allowing a toad to eat out of her mouth, the way people will let a canary take a piece of sugar. The horrid fat sea-snakes she called her 'little chicks', and she would let them romp on her big, spongy breast.

'I know what you want!' said the sea-witch. 'It's very silly of you! Still, you shall have your way, and it'll bring you to mischief, my lovely princess. You want to get rid of your fish's tail and instead have two stumps to walk on, like human beings, so that the young prince will fall in love with you and you can marry him and get an immortal soul.' And the witch gave such a loud and horrid laugh that the toad and the snakes dropped to the ground and lay there wallowing. 'You've come in the nick of time,' said the witch. 'After the sun has risen tomorrow I shouldn't be able to help you for another year. I'll make you a drink; and before the sun rises you must swim ashore with it and sit on the shore and drink it. Your tail will then split in two and shrivel into what human beings call nice little legs. But it'll hurt: like having a sharp sword go through you. All who see you will say you are the loveliest little human being they've ever seen! You'll keep your graceful movements, and no dancer will be as graceful. But every step you take will be like treading on a sharp knife which draws blood. If you're ready to suffer all this, I'm willing to help you.'

'Yes!' said the little mermaid in a trembling voice, thinking of the prince and of winning an immortal soul.

'But remember this,' said the witch: 'when once you have gained human form, you can never more become a mermaid! You will never be able to come down into the sea to your sisters and your father's palace; and unless you win the prince's love, so that for your sake he forgets father and mother, and clings to you with all his heart and allows the clergyman to place your hands together so that you become husband and wife, you will never win an immortal soul! The morning after he marries another, your heart will break and you will become foam on the water.'

'I'm willing!' said the little mermaid, turning as pale as death.

'But I want my payment as well,' said the witch. 'And the charge I make isn't a small one. You have the loveliest voice of any at the bottom of the sea. You think you're going to charm him with it, but that voice you must give to me. The best you possess is my price for the precious drink. I shall have to put my own blood into it, to make the drink as sharp as a two-edged sword.'

'But when you take my voice,' said the little mermaid, 'what shall I have left?'

'Your lovely figure,' said the witch; 'your graceful motions and your expressive eyes. You should charm a human heart with those. Well, have you lost heart? Put out your little tongue; then I'll cut it off in payment, and you shall have the magic drink!'

'Very well!' said the little mermaid; and the witch put on her cauldron to boil the magic drink. 'Cleanliness is next to godliness!' she said, wiping the cauldron with the snakes, which she tied into a knot; then scratching herself on the chest, she allowed her black blood to drip into the cauldron. The steam formed the weirdest shapes, which were enough to make anybody frightened. The witch kept on putting fresh things into the cauldron, so that when it was properly boiling it was like a crocodile shedding tears. At last the drink was ready, and then it looked like pure water.

'There you are, then!' said the witch; and she cut off the little mermaid's tongue, so that she was dumb and could neither sing nor speak.

'If the polyps should seize you on your way back through my wood,' said the witch, 'just throw one drop of this drink on them, and their arms and fingers will snap into a thousand pieces!' But there was no need for the little mermaid to do this; the polyps shrank from her in fear when they saw the bright drink, which glistened in her hand like a sparkling star. And so she soon got through the wood, the swamp, and the roaring whirlpools.

She could see her father's palace; the fires in the big ballroom were out, and she thought they must all have been asleep there, though she did not dare to look for them: she was dumb now and was leaving them for ever. She was almost heartbroken with grief. She stole into the garden, took one flower from each sister's flower-bed, and, throwing a thousand kisses in the direction of the palace, floated up through the dark-blue sea.

The sun hadn't yet come out when she saw the prince's palace and climbed the splendid marble stairs. The moon was shining beautifully. The little mermaid drank the burning sharp drink, and it was just as if a two-edged sword passed through her delicate body; she fainted and lay as though dead. When the sun shone out across the sea, she woke up, feeling a burning pain; but there in front of her stood the lovely young prince, fixing her with his jet-black eyes. Casting her own eyes down, she saw that her fish's tail was gone and that she had the nicest little white legs any little girl could have; but she was quite naked, and so she wrapped herself in her mass of long hair. The prince asked who she was and how she had got there, and she looked at him sweetly though sadly with her dark-blue eyes; of course, she couldn't speak. Then, taking her by the hand, he led her into the palace. Every step she took felt, as the witch had told her it would, like treading on pointed needles and sharp knives, but she bore it gladly. Holding the prince's hand, she rose as lightly as a bubble; and he and everyone else marvelled at her graceful, gliding walk.

Rich dresses of silk and muslin were given her to put on. She was the most beautiful of any in the palace; but she was dumb, and could neither sing nor speak. Lovely slave-girls, clad in silk and gold, came forward and sang for the prince and his royal parents; there was one who sang more beautifully than all the rest, and the prince clapped his hands and smiled at her. It made the little mermaid so sad, because she knew that she had sung far more beautifully. She thought: 'If only he knew that I have given my voice away for ever, so as to be with him!'

The slave-girls then danced, in graceful, gliding dances to most glorious music; and seeing them, the little mermaid lifted her pretty white arms, raised herself on tiptoe, and glided across

W HEATH ROBINSON

the floor, dancing as no one had danced yet. At every movement her loveliness became even more striking, and her eyes spoke more deeply to the heart than the singing of the slave-girls.

Everyone was delighted by it, especially the prince, who called her his little foundling; and so she danced more and more, though every time her foot touched the ground it was like treading on sharp knives. The prince said that she was always to be with him, and she was allowed to sleep outside his door on a velvet cushion.

He got her to make men's clothes, so that she could go with him on horseback. They would ride through the sweetly scented woods, where green branches would touch her shoulders and little birds sing behind the fresh leaves. With the prince she climbed high mountains; and though her delicate feet would bleed for all to see, she would laugh and follow him till they saw the clouds sailing beneath them like a flock of birds making their way to foreign lands.

At home in the prince's palace, in the night when the others were asleep, she would go out on to the broad marble steps, and it would cool her burning feet to stand in the cold sea-water; she would then think of those down below.

One night her sisters came up arm in arm, singing so sadly as they swam across the water; and she waved to them, and they knew her and told her how unhappy she had made them all. They visited her every night after that; and one night she saw, a long way out, her old grandmother, who hadn't been above the surface for many years, together with the merman king wearing his crown. They stretched their hands towards her, but didn't venture so near land as her sisters.

She grew fonder of the prince day by day. He liked her as one likes a good, sweet child; but the idea of making her his queen never entered his head. And his wife she had to be; otherwise she would never get an immortal soul, but on his wedding morning would become foam on the sea.

'Don't you like me most of any of them?' the little mermaid's eyes seemed to say when he took her in his arms and kissed her pretty forehead.

'Yes, you are dearest to me,' said the prince; 'for you are the best-hearted of them all. You are the most devoted to me; and you remind me of a young woman I once saw, but am never likely to see again. I was on a ship which was wrecked; the waves washed me ashore by a holy temple, where some young women served. The youngest of them found me by the shore and saved my life; I saw her only twice. She is the only woman in the world I could love; but you are like her, and you have nearly taken her place in my heart. She belongs to the holy temple, and so good fortune has sent me you; we will never part!'

'Alas, he doesn't know that I saved his life!' thought the little mermaid. 'I took him across the sea to the wood where the holy temple stands, and hid behind the foam, watching to see if anyone would come. I saw the beautiful young woman he loves more than me!' And the mermaid gave a deep sigh; she couldn't cry. 'The young woman belongs to the holy temple, he says; she'll never come out into the world; they'll never meet again. I am with him, seeing him every day; I'll care for him, love him, give my life to him!'

But now the prince was to marry and have the lovely daughter of the neighbouring king for his wife, people said. That was why he was fitting out such a splendid ship. 'The prince is going to see the land of our neighbouring king, they say, but it's to see the neighbouring king's daughter; he's taking many attendants with him.' But the little mermaid shook her head and laughed; she knew the prince's mind much better than all the rest. 'I must go!' he had said to her. 'I must see the beautiful princess; my parents insist on it. But they shall never make me bring her home as my bride; I'll never love her! She doesn't remind me of the beautiful young woman in the temple, as you do. If ever I choose a bride, it's more likely to be you, my dumb foundling with the expressive eyes!' And he kissed her red lips, played with her long hair, and laid his head on her heart, making it dream of human happiness and an immortal soul.

'Why, you don't seem afraid of the sea, my dumb child!' he said, as they stood on the splendid ship that was to take him to the lands of the neighbouring king. And he told her of storms and calm weather, of weird fishes in the deep, and of what the diver had seen there; while she smiled at all he told, knowing, of course, more about the bottom of the sea than anyone.

In the moonlit night when everyone was asleep apart from the ship's mate who stood at the helm, she would sit by the rail, gazing into the clear water and imagining that she saw her father's palace; her old grandmother would be nearest, wearing her silver crown and gazing up through the swift currents towards the ship's keel. Then her sisters would rise to the surface, gazing sorrowfully at her and wringing their white hands. She would wave to them, smiling, wanting to tell them that she was quite well and happy; but then the cabin boy would come along and the sisters would dive below, leaving him to think that the white he had seen was foam on the sea.

Next morning, the ship sailed into the harbour of the neighbouring king's splendid city. The church bells were all ringing, and trumpets were blown from the tall towers as soldiers stood with flags flying and bayonets flashing. Every day was celebrating. Balls and parties followed one another, but the princess wasn't there yet; she was being educated, they said, a long way off in a holy temple where she was learning all the royal virtues. At long last she arrived.

The little mermaid was eager to see her beauty, and was forced to admit that she had never seen a more graceful figure. Her skin was so pure and delicate; and smiling behind long dark eyelashes were two blue-black, steadfast eyes.

'It's you!' said the prince. 'You who saved me when I lay almost dead on the shore.' And he clasped his blushing bride in his arms. 'Oh, how overjoyed I am!' he said to the little mermaid. 'The best, the thing I never dared hope for, has come true for me. You will be glad at my good fortune, for you are fonder of me than any of them!' And the little mermaid kissed his hand, while all the time she felt that her heart would break. His wedding morning would bring death to her, changing her into foam on the sea.

The church bells all rang; the heralds rode through the streets proclaiming the betrothal. Sweet-scented oils in rich silver lamps burnt on every altar. The priests swung their incense vessels, and the bride and bridegroom held hands and were blessed by the bishop. The little mermaid, dressed in silk and gold, stood holding the bridal train, but her ears were deaf to the festive music, her eyes blind to the sacred ceremony she was thinking of her last night, and of everything in this world she had lost.

That very evening the bride and bridegroom went aboard the ship; guns were fired, flags all waved, and in the middle of the ship was pitched a royal tent of gold and purple, with the loveliest of cushions for the bridal couple to sleep on in the cool, still night.

The sails swelled in the breeze, and the ship glided lightly and easily across the clear ocean.

As darkness fell, lamps of many colours were lit and the sailors danced merry dances on deck. The little mermaid was reminded of the first time she had come to the surface and seen the same splendour and rejoicing; and she reeled in the dance herself, gliding as the swallow glides when it is being chased, while all cried out in admiration of her, for she had never danced so splendidly. It was as if sharp knives cut into her feet, though she never felt them; they cut more painfully into her heart. She knew this was the last evening that she would see the one for whom she had left her home and her family, giving up her lovely voice and daily suffering endless pains all unknown to him. It was the last night she would breathe the air he breathed, see the deep ocean and the starry blue sky. An everlasting night, mindless and dreamless, awaited her who had no soul, no hope of winning one. On the ship all was rejoicing and merrymaking till well over midnight, while she laughed and danced with the thought of death in her heart. The prince kissed his lovely bride, and she played with his black hair; and arm in arm they went to rest in the splendid tent.

The ship grew hushed and silent, with only the mate at the helm, as the little mermaid laid her white arms on the rail and looked eastward for the dawn, knowing that the first ray of daylight would kill her. All at once she saw her sisters come to the surface, as pale as she was herself. Their beautiful long hair no longer streamed in the wind; it had been cut off.

'We gave it to the witch, so that she would bring help that will save you from dying tonight. She gave us a knife. Here it is! See how sharp it is! Before the sun rises you must stab it into the prince's heart, and when his warm blood splashes your feet, they will grow together into a fish's tail and you'll be a mermaid again, able to come down below to us and live out your three hundred years before becoming dead, salt-sea foam. Hurry! He or you must die before the sun rises! Our old grandmother is so full of grief that her white hair has fallen out, as ours fell to the witch's scissors. Kill the prince and come back! Hurry! Don't you see the red strip in the sky? In a few minutes the sun will rise, and you must die!' And, giving a strange, deep sigh, they sank into the waves.

The little mermaid drew back the purple curtain from the tent door and saw the lovely bride asleep with her head on the prince's breast; and, stooping down, she kissed him on his beautiful forehead, looked up at the sky where the dawn was growing brighter and brighter, looked at the sharp knife, and again turned her gaze on the prince, who murmured in his dreams the name of his bride. She alone was in his thoughts, and the hand which held the knife trembled. But then all at once she threw it far into the waves, which shone red where it fell, as though drops of blood were trickling from the water. Once more she looked, with half-glazed eyes, at the prince; then she plunged into the sea, feeling her body melt into foam as she did so.

The sun now rose from the sea, its beams falling gently and warmly on the deadly cold foam. The little mermaid had no feeling of death, but saw the bright sun and, soaring above her, hundreds of lovely transparent creatures; through them she could see the ship's white sails and the red clouds in the sky; their voice was music, but so spiritual that no human ear could hear it, just as no earthly eye could see them. They glided through the air without wings by their own lightness. The little mermaid saw that she had a body like theirs, which rose higher and higher out of the foam.

'To whom am I coming?' she said; and her voice sounded like that of the other beings, so spiritual that no earthly music can reproduce it.

'To the daughters of the air!' they replied. 'A mermaid never has an immortal soul, and can never get one unless she wins the love of a human being! Her everlasting life depends on a strange power. The daughters of the air have no everlasting soul either, but by good deeds they can create one for themselves. We fly to the hot countries, where the warm, plague-filled air kills human beings, and there we waft cool breezes. We spread through the air the scent of flowers, bringing refreshment and healing. When for three hundred years we have striven to do all the good we can, we get an immortal soul and share in the eternal happiness of human beings. You have striven, poor little mermaid, with all your heart for the same as we have striven for; you have suffered and borne, and have raised yourself up into the world of the aerial spirits. Now, through your own good deeds, you can create an immortal soul for yourself in three hundred years' time.'

And, lifting her clear arms towards God's sun, the little mermaid, for the first time, felt tears.

There was noise and bustle on the ship again, and she saw the prince with his beautiful bride, gazing sadly at the bubbling foam as though they knew that she had plunged into the waves. Invisible now, she kissed the bride's forehead, smiled to the prince, and with the other children of the air soared up on to the rose-red cloud which was sailing above.

'In three hundred years we shall float like this into God's heaven.'

'We can even get there earlier!' one of them whispered. 'We float invisibly into human houses where there are children, and for every day on which we find a good child who pleases his parents and earns their love, God shortens our time of trial. The child never knows when we fly through the room; and when we smile with pleasure at him, a year is taken off the three hundred. But if we see a naughty and wicked child, then we must weep tears of sorrow, and each tear adds a day to our time of trial!'

THE EMPEROR'S NEW CLOTHES

MANY years ago there lived an emperor so tremendously fond of fine new clothes that he spent all his money on rigging himself out. He cared nothing for his soldiers or for going to the theatre or for driving in the country, unless it was to show off his new clothes. He had a robe for every hour of the day; and, just as we say of a king that he is 'in council', so they would say of him: 'The emperor's in the wardrobe'.

In the big city where he lived it was always lively, and every day there were many visitors. One day two impostors came. They passed themselves off as weavers and said they could weave the loveliest cloth imaginable. Not only were the colours and the patterns so very beautiful, but clothes made from the material had the magic power of being invisible to anyone not fit for his post or hopelessly stupid.

'H'm, these clothes sound rather good,' thought the emperor. 'By wearing them, I could find out which of my people were unfit for their posts and should be able to tell the clever ones from the stupid. Yes, that cloth must be woven for me at once!' And he paid the impostors a large sum of money in advance, so that they could start work.

Sure enough, they set up two looms and pretended to be working, though there wasn't a thing on the looms. They coolly demanded the finest silk and the richest gold thread; and stuffing this into their bags, they worked away at the empty looms till well into the night.

W HEATH ROBINSON

'I wonder how far they've got with that material,' thought the emperor. But he had rather a queer feeling inside him when he thought that anyone stupid or unfit for his post wouldn't be able to see it. Of course, he saw no reason to be afraid himself; still, he thought he would send somebody else first, just to see how things stood. The whole city had heard about the magic power of the material, and everybody was eager to see how hopeless or stupid his neighbour was.

'I'll send my honest old minister to the weavers,' thought the emperor. 'He's the best person to see what the cloth looks like, for he's a man of sense, and nobody attends to his job better than he does.'

So off went the worthy old minister to the room where the two impostors sat working at the empty looms. 'Good gracious!' thought the old minister, opening his eyes wide. 'I can't see a thing!' But he didn't say so.

The two impostors said would he please come a little nearer, and didn't he think it had a beautiful pattern and lovely colours. They then pointed to the empty loom, and the poor old minister opened his eyes wider than ever. But he couldn't see anything, for there was nothing to see. 'Goodness me!' he thought. 'Does that mean I'm stupid? I never thought I was—and nobody must ever know it. Surely I can't be unfit for my post! No, it would never do for me to let on that I can't see the cloth.'

'Well, have you nothing to say about it?' said the one who was weaving.

'Oh, it's lovely! Simply delicious!' said the old minister, peering through his spectacles. 'This pattern—and these colours! I shall tell the emperor I am indeed delighted with it.'

'We're pleased to hear it,' said the two weavers; and they named the colours and the singular pattern.

The old minister listened carefully, so as to be able to repeat the names when he got back to the emperor, which he did.

The impostors now asked for more money, and more silk and gold thread, saying they wanted it for weaving. It all went into their own pockets; not a thread was put on the loom, and they went on weaving at the empty loom as before.

Soon the emperor sent another trusted official to see how the weaving was getting on, and if the cloth would soon be ready. The same thing happened to him as to the minister: he looked and looked, but as there was nothing there but the empty looms, he couldn't see anything.

'There, isn't it a beautiful piece of cloth?' said the two impostors, pointing out the lovely pattern which wasn't there.

'I'm not stupid,' thought the man; 'so it must be because I'm not fit for my post! That's funny! But I must take good care not to show it.' And so he praised the material he couldn't see and assured them how delighted he was with the pretty colours and the lovely pattern. 'Yes, it's simply delicious!' he told the emperor.

The whole town was talking about the splendid material.

Now the emperor thought he would see it for himself, while it was still on the loom. With a large body of chosen men, among them the two worthy old officials who had been there already, he went to where the two wily impostors were now weaving for all they were worth, but without a thread or a stitch on the loom.

'Isn't it simply superb!' said the two worthy officials. 'See what a pattern, your majesty, and what colours!' And they pointed to the empty loom, thinking that the others could see the material.

'What on earth!' thought the emperor. 'I don't see a thing!

Why, this is terrible! Am I stupid? Am I unfit to be emperor? This is the most dreadful thing that could have befallen me!' . . . 'Oh, it's beautiful!' said the emperor. 'It has my most gracious approval!' And he nodded with satisfaction as he looked at the empty loom; he wasn't going to say he couldn't see anything. All the courtiers who were with him looked and looked, but with as little result as all the rest, though, like the emperor, they said: 'Oh, it's very beautiful!' And they advised him to try out some clothes made from this splendid new material in the grand procession that was shortly to take place. 'It's superb! Ravishing! Magnificent!' they all declared. They were one and all most thoroughly delighted with it. The emperor gave each of the impostors a medal to pin on his coat, and the title of Lord High Weaver.

Before the morning of the procession the impostors sat up all night with over sixteen candles burning. People could see they were busy finishing the emperor's new clothes. They pretended to take the cloth off the loom, they clipped at the air with their great scissors, they sewed with needles that weren't threaded, and then at last they said: 'There, now the clothes are ready!'

The emperor and his chief gentlemen in waiting went there in person, and each of the weavers raised his arm as though holding something, and said: 'Here you have the breeches! Here's the coat! Here's the cloak!' And so they went on. 'They're as light as gossamer! You wouldn't think you had anything on—that's the beauty of them!'

'Yes, indeed!' said all the gentlemen in waiting. But they couldn't see anything, for there wasn't anything to see.

'If it would graciously please your imperial majesty to take off your clothes,' said the impostors, 'we will help you on with the new ones, here in front of the mirror.'

The emperor took off all his clothes, and the impostors pretended to help him on with each of the new garments they were supposed to have made. Then they put their hands round his waist as if they were fastening something round—that was the train. And the emperor turned and twisted in front of the mirror. 'How becoming they are! What a beautiful fit!' they all of them cried. 'What a pattern! What colours! What sumptuous robes they are!'

'The canopy to be carried over your majesty in the procession is waiting outside,' said the master of ceremonies.

'Very well, I'm ready,' said the emperor. 'Isn't it a good fit?' And he turned round once more in front of the mirror, pretending to be having a really good look at his finery.

The chamberlains who were to bear the train fumbled about the floor as if they were picking the train up; and they walked along holding their hands in the air, not daring to let on that they couldn't see anything.

So off marched the emperor in the procession under the

beautiful canopy, and everybody in the street and at the windows cried: 'Aren't the emperor's new clothes wonderful! What a lovely train he has to his robe! What a splendid fit!' Nobody would let on that he couldn't see anything, because then he would have been unfit for his job or very stupid. Never had the emperor's clothes been such a success.

'But he hasn't got anything on!' cried a little child.

'Dear me! Listen to what the pretty innocent says!' cried its father. And it was whispered from man to man what the child had said.

'"He hasn't got anything on," says a little child. "He hasn't got anything on!"'

'Why, but he hasn't got anything on!' they all shouted at last. And the emperor winced, for he felt they were right. But he thought to himself: 'I must go through with the procession now.' And he drew himself up more proudly than ever, while the chamberlains walked behind him, bearing the train that wasn't there.

THE STEADFAST TIN SOLDIER

ONCE upon a time there were twenty-five tin soldiers, all of them brothers, for they had all sprung from an old tin spoon. They shouldered their rifles and faced eyes forward; and their uniforms, red and blue, looked really splendid. The first words they ever heard in this world, when the lid was taken off the box in which they lay, were: 'Tin soldiers!' It was the cry of a little boy as he clapped his hands; they had been given to him for his birthday, and he was standing them on the table. Each soldier was the living image of the next, except for one who was a little bit different. He had only one leg, as he was the last to be made and there hadn't been enough tin to go round. But he stood just as firmly on his one leg as the others did on two, and he was the one that was to stand out from the rest.

There were many other toys on the table where they were placed, but the one which caught the eye first was a splendid paper castle. Through the tiny windows you could see right into the rooms. In front of it were some small trees standing round a little mirror which was supposed to be a lake, and some wax swans swimming on it were reflected in the water. It was all very pretty, but prettier than all the rest was a little lady who stood at the open door of the castle. She too had been cut out of paper, but she was wearing a skirt of the brightest muslin and a narrow blue ribbon over her shoulder like a scarf, and in the middle of this was a glistening spangle the size of her face. The little lady was stretching out both her arms, for she was a dancer; and she had raised one of her legs so high in the air that the tin soldier couldn't make out where it was and so thought that she had only one leg, like himself.

'She'd make a wife for me!' he thought. 'But she's a very fine lady, she lives in a castle. I only have a box, and there are twenty-five of us to that—it's no place for her. Still, I must see about getting to know her!' And so he lay all his length behind a snuff-box which stood on the table, from where he had a good view of the pretty little lady, who kept on standing on one leg without losing her balance.

Late in the evening all the other soldiers got back in their box and the people of the house went to bed. The toys then began to play—at visiting, at fighting battles, and at having parties. The tin soldiers rattled their box because they wanted to join in but couldn't get the lid off. The nutcrackers turned somersaults and the slate pencil had fun on the slate. They all made such a noise that they woke the canary up and he began to join in, chirruping away in verse. The only two who never budged were the tin soldier and the little dancer. She stood straight up on tiptoe with both her arms stretched out, and he was just as steadfast on his one leg, never for a moment taking his eyes off her.

Then the clock struck twelve, and smack! went the lid of the snuff-box. But there wasn't any snuff in; only a little black goblin, a tricky little jack-in-the-box.

'Tin soldier,' said the jack-in-the-box, 'just you keep your eyes to yourself!'

But the tin soldier pretended not to hear him.

'All right, you wait till the morning!' said the jack-in-the-box.

Now, when the morning came and the children got up, the tin soldier was put on the window-sill; and, whether it was the jack-in-the-box or only a draught that did it, all of a sudden the window sprang open and the soldier fell head first from the third floor. It all went at a dreadful speed, and he turned his leg up in the air and came to rest on his helmet, with his bayonet sticking between the paving-stones.

The maid and the little boy went straight down to look for him: but though they very nearly trod on him, they didn't see him. Had the soldier cried 'Here I am!' they would most likely have found him, but he didn't think it proper to shout out when he was in uniform.

Then it started to rain, and the drops fell faster and faster till it became a regular downpour. When it was over, two street-boys came along.

'Hey, look!' said one of them. 'There's a tin soldier! We'll give him a sail!'

So they made a boat out of newspaper, put the tin soldier in the middle, and sent him sailing away down the gutter, while they both ran alongside, clapping their hands. Dear me, what big waves there were in that gutter, and what a current! But then it had just been pouring. The paper boat kept bobbing up and down, and every now and then it would twirl right round, making the soldier feel quite giddy. But he remained steadfast and never flinched, eyes forward and shouldering his rifle.

All of a sudden the boat was swept under a covered drain; it became as dark as it was at home in his box.

'I wonder where I shall get to now!' he thought. 'Ah yes, the jack-in-the-box is to blame for this. Oh, if only the little lady were in the boat with me, it could be twice as dark for all I'd care!'

Just then along came a big water-rat that lived in the drain.

'Have you got a passport?' demanded the rat. 'Show your passport!'

But the tin soldier never said a word; only clutched his rifle more tightly than ever. The boat tore along, with the rat after it. Ugh! How it gnashed its teeth and shouted out to sticks and straws: 'Stop him! Stop him! He hasn't paid the toll. He hasn't shown his passport!'

But the current grew stronger and stronger. The soldier could already see daylight ahead, where the drain ended; though he could also hear a roaring noise fit to frighten any brave man. Just think of it—where the gutter ended, the drain emptied itself into a great canal; and that was as dangerous for him as sailing down a big waterfall would be for us!

Already he was so close that he couldn't stop. Then out rushed the boat, with the poor tin soldier holding himself as stiffly as he knew how—no one was going to say that he'd blinked! Three or four times the boat spun round, and by now it was full of water to the very top—sink it must! The tin soldier was up to his neck in water, and deeper and deeper sank the boat. The paper came further and further apart, and now the water closed over the soldier's head. At this moment his thoughts turned to the pretty little dancer whom he was never to see more, and in the tin soldier's ears rang the old song:

> On, on, warrior!
> Forward to your death now!

And then the paper came to pieces and the tin soldier tumbled through—to be instantly swallowed by a great fish.

My word, it was dark in there! It was worse even than in the drain—and so cramped! But the tin soldier remained steadfast, lying full length, shouldering his rifle . . .

The fish dashed about, making the most horrible twists and turns. But then at last it lay perfectly still, and all at once it was as if a flash of lightning had passed through it. The light shone quite brightly, and suddenly there was a cry of 'Tin soldier!' The fish had been caught, taken to market, sold, and brought into the kitchen, where the maid had cut it open with a big knife. She picked the soldier up by the waist with her finger and thumb and took him into the sitting-room, where everybody was eager to see this remarkable man who had been travelling about inside a fish. But it was nothing to the tin soldier. They stood him on the table, and there . . . well now, what a strange world it is! The tin soldier was in the very room he had been in before; there were the very same children, and the toys standing on the table: the splendid castle with the pretty little dancer still standing on one leg with the other high up in the air —she too had been steadfast. The tin soldier was so touched that he could have wept tin tears, only that wouldn't have done at all. He looked at her and she looked at him, but neither said a word.

All of a sudden one of the little boys took the soldier and threw him straight into the fire, without as much as saying why—it was definitely the jack-in-the-box that was to blame.

The tin soldier was all aglow and felt dreadfully hot, but whether it was with the real flames or with love he couldn't have said. His colours were all gone, but whether they had gone on the journey or from grief nobody could tell. He looked at the little lady and she looked at him, and he felt himself melting away, but still he remained steadfast as he shouldered his rifle. Then all at once the door opened, the wind caught the little dancer, and she flew like a fairy straight into the stove to the tin soldier, where she burst into flames and was gone. And then the tin soldier melted away to a lump; and when the maid cleared out the ashes the next day she found him in the shape of a little tin heart. But all that was left of the dancer was the spangle, and that was as black as a cinder.

W.H.R
THE : WILD : SWANS

THE WILD SWANS

A LONG way from here, in the land the swallows fly to when we are having winter, there lived a king who had eleven sons and one daughter, called Eliza. The eleven brothers—princes, they were—went to school with stars on their breasts and swords at their sides; they wrote on golden slates with diamond pencils and had their lessons off by heart as well as in their heads, so you could hear straight away they were princes. Their sister Eliza sat on a little stool made from mirror-glass, and she had a picture-book which had cost half the kingdom.

Oh, they were well off, these children! But it wasn't always to be so.

Their father, the king of the whole country, married a wicked queen who was not a bit nice to the poor children, as they found out on the very first day. There were great goings-on all over the palace, and the children were playing at visitors; but instead of having all the cakes and roasted apples they could eat, all she gave them was a cupful of sand, telling them they could fancy they were having something.

The following week she sent the little sister Eliza into the country to stay with some farm people, and before very long she had put so many ideas into the king's head about the poor princes that he no longer cared for them.

'You go off into the world and shift for yourselves!' said the wicked queen. 'Go flying off, big birds without voices!' Yet she couldn't make it as bad for them as she would have liked, for they changed into eleven lovely wild swans. With a strange cry they flew out of the palace windows and away over the park and the wood.

Very early in the morning they came flying past where their sister Eliza lay fast asleep in the farmer's cottage; and here they glided over the roof, craning their long necks and flapping their wings, though no one either heard or saw them. Off again they had to go, high up into the clouds, far away into the wide world; and there they flew into a big dark wood which stretched right down to the shore.

Poor little Eliza stood in the farmer's cottage playing with a green leaf; she had no other plaything. And pricking a hole in the leaf she looked through it at the sun and seemed to see the bright eyes of her brothers, while whenever the warm sunbeams shone on her cheeks she would think of all their kisses.

One day passed like another. Whenever the wind blew through the big rose-hedges outside the house, it would whisper to the roses: 'Who can be more beautiful than you?' And shaking their heads the roses would say: 'Eliza!' And whenever the old wife sat at her door on a Sunday reading her prayer-book, the wind would turn the leaves and say to the book: 'Who can be more good than you?' 'Eliza!' the prayer-book would say. And what the roses and the prayer-book said was the simple truth.

When she was fifteen it was time for her to go home; and seeing how beautiful she was the queen was cross and spiteful with her. She would have loved to turn her into a wild swan just like her brothers, only she didn't dare to straight away, as the king was wanting to see his daughter.

Early one morning the queen went into the bathroom. It was built of marble and decorated with soft cushions and the loveliest of carpets. And taking three toads and kissing them she said to one of them 'You sit on Eliza's head when she gets into the bath and make her as sluggish as you!' and to the second 'You sit on her forehead and make her as ugly as you, so that her father won't know her!' while to the third she whispered 'You give her a bad temper that will cause her suffering!' Then putting the toads in the clear water, which instantly turned a greenish colour, she called Eliza, undressed her, and made her get into the water; and as she ducked in one of the toads sat on her hair, the second on her forehead, and the third on her breast, only without Eliza seeming to notice it. As she got up three crimson poppies floated on the water. If the creatures hadn't been poisonous and been kissed by the witch, they would have been turned into red roses; but flowers they had become, from settling on her head and at her heart. She was too good and innocent for the magic to have any power over her.

When she saw this, the wicked queen rubbed her over with walnut-juice, which made her all black and brown, smeared her pretty face with a smelly ointment, and made her hair all tangled. You wouldn't have known the beautiful Eliza again.

And so when her father saw her he got quite a shock and said that she wasn't his daughter. No one else would own to her either, excepting only the watch-dog and the swallows; but then they were poor creatures and had no say in the matter.

This made poor Eliza cry, and she thought of her eleven brothers who were all gone. Sadly she stole out of the palace and walked all day over meadow and common and into the big forest. She had no idea where she was making for, but she felt so very sad and longed for her brothers; like herself, she thought, they had been driven out into the world, and she meant to try to find them.

She hadn't been long in the forest when night fell; and she had left every path and track behind. Lying down on the soft

W. HEATH
ROBINSON

moss, she said her prayers and laid her head against a tree-stump. It was so silent, the air was so mild, and shining like green fire round about the grass and moss were hundreds of glow-worms; she had only to touch a branch very gently with her hand and the glowing insects dropped down to her like shooting stars.

All that night she dreamt of her brothers; they played like children again, and they wrote with diamond pencils on gold slates and looked at the lovely picture-book that had cost half the kingdom; only they no longer made simple lines and noughts, but wrote down their boldest adventures and all they had seen and heard. And everything in the picture-book was alive; the birds sang and people came out of the book and talked to Eliza and her brothers. But when she turned the page they jumped straight back again, so that the pictures shouldn't get jumbled up.

When she awoke the sun was already well up. She couldn't actually see it, for the tall trees spread their branches thick and close; but the rays shimmered there like fluttering golden gauze. There was a fresh smell of green things and the birds very nearly perched on her shoulders. She heard the splashing of water; for there were many large springs which all ran out into a lake with the loveliest sandy bottom. There were certainly some thick bushes growing round about; but in one place the stags had nibbled a large opening, and here Eliza went down to the water, which was so clear that if the wind hadn't stirred leaves and bushes, making them wave, she would have thought they had been painted on the bottom, so plainly was every leaf reflected, both those which the sun shone through and those right in the shade.

At the sight of her own face she was quite frightened, it was so brown and nasty; but when she wetted her little hand and rubbed her eyes and forehead, the white skin shone through again. Then, taking off all her clothes, she went into the fresh water; and a lovelier princess than she there never was in all the world.

When she had got dressed again and had plaited her long hair, she went to the gushing spring, drank from the hollow of her hand, and wandered deeper into the forest, not knowing where to. She thought of her brothers, and she thought of the good Lord, who surely would not desert her. He made the wild crab-apples grow as food for the hungry; and He showed her one such tree, its branches weighed down with fruit. Here she made her first midday meal and then, after propping up its branches, walked on into the darkest part of the forest. There it was so still she could hear her own footsteps and every little withered leaf that yielded to her foot; not a bird was to be seen there, not a sunbeam could force its way through the great leafy branches. The tall trunks grew so very close together that when she looked straight ahead it seemed to her as though she were surrounded by one wooden fence standing behind another. Oh, the loneliness here was like nothing she had ever known!

The night grew so dark, and not one little glow-worm shone out from the moss as sadly she lay down to sleep. Then suddenly the branches above her head seemed to her to part, and our Lord looked down with gentle eyes upon her, while little angels peeped out from above His head and from under His arms.

When she woke up in the morning she couldn't tell whether she had dreamt it or it was all really true.

Going a few steps further on, she met an old woman with some berries in a basket, and the woman gave her some of these. Eliza asked her whether she had seen eleven princes riding through the forest.

'No,' said the woman. 'But yesterday I saw eleven swans with golden crowns on their heads swimming down a river near here!'

And she took Eliza a little further on till they came to a bank, where down below there was a winding river. The trees by its shores stretched their long, leafy branches across to one another; and where they were unable to reach by their own natural growth, they had torn their roots loose from the soil and were leaning across the water with their branches interlaced.

Taking leave of the old woman, Eliza walked alongside the river to the point where it flowed out to the wide open shore.

Lying outstretched before her was the beautiful sea. But not a sail was in sight, not a boat was to be seen. How was she to make her way on from there? She looked at the countless pebbles that lay on the beach; all had been worn smooth and round by the sea. Glass, iron, stones—everything washed up there had been shaped by the sea, which yet was far softer than her delicate hand. 'It rolls on tirelessly, smoothing down what is rough. I'll be just as tireless. Thank you for your lesson, you clear, rolling waves! The time will come, as I know in my heart, when you will bear me to my dear brothers.'

Lying on the seaweed washed up on the beach were eleven white swans' feathers. She gathered them into a bunch, and there were drops of water on them; whether dew or tears no one could tell. Lonely though it was by the shore, she didn't feel it; for the sea was ever-changing, showing more changes in a few hours than freshwater lakes in a whole year. If a large black cloud appeared, the sea would seem to say 'I can look black as well'; and then the wind would blow and the waves would show white. But if the clouds gleamed red and the wind slept, the sea would be like a rose-petal, now green, now white. But no matter how calmly it rested there would be gentle motion by the shore; the water would softly rise and fall like the breast of a sleeping child.

The sun was about to set when Eliza caught sight of eleven wild swans with golden crowns on their heads flying towards land, one gliding behind the other; they looked like a long white ribbon. Climbing on to the bank Eliza hid behind a bush; and the swans settled near her, flapping their big white wings.

When the sun had sunk into the sea the swans suddenly shed their feathers, and there stood eleven lovely princes, Eliza's brothers. She gave a loud cry; for though they had greatly changed she knew that it was they, that it must be they. And she flung herself into their arms, calling them by name; and they were so happy when they saw and knew their little sister, who had grown so big and lovely. They laughed and they cried; and soon they had told one another how wicked their step-mother had been to them all.

'We brothers,' said the eldest, 'fly as wild swans while the sun is in the sky; when it has gone down we get back our human form. And so at sunset we must take care to have a resting-place for our feet; for if we were flying up to the clouds we should, as human beings, plunge into the deep. This is not our home; across the sea there is a land just as beautiful as this. But the way to it is long; we have to cross the great ocean and there isn't an island on our way where we can spend the night, only a lonely little rock jutting up in the middle. It's just big enough for us to rest on side by side. In a rough sea the spray washes right over us; and yet we thank our God for it. There we spend the night in our human form; without it we should never be able to visit our own dear country, for we must have two of the longest days of the year for our flight. Only twice a year is it given to us to visit our home; eleven days are allowed us, and then we fly across this big forest, from where we can get a glimpse of the palace where we were born and where our father lives, and can see the tall tower of the church where Mother is buried. Here we feel that trees and bushes are related to us; here the wild horses gallop across the plains as we saw them in our childhood; here the charcoal-burner sings all the old songs we danced to as children; here is our native land; here is the place we are drawn to; and here we have found you, dear little sister. Two more days may we stay here, and then we must be off across the sea to a lovely land, but one that is not our own. How can we take you with us? We have neither ship nor boat.'

'How can I rescue you?' said their sister.

And they talked together nearly all night long, dozing for only a few hours.

Eliza woke to the sound of swans' wings whirring over her head. Her brothers had changed again, and they flew circling round and round and soon were far away; all but one, the youngest of them, who stayed behind. And this one laid his head in her lap and she stroked his white wings; all day long they were together. Towards evening the others returned, and when the sun had gone down they were back in their natural form.

'Tomorrow we shall fly away from here and may not return for a whole year; only we can't leave you like this! Have you the heart to go with us? My arm is strong enough to carry you through the forest; then surely we all have wings that are strong enough to fly you across the sea.'

'Yes, take me with you!'

All that night they spent weaving a net of supple willow-bark and tough rushes; and it was a big and strong one. Eliza lay down on this; and when the sun rose and the brothers were transformed into wild swans, they took the net in their beaks and flew up into the clouds with their dear sister, while she was still asleep. As the rays of sunshine fell right on her face, one of the swans flew over her head, so that his broad wings would shade her . . .

They were a long way from land when Eliza woke up; and she thought that she was still dreaming, so strange did it seem to her to be borne across the sea, high up in the air. By her side lay a spray of lovely ripe berries and a bunch of tasty roots; her youngest brother had gathered these and put them there for her, and she gave him a grateful smile, for she knew that he was the one flying straight over her head and shading her with his wings.

They were so high up that the first ship they saw below them seemed like a white seagull floating on the water. Behind them was a big cloud, the size of a mountain, and on it Eliza saw the reflection of herself and the eleven swans; and they were like giants. It made a picture more splendid than anything she had ever seen before; but as the sun rose higher and the cloud fell further back, the floating shadow-picture vanished.

All that day they flew on their way as an arrow whizzes through the air, though they were slower than usual, now they had their sister to carry. Then a storm arose as evening drew on; in dread Eliza saw the sun sink down, while still there was no sign of the lonely rock in the sea.

The swans seemed to her to be beating their wings faster now. Alas, it was her fault that they were not going quickly enough! When the sun set they would become human beings, and would plunge into the sea and be drowned. And so from the bottom of her heart she said a prayer to our Lord, while still there was no rock in sight. The black cloud came nearer; strong gusts of wind foretold a storm; the clouds formed into a single big, threatening wave which rolled solidly on like lead; lightning flash followed lightning flash.

Now the sun was down to the edge of the sea. Eliza's heart trembled. Then all at once the swans shot downward, so fast that she thought she was falling. But then once more they were gliding. The sun was half way in the sea; and now, for the first time, she sighted the little rock below her, looking no bigger than a seal sticking its head out of the water. The sun sank so

fast; now it seemed no more than a star. Then all at once her foot touched firm ground; and the sun went out like the last spark of burning paper. Round her, standing arm in arm, she saw her brothers; but there was just room for them and herself, and no more. The waves dashed against the rock, washing over them and drenching them, while the sky glowed in a blaze of fire and the thunder rolled in peal after peal. But sister and brothers, holding one another by the hand, sang a hymn, and this gave them comfort and courage.

At dawn the air was pure and still; and as soon as the sun had risen the swans flew with Eliza away from the island. The sea was still very rough, and it looked, when they were high up in the air, as if the white foam on the dark green waves was millions of swans floating on the water.

As the sun rose higher Eliza saw in front of her, half-floating in the air, a mountainous country with sparkling clumps of ice on its peaks; and right in the middle stood a palace, stretching, she thought, for miles, with rows of soaring pillars built one on top of the other. Down below were waving palm forests and gorgeous flowers the size of mill-wheels. She asked if this was the country she was bound for; but the swans shook their heads, for what she saw was a lovely castle in the air, an ever-changing mirage; they could take no one in there. Eliza gazed at it; and all at once mountains, forests, and palace tumbled down and there stood twenty glorious churches, every one alike, with tall towers and pointed windows. It seemed to her that she heard the pealing of the organ, but it was only the sea. Now she was very near to the churches; and all at once they became a fleet of ships which sailed away beneath her. She looked down; and then they were only fog drifting across the sea. Yes, she had an ever-changing sight before her eyes; and then she saw the real land, the country she was going to. Lovely blue mountains rose up, with cedar forests and cities and palaces. Long before the sun had gone down she was sitting on the mountainside in front of a big cave overgrown with slender green climbing plants; she was reminded of embroidered carpets.

'Now we'll see what you dream about tonight,' said the youngest brother, showing her to her bedroom.

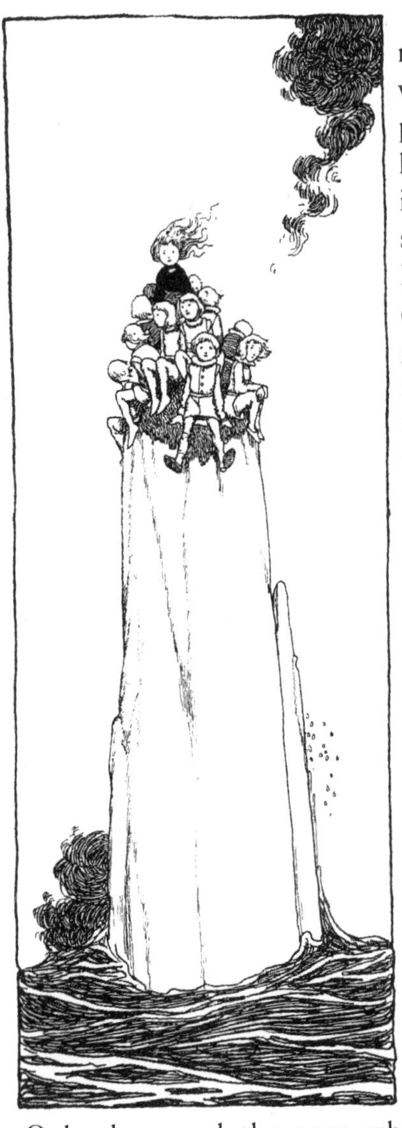

'If only I might dream how to rescue you!' she said. And she was so full of the idea that she prayed fervently to God for His help, and went on praying even in her sleep. And then it seemed to her that she flew high up into the air to the castle of the mirage, and that the fairy godmother came forward to meet her so pretty and so shining, and yet resembling the old woman who had given her berries in the wood and told her about the swans wearing the gold crowns.

'Your brothers can be saved!' she said. 'But have you courage and perseverance? The sea may be softer than your delicate hands and yet able to smooth the rough stones; but it never feels the pain your fingers will feel. It has no heart, and does not suffer the pain and sorrow that you must endure. Do you see this stinging nettle I am holding in my hand? There are lots of this kind growing round the cave where you are sleeping. Only those and the ones which spring up on graves in the churchyard will do; bear this in mind. These you must gather, though they will nettle and blister your skin. Trample the nettles with your feet and you'll have flax; and with this you must weave and make up eleven shirts of mail with long sleeves, and if you throw these over the eleven wild swans the spell will be broken. Only be sure and remember that from the moment you begin this work and until it is finished, even though it takes years, you mustn't speak. The first word you say will strike like a fatal dagger into your brothers' hearts; on your tongue depends their lives. Bear all this in mind!'

And so saying she touched her hand with the nettle; and it was like burning fire and woke Eliza up. It was broad daylight, and close by where she had slept was a nettle like the one she had seen in her dream. Falling on her knees, she thanked our Lord and went out of the cave to begin her work.

With her delicate hands she plucked at the horrible nettles, and they were like fire. Big blisters came out on her hands and arms; but she was ready to suffer this so long as she could save her dear brothers. Trampling on all the nettles with her bare feet she wove the green flax.

When the sun had gone down her brothers returned; and they were frightened to find her so silent, thinking that this was a fresh spell of their wicked stepmother's. But on seeing her hands they realized what she was doing for their sakes, and the youngest brother cried; and where the tears fell she felt no pain and the smarting blisters disappeared.

That night she spent at her work; for she had no rest until she had saved her dear brothers. The whole of the next day, while the swans were away, she sat in her solitude; but never did time fly so quickly. One shirt of mail was already finished, and now she started on the next.

All at once there came the sound of a hunting-horn away among the mountains; and she was terrified. The sound came nearer, she heard the dogs bark; and, frightened, she made for her cave, tied the nettles which she had gathered and dressed into a bundle, and sat on them.

Just then a big dog came bounding out of the thicket, and just after another, and yet another. They gave a loud bark, ran back, and came on again. It wasn't many minutes before all the huntsmen stood outside the cave, the most handsome among them being the king of the country. And he went over to Eliza; he had never seen a more beautiful girl, he thought.

'How did you get here, you lovely child?' he said. Eliza shook her head; for of course she couldn't speak, for the sake of her brothers' lives and their release. And she hid her hands under her apron, so that the king shouldn't see what she was having to suffer.

'Come with me!' he said. 'This is no place for you. If you are good as you are pretty, I'll dress you in silks and velvet, put a golden crown on your head, and allow you to make your home in the richest of my palaces!' And he lifted her up on to his horse. She cried and wrung her hands, but the king said: 'I've only your happiness at heart. Some time you'll thank me for it!' And with this he galloped off among the mountains, holding her on in front, his huntsmen hurrying after him.

As the sun went down the splendid royal city with its churches and domes lay before them; and the king led her into the palace, where big fountains were splashing in lofty marble halls and where walls and ceiling were resplendent with paintings; but she had no eyes for them, and cried and grieved. Submissively she allowed the women to dress her in royal clothes, braid her hair, and draw splendid gloves over her nettled fingers.

As she stood there in all her glory she was so dazzlingly beautiful that the Court bowed ever lower to her and the king chose her for his bride, although the archbishop shook his head and whispered that the pretty girl from the forest was surely a witch, the way she dazzled their eycs and captivated the king's heart.

But refusing to listen the king ordered the music to play, the costliest dishes to be served, and the loveliest girls to dance around her; and she was led through fragrant gardens into splendid galleries. But never a smile crossed her lips or played in her eyes; sorrow had taken up its home there. And then the king opened a small chamber near where she was to sleep; it was decorated with costly green carpets and was just like the cave where she had been before. On the floor lay the bunch of flax she had spun from the nettles, and from the ceiling hung the shirt of mail that had been finished. All had been gathered up by one of the huntsmen as curiosities.

'Here you will be able to imagine yourself back in your old home!' said the king. 'Here's the work which kept you busy there; now, in all your glory, it will amuse you to turn your mind back on those days.'

When Eliza saw the thing which was so near and dear to her a smile played on her lips and the blood returned to her cheeks; thinking of her brothers' release she kissed the king's hand, and he pressed her to his heart and commanded all the church bells to proclaim the wedding feast. The lovely, dumb girl from the forest was queen of the land.

The archbishop whispered evil words in the king's ear; but they failed to reach his heart. The wedding was fixed and the archbishop himself had to place the crown on her head; and with a malicious heart he pressed the close-fitting circle tightly over her forehead and made it hurt. But there was a heavier circle round her heart, her grief for her brothers; and she did not feel the bodily pain. Her lips were silent, for a single word would have brought her brothers' lives to an end; but her eyes spoke affection for the good and handsome king who did everything to please her. With all her heart she was more and more good to him every day. If only she had been able to confide in him and tell him her sufferings! But silent she must be, and silently complete her work. And so at night she would steal from his side and, going into the little closet that was arranged like the cave, she finished one shirt of mail after the other. But when she came to the seventh she had no more flax.

Growing in the churchyard, as she knew, were the nettles that she needed, but she had to gather them herself. How was she to get there?

'Oh, what is the pain in my fingers to the sufferings of my heart?' she thought. 'I must venture it! Our Lord will not let me down!'

With a heart of fear, as though about to do something wicked, she stole in the moonlit night down into the garden and went through long avenues into the deserted streets and to the churchyard. There, sitting on one of the broadest tombstones, she saw a group of lamiae, ugly witches. They were taking off their rags as though they were going to bathe and were digging with long, lean fingers into the fresh graves, taking out the bodies and eating their flesh. Eliza had to go straight past them, and they fixed her with their evil eyes; but she said a prayer, and gathering the stinging-nettles took them home to the palace.

One person only had seen her and that was the archbishop; he was up when other people were asleep. Now, he thought, he had been proved right and all wasn't as it should be with the queen; she was a witch, and she had enchanted the king and the whole people.

In the confessional he told the king what he had seen and what he feared; and as the harsh words fell from his lips the

carvings of saints shook their heads as much as to say: 'It isn't true; Eliza's innocent.' Only the archbishop read the sign differently, thinking that they were witnessing against her and shaking their heads at her sins. And two heavy tears rolled down the king's cheeks, as he went home with doubt in his heart. In the night he pretended to sleep, but peaceful sleep never came to his eyes. He noticed how Eliza got up and that she did so every night; and each time he softly followed her and saw her disappear into her closet.

Day by day his looks grew darker. Eliza saw it but did not realize why. But it alarmed her, and she suffered in her heart for her brothers. Her salt tears fell on the royal velvet and purple and lay there like glistening diamonds; yet all who saw this rich splendour wished that they were queen. Soon, however, she had reached the end of her work and only one shirt of mail remained to be done; but she had no more flax and not a single nettle left. And so once more, for the last time, she would have to go to the churchyard and gather a few handfuls. She thought in fear of the lonely walk and the dreadful lamiae; but her resolution was firm, like her trust in our Lord.

And so Eliza went. But the king and the archbishop followed her and saw her disappear at the entrance gate of the churchyard; and when they got there they saw on the gravestone the lamiae, sitting as Eliza had seen them, and the king turned away; for among them he imagined to himself the one whose head had rested that very evening on his breast.

'The people must judge her!' he said. And the people judged and said: 'She shall be burnt in flames of fire!'

From the splendid royal halls she was taken to a damp and dark dungeon where the wind came whistling in through the grated window. In place of velvet and silk they gave her the bunch of nettles she had gathered; on this she could lay her head. The rough, smarting shirts of mail she had woven were to be her eiderdown and blanket. But they could have given her nothing more dear to her; she took up her work again and prayed to God. Outside, the boys sang mocking verses about her; no one comforted her with a loving word.

Towards evening, however, there sounded, close to the grating, the swish of a swan's wing; the youngest of the brothers had found his sister. And she sobbed aloud for joy, though she knew that the night which was coming might be the last that she had to live. But then the work was nearly finished, and her brothers were there.

The archbishop came in order to spend the last hour with her, as he had promised the king to do; but she shook her head and begged him with her eyes and looks to go. That night she would have to finish her work, or all would have been of no avail: all—the pain, the tears, and the sleepless nights. The archbishop left her with harsh words; but poor Eliza, knowing she was innocent, went on with her work.

The little mice ran about the floor, dragging the nettles to her feet so as to give her a little help; and the thrush sat at the grating of her window and sang all night as merrily as it could so that she shouldn't lose heart.

The dawn was just breaking, and it was another hour to sunrise, when the eleven brothers arrived at the palace gate and demanded to be taken to the king. But this was impossible, they were told, as it was night yet; the king was asleep and couldn't be disturbed. They pleaded and they threatened; and the watch came and then the king himself appeared and asked what it was all about. At that very moment the sun rose and no brothers were to be seen, but flying over the palace were eleven wild swans.

Streaming through the city gate went all the people, going to see the burning of the witch. A miserable horse pulled the cart in which she sat. She had been dressed in a smock made from coarse sacking. Her lovely hair hung loose round her pretty face; her cheeks were deathly pale, her lips moving softly, as her fingers wove the green flax. Even on the way to her death she never left off the work she had begun; ten shirts of mail lay at her feet and she was weaving the eleventh. The mob were mocking her.

'Look at the mumbling witch! That's not a hymn-book she's

holding in her hand; she's at her horrible magic. Snatch it from her and tear it into a thousand pieces!'

And, crowding round her, they were about to tear up her work, but at that moment eleven white swans flew up and settled, beating their wings, round her on the cart. At this the crowd gave way, terrified.

Now the executioner seized her by the hand; but hastily she flung the eleven shirts over the swans, and there stood eleven handsome princes; only the youngest of them had in place of one arm a swan's wing, his shirt of mail being a sleeve short as she hadn't managed to finish it.

'Now I may speak!' she said. 'I am innocent!'

And seeing what had taken place, the people bowed before her as to a saint. But she sank swooning into her brothers' arms from the fear and the excitement and the suffering.

'Yes, she is innocent!' said the eldest brother; and he told them the story of all that had happened. And while he spoke there arose a fragrance as of millions of roses, for every faggot of the bonfire had taken root and grown branches, and there stood a sweet-smelling hedge, so very high and big, of red roses. At the top was a single bloom, a white and glowing one which shone like a star. Breaking this off the king placed it on Eliza's breast; and she woke with peace and happiness in her heart.

And every church bell rang of its own accord and birds came flying up in big flocks. It was a wedding procession back to the palace such as had never been seen by any king before.

THE FLYING TRUNK

ONCE upon a time there was a merchant; a man so rich that he could have paved the whole street and most of a small alley with silver. But he didn't; he had other uses for his money. If he spent a penny he got a shilling in return; that was the sort of merchant he was. And then one day he died.

All this money now went to his son, and he lived merrily, going to carnivals every night, making kites out of paper money, and playing ducks and drakes on the pond with sovereigns instead of stones. That was a sure way of getting money to go—and it went. All he had left in the end was fourpence, and his clothes were a pair of slippers and an old dressing-gown. His friends no longer cared for him now, for of course they couldn't walk the street together; but one of them, who was kind, sent him an old trunk saying: 'Pack up!' Now that was all very well, but he had nothing to pack. And so he got into the trunk himself.

It was a peculiar trunk. At the first touch of the lock it would fly. And that's what it did: swish! it flew through the chimney with him right up above the clouds, farther and farther away. The bottom creaked and he was terrified it would fall to pieces; he'd have come a nice little cropper if it had, and no mistake! And so in time he arrived in the land of the Turks. Hiding his trunk under some dead leaves in the wood he went into the town, which he was able to do there because among the Turks everybody of course wore a dressing-gown and slippers like him.

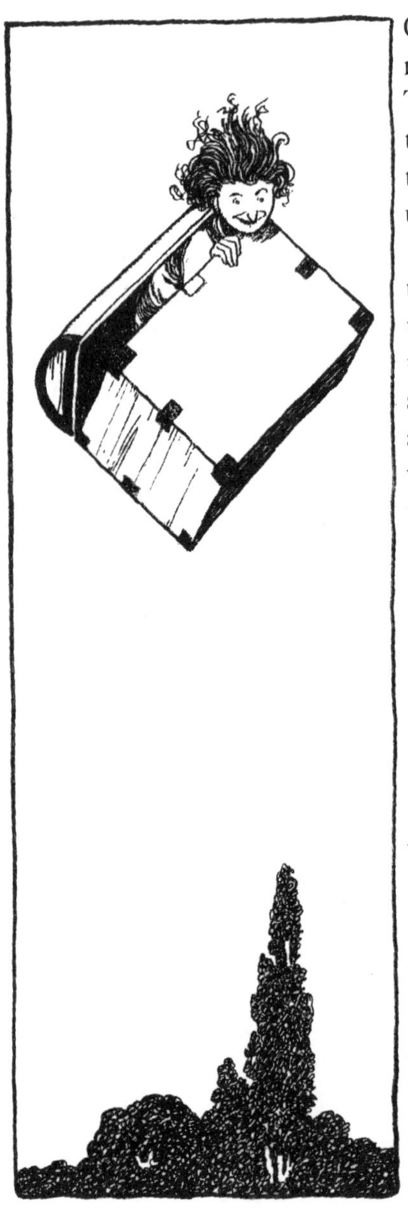

On the way he met a nursemaid with a baby. 'I say, you Turkish nurse!' he said. 'What's this big palace here, by the town? The windows are so high up.'

'The king's daughter lives there,' she said. 'A fortune-teller has said that she's going to be very unhappy over a sweetheart, and so nobody's allowed to visit her except when the king and queen are there.'

'Right!' said the merchant's son; and, going into the wood, he got into his trunk, flew on to the roof, and climbed in to the princess through the window.

She was fast asleep on the sofa; and she was so lovely that the merchant's son was forced to kiss her. She woke up at this and was rather frightened; but he said that he was the Turkish god who had come down to her through the air, and she liked that.

So they sat side by side, and he told her stories about her eyes: they were 'the loveliest

misty lakes and her thoughts swam on them like mermaids'. And he told her about her forehead: it was 'a snowy mountain with the most gorgeous halls and pictures in it'. And he told her about the stork, which brings sweet little babies.

Yes, they were lovely stories! And then he proposed to the princess, and she at once said 'Yes'.

'But you must come again on Saturday,' she said, 'when the king and queen will be taking tea with me. They'll be very proud that I'm to marry the Turkish god. But mind that you know a really nice fairy tale to tell, as my parents are most fond

of them; my mother likes them to be moral and refined, and my father merry so as to make you laugh.'

'The only wedding present I shall bring, then, will be a fairy tale!' he said, and so they parted, the princess giving him a sword studded with gold coins—and he knew what to do with those.

Flying off, he bought himself a new dressing-gown and then sat in the wood making up a fairy tale. It was to be ready by Saturday, and it isn't as easy as all that.

Soon he had finished, and soon it was Saturday.

The king, the queen, and the whole Court were waiting with tea at the princess's. He was so nicely received.

'Now please tell us a fairy tale!' said the queen. 'One with a deep meaning and a moral.'

'But one to laugh at as well!' said the king.

'Certainly,' he said, and he began his story. Now, listen carefully.

'Once upon a time there was a box of matches, and they were extremely proud of themselves because of their high birth; their family tree—that is to say, the big pine-tree of which each of them was a little splinter—had been a great old tree in the forest. The matches now lay on the shelf between a tinder-box and an old iron pot, and they were telling them of their youth. "Yes," they said, "we were on top of the world when we were on top of the tree. We had diamond tea (that was the dew) every morning and evening, and sunshine (when there was any sunshine) all day long, while all the little birds had to tell us stories. And we could feel we were rich, because the other trees were only dressed in summer, while our family could afford green clothes both summer and winter. But then came the woodcutters (that was the Great Revolution), and our family was split up. Our parent tree got a place as the mainmast of a splendid ship, which could sail round the world when it wanted. Other branches found other places to go to, and our task is to bring light to the common people. That's how persons of quality like us come to be in the kitchen."

'"Well, now, it's different with me!" said the iron pot, which was next to the matches. "Ever since I was born I've been scrubbed and boiled over and over again. My business is the solid things of life and, as a matter of fact, I come before anyone in the house. My one pleasure is to stand after meals clean and tidy on the shelf, having a sensible talk with my friends; but, excepting for the bucket, which once in a while goes into the yard, we always live indoors. Our only news-bringer is the peat basket, but he talks so disturbingly about the Government and people. Why, only the other day an old pot was so frightened by it that it fell down and broke itself! He's a regular radical, I can tell you."

'"Now, you're too talkative!" said the tinder-box; and the steel struck the flint so that it gave out sparks. "Why don't we have a pleasant evening?"

'"Yes; let's talk about which of us comes of the best family!" said the matches.

'"No, I don't care for talking about myself," said the earthenware pot. "Let's have an evening's entertainment! I'll begin. I'll tell the sort of thing we've all of us known. It's so easy to imagine, and such good fun! . . . On the Baltic where the Danish beech-woods grow——"

'"That's such a nice beginning!" cried all the plates. "This is going to be a story I shall like."

'"Well now, it was there, in the home of a quiet family, that I spent my youth. The furniture was polished, the floor washed, and clean curtains hung up once a fortnight."

'"Aren't you an interesting story-teller!" said the broom. "It's easy to tell you're a lady; the tone of your tale is so clean."

'"Yes, you can feel that!" said the bucket; and it gave a little skip of delight and rattled on the floor.

'And the pot went on with its story, the end of which was just as good as the beginning.

'All the plates clattered for joy, and the broom took some parsley from the bin and crowned the pot with it, knowing that this would annoy the others, and thinking: "If I crown her today, she'll crown me tomorrow."

'"I'm going to dance!" said the fire-tongs, and did so. Gracious me, the way she kicked her leg into the air. The old chair-cover over in the corner burst at the sight of it. "Please may I be crowned?" said the tongs; and she was.

'"They're only riff-raff!" thought the matches.

'The tea-urn was then called upon to sing, but she had a cold, she said, and couldn't, except when she was on the boil. But she was only giving herself airs; she didn't want to—only when she was on the mistress's table.

'Sitting on the window-sill was an old quill-pen, one the maid used to write with. The only thing remarkable about it was that it had been dipped too far into the ink-well, but that only made *it* stuck up. "If the tea-urn won't sing," it said, "she can do without! Hanging outside in a cage is a nightingale; that

can sing. It's true that it hasn't learnt anything, but we won't speak ill of that tonight."

'"I think it most improper," said the kettle, who was kitchen-singer and half-sister to the tea-urn, "that we should have to listen to such a foreign bird. Is it patriotic? I'll leave it to the shopping-basket to judge!"

'"I'm just annoyed!" said the shopping-basket. "I'm as annoyed as anyone can imagine! Is this a proper way to spend the evening? Wouldn't it be better to set the house to rights?

That would put everybody in his place, and I'd be in charge of the whole pack of you. You'd see a change then!"

'"Yes, let's have a row!" they all said. At that moment the door was opened. It was the housemaid, and all at once they were silent, nobody breathing a word. But there wasn't a pot among them but knew what it could do and how genteel it was. "Yes," they thought, "if only I'd wanted, it *would* have been a pleasant evening!"

'The maid took the matches and struck them. Dear me, how they spluttered and flared up!

'"Surely everybody can see now," they thought, "that we're number one. How brilliant we are! What a light!" And with that they were burnt out.'

'What a lovely fairy tale that was!' said the queen. 'I felt exactly as though I were in the kitchen along with the matches. Yes, now you shall marry our daughter.'

'Yes, indeed!' said the king. 'You shall marry our daughter on Monday.' And they called him by his first name, now that he was to join the family.

The wedding having been decided, the whole city was illuminated the evening before. There was scrambling for buns and cakes; and the street-boys, standing on tiptoe, cheered and whistled through their fingers. It was simply gorgeous.

'Well, I suppose I ought to be doing something, too!' thought the merchant's son; and so he bought rockets, bombshells, and all the fireworks imaginable, and, putting them into his trunk, flew off into the air with them.

Whoops, how they flashed, and how they banged!

It sent all the Turks jumping into the air with their slippers flying about their ears; they'd never seen a show like it. Now they did know it was the Turkish god himself who was going to marry the princess.

As soon as the merchant's son was back in the wood he thought to himself: 'I think I'll go into the town and hear how it all went off.' And of course it was only natural that he should want to.

The stories that people were telling! Every single person he asked about it had seen it his own way, though all had thought it grand.

'I saw the Turkish god himself,' said one. 'He had eyes like shining stars and a beard like foaming waves!'

'He flew in a cloak of fire,' said another. 'The loveliest little cherubs peeped out from beneath its folds!'

Oh yes, they were lovely things he heard; and the next day was to be his wedding day.

He then went back to get his trunk—but where was the trunk? It was burnt up. A spark from a firework had got into it and had set it alight, and it was in ashes. He could fly no more; no more go to his bride.

She stood waiting on the roof all day. She's waiting still, while he goes round the world telling fairy tales. But they are no longer as merry as the one he told about the matches.

THE STORKS

ON THE last house of a small town there was a storks' nest. The mother stork sat on the nest with her four little ones, who were poking out their heads with their little black beaks, for they had not yet turned red. A little way off, stiff and straight on the roof-ridge, stood father stork, who had drawn up a leg so as to have at least some inconvenience as he stood on sentry duty. You might have thought he was carved out of wood, so still he stood. 'It must look rather grand, my wife having a sentry by her nest!' he thought. 'They won't know I'm her husband; they'll think I've been commanded to stand here. How splendid it looks!' And he went on standing on his one leg.

In the street below a crowd of children were playing; and when they saw the storks one of the boldest of the boys, followed soon by all the others, began to sing an old song about the storks, though they sang it in the way he remembered it:

> 'Daddy, Daddy Bony-knee,
> Fly home to your family!
> Your wife's waiting there for you
> With four big baby storks.
> One shall be hanged,
> Another shall be banged,
> The third shall be burned,
> The fourth shall be turned!'

'Just listen to what the boys are singing!' said the little baby storks. 'They say we're going to be hanged and burned.'

'You shouldn't take any notice of that!' said the mother stork.

'Don't listen to them, and you'll be all right.'

But the boys went on singing, and pointed their fingers at the storks. Only one boy, whose name was Peter, said that it was a shame to make fun of the creatures, and he wouldn't join in. And the mother stork comforted her young ones, saying: 'Don't take any notice! Just look how calmly your father stands, and on one leg at that.'

'We're so frightened!' said the young ones, burying their heads inside the nest.

Next day, when the children met again to play and saw the storks, they began their song again:

'One shall be hanged,
Another shall be burned . . .'

'Are we really going to be hanged and burned?' asked the young storks.

'Of course not!' said their mother. 'You must learn to fly. I'll drill you. Then we'll go into the meadow and call on the frogs. They'll curtsy to us in the water, singing "Ko-ax! Ko-ax!" And then we'll eat them up, and it'll be ever such fun!'

'And what then?' asked the young storks.

'Then all the storks there are in the whole country will get together and the autumn manoeuvres will begin. You have to be a good flyer then. It's of very great importance, because anyone who can't fly gets stabbed to death by the general's beak. So take good care to learn something when the drilling begins.'

'Then we *shall* be hanged, just as the boys said. And listen, now they're saying it again!'

'Listen to me and not to them,' said mother stork. 'After the big manoeuvres we shall fly to the warm countries—oh, ever such a long way from here, over mountains and forests. We shall fly away to Egypt, where there are three-cornered houses built

of stone which end in a point up above the clouds. They're called pyramids, and they're older than any stork can imagine. There's a river there which overflows, leaving the land all mud. You walk in mud and eat frogs.'

'Oh!' said all the young oncs.

'Oh yes, it's lovely there! You do nothing but eat all day. And while we are having such a good time, there won't be a green leaf on the trees in this country. It'll be so cold here that the clouds will freeze to bits and fall down in little white scraps.' (She meant the snow, only she couldn't explain it any better.)

'Do the naughty boys freeze to bits as well?' asked the young storks.

'No they don't freeze to bits! But they nearly do, and have to sit moping in a dark parlour. You, though, are able to fly about in a strange land where there are flowers and warm sunshine.'

Now, time passed and the young ones were big enough to be able to stand up in the nest and see far and wide; and father stork came flying home every day with nice frogs, little snakes, and all the stork delicacies he could find. Oh, what fun they had watching the tricks he did for them! He would stick his head behind his tail and clack his beak just like a little rattle; and then he would tell them stories, all from the marsh.

'I say, you must learn to fly,' said mother stork one day; and all four of the young ones had to go out on the ridge. Oh, how they wobbled! How they balanced with their wings, and yet very nearly fell down!

'Now just watch me!' said their mother. 'This is the way to hold your head. This is the way to place your feet. Left, right! Left, right! This will help you to make your way in the world!' So saying she flew off a little way. And the young ones made a clumsy little hop. Flop! There they lay; for they were heavy in the body.

'I don't want to fly,' said one of the young ones; and he crept back into the nest. 'I don't care for going to the warm countries.'

'Do you want to stop here and freeze to death when winter comes? Do you want the boys to come and hang and burn and turn you? I'll call them!'

'Oh no!' said the young stork. And he hopped out on to the roof again like the others. On the third day they could really fly a little; and so they thought they could also sit down and rest in the air. They tried to do, but—flop! They had tumbled down. And then they had to work their wings again. Now the boys appeared in the street below, singing their song:

'Daddy, Daddy Bony-knee!'

'Supposing we were to fly down and peck their eyes out?' said the young ones.

'No, don't!' said their mother. 'Just listen to me; it's a lot more important. One, two, three! Now right turn, fly! One, two, three! Now left turn round the chimney. There, that was all right! That last beat of your wings was so nice and correct that you may come with me into the marsh tomorrow. There'll be several respectable stork families there with their children, so let me see that mine are the nicest and that you can hold your heads up. That looks well, and earns respect!'

'Yes, but aren't we to get our own back on the naughty boys?' asked the young storks.

'Leave them to shout what they like! You'll be flying with the clouds and going to the land of the pyramids when they must freeze and never have a green leaf or a sweet apple.'

'Yes, but we will get our own back!' they whispered to one another. And then there was more drilling.

Of all the boys in the street there was none worse at singing the mocking song than the very one who had started it, and he was a very little one—he can't have been more than six. The young storks, it is true, took him to be a hundred, for, of course, he was so much bigger than their mother and father; and what did they know about how old children and big human beings could be? They meant to have all their revenge on this boy; he had started it all, and he always went on. The young storks were so annoyed, and the bigger they grew the less they would put up with it. In the end their mother had to promise them their revenge, only she said she wouldn't take it until the last day they were in the country.

'We shall first have to see how you get on in the big manoeuvre. If you do badly in it the general will thrust his beak into your breasts, and then the boys will be right, at least in a way. Now, let's see!'

'All right, you shall see!' said the young ones. And then they did try hard! They practised every day, flying so prettily and easily they were a delight to watch.

Then autumn came. All the storks began to gather together in order to fly away to the warm countries while we have winter. That was a manoeuvre! They had to fly over woods and towns just to see how well they could fly, for of course it was a big journey which lay before them. The young storks managed so nicely that they were given Very Good, with frog and snake. This was top marks, and they were allowed to eat the frog and the snake, which they did.

'Now we're going to gct our own back,' they said.

'Of course!' said the mother stork. 'What I've thought of is just the very thing! I know where the pond is where all the little human children lie till the stork comes and brings them to their parents. The pretty little children sleep and dream there lovelier than they ever dream again. All parents want such a little baby, and all children want a sister or a brother. Now we'll fly off to the pond and bring one for each of those children who haven't sung the wicked song and made fun of the storks—for *these* children are not going to have one.'

'But the one who started the singing, the horrid bad boy!' cried the young storks. 'What are we going to do with him?'

'Lying in the pond is a dead little baby which has dreamt

itself to death. We'll take that to him, and then he'll cry because we've brought him a dead little brother. But the good boy (you surely haven't forgotten him, the one who said "It's a shame to make fun of the creatures!"), we'll take him both a brother and a sister. And as this boy's name was Peter you shall all of you be called Peter too!'

And it was as she had said: all the storks were given the name of Peter, and they are called so to this day.

LITTLE SHUTEYE

In all the world there's no one who can tell so many stories as Little Shuteye. He's a proper story-teller.

Late in the evening, when children are sitting as good as gold at the table or on their stools, in comes Little Shuteye. He comes very, very quietly up the steps, walking in his stockinged feet. Very softly he opens the door, and then—puff! he squirts some milk into the children's eyes: so very, very gently, and yet always enough that they can't keep their eyes open, and so can't see him. Stealing right up behind them, he blows them softly on the neck, and they get heavy-headed. Oh yes! But it doesn't hurt, for Little Shuteye does it for their own good; he only wants them to be quiet, and they're always quietest when they've been put to bed. They've got to be quiet so he can tell them stories . . .

When the children have gone to sleep, Little Shuteye sits down on the bed. He's well dressed, his coat being made of silk; though it's impossible to say what colour it is, because it shines green, red, and blue, all according to the way he turns. Under each arm he holds an umbrella, one with pictures on it which he puts up over the good children, making them dream the loveliest of stories all night long, and one with nothing on at all; this one he puts up over the naughty children, making them sleep stupidly, so that they wake in the morning without having dreamt a thing.

Now let's hear how Little Shuteye came every night for a whole week to a little boy called Hjalmar, and what he told him!

There'll be seven stories altogether, there being seven days in a week.

MONDAY

'Now then,' said Little Shuteye in the evening, when he'd got Hjalmar off to bed, 'I'm going to brighten things up!' And with that all the flowers in the plant-pot grew into big trees, reaching up with their long branches under the ceiling and along the wall, and making the whole room look like the loveliest summer-house. And all the branches were full of flowers and every flower was more beautiful than a rose, smelling so deliciously, and, if you felt like eating it, tasting sweeter than jam. The fruit glittered like gold; and then there were buns bursting with currants—it was marvellous! But all at once a dreadful wailing sounded from the table drawer, where Hjalmar's school books were kept.

'Whatever's that?' said Little Shuteye, going to the table and opening the drawer. It was the slate; so terribly upset because it had got a wrong figure in its sum, and quite ready to come to pieces. The pencil was jumping and skipping at the end of its string for all the world like a little dog: it was wanting to help with the sum, but couldn't. And there was Hjalmar's copy-book, wailing away inside its covers something dreadful! Standing down the side of each page were all the capital letters, each with a small one alongside: a whole column of them. It was a copying exercise, and alongside these letters were some others which pretended to look like them, and which Hjalmar had written. They looked almost as though they had fallen over the pencil line which they were supposed to be standing on.

'Look, this is the way to carry yourselves!' said the copy letters. 'Look, sloping like this, and with a brisk flourish!'

'Oh, how we'd like to,' said Hjalmar's letters; 'but we can't, we feel so poorly.'

'Then you must have a pick-me-up,' said Little Shuteye.

'Oh no!' they cried; and they stood up so straight it was a pleasure to see them.

'H'm, now there'll be no story-telling,' said Little Shuteye. Now I shall have to make them practise.' Left, right! Left, right! And he made the letters practise, and they stood as straight and as correctly as any copy-book letters could stand. But when Little Shuteye had gone and Hjalmar went to look at them next morning they were just as poor as they had been before.

TUESDAY

The moment Hjalmar was in bed, Little Shuteye touched all the furniture in the room with his little magic squirt and every piece at once began to talk, all talking about themselves except the spittoon which said nothing, annoyed that they could be so conceited as only to talk about themselves and only think about themselves, never giving a thought to the one who stood humbly in his corner, letting himself be spat upon.

Hanging over the chest of drawers was a large painting in a gilt frame; it was a landscape, and it showed tall old trees, flowers among grass, and a large lake with a river flowing behind the wood, past many castles right out to the wild ocean.

Little Shuteye touched the painting with his magic squirt; and the birds in the picture began to sing, the branches of the trees stirred, and the clouds went flying along, casting their shadows across the landscape.

Little Shuteye then lifted little Hjalmar up to the frame, and Hjalmar put his feet into the picture, straight into the tall grass, and stood up in it, the sun shining down on to him through the branches of the trees. Running to the water, he got into a little boat which lay there, a red-and-white one. The sails shone like silver, and six swans, all with gold crowns round their necks and a sparkling blue star on their heads, pulled the boat past the green woods, where the trees told tales of robbers and witches, and the flowers of the pretty little elves and what the butterflies had told them.

The loveliest fishes, with scales like silver and gold, swam after the boat, leaping into the air from time to time and making the water say 'Plop!' while the birds, red ones and blue ones, big ones and little ones, flew in two long rows behind, the midges danced, and the cockchafer cried 'Buzz, buzz!' They all wanted to go with Hjalmar, and every one of them had a story to tell.

This was a proper sail! Now the woods would be as dense as dense and as dark as dark, and now they would be like the loveliest garden full of sunshine and flowers, and there would be big castles of glass and of marble. Princesses would be standing on the balconies, all of them little girls whom Hjalmar knew well, having played with them before. They would hold out their hands with the nicest sugar-pigs that any sweet-shop ever sold, and Hjalmar as he sailed past would catch hold of one end of the sugar-pig while the princess held on to the other, and each of them would get a piece of it, she the smaller one and Hjalmar easily the bigger piece. Little princes would stand sentry at each castle, shouldering their gold swords and showering raisins and tin soldiers. They were proper princes!

Now Hjalmar would be sailing through woods, and now would seem to pass through large halls or through the middle of a town, also through the one where his nurse lived; she who had carried him as a tiny little boy and had been so fond of him. And she nodded and waved, and sang the pretty little verse she had made up herself and sent to Hjalmar:

'My own dear Hjalmar, your smile I've missed
This many and many a day:
Your rosy cheeks and the lips I kissed;
The games that we used to play.

I loved you and cherished you right from birth,
But soon had to bid you Goodbye
God bless you and keep you here on earth,
You angel sent down from on high!'

And all the birds joined in the song, the flowers danced on their stalks, and the old trees nodded as though Little Shuteye were telling them stories as well.

WEDNESDAY

Dear me, how it poured down outside! Hjalmar could hear it in his sleep; and when Little Shuteye opened a window, the water was right up to the windowsill. Outside there was a regular sea, with a splendid ship lying alongside the house.

'Would you like a sail, little Hjalmar?' said Shuteye. 'You can get to foreign countries tonight and be back here again tomorrow!'

And all at once Hjalmar found himself in his Sunday best, standing in the middle of the splendid ship; and soon the weather was fine again, and they sailed through the streets, beating their way round the church, and found themselves on the wide open sea. They sailed on till there was no more land to be seen, and then caught sight of a flock of storks which were also leaving home, bound for the warm countries. One of the storks was behind the rest, and they had already flown such a long, long way that this one was so very tired and his wings would hardly bear him any longer. He was the last of the whole row and soon was a long way behind, dropping farther and farther down on his outstretched wings and flapping them a few more times. But all to no use: now his feet were touching the ship's rigging, now he was slipping down the sail, and now—bump!—he was on the deck.

The cabin-boy picked him up and put him in the hen-house along with the hens, ducks, and turkeys. The poor stork stood among them quite down-hearted.

'What a freak!' said all the hens.

And the turkey-cock puffed himself up as fat as he could and asked who he was; and the ducks walked backwards nudging one another, and saying: 'Quack! Quack! Quick! Quick!'

And the stork told them all about warm Africa; about the pyramids, and about the ostrich which runs like a wild horse across the desert. But the ducks didn't understand a word of what he said, and, nudging one another, said: 'Why, isn't he silly?'

'Of course he's silly!' said the turkey-cock, with a gobble. And the stork held his tongue and thought of his Africa.

'Nice thin legs you've got there!' said the turkey. 'How much a yard?'

'Quack! Quack! Quack!' chortled the ducks. But the stork pretended not to hear.

'You can join in!' the turkey said to him. 'Because that was a very witty remark! Or can it have been too low for him? Alack, alack! He isn't all there! Let's go on showing off among ourselves.' And the hens clucked and the ducks quacked 'Click-clack! Click-clack!' They themselves thought it terribly funny.

But Hjalmar went to the hen-house and, opening the door, called the stork, and it hopped out on the deck to him. It had rested now, and seemed as though it nodded to Hjalmar as if thanking him. Then it spread its wings and flew off to the warm countries, while the hens clucked, the ducks quacked, and the turkey-cock went red in the face.

'We'll make broth of you tomorrow!' said Hjalmar—and then he woke up and found himself in his cot. What a wonderful journey Little Shuteye had taken him on that night!

THURSDAY

'I say!' said Little Shuteye. 'Now don't be frightened. Just look at this little mouse!' And he held out his hand with the pretty little creature in it. It's come to invite you to a wedding. Two little mice here mean to enter into matrimony tonight. They live underneath your mother's pantry floor, which they say makes such a lovely home!'

'But how can I get through the little mouse-hole in the floor?' asked Hjalmar.

'Leave that to me,' said Little Shuteye. 'I'll make you small!' And he touched Hjalmar with his magic squirt, making him at once grow smaller and smaller, till in the end he was less then the size of a finger. 'Now you can borrow the tin soldier's clothes; I expect they'll fit you, and it's so smart to wear a uniform when you're at a party.'

'All right!' said Hjalmar; and in less than no time he was dressed like the nattiest little tin soldier.

'Now, would you please get into your mother's thimble,' said the little mouse, 'and I'll have the honour to pull you!'

'I say, you are going to a lot of trouble!' said Hjalmar. And off they drove to the mouse-wedding.

First they went underneath the floor in a long passage, which was only just high enough for them to drive in with their thimble, and which was lit up all the way with touchwood.

'Isn't there a lovely smell here?' said the mouse which was pulling him. 'The whole passage has been rubbed down with bacon rind. It couldn't be nicer!'

They then entered the wedding-hall. Here, standing on the right, were all the little lady mice, whispering and tittering as though making fun of one another. Standing on the left, stroking their whiskers with their paws, were all the gentlemen mice, while in the middle of the hall were the bride and bridegroom. They were standing in a scooped-out cheese rind, kissing each other such a lot in front of everybody, now they were engaged and about to be married.

More visitors kept on coming all the time; every mouse there was very nearly crushing the one next to him to death, and the bride and bridegroom had taken up a position in the doorway, so there was no getting either in or out. The whole room, like the passage, had been rubbed down with bacon rind; that was the only refreshment, except that, for dessert, they brought out a pea, in which a little mouse belonging to the family had nibbled the names of the bride and bridegroom—or rather, the initials. This was something quite out of the ordinary.

All the mice said what a lovely wedding it was, and how good the conversation had been.

And then Hjalmar drove home again. He'd certainly been in fashionable company, even though he had been forced to shrink such a lot, to make himself small and dress up in a tin soldier's uniform.

FRIDAY

'It's astonishing the number of older people there are who'd like to get hold of me!' said Little Shuteye. 'Especially those who've done something wrong. "Dear Little Shuteye," they'll say to me, "we can't get a wink of sleep, and we lie all night long looking at our bad deeds sitting like ugly little goblins on the edge of the bed, squirting hot water all over us. Please will you come and chase them away, so we can get a good night's rest." And then they'll heave a big sigh and say: "We're quite willing to pay you. Good night, Shuteye! The money's on the window-sill!" But I won't do it for money,' said Little Shuteye.

'Now, what have we got on for tonight?' asked Hjalmar.

'Well now, I wonder whether you'd like to go to another wedding tonight; a different sort from yesterday's. Your sister's big doll, the one that looks like a man and is called Herman, is to be married to the doll Bertha; besides which, it's the doll's birthday, and so there'll be no end of presents.'

'Yes, I know all about that.' said Hjalmar. 'Whenever the dolls need new clothes, my sister lets them have a birthday or a wedding. It must have happened a hundred times!'

'Ah yes, but tonight's wedding is the hundred and first, and when the hundred and first's over, that's the end of everything! That's another reason why this is going to be so wonderful. Just look!'

Hjalmar looked across at the table; and there stood the little cardboard house with lights in the windows, and all the tin soldiers presenting arms outside. The bride and bridegroom sat on the floor, leaning against the table-leg full of thought, as, of course, they had every reason to be. It was Little Shuteye, dressed in Grandma's black skirt, who married them; and when the wedding was over, all the furniture in the room joined in singing the following pretty song, which had been written by the pencil and went to the tune of the tattoo:

'Three cheers for the bride and the groom,
As they march arm in arm through the room;
As straight as two pokers in love,
As stiff as a newly washed glove!
Hurrah! Hurrah! for poker and clout!
Come, sing it again; let our cheers ring out!
Hurrah! Hurrah! for poker and clout!
Come, sing it again; let our cheers ring out!'

And then the presentations were made; but there were no eatables 'by request', as they had enough in their love.

'Now, shall we have a honeymoon in the country, or go abroad?' asked the bridegroom. And they turned for advice to the swallow, who'd been a big traveller, and to the old farmyard hen, who'd hatched out five broods of chicks. The swallow told them all about the lovely warm countries, where the grapes grew so big and heavy, where the air was so mild, and the mountains had colours the like of which we never see.

'Ah, but then they haven't got our cabbage!' said the hen. 'I remember the summer I spent in the country with all my chicks. There was a gravel-pit we could go scratching in, and we were also allowed into a garden full of cabbages. Oh, wasn't it green! I can't imagine anything so pretty.'

'But one cabbage-stalk looks just like another,' said the swallow. 'And it's often such bad weather here!'

'Oh, we're used to that,' said the hen.

'But it's so freezing cold here!'

'Good for cabbages!' said the hen. 'Besides, sometimes it's warm. Wasn't there a summer, four years ago, that lasted five weeks? It was so hot you couldn't breathe! And then we haven't got all those poisonous animals they have abroad. And we're safe from robbers. Anybody who doesn't think our country's the nicest is a good-for-nothing wretch!' And the hen burst into tears. 'I've travelled myself. I rode over fifty miles in a barrel. There's no fun at all in travelling!'

'Why, the hen's a sensible woman!' said Bertha the doll. 'I don't like mountain travel, either; for first you have to go up, and then you have to go down. No, we'll move out to the gravel-pit, and walk in the cabbage patch.'

And that was an end of it.

SATURDAY

'Any stories for me tonight?' said little Hjalmar, as soon as Little Shuteye had got him to bed.

'We've no time for that tonight,' said Little Shuteye, spreading his prettiest umbrella over him. 'Have a look at these Chinamen!' And the umbrella looked just like a big Chinese bowl on which were blue trees and pointed bridges where little Chinamen stood nodding their heads. 'We must see about brightening up the world for tomorrow,' said Little Shuteye. 'It's a holiday, you know—Sunday. I'm going up into the church tower to see if the little church brownies are polishing the bells to make them ring nicely; I'm going into the field to see if the winds are blowing the dust off the grass and leaves; and, the biggest job of all, I'm going to take all the stars down to polish them. I put them in my apron; but first they each have to be numbered, so that they can be put back in their proper places, or else they wouldn't stick fast and we should have too many shooting-stars, with one dropping down after the other.'

'Now, look here, Mr Shuteye!' said an old portrait that hung on the wall by Hjalmar's bed. 'I'm Hjalmar's great-grandfather. Thank you for telling the boy stories; but you mustn't confuse his ideas. The stars can't be taken down and polished. The stars are planets like our Earth, and that's the fact of the whole matter!'

'Much obliged to you, old great-grandfather!' said Little Shuteye. 'Much obliged! You're the head of the family—you're the "great" head of the family—but I'm older than you. I'm an old pagan; the Greeks and the Romans called me the dream god. I've visited all the best houses, and I still do. I can get on with both the great and the small. Now you can tell stories!' And off went Little Shuteye, taking his umbrella with him.

'A man can't even speak his own mind now!' said the old portrait.

And there Hjalmar woke up.

SUNDAY

'Hello!' said Little Shuteye. And with a nod Hjalmar jumped out of bed and turned great-grandfather's portrait with its face to the wall, so as to stop it from butting in like the day before.

'Now tell me some stories: about the five green peas living in one pod; and about the cock bone that made love to the hen bone; and about the darning-needle that was so fine in her ways she fancied herself a sewing-needle.'

'One can have too much of a good thing!' said Little Shuteye. 'I'd rather show you something, you know. I'll show you my brother; he's called Little Shuteye as well, but he never visits anybody more than once, and when he does he takes them away on his horse and tells them stories. He only knows two: one so marvellously lovely that nobody in the world can imagine it; and one so horrid and nasty that—well, there's no describing it!' And Shuteye lifted little Hjalmar up to the window, and said: 'Look, there's my brother, the other Little Shuteye! They also call him Death. You see, he doesn't look half as bad as he does in the picture-books, where he's all ribs and bone. Why, there's silver embroidery on his coat; it's the very nicest hussar's uniform. A cloak of black velvet is streaming out over his horse's back. Look at the way he gallops!'

And Hjalmar saw Little Shuteye riding along, picking up young people and old on to his horse and; putting some in front and others behind, but always asking first: 'What's your report like?' 'Good!' they would all say. 'All right, let me have a look!' he would say, and they would have to show him the book. And all who had 'Very Good' and 'Excellent' were seated in front of the horse and told the nice story, while those who had 'Fair' and 'Poor' had to sit behind and hear the horrid story. They would tremble and cry and want to jump off the horse, but wouldn't be able to, because they would at once have grown fast to it.

'Why, but Death is the nicest Little Shuteye!' said Hjalmar. 'I'm not afraid of him.'

'And you shouldn't be, either,' said Little Shuteye. 'Only see that you have a good report!'

'Now, that's education!' murmured great-grandfather's portrait. 'It does some good, after all, to speak one's mind.' And he was so pleased.

There, now that's the story of Little Shuteye. He'll be able to tell you more himself, tonight.

THE ROSE ELF

IN THE middle of a garden there grew a rose-tree which was quite full of roses; and in one of these, the most beautiful of them all, lived an elf. He was so tiny that no human eye could see him. Behind every petal of the rose he had a bedroom. He was as shapely and as lovely as any child could be, and had wings reaching down from his shoulders to his feet. Oh, what a scent there was in his rooms; and how bright and beautiful were the walls! They, of course, were the delicate pale pink rose-petals.

All the day he revelled in the warm sunshine, flitting from flower to flower, dancing on the butterfly's wings as it flew, and measuring how many steps it took him to run across all the roads and footpaths there were on a single lime leaf. They were what we call the veins of the leaf that he took for roads and footpaths; and indeed to him they were never-ending roads! Before he had finished the sun had set; he had been too late in starting.

It turned so very cold; the dew was falling and there was a wind. He had better see about getting home. He hurried for all he was worth; but the rose had closed and he couldn't get in. Not one rose was open. The poor little elf got so frightened; he had never been out at night before and had always slept so sweetly behind the snug rose-petals. This would be the death of him, he thought!

At the other end of the garden he knew there was an arbour of lovely honeysuckle, with blossom which looked like large painted horns. He would creep into one of these and sleep there till the morning.

So off he flew. Ssh! There were two people in there: a handsome young man and the loveliest of girls. They sat side by side, wishing never more to be parted; they were so very fond of each other, much more than even the best of children are fond of their mothers and fathers.

'Yet part we must!' said the young man. 'Your brother isn't good to us, and so is sending me on an errand, far away over mountains and seas. Goodbye, my sweet bride, for that is what you are!'

And then they kissed each other, and the young woman wept and gave him a rose. But before handing it to him she pressed it to her lips and kissed it so firmly and warmly that the flower opened. Seeing this, the little elf flew into it and rested his head against the delicate fragrant walls. But he could plainly hear them saying 'Goodbye! Goodbye!' and he felt that the rose was placed on the young man's breast. Oh, how the heart did beat in there! The little elf just couldn't fall asleep for its beating.

It wasn't long that the rose lay undisturbed on the man's breast; he took it out, and as he walked alone through the dark woods he kissed the flower: so often and so passionately that the little elf was very nearly crushed to death. He could feel through the petals how the young man's lips burnt, and the rose had opened out as in the hottest midday sun.

Suddenly another man appeared, dark and angry. He was the beautiful girl's wicked brother. Out came his big sharp knife, and as the other kissed the rose the wicked man stabbed him to death; then cutting off his head he buried it with the body in the soft earth under a lime-tree.

'Now he's dead and gone,' thought the wicked brother. 'He'll never come back any more. It was a long journey he was making, over mountains and seas, where it is easy to lose one's life; and he's lost it. He won't return, and my sister will never dare to ask me about him.'

Then with his foot he scraped dead leaves over the disturbed soil and went off home in the darkness of night. But he didn't go alone, as he believed: the little elf went with him. He sat in a withered, rolled-up lime leaf which had fallen on to the wicked man's hair when he was digging the grave. His hat was over him now. It was so dark in there; and the elf was trembling with fear and anger at the foul deed . . .

Early in the morning the wicked man arrived home. He took his hat off and went into his sister's bedroom. There lay the beautiful girl in the bloom of youth, dreaming about him of whom she was so fond, and who she believed was going over mountains and through forests. And, stooping over her, the wicked brother gave an ugly laugh, such as a demon might laugh. At that moment the dead leaf fell from his hair on to the counterpane, but he did not notice it and went out to get a little early morning sleep himself. The elf, however, slipped out of the dead leaf, crept into the sleeping girl's ear, and as though in a dream told her of the dreadful murder, described to her the place where her brother had killed the man and left his body, and told her about the lime-tree which blossomed close by, saying: 'To prove to you that it is not just a dream that I have told you, you will find on your bed a dead leaf!' And when she woke up she did find it.

And oh, the salt tears that she wept! And to no one dared she tell her grief. The window stood open all day long and the little elf could easily have got out into the garden to the roses and all the other flowers, only he hadn't the heart to leave her so sad. On the window sill was a bush of monthly roses, and settling there in one of the roses he sat and watched the poor girl. Her brother came into the room many times and was so merry and wicked; but she didn't dare to say a word about her great grief.

As soon as it was night she stole out of the house; and going into the wood to the place where the lime-tree grew, she swept the leaves off the ground, dug down into it, and found at once the one who had been killed. Oh, how she cried and prayed to the Lord that she, too, might soon die!

Gladly would she have carried the body home, had she been able to; but she took the pale head with the closed eyes, kissed the cold lips, and shook the soil out of his handsome hair. 'This I shall keep!' she said. And when she had placed earth and leaves over the dead body, she took home the head, together with a small sprig of the mock-orange which blossomed in the wood where he had been killed.

Back in her room, she fetched the biggest flower-pot she could find; and placing the dead man's head in this, she put soil on it and then planted the sprig of mock-orange.

'Goodbye! Goodbye!' whispered the little elf. He could no longer bear to see all this sorrow, and so he flew into the garden to his rose. But this had faded, and only a few wan petals clung to the green hip.

'Ah, how soon all that is beautiful and good passes away!' sighed the elf. At length he found another rose. He made this his house, and behind its fragrant, delicate petals he settled down to live.

Every morning he would fly across to the poor girl's window, and always she would be standing there by the flower-pot, weeping. The salt tears fell on to the mock-orange, and for every day that she grew paler and paler the sprig got fresher and greener. One shoot grew out after the other, little white buds turned into blossom, and she would kiss them. But the wicked brother would scold her and ask if she had lost her wits. He didn't like her to be always crying over the flower-pot, and couldn't understand why she did. Little did he know of the eyes that were closed and the red lips that had turned to earth. And she bent her head towards the flower-pot, and the little elf from the rose found her there asleep. Climbing into her ear, he spoke to her about the evening in the arbour, about the fragrance of the rose and the love of elves. So sweetly did she dream; and as she dreamt her life slipped away. She had died a peaceful death and was in heaven with the one she held dear.

And the orange-blossoms opened their big white bells, smelling so wonderfully sweet; this was their only way of weeping for the dead.

But seeing the beautiful blossoming tree, the wicked brother took it as an heirloom for himself and placed it in his bedroom close to his bed; for it was lovely to look at and the scent was so sweet and delicious. The little rose elf went with it, flying from blossom to blossom. There lived a little soul in every one, and to each of them he told the story of the murdered young man whose head was now earth under the earth, and of the wicked brother and the poor sister.

'We know about it!' said all the creatures in the flowers. 'We know about it! Didn't we grow up from the dead man's eyes and lips? We know about it! We know about it!' And they nodded their heads so strangely.

The rose elf couldn't make out why they took it so calmly, and he flew out to the bees gathering honey and told them the story of the wicked brother. And the bees told it to their queen, who commanded them all to kill the murderer the next morning.

But in the night—it was the first night after the sister's death—when her brother was asleep in bed near to the fragrant orange-blossom, each flower opened its cup, and invisibly, but bearing poisoned spears, the flower spirits came out. Sitting first at his ear they told him evil dreams, and then they flew over his lips and stabbed his tongue with the poisoned spears. 'Now we have avenged the dead!' they said; and they went back into the white bells of the orange-blossom.

When morning came and the window of the bedroom was thrown open, the rose elf with the queen bee and the whole swarm of bees hurried in to kill him.

But he was already dead; people were standing round the bed and saying: 'The scent of the orange-blossom has killed him!'

Then all at once the rose elf understood the flower's revenge; and he told it to the queen of the bees, and with her whole swarm she flew buzzing round the flower-pot. Then a man took the flower-pot away and one of the bees stung his hand, making him drop the pot and break it.

And then they saw the whitened skull, and knew that the dead man in the bed was a murderer.

And the queen bee hummed in the air and sang of the blossom's revenge and of the rose elf, and of how behind the smallest petal there lives one who can tell and can avenge a wrong.

THE SWINEHERD

ONCE upon a time there was a poor prince. He had a kingdom which was rather small, but, small or not, it was large enough to marry on, and marry he would.

Now, it was really rather forward of him, daring to say to the emperor's daughter: 'Will you have me?' But he did dare, for his name was famous everywhere. There were hundreds of princesses who would have said 'Yes' and been glad of him. But do you think she did?

Well now, just listen.

Growing on the grave of the prince's father was a rose-tree—such a lovely rose-tree! It flowered only once every five years, and even then it only had one bloom; but this rose was so sweet that to smell it made you forget all your troubles and worries. And then he had a nightingale, which could sing as though every lovely melody sat in its little throat. The rose and the nightingale were for the princess; and so they were both placed in big silver caskets and sent to her.

The emperor had them carried before him into the great hall where the princess was playing 'visitors' with her maids of honour—they never did anything else. And when she saw the big caskets with the presents inside, she clapped her hands for joy.

'I do hope it's a little pussy-cat!' she said. But then out came the beautiful rose.

'Oh, isn't it pretty!' cried all the maids of honour.

'It's more than pretty,' said the emperor; 'it's nice!'

But then the princess felt at it, and she could have cried.
'Ugh, daddy!' she cried. 'It isn't an imitation one: it's real!'
'Ugh!' cried all the maids of honour. 'It's a real one!'

'Now, let's see what's in the other casket before we start getting cross,' suggested the emperor. And then out came the nightingale; and so beautifully did it sing that for the moment nobody could find any fault with it.

'*Superbe! Charmant!*' cried all the maids of honour; because they all spoke French, the one worse than the other.

'How the bird reminds me of the late lamented empress's musical-box!' said an old courtier. 'Why yes, it's exactly the same tone, the same expression.'

'Yes, it is!' said the emperor; and he cried like a child.

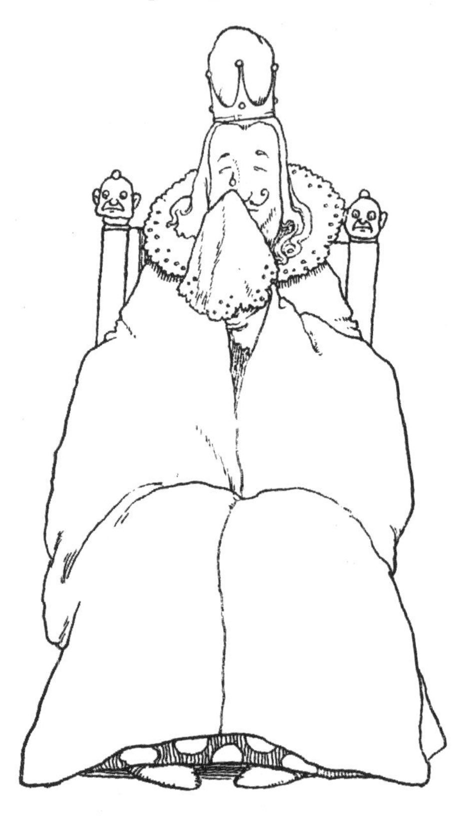

'I don't believe that's a real one,' said the princess.

'Oh yes, that's a real bird,' said the men who had brought it.

'Then away with the creature!' said the princess. And she wouldn't hear of allowing the prince in.

But he wasn't to be put off like that. He smeared his face black and brown, pulled his cap down over his eyes, and knocked at the gate.

'Good morning, emperor!' he said. 'Have you a job for me at the palace?'

'Well, we get so many coming asking for jobs,' said the emperor. 'But let me see—I could do with somebody to look after the pigs. We've got plenty of them.'

And so the prince was taken on as Imperial Swineherd. He was given a wretched little room down by the pigsty, and there he had to stay. But he sat working away all day long, and by evening he had made a nice little cooking-pot. All round it there were little bells, and as soon as the pot started to boil they would tinkle away so prettily, playing the old tune of:

Ah, my darling Augustine,
Everything's lost, lost, lost!

But the oddest thing of all was that if you held your finger in the steam which came from the pot, you could immediately smell what was being cooked in every oven in the town. Well now, that was a different thing altogether from a rose.

Now, the princess was walking past with all her maids of honour, and when she heard the tune she stood still and looked very pleased, because she too could play 'Ah, my darling Augustine'. It was the only tune she could play, but then she played it with one finger.

'Why, that's the tune I know,' she said. 'Then he must be a well-bred swineherd. I say! Go in and ask him the price of that instrument.'

And so one of the maids of honour had to run in and ask. But she put pattens on first.

'What will you take for that pot?' asked the maid of honour.

'I'll take ten kisses from the princess,' answered the swineherd.

'Good gracious me!' said the maid of honour.

'Nothing else will do,' said the swineherd.

'Well, what's he say?' asked the princess.

'I really can't tell you,' said the maid of honour. 'It's so shocking!'

'Then whisper it to me.' And so she whispered it.

'How very rude he is!' said the princess, walking away at once. But she hadn't gone very far when the bells began tinkling beautifully:

> Ah, my darling Augustine,
> Everything's lost, lost, lost!

'Look here!' said the princess. 'Ask him if he'll take ten kisses from my maids of honour.'

'No, thanks!' said the swineherd. 'Ten kisses from the princess, or I stick to my pot.'

'How very tiresome!' said the princess. 'But then you must all of you stand round me, so nobody sees.'

And so the maids of honour all stood round her, spreading out their dresses; and the swineherd got his ten kisses, and she her pot.

And then they did have some fun! The whole of that evening and all next day the pot was kept on the boil. There wasn't an oven in the whole town but they knew what was being cooked there, from the chamberlain's to the cobbler's. The maids of honour danced and clapped their hands in delight.

'We know who's going to have soup and pancakes! We know who's going to have roast and rice pudding! How very interesting it is!'

'Most interesting!' said the lady stewardess.

'Yes, but no telling! Because I'm the emperor's daughter.'

'We'd never dream,' they all said.

The swineherd—that is to say, the prince, but of course they had no idea that he wasn't a real swineherd—the swineherd never missed a day without doing something. And now he made a rattle. When he swung it round, it played all the waltzes, jigs, and polkas that had ever been known.

'Oh, isn't it *superbe*!' cried the princess, as she was passing. 'I never heard such a lovely composition. Look here, go in and ask him the price of that instrument. But there'll be no kissing!'

'He wants a hundred kisses from your royal highness,' said the maid of honour who had been to ask.

'The fellow must be mad!' said the princess, and she walked off. But she had not gone very far when she stopped. 'We must encourage the arts!' she said. 'And I'm the emperor's daughter. Tell him he shall have ten kisses, the same as yesterday. The rest he can take from my maids of honour.'

'Oh, but we wouldn't like him to,' said the maids of honour.

'Nonsense!' said the princess. 'If I can kiss him, so can you. Bear in mind that I give you your board and wages.' And so the maid of honour had to go in again.

'A hundred kisses from the princess,' he said; 'or we both keep what we've got.'

'Stand round!' she said. And so all the maids of honour stood round, and he began his kisses.

'What on earth is all that commotion down by the pigsty?' said the emperor, who had stepped out on to the balcony; and he rubbed his eyes and put on his spectacles. 'If it isn't the maids of honour up to their tricks! I'll have to see to them.' And he pulled his slippers up behind; you see, they were trodden down at the heel.

My word, how he hurried!

As soon as he got down into the courtyard, he crept along

very quietly; and the maids of honour were so busy counting the kisses to see that all was fair, and that he didn't get too many nor too few, that none of them noticed the emperor. He drew himself up on tiptoe.

'Whatever's this?' he said, when he saw them kissing; and he swiped them over the head with his slipper, just as the swineherd was having his eighty-sixth kiss. 'Get out!' cried the emperor, for he was wild. And both the swineherd and the princess were turned out of his kingdom.

And so there she stood, crying, with the swineherd scolding, and the rain pouring down.

'Oh, how miserable I am!' said the princess. 'If only I'd taken the handsome prince! Oh, I'm so unhappy!'

And, going behind a tree, the swineherd wiped the black and brown off his face, threw away his nasty clothes, and stepped forward in his prince's dress, looking so handsome that the princess curtsied when she saw him.

'I've learnt to despise you, my dear!' he said. 'You wouldn't have an honest prince. The rose and the nightingale meant nothing to you. But the swineherd you could kiss for a musical-box. Now you can make the best of it!'

And going into his kingdom, he shut and bolted the door, leaving her standing outside to sing away to her heart's content:

> Ah, my darling Augustine,
> Everything's lost, lost, lost!

THE BUCKWHEAT

WHEN you pass a field of buckwheat after a thunderstorm you will often find it singed and turned quite black. It is just as if a fire has passed over it, and the farmer will say: 'The lightning did that to it!' But why did it do that to it?

I shall tell you what the sparrow told me; it is a story which the sparrow had heard from an old willow-tree that grew near to a buckwheat field, and which grows there still. It's a most respectable old willow-tree, as well as being a big one, but it's old and crinkled; it's split right down the middle of it and grass and brambles are growing out of the crack. The tree bends forward, its branches hanging right down to the ground and looking for all thc world like green hair.

Growing in all the fields round about was corn—rye and barley and oats, the lovely oats which when ripe look like a crowd of yellow canaries perching on a branch. The corn grew ever so beautifully; and the heavier it got, the deeper it bowed down in humbleness.

But there was also a field of buckwheat which happened to be facing the old willow-tree. The buckwheat didn't bow its head like the rest of the corn; it swaggered proud and erect.

'I fancy I'm as rich as the wheat,' it said. 'Besides, I'm a lot more handsome. My flowers are as beautiful as the blossom on the apple-tree. I and my family are a delight to the eye. Do you know anybody grander than we are, old willow-tree?'

And the willow-tree nodded his head as if to say: 'Why yes, indeed I do!' But the buckwheat was so bursting with pride that it said: 'The silly tree! It's so old the grass is growing in its stomach.'

All at once a dreadful storm arose. All the flowers of the field folded up their petals or bowed their delicate heads as the storm swept over them. But the buckwheat swaggered with pride.

'Bow your head like us!' said the flowers.

'I've no need to,' said the buckwheat.

'Bow your head like us!' cried the corn. 'Here's the spirit of the storm! He has wings which reach down from the clouds to the earth, and he'll cut you in two before you can beg for his mercy.'

'Well now, I won't bow my head!' said the buckwheat.

'Shut your flowers and bow your stalks!' said the old willow-tree.' Don't look up at the lightning when the cloud bursts. Not even human beings dare to; for looking into the lightning you will see heaven, and that's a sight to blind even humans. So what would happen to us ground things if we dared to? We who are so much humbler.'

'So much humbler?' said the buckwheat. 'Now I'm going to look into heaven!' And so, in its pride and conceit, it did. It was exactly as if the world were ablaze, the way it lightened.

When in time the storm had passed over, the flowers and the corn stood in the calm clear air, so very refreshed after the rain. But the buckwheat had been burnt by the lightning as black as a cinder; it was dead and useless, a weed in the field.

And the old willow-tree stirred its branches in the wind and from its green leaves fell big drops of water, as though it were weeping. And the sparrows asked: 'What are you crying for? It's so lovely here! See how the sun is shining! See how the clouds are passing over! Do you smell the scent of flowers and bushes? What are you crying for, old willow-tree?'

And the willow-tree told them about the buckwheat's pride, conceit, and punishment, which always follows. I who am telling the story heard it from the sparrows; they told it to me one evening when I asked them for a fairy tale.

THE NIGHTINGALE

In China, you know, the emperor's a Chinaman, and all his courtiers and people are Chinamen. Now, this was all many years ago, but that's just why the story's worth telling, before it gets forgotten.

The emperor's palace was the most gorgeous palace in the world, built entirely of fine porcelain: so precious, but so brittle, so delicate to touch, that you had to be very careful indeed. In the garden were the most wonderful flowers, and tied to the most marvellous of them all were silver bells, which used to tinkle so that you wouldn't go past without noticing them. Yes, everything in the emperor's garden was most carefully worked out, and it was of such a length that the gardener himself had no idea where it ended. If you kept on walking, you came to the loveliest wood, full of tall trees and deep lakes. The wood went straight down to the sea, which was blue and deep. Big ships could sail right in under the branches; and in these there lived a nightingale, which sang so beautifully that even the fisherman, though he had so much else to do, would lie still and listen when he was out drawing in his net at night and he happened to hear it. 'My word, isn't it grand!' he would say. But then he would have to see to his things and would forget all about the bird; though on the next night that it sang and the fisherman happened to be there, he would say the same thing: 'My word, isn't it grand!'

Travellers from all over the world came to see the emperor's city, and they would admire the town, the palace, and the

garden. But when they heard the nightingale, they would all say: 'Ah, but that's the best!'

And the travellers told about it when they got home, and scholars wrote many books about the city, the palace, and the garden, not forgetting the nightingale but placing it at the top of the list. And those who could write poetry made up the loveliest poems, all about the nightingale in the wood by the deep lake.

These books went round the world, and in time some of them reached the emperor. He sat in his golden chair, reading and reading, and every now and then nodding his head; he was so delighted by the splendid descriptions of the city, the palace, and the garden. 'Ah, but the best of all is the nightingale!' he read.

'What!' cried the emperor. 'The nightingale! Why, I never heard of it! Is there such a bird in my empire? And in my own garden at that? I never heard tell of it! This is the sort of thing I have to get out of books.'

And he called for his gentleman in waiting, who was so grand a person that when anyone of lower rank ventured to speak to him or ask him a question, the only answer he would give was 'P!' and that has no meaning at all.

'I hear reports of a highly remarkable bird called a nightingale,' said the emperor. 'They say it's the best thing in my great empire! How is it that I have never been told about it?'

'I have never heard it mentioned,' said the gentleman in waiting. 'It has never been presented at Court.'

'I wish it to come here tonight and sing for me,' said the emperor. 'Here's all the world knows what I've got, and I don't!'

'I have never heard it mentioned,' said the gentleman in waiting. 'I'll seek it out! I'll find it!'

But where was it to be found? The gentleman in waiting ran

up and down all the stairs, and through halls and corridors; among all the people he met none had heard tell of the nightingale, and the gentleman in waiting ran back to the emperor, and said that it must be one of those tales made up by people who write books. 'Your imperial majesty should never believe what's written in books! It's all invented; what they call black magic.'

'But the book I read it in,' said the emperor, 'was sent to me by the illustrious emperor of Japan, and so it can't be untrue. I *will* hear the nightingale! It must be here tonight! It has my most gracious favour! And if it doesn't come, then the whole Court shall be punched in the stomach, after eating their supper!'

'Tsing-pe!' said the gentleman in waiting; and off he ran again, up and down all the stairs and through all the halls and corridors, half the Court running with him, because they didn't want to be punched in the stomach. They all inquired after the strange nightingale which everyone in the world knew of, though nobody at Court.

At last they found a poor little girl in the kitchen. She said: 'Why, yes, the nightingale! I know it well. My word, it can sing! Every night I'm allowed to take a few scraps from the table home to my poor sick mother, who lives down by the shore. And on my way back, when I'm tired and rest in the wood, I hear the nightingale sing. It brings the tears to my eyes, just as if my mother was kissing me!'

'Little kitchen-maid,' said the gentleman in waiting, 'I'll get you a permanent job in the kitchen and permission to watch the emperor eat, if you'll lead us to the nightingale; for it's been summoned to appear tonight.'

And so off they all went into the wood where the nightingale used to sing; half the Court was there. Now, as they were walking along a cow began to bellow.

'Ah,' said the Court officials, 'there we have it. What remarkable power for such a small creature! I'm pretty certain I've heard it before!'

'Why, that's the cow mooing!' said the little kitchen-maid. 'We've a long way to go yet.'

Next the frogs in the pond began to croak.

'Lovely!' said the Chinese chaplain. 'Now I hear her! It's like the ringing of little church bells.'

'Why, that's the frogs!' said the little kitchen-maid. 'But I think we shall soon be hearing it now.'

And then the nightingale began to sing.

'That's it!' said the little maid. 'Listen! Listen! And there it is.' And she pointed to a grey little bird up in the branches.

'Is it possible?' said the gentleman in waiting. 'I'd never imagined it would be like that! How common it looks. I expect it's lost its colour from seeing so many important people round it.'

'Little nightingale,' cried the little kitchen-maid in a loud voice, 'our gracious emperor wants you to sing for him!'

'With the greatest of pleasure!' said the nightingale, singing for all it was worth.

'It's like the tinkling of glass bells!' said the gentleman in waiting.' And just look at the way its little throat's going! It's strange that we've never heard it before. It'll be a big success at Court.'

'Shall I sing for the emperor once more?' said the nightingale, thinking that the emperor was there.

'My excellent little nightingale,' said the gentleman in waiting, 'it is my great pleasure to summon you to a Court fête tonight, when you will charm his exalted imperial highness with your enchanting song!'

'It sounds best here in the open!' said the nightingale; but it gladly went with them on hearing that this was the emperor's wish.

The palace had been made all bright and cheerful. Walls and floor, which were of porcelain, glistened in the light of thousands of gold lamps. The loveliest of flowers, all able to tinkle, had been set out along the corridors; with the hurrying and the scurrying the bells all tinkled away, and nobody could hear a word that was said.

In the middle of the big hall where the emperor sat a golden perch had been set up for the nightingale to stand on. The whole Court was there, and the little kitchen-maid had been allowed to stand behind the door, now she had the title of regular kitchen-maid. Everyone was dressed in his best, and all looked at the little grey bird, which the emperor nodded to.

And the nightingale sang so deliciously that the tears came into the emperor's eyes and rolled down his cheeks, and then the nightingale sang even more beautifully; its song went straight to the heart. And the emperor was most pleased, and said that the nightingale should have his gold slipper to wear

round its neck. But the nightingale said 'Thank you!' it had been well rewarded already.

'I've seen tears in the emperor's eyes, and I treasure that more than anything. There's strange power in an emperor's tears! Indeed, I've been well rewarded.' And it sang with its sweet and heavenly voice again.

'As pretty a piece of showing off as ever was!' said all the ladies round about. And they filled their mouths with water to cluck with when anybody spoke to them, thinking that they, too, were nightingales; while, as for the footmen and chambermaids, they gave it out that they also were pleased, and that's saying a lot, because they are the hardest of all to satisfy. Oh yes, the nightingale was certainly a success.

It was decided that it should stay at Court and have a cage of its own, with freedom to go out twice a day and once a night. It had twelve servants to go with it, each holding on to it by a silk ribbon round its leg. There was no fun at all in those walks.

The remarkable bird was the talk of the town, and when two people met, one would say nothing but 'Night!' and the other only 'Gale!'—and then they would sigh and understand each other. Eleven grocers' children were even called after it, though none of them was the slightest bit musical . . .

One day a large parcel arrived for the emperor, with the word 'Nightingale' written on the outside.

'This'll be a new book about our famous bird!' said the emperor. But it wasn't a book; it was a sort of toy packed in a box, an artificial nightingale made in imitation of the live one but studded all over with diamonds, rubies, and sapphires. When the artificial bird was wound up, it would sing one of the pieces the real one sang, while wagging its tail up and down and glittering with silver and gold. Round its neck was a little rib-

bon, and on it was written: 'The emperor of Japan's nightingale is poor compared to the emperor of China's.'

'How lovely!' they all said; and the one who had brought the artificial bird was immediately given the title of Chief Imperial Nightingale Bringer.

'Now they must sing together: what a duet it'll be!'

And so they had to sing together, though it wasn't really a success, for the real nightingale sang in its own way and the artificial bird ran on rollers. 'It isn't to blame,' said the music-master. 'It keeps perfect time, and is quite after my own style.' So the artificial bird had to sing by itself . . . It was as great a success as the real one; and then, of course, it was so much prettier to look at, sparkling just like bracelets and brooches.

It sang the same tune over and over thirty-three times, and

never grew tired. Some would have liked to hear it through once more, but the emperor thought that the real nightingale should be given a turn . . . But where was it? Nobody had noticed it when it had flown out through the open window, off to its own green woods.

'Why, what's the meaning of this?' said the emperor. And all the courtiers called it names, saying what an ungrateful creature the nightingale was. 'We still have the best bird, though!' they said. And the artificial bird had to sing once more; it was the thirty-fourth time they had heard the same piece, but they didn't quite know it yet, as it was a hard one. And the music-master was full of the highest praise for the bird, declaring even that it was better than the real nightingale, not only for its dress and its lots of lovely diamonds, but inside as well.

'For you see, my lords and ladies—and your imperial highness above all—with the real nightingale you can never know what to expect. But with the artificial bird everything is fixed. Just so, and no other way! It can be explained. You can rip it open and show the working of the human mind, how the mechanism is arranged, how it goes, and how one thing follows another . . .'

'That's exactly what I think,' they all said; and the music-master was allowed, the following Sunday, to put the bird on show to the people. They were also to hear it sing, said the emperor. And they did hear it; and were as pleased as though they'd made themselves merry drinking tea, which is so very Chinese. And they all said 'Ah!' and held up the finger called 'Lickpot' and nodded. But the poor fisherman who had heard the real nightingale said: 'It sounds nice enough and it's rather like it, but there's something missing: what, I can't tell!'

The real nightingale was banished from the empire.

The artificial bird had its place on a silken cushion close to the emperor's bed; all the presents it had received, in gold and precious stones, lay round about it, and it had been honoured with the title of High Imperial Bedside Table Singer, ranking number one on the left; for the emperor regarded the side of the heart as the more important, and the heart is on the left side even in an emperor. And the music-master wrote twenty-five volumes about the artificial bird. They were so long and so learned, and full of the most difficult Chinese words; and everybody said they had read them and understood them, for if they hadn't they would have been stupid and would have been punched in the stomach.

And so a whole year went by. The emperor, the Court, and every other Chinaman knew by heart every little cluck in the artificial bird's song, but that was exactly why they liked it best: they could join in the singing, as they did. The boys in the street would sing 'Ze-ze-ze! Cluck-cluck-cluck!' and so would the emperor. Yes, indeed, it was lovely!

But one evening the artificial bird was singing away, and the emperor was lying in bed listening to it, when there was a 'Zup!' inside the bird; something snapped with a 'whir-r-r-r!', all the wheels went round, and the music stopped.

The emperor jumped straight out of bed and sent for his physician; but what good could he do? They then called in the watchmaker, and after a lot of talk and much looking into it he got the bird fairly well mended, but said that they would have to go very carefully with it, as the works were so worn and it wasn't possible to put new ones in so it would be sure to sing. This was a great blow. They didn't dare to let the artificial bird sing more than once a year, and even that was bad enough. But then the music-master would make a short speech with his hard words, saying that it was as good as it had been before—and it *was* as good as it had been before.

Five years had now passed by and suddenly the whole country was in great grief. In their hearts they all loved their emperor; and now he was ill and wouldn't live, it was said. A new emperor had already been chosen, and outside in the street people were asking the gentleman in waiting how the old emperor was getting on.

'P!' he said, shaking his head.

Cold and pale the emperor lay in his large and splendid bed. The whole Court thought him dead, and everyone ran off to greet the new emperor; the servants of the bedchamber ran out to talk about it, and the palace maids gave a big party. Cloth had been laid on the floors of all the halls and corridors to deaden the sound of footsteps, and it was so very, very quiet. But the emperor wasn't dead yet; stiff and pale he lay in the splendid bed with the long velvet curtains and the heavy golden tassels.

A window was open up above, and the moon was shining in on the emperor and the artificial bird.

The poor emperor could hardly breathe; there seemed to be something on his chest. Opening his eyes, he saw that it was Death sitting on his chest, and it was wearing his gold crown and holding his gold sword in one hand and his splendid banner in the other. And out of the folds of the big velvet curtains strange heads were peeping, some very ugly and others looking so very gentle: they were all the emperor's bad deeds and good deeds, watching him while Death sat on his heart.

'Do you remember?' they whispered one after another. 'Do you remember?' And they told him so many things that the sweat stood out on his forehead.

'I never knew!' said the emperor. 'Music, music! The great Chinese drum!' he cried. 'Stop me hearing all the things they say!'

And they kept on, with Death nodding like a Chinaman at all that was said.

'Music, music!' screamed the emperor. 'You precious little golden bird, sing for me, sing! I gave you gold and precious things; with my own hands I hung my gold slipper round your neck. Sing for me, sing!'

But the bird stood silent; there was no one to wind it up, and it never sang without. And Death kept on staring the emperor in the face with its great empty sockets, and there was silence, dreadful silence.

Then all at once, from near the window, there came the loveliest singing. It was the little, live nightingale, sitting on the branch outside; hearing of its emperor's distress, it had come to sing hope and comfort to him. And as it sang, the figures grew fainter and fainter, the blood flowed faster and faster in the emperor's feeble body, and, listening, Death itself said: 'Keep on, little nightingale, keep on!'

'Then will you give me the splendid gold sword? Then will you give me the rich banner? Will you give me the emperor's crown?'

And Death gave up each of his treasures for a song while the nightingale went on singing, singing of the silent churchyard where the white roses grow, where the elder-tree sweetly smells, and where the fresh grass is wetted by the tears of the mourners; and, growing homesick for his garden, Death floated, like a cold, white mist, out of the window.

'Thank you! Thank you!' said the emperor. 'You heavenly little bird, I know you! I drove you from my country and my empire, and yet you have sung away the evil visions from my bed and sent Death away from my heart. How shall I reward you?'

'You have rewarded me!' said the nightingale. 'I got tears from your eyes the first time that I sang, and for that I'll never forget you. They are the jewels which cheer a singer's heart. But sleep now, and grow well and strong! I will sing for you!'

And it sang—while the emperor fell into a sweet sleep, a sleep so gentle and refreshing.

The sun was shining in to him through the windows when he woke refreshed and well. None of his servants had returned yet, thinking that he was dead, but the nightingale was singing away there still.

'You must stay with me for ever,' said the emperor. 'You need only sing when you want to, and I'll smash the artificial bird into a thousand pieces!'

'Don't do that!' said the nightingale. 'It did what good it could. Keep it as before. I can't settle down in the palace; but let me come whenever I feel like coming, and I'll sit in the evening on the branch by your window and sing for you, making you cheerful as well as thoughtful. I'll sing of people who are happy and of those who suffer; I'll sing of good and evil hidden round about you. The little singing-bird flies far and wide; to the poor fisherman, to the roof of the cottager, to all so far away from you and your Court. I love your heart better than your crown, and yet there's something holy about your crown. I will come. I will sing for you. But one thing you must promise me!'

'Everything!' said the emperor, standing up in the imperial robes in which he had dressed himself and holding the sword, heavy with gold, towards his heart.

'One thing I ask of you. Let no one know that you have a little bird which tells you everything, and then all will be even better!'

And the nightingale flew off.

The servants came in to see to their dead emperor and—well, there they stood, and the emperor said: 'Good morning!'

SWEETHEARTS

(The Top and the Ball)

THE TOP and the ball lay in a drawer together, along with other toys, and one day the top said to the ball: 'Why don't we be sweethearts, seeing that we're in the same drawer together?' But the ball, who was made of morocco leather and as conceited as any young lady, wasn't going to answer such talk.

Next day, along came the boy who owned the toys; he took the top and painted it red and yellow all over, and then he hammered a brass nail through the middle of it. It was a splendid sight to see the top, the way it went spinning round.

'Look at me!' he said to the ball. 'What do you say now? Shall we be sweethearts, then? We go so very well together, you bouncing and I skipping! There couldn't be a happier couple than us two.'

'That's what you think!' said the ball. 'You don't seem to know that my father and mother were moroccan slippers, and that I've a cork in me.'

'Ah, but then I'm mahogany!' said the top. 'And the Lord Mayor himself made me! He has his own workshop and he got such a lot of fun out of me!'

'So you expect me to believe that?' said the ball.

'May I never be whipped again if I'm telling a lie!' replied the top.

'You give a good account of yourself,' said the ball. 'But, you see, I can't; I'm practically half engaged to a swallow. Every time

I go into the air he pops his head out of the nest and says: "Will you? Will you?" And now I've told myself I will, and that's practically a half-engagement. But I promise never to forget you.'

'A lot of good that will be!' said the top. And from then on they never spoke to each other.

The next day the ball was taken out. The top watched her fly right into the air like a bird, until at last she was clean out of sight. Each time she came back again, but when she touched the ground she would take a high bounce into the air; either from longing or because she had a cork in her. The ninth time she went up she never came back again; and though the little boy searched and searched, she was gone.

'I could say where she is!' sighed the top. 'She's in the swallow's nest, and has married the swallow!'

The more the top thought it over, the more he lost his heart to the ball. The very fact that he couldn't have her made him love her all the more. The puzzling thing about it was that she should have chosen someone else. And the top went on spinning and humming, while all the time his thoughts were of the ball, who grew more and more beautiful in his imagination. And so many years passed—and it was just an old love affair.

And the top was no longer young . . . But then one day he was painted from head to foot with gold paint; never had he looked so handsome! He was a gold top now, and he skipped till the air fairly whistled. This was just the thing! Then all of a sudden he had skipped too high and—he was gone!

They searched and searched, even in the basement, but he was nowhere to be found.

. . . Wherever was he?

He had jumped into the dustbin, down among all sorts of stuff—cabbage stalks, sweepings, and rubbish from the gutter-spout.

'I've landed in a proper place now. I shan't keep my gilt long here. And what's all this riff-raff that I've got among?' And he stole a look at a cabbage stalk which hadn't a picking on it, and at a funny round thing that looked like an old apple. Only it wasn't an apple: it was an old ball which had lain for years in the gutter and got all sodden.

'Thank goodness, there's somebody of my own class to talk to at last!' said the ball, with a glance at the gilded top. 'Actually, I'm of morocco leather and was stitched by a gentlewoman, and I have a cork in me, though you wouldn't think it to look at me. I was just going to marry a swallow when I fell in the gutter, and I've lain there sopping wet these five years. It's a long time, I can tell you, for a lady!'

But the top made no answer; he was reminded of his old sweetheart, and the more he listened, the more he was certain that this was she.

Presently the maid came to empty the dustbin. 'Hello!' she cried. 'Here's the gold top!'

And so the top was restored to his former honour in the house. But nothing was heard of the ball, and the top never spoke of his old love again. That dies when your sweetheart has lain for five years sopping wet in a gutter; and you never know her again if you meet her in the dustbin.

THE UGLY DUCKLING

IT WAS so lovely in the country! It was summer. The wheat was yellow, the oats green; the hay was stacked up in the grassy meadows; and there went the stork on his long red legs, jabbering away in Egyptian, which was the language he had learnt from his mother. All round the fields and meadows were large woods, and in the middle of the woods there were deep lakes. Yes, it *was* lovely there in the country! Standing in the sun was an old manor-house with a deep moat round it, and from the wall down to the water's edge grew great big burdocks, which were so tall that little children could stand upright under the largest of them. The place was as wild as the densest forest, and in there a duck was sitting on her nest. She was busy hatching her little ducklings, but was getting rather tired of it because it was taking so long and she seldom had visitors; the other ducks thought more of swimming about on the moat than of coming in and sitting under a burdock leaf quacking to her.

At long last the eggs began to crack, one after the other. 'Cheep! Cheep!' they said. Every yolk among them had come to life and was popping its head out.

'Quack! Quack!' she said. 'Quick! Quick!' And they were as quick as they knew how, peeping about under the green leaves on all sides, their mother letting them look as much as they pleased because green is so good for the eyes.

'Oh, what a big world it is!' cried all the ducklings. And of course they did have a lot more room than in the eggs.

'Don't think this is all the world!' said their mother. 'It

stretches a long way past the other side of the garden, right over to the parson's field, but that's a place I've never been to. Well now, I hope you're all here.' And she got up to have a look. 'Why no, I haven't got you all yet! The biggest egg's still there. How long is this going to take? I'm just about sick of it!' And she settled herself down again.

'Well, how's it going?' asked an old duck who had dropped in to see her.

'It's taking ages with one of these eggs!' said the duck on the nest. 'I can't get it to crack at all. But just have a look at the others. They're the darlingest ducklings I've ever seen! Every one of them takes after its father! The wretch, he never comes near me!'

'Let's have a look at the egg that won't crack,' said the other. 'Take my word for it, it's a turkey egg! I was taken in that way once. And what a bother I had with those youngsters! They're frightened to death of water! I *couldn't* get them into it. I quacked and I clacked, but it wasn't a bit of use! Let me have a look. Yes, it's a turkey egg all right! You leave it where it is and teach the other ones to swim.'

'I think I'll stick at it for a bit!' said the duck. 'I've sat here so long I can just as well sit on a bit longer.'

'As you please,' said the old duck. And she waddled off.

At long last the big egg cracked open. 'Cheep! Cheep!' said the young one as it tumbled out. He was a big, ugly fellow. The duck looked at him and said: 'That's a monstrous duckling! He's not a bit like the others. Surely it wouldn't be a turkey chick. Well, we'll soon find out! He'll go in the water, if I have to kick him in!'

It was really glorious weather the next day; the sun shone down on every green burdock. The mother duck turned out at the waterside with all her family. Splash! She was in the water.

'Quack! Quack!' she said; 'Quick! Quick!' And one after the other the little ducklings plumped in. The water closed over their heads, but they came straight up again and floated along beautifully, their legs going by themselves. And every one of them was in, the ugly grey fellow swimming along with the rest.

'He's no turkey!' she said. 'See how beautifully he uses his legs, and how straight he holds himself. He's my own little duck! And he isn't so bad-looking, either, when you come to think of it. Quack! Quack! Come along, all of you, and I'll take you into the world and introduce you to the duck-yard! But mind you keep close to me, so that nobody treads on you. And keep a sharp look-out for the cat!'

And so they went into the duck-yard. There was a terrible

noise in there, as two families were having a fight over an eel's head—and in the end the cat got it.

'There now, that's the way of the world!' said the mother duck, licking her bill, for she, too, fancied eel's head. 'Now hurry along!' she said. 'Show how sharp you can be and bow nicely to the old duck over there. She's the most select of anybody here. She's of Spanish blood, and that's why she's so plump. And do you see that red rag she has round her leg? That's something very grand, the greatest distinction a duck can have. It's a sign that they don't intend to part with her, and to mark her out for people and animals. Look smart now, and don't turn your toes in! A well-brought-up duckling keeps his toes well apart, like Father and Mother. Now then! Bow nicely, dears, and say "Quack!"'

And they did as they were told. But the other ducks that were gathered there looked at them and said out loud: 'Just look! Now we're getting that rabble. As if there weren't enough of us already! And, my, what an object that one is. We're not putting up with him.' And one duck flew straight at him and bit him in the neck.

'Leave him alone!' said the mother. 'He's doing no harm.'

'No, but he's too big and gawky,' said the duck that had bitten him. 'So he's going to get it!'

'You've got some pretty ones there, my dear,' said the old duck with the rag round her leg. 'All excepting that one; he hasn't come out at all well. What a pity you can't make him afresh!'

'It can't be helped, your ladyship,' said the ducklings' mother. 'He's not pretty, but he has a good disposition and he swims as nicely as any of the others—a little better, if anything! I fancy he'll grow better-looking in time, or else not so big. He was too long in the egg, and it's affected his figure.' And as she spoke she preened his neck and smoothed his feathers down. 'Besides, he's a drake,' she said, 'and so it doesn't matter so much. I expect he'll turn out strong enough to give a good account of himself!'

'The other ducklings are charming!' said the old duck. 'Make yourselves at home, dears; and if you come across an eel's head, just bring it along to me.'

And so they made themselves at home.

But the poor duckling that had been the last to hatch and was so ugly to look at was pecked, jostled and made fun of by the ducks and the hens. 'He's too big!' they all said. And the turkey cock, who had been born with spurs on and so fancied himself emperor, puffed himself out like a ship in full sail and, making straight for him, gobbled at him till he was quite red in the face. The poor little duckling scarcely knew which way to turn, and was so very miserable because he looked so ugly and was the laughing-stock of the duck-yard.

That was the way things went from the first day, and later it got worse and worse. The poor duckling was pushed around by every one of them. Even his brothers and sisters were unkind to him, and they would say: 'If only the cat would get you, you ugly thing!' And his mother said: 'I wish you were far enough away!' And the ducks bit him and the hens pecked him and the maid who fed the poultry let fly at him with her foot.

So one day he fluttered away over the hedge, causing all the little birds in the bushes to fly frightened into the air. 'That's because I'm so ugly!' thought the duckling, shutting his eyes as he ran on. And so in time he came to the great marshes where the wild ducks lived. There he lay all night, he was so tired and weary.

In the morning the wild ducks flew up and came to have a look at their new companion. 'What do you think you are?' they asked. And the duckling turned and bowed all round as well as he could.

'You're an ugly object!' said the wild ducks. 'But it's all the same to us, so long as you don't marry into our family.' Poor thing! He hadn't the least intention of marrying! If only they would allow him to lie among the rushes and drink a little marsh water.

For two whole days he lay there, and then along came two wild geese—or rather wild ganders, for they were males. They hadn't been long out of the egg, which explains why they were so cocky.

'Look here, my lad!' they said. 'You're so ugly that we rather like you. Why not fly in with us? In another marsh not far from here there are some really adorable wild geese, all maiden ladies, and nice quackers. You'd make a hit, with your ugliness!'

'Bing! Bang!' A sudden shot rang out, and the two wild ganders fell dead among the rushes, while the water turned blood-red. 'Bing! Bang!' Another shot, and whole flocks of wild geese flew up from the rushes, followed by yet another crack. There was a big shoot on. The men were all round the marsh, and some were even perched in branches of trees which hung right over the rushes. Blue smoke drifted like clouds among the darker trees and hung far out over the water. The gun dogs came flop-flopping through the mud, and reeds and rushes swayed in all directions. It was terrifying for the poor duckling, and he turned his head to hide it under his wing. And then all of a sudden there stood right next to him an enormous dog; its tongue was lolling right out and its eyes gleamed horribly. It thrust its jaws right down towards the duckling, baring its sharp teeth as it did so. And then—splash, it had gone without getting him!

'Thank heaven!' sighed the duckling. 'I'm so ugly that even

the dog doesn't fancy me.'

And he lay there perfectly still, while the shot whistled among the rushes and the guns cracked and banged.

It was late in the day before all was quiet again, but the poor duckling was too scared to get up even then, and he waited for a few more hours before daring to look round. Then he scampered away from the marsh as fast as his legs would carry him; over fields and meadows he ran, though there was such a wind that he had hard work fighting his way against it.

Towards evening he came to a poor little cottage; it was so wretched that it couldn't make up its mind which way to fall and so remained standing. The wind swept so fiercely around the little duckling that he had to squat on his tail so as not to be blown over—and it got worse and worse. And then he noticed that the door had come off one of its hinges, and was so crooked that it was possible to slip through the crack into the house, and this he did.

In the house lived an old woman, with her cat and her hen. The cat, which she called Sonny, could arch its back and purr and it could also make sparks fly, but for that you had to stroke it the wrong way. The hen had short little legs and so was called Chickabiddy Dumpy. It was a good layer and the woman was as fond of it as of her own child.

The next morning the strange duckling was noticed at once and the cat began to purr and the hen to cluck.

'What's all the fuss?' said the woman, looking round. But her eyesight was poor, and so she took the duckling for a plump duck that had gone astray. 'This is a catch!' she said. 'I'll have duck eggs now—that is, if it isn't a drake. We must give it a trial.'

And so the duckling was taken on trial for three weeks; but no eggs arrived. Now, the cat was master in that house and the

hen was mistress, and they always used to say: 'We and the world!' thinking they were half of it, and that the better half. The duckling thought there might be two opinions about this, but the hen wouldn't have it.

'Can you lay eggs?' she asked.

'No.'

'Very well, then, will you hold your tongue!'

And the cat said: 'Can you arch your back and purr and make sparks fly?'

'No.'

'Very well, then, don't pretend to opinions when sensible people are speaking!'

And the duckling sat in a corner and was thoroughly downhearted. Then all at once he remembered the fresh air and the sunshine; and he felt such a strange longing to float on the water that in the end he just couldn't help himself and had to tell it to the hen.

'What's come over you?' she asked. 'You have nothing to do, and that's why you get these ideas into your head. Lay some eggs or purr, and they'll go over!'

'But it's so grand to float on the water!' said the duckling. 'So grand to get your head under and duck to the bottom.'

'H'm, very delightful, I'm sure!' said the hen. 'You must have taken leave of your senses! Ask the cat—he's the wisest person I know—if he likes floating on the water or ducking under! I won't say what I think. Go and ask the old woman, our mistress! There's nobody any wiser than she is. Do you think she likes floating on water and ducking her head under?'

'None of you understand me!' said the duckling.

'And if we don't understand you, who would, I would like to know? You're surely not making yourself out to be wiser than the cat and the old woman—to say nothing of me! Don't take on so, child! And give thanks to your Maker for all the kindnesses shown to you. Didn't you come into a warm room, in company you can learn from? But you're a muddle-head and it's got past a joke having to live with you. Now mark what I say! It's for your own good. I'm being disagreeable, but that's the way to tell your real friends. Now look to it and lay some eggs and learn to purr and make sparks fly!'

'I think I'll go out into the wide world,' said the duckling.

'All right then, go!' said the hen.

So off he went. And he floated on the water and he ducked under it, but was cut by everybody because of his ugliness.

And so autumn came round. The leaves on the trees turned brown and yellow, and the wind caught them and sent them dancing; there was a chill look in the air; the clouds were heavy with hail and sleet; and the raven stood on the fence and squawked 'Ow! Ow!' from sheer cold. The very thought of it was enough to give one the shivers. The poor duckling did have a bad time!

One evening with a glorious sunset a whole flock of handsome large birds came out of the bushes. The duckling had never seen any so beautiful; they were gleaming white and had long graceful necks. They were swans. They uttered the strangest of cries, spread their magnificent long wings, and flew off from these cold parts to warmer lands with open water. They soared so high, so high, that the ugly little duckling felt a queer feeling come over him; he spun round on the water like a wheel, stretched his neck after them in the air, and let out a cry so loud and strange that he frightened himself. He couldn't get the handsome birds, the lucky birds, out of his head, and as soon as they were out of sight he dived straight to the bottom; and when he came up again he was almost beside himself. He had no idea what the birds were called or where they went to, but he loved them as he had never loved anyone before. He wasn't at all jealous of them, for how could he dream of wishing for such splendour? He would have been glad only to have the ducks put up with him—the poor ugly creature!

The winter was so cold, so bitterly cold. The duckling had to swim about so as to keep the water from freezing up altogether. But every night the hole he was swimming in grew smaller and smaller, and the top of the ice cracked in the frost. The duckling had to keep his legs going all the time to stop the gap from closing up. In the end he grew quite faint, lay perfectly still, and froze fast in the ice.

Early the next morning a farmer came along and saw him, and going out to him he broke the ice with his clog and took him home to his wife. There he revived.

The children wanted to play with him, but the duckling was afraid they were going to hurt him and flew terrified into the milk-pan, slopping the milk all over the room. The woman screamed and waved her arms, and this made him fly into the butter-tub, and down from there into the flour-bin and up again. He did look a sight! The woman screamed and let fly at him with the tongs, and the children fell over one another trying to catch him, shrieking with laughter. Luckily the door was open and he scrambled out among the bushes into the freshly fallen snow, where he lay all in a daze.

But it would make too dismal a story to tell of all the misery and hardship he had to undergo that hard winter. He was lying on the marsh among the rushes when the warm sun began shining again. The larks were singing—it was lovely spring!

Then all at once he lifted his wings. They were stronger now than before and bore him along easily, and before he was aware of it he was in a large garden, where the apple-trees were in

W.
HEATH
ROBINSON

blossom and sweet-smelling lilac hung down on long green branches over the winding streams. Oh, how fresh and spring-like it was! And from the thicket straight in front of him came three beautiful white swans, spreading their wings and floating so lightly on the water. The duckling knew the splendid birds and a strange sadness came over him.

'I'll fly over to the royal birds. And they'll peck me to death for being so ugly and daring to go near them! But what do I care? Rather be killed by them than pinched by the ducks, pecked at by the hens, kicked by the girl who looks after the poultry, and suffer hardship in winter!' And so he flew into the water and swam towards the splendid swans; and seeing him they ruffled their feathers and went to meet him. 'Have done with me!' said the poor creature, as he bowed his head towards the water and waited for death. But what was this he saw in the clear water? There, beneath him, was his own reflection; but he was no longer a clumsy, grey-black bird, plain and ugly—he was a swan himself!

It doesn't matter being born in a duck-yard, when you have been hatched out of a swan's egg!

He felt really happy about all the trouble and hardship he had been through, and able to appreciate all the happiness and all the delight which were coming to him. And the big swans swam round him and stroked him with their beaks.

Some little children came into the garden and threw bread and meal in the water, and the smallest of them cried: 'There's a new one!' And the other children chimed in: 'Yes, there's a new one come!' And they clapped their hands and danced about and ran for Father and Mother; and bread and cakes were thrown into the water, and everybody said: 'The new one is the nicest—so young and so handsome!' And the old swans curtsied to him.

It made him feel quite bashful and tuck his head under his wing, not knowing what to do. He was so very happy, and yet not at all proud, for a good heart is never proud; but he was thinking of how he had been despised and disdained, while now everyone was saying he was the loveliest of all lovely birds. And the lilacs bowed their branches down to the water for him, and the sun shone so kindly and so warmly that, ruffling his feathers and raising his slender neck, he rejoiced with all his heart: 'I never dreamt of so much happiness, when I was the ugly duckling!'

THE FIR-TREE

THERE was such a pretty little fir-tree standing in the wood. It grew in a good place, able to catch the sun, getting plenty of fresh air; and many bigger companions grew round about, both firs and pines. But the little fir-tree was so impatient to grow; it thought nothing of the warm sunshine and the fresh air; it cared nothing for the village children, prattling away as they gathered strawberries or raspberries. Often they would come along carrying a whole jugful or a string of strawberries threaded on straw, and, sitting down by the little tree, would say: 'Isn't it a pretty little one!' The tree hated to hear it.

By the next year it had grown a long shoot bigger, and the next year again an even longer one. You see, from the number of joints on a fir-tree you can always tell how many years it has been growing.

'Oh, if only I were such a big tree like the others!' sighed the little tree. 'I'd be able to spread my branches right out and from my top see into the wide world. The birds would come and build their nests in my branches, and when the wind blew I'd be able to nod as grandly as they all do.'

It got no pleasure at all out of the sunshine, or the birds, or the crimson clouds which sailed over its head in the morning and evening.

Often in the winter-time, when the snow lay glistening white all around, a hare would come bounding along and leap right over the little tree—and how that did annoy it! But two winters went by, and by the third the tree was so big that the hare had to go round it. Oh, to grow, to grow, to get big and old! That was the only nice thing in all the world, thought the tree.

In the autumn the woodcutters always came and felled some of the tallest trees. This happened every year; and the young fir-tree, which by now was quite well grown, trembled to see it, for the magnificent trees would fall creaking and crashing to the ground. Then their branches would be cut away, and they would look altogether bare and long and narrow; one hardly knew them again. And they would be laid on wagons, and horses would pull them away out of the wood.

Where were they going? What was in store for them?

When the swallow and the stork came, in the spring, the tree said to them: 'Don't you know where they were taken? Didn't you meet them?'

The swallows knew nothing, but the stork, looking thoughtful, nodded its head and said: 'Well, I believe so! I met lots of new ships on my flight from Egypt, and there were splendid masts on them. I dare say they were the ones—they smelt of fir. I can give you news of them—they've come out on top!'

'Oh, if only I were big enough to fly away over the sea! What's it really like, this sea? What does it look like?'

'Well, that would take too much explaining,' said the stork, and off it went.

'Be glad of your youth!' said the sunbeams. Be glad of your healthy growth, of that young life that's in you!'

And the wind kissed the tree and the dew shed tears over it, but the fir-tree didn't understand.

Now, at Christmas-time quite young trees would be felled, trees which often were not even as big or as old as this fir-tree which knew neither peace nor rest but was for ever wanting to push on. These young trees—and they were the nicest ones of all—were always left with their branches on. They were placed on wagons, and pulled off out of the wood by horses.

'Where are they going?' asked the fir-tree. 'They're no bigger than I am, and one of them was even a lot smaller. Why were they left with all their branches on? Where are they going to?'

'We'll tell you where! We'll tell you where!' chirruped the sparrows. 'We've been in the town, looking in through the windows. We know where they go to. Why, they go to the greatest honour and glory you can think of! We've peeped in through the windows and seen them planted in the middle of the warm room and decorated with the loveliest of things, such as golden apples, gingerbread, toys, and hundreds and hundreds of candles!'

'And then . . . ?' asked the fir-tree, trembling in all its branches. 'And then? What happens then?'

'Why, that's all we saw. It was marvellous!'

'I wonder if I was born for this glorious life?' thought the tree joyfully. 'It's even better than crossing the sea. I'm just dying for it. I do wish it was Christmas! I'm as tall and spreading as the ones who were taken away last year. Oh, if only I were on the wagon now! I do wish I were in the warm room with all the honour and glory! And then . . . ? Why, then there'll be something even better, even finer, or why should they decorate me so? There must be something even greater, even grander! But what? I'm yearning! I'm pining! I can't think what's come over me!'

'Be glad of me!' said the air and the sunshine. 'Be glad of your healthy youth, here in the open!'

But it wasn't a bit glad, though it grew and grew. Winter and summer, it was always green, dark green; and people who saw it said: 'That's a nice tree!' And at Christmas it was the first of all to be felled. The axe cut deep into its marrow and it fell with a sigh to the ground, feeling a pain and faintness, and quite unable to think of anything happy. It was so sad at the thought of parting from home, from the spot where it had grown up, knowing that it would never more see its dear old companions, the little bushes and the flowers that grew round it, nor even, perhaps, the birds. Going away wasn't a bit pleasant.

It came to itself in the yard when, unloaded with the other trees, it heard a man say: 'That's a beauty! We'll have that one!'

Now two servants in full dress came and took the tree into a lovely big room. There were portraits hanging on the walls, and standing by the fireplace were big Chinese vases with lions on the lids. There were rocking-chairs, silk sofas, and big tables piled with picture-books and toys worth a hundred times a hundred shillings—or so the children said. The fir-tree was stood up in a big barrel filled with sand; though nobody could see it was a barrel, as green cloth was hung round it and it stood on a big gaily coloured carpet. How the tree trembled! Whatever was going to happen? Servants and young ladies both began to decorate it. On the branches they hung little bags cut out of coloured paper, each one filled with sweets. Golden apples and walnuts hung as though they had grown there, and over a hundred red, blue and white candles were fixed on to the branches. Dolls that were the living image of people (and that the tree had never seen the like of) hung among the greenery, and right at the very top was a big star made of gold tinsel. It was gorgeous, positively gorgeous!

'Tonight,' they all said, 'tonight it's going to be all lit up!'

'Oh,' thought the tree, 'if only it was tonight! If only the lights would soon go on! And I wonder what will happen then? Will trees come from the wood to look at me, I wonder? Will the sparrows fly about the window, I wonder? Shall I grow fast here and stand decorated winter and summer, I wonder?'

Oh yes, it had the right ideas. But the sheer longing had given it a proper bark-ache; and bark-ache is as bad for a tree as headache is for us.

At last the candles were lit. What splendour, what magic! The glory of it made the tree tremble in every limb; so much that one of the candles set fire to the greenery; it hurt horribly.

'Goodness gracious!' cried the young ladies, hastening to put it out.

The tree was too frightened even to tremble now. It was really horrid! It was so afraid of losing some of its finery, and was quite bewildered by all the glory. And then all at once the folding-doors were opened and a crowd of children came rushing in, as though they would upset the whole tree; the older people quietly followed them. The little ones stood perfectly still, but only for a moment; for then they all shouted for joy, making the whole place ring with their cries. They danced round the tree, while presents were picked off one after another.

'What are they up to?' thought the tree. 'What's going to happen?' The candles burnt right down to the branches, and as they did so they were blown out and afterwards the children were allowed to strip the tree. And the way they rushed at it, making it creak in all its branches! If it hadn't been fastened to the ceiling by its tip and its golden star it would have crashed.

The children were skipping around with their splendid toys, nobody looking at the tree except the old nurse, who went peering in among the branches, though only to see whether a fig or an apple had been forgotten.

'A story! A story!' cried the children, pulling a fat little man over towards the tree. And sitting down underneath it, he said: 'Now we're in the wood, and it won't do the tree any harm to listen to it. But I'm only going to tell one story. Would you like the one about Imsy Whimsy, or the one about Willy Nilly, who fell downstairs and yet came out top and married the princess?

'Imsy Whimsy!' cried some. 'Willy Nilly!' cried others. There never was such shouting and screaming! Only the fir-tree held its tongue, thinking to itself, 'Don't I come in here! Don't I have a part?' Of course it had been in it; it had played its part.

And then the man told the story of Willy Nilly, who fell downstairs and yet came out top and married the princess. And the children clapped their hands and shouted: 'Go on! Go on!' wanting 'Imsy Whimsy' as well, but getting only 'Willy Nilly'. The fir-tree stood perfectly still and full of thought: the birds in the wood had never told anything of this sort. 'Willy Nilly fell downstairs and yet married the princess! Ah yes, that's the way of the world,' thought the fir-tree, believing the story to be true because such a nice man had told it. 'Ah yes, who knows?' Perhaps *I* shall fall downstairs and marry a princess!' and it looked forward to being dressed in candles and toys and in gold and fruit the next day.

'I won't tremble tomorrow,' it thought. 'I'll really enjoy all my splendour. I shall hear the story of Willy Nilly again tomorrow, and perhaps the one about Imsy Whimsy as well.' And the tree stood silent and thoughtful all night.

In the morning the servants came in.

'Now for the finery again!' thought the tree. But they dragged it out of the room and upstairs into the attic, where, in a dark corner, without a gleam of daylight, they left it. 'What's the meaning of this?' thought the tree. 'I wonder what I'm going to do here? I wonder what I'm going to be told here?' And, leaning up against the wall, it stood thinking and thinking. And it had plenty of time for it, for days and nights went by. Nobody came; and when at long last somebody did, it was only to put some big boxes away in a corner. The tree stood quite hidden; anyone would have thought it was clean forgotten.

'It'll be winter outside,' thought the tree. 'The ground will be hard and covered with snow; they won't be able to plant me. So they'll be leaving me here in shelter till the spring. How very thoughtful of them! How good human beings are! If only it wasn't so dark—and so dreadfully lonely. Not even a little hare! It was really so nice in the wood when the snow lay round about and the hare bounded past; yes, even when it jumped over me, though then I didn't use to like it. It's so awfully lonely up here!'

'Squeak, squeak!' said a little mouse just then, popping out of its hole, followed by another one. They came sniffing at the fir-tree and slipping in and out among its branches.

'Isn't it horribly cold?' said the little mice. 'It's a heavenly place, though, except for that! Isn't it, old fir-tree?'

'I'm not at all old!' said the fir-tree. 'There are plenty a lot older than I am.'

'Where do you come from?' asked the mice. 'And what do you know?' (They were so dreadfully inquisitive.) 'Tell us, please, about the loveliest place on earth! Have you been there? Have you been in the larder, where there are cheeses on the shelves and hams hanging under the ceiling; where life's a bed of tallow-candles, and where you go in lean and come out fat?'

'I don't know the place,' said the tree. 'But I know the wood where the sun shines, and where the birds sing.' And it told the whole story of its youth. The mice had never heard the like of it, and they listened and they said: 'Why, what a lot you've seen! How happy you have been!'

'Have I?' said the fir-tree, thinking over the story it had been telling. 'Why yes, they were rather pleasant times, when you come to think of it.' And then it went on to tell of Christmas Eve, when it had been decorated with cakes and candles.

'Oh,' said the little mice, 'how happy you've been, old fir-tree!'

'I'm not old at all,' said the tree. 'I only came out of the wood this winter. I'm in my prime and have only had my growth checked.'

'What a lovely story-teller you are!' said the little mice; and the next night they brought four other little mice to listen to the tree. And the more it told, the more clearly it remembered everything; and it thought to itself: 'Yes, they were rather pleasant times! Willy Nilly fell downstairs and yet married the princess, and perhaps *I* may marry a princess.' And the fir-tree's thoughts turned to a birch-tree—such a pretty little birch-tree—which grew in the wood; to the fir-tree this was a real, lovely princess.

'Who's Willy Nilly?' asked the little mice. And the fir-tree told them the whole fairy tale; it remembered every single word of it. And the little mice were ready to jump right to the top of the tree for very joy. The next night many more mice came, and on the Sunday even two rats. But they said that the story wasn't amusing, and this saddened the little mice, for now they, too, thought less of it.

'Is that the only story you know?' asked the rats.

'That's all!' answered the tree. 'I heard it on the happiest evening of my life; only then I never realized how happy I was!'

'It's an extremely bad story! Don't you know any with bacon and tallow candles in? No pantry stories?'

'No,' said the tree.

'Then you can keep it!' said the rats, and in they went.

In the end the little mice also stayed away, and the tree sighed: 'It was so nice when the nimble little mice used to sit round me, listening to my story. Now even that's all gone. But I'll remember to enjoy myself when I'm taken out again.'

But when would that be . . . ? Well now, one morning somebody came rummaging about in the attic. The boxes were moved and the tree was pulled out. It was rather rough, the way they threw it on the floor, but then all at once a man dragged it towards the stairs where the daylight shone.

'Now for a new life!' thought the tree. It could feel the fresh air and the first sunbeam—and now it was out in the yard. It was all so quick; the tree clean forgot to look at itself, there was so much to see round about. The yard was next to a garden, and everything there was in bloom. Roses hung fresh and fragrant over the little railing, the lime-trees were blossoming, and the swallows were flying about saying: 'Twitter-twitter-tweet, my husband's come!' But they didn't mean the fir-tree.

'Now I shall live!' it cried joyfully, spreading wide its branches. But, alas, they were all withered and yellow; and it lay in a corner among weeds and nettles. The gold paper star was still at the top, glittering now in the brilliant sunshine.

Playing in the yard were a few of the merry children who had danced round the tree at Christmas-time and had been so delighted with it. One of the smallest rushed up and tore off the gold star.

'Look what's still on the ugly old Christmas-tree!' he said, trampling on its branches and crunching them under his boots.

And the tree looked at all the glorious flowers and fresh growth in the garden, and it looked at itself; and it wished that it had stayed in its dark corner of the attic. It thought of the freshness of youth in the wood, of the merry Christmas Eve, and of the little mice that had listened so delighted to the story of Willy Nilly.

'All, all over!' said the poor little tree. 'If only I'd been happy when I could have been. All, all over!'

And the servant came and chopped the tree into little bits; a whole bundle of them. It made a lovely blaze under the scullery copper; and it sighed so deeply, every sigh like a little crackle.

So the children playing in the yard ran inside and sat down in front of the fire, looking into it and crying 'Bing, bang!' while at each crackle, which was a deep sigh, the tree thought of a summer's day in the wood, or a winter's night when the stars were shining. It thought of Christmas Eve and of 'Willy Nilly', the only fairy tale it could tell or had ever heard—and so in time it was burnt out.

The boys played in the yard, the smallest wearing on his breast the gold star which the tree had borne on its happiest evening. Now that was all over, and it was all over with the tree, and the story's over as well. All, all over! And so it is with every story!

THE SNOW QUEEN

A Fairy Tale in Seven Stories

First Story, telling all about the Looking-glass and the Broken Bits

NOW THEN, here's where we begin! When we get to the end of the story we shall know more than we know now. It's about a wicked imp. He was one of the wickedest of them all, the very Devil himself. One day he was in a thoroughly good humour, having made a looking-glass which had the magic power of making anything good and beautiful that looked into it shrink to next to nothing, while what was no good or was ugly stood out well and grew even worse. The loveliest landscapes would look just like boiled spinach, and the nicest people would become nasty or would stand on their heads without any stomachs. Their faces would be so twisted that one didn't know them again, and if you had a freckle you could be pretty certain that it would spread all over your nose and mouth. This was great fun, thought Old Nick. If a nice, kindly thought passed through anybody's head, the looking-glass would show such a grin that the demon couldn't help but laugh at his curious trick. Everyone who went to the Imps' School (he kept an imps' school) used to go about saying that a miracle had happened; for the first time, they said, you could now see what the world and human beings really looked like. They would run about with the looking-glass, and in the end there wasn't a country or a person anywhere that hadn't been distorted in it. They next thought that they would fly up

W HEATH ROBINSON

towards Heaven itself, so as to make fun of the angels and Our Lord. The higher they flew with the looking-glass, the more it grinned, and they could hardly hold on to it. Higher and higher they flew, getting nearer to God and his angels. Then all at once the looking-glass gave such a dreadful twitch while grinning that it shot out of their hands and crashed to the ground, where it broke into hundreds of millions, billions, and even more bits, causing more mischief than before; for some of the bits were scarcely as big as a grain of sand, and these went flying round the world, and if they got into anyone's eyes would stick there, the people then seeing everything wrong or having an eye only for what was bad in anything, each little bit having the same power as the whole looking-glass had had. Some people even got a little bit in their hearts, and this was really dreadful, for then their hearts would be like a lump of ice. Some pieces were large enough to be used as window-panes, but it was a mistake to look through these at your friends. Other pieces were used in spectacles, and then everything would go wrong when people put them on in order to see properly and fairly, while the Evil One would laugh till his sides split—it was lovely the way this tickled. But other little bits went on floating about in the air. Now, just listen to this!

Second Story. A Little Boy and a Little Girl

In the middle of the city, where there are so many houses and so many people that there isn't room for everyone to have a little garden, and where most people therefore have to make do with flowers and pot plants, there lived at least two poor children who had a garden rather larger than a plant-pot. They weren't brother and sister, but were as fond of each other as if they had been. Their parents were near neighbours. They lived in two attics; and where the roof of one house touched the other and a gutter ran along the eaves there was a little window opening out from each house. You had only to step across the gutter in order to get from one window to the other.

The parents had a big wooden box standing outside their windows, and here grew the vegetables which they used, together with a little rose-tree; there was one in each box, and it grew beautifully. The parents now had the idea of placing their boxes across the gutter, so that they almost reached from one window to the other and looked exactly like two flower-beds. The peas hung down over the boxes, and the rose-trees, making long growths, twined round the windows, bending over to each other; it was rather like a wedding arch of greenery and flowers. As the boxes were very high and the children knew they hadn't to climb up them, they were often allowed to step out to each other, and then, sitting on their little stools under the roses, they would play together beautifully.

In winter, of course, this fun all stopped. The windows would often be quite frozen up; but then they would warm pennies by the fire, and, pressing them against the frozen pane, would make lovely little peep-holes, as round as could be. A sweet little eye would peep out from behind each of them; and this would be the little boy and the little girl. He was called

Kay, and she was called Gerda. In summer they could get to each other at a bound; but in winter they first had to go all the way downstairs and then all the way upstairs again, while outside drifted the snow.

'That's the swarming of the white bees,' said Old Grandmother.

'Have they a queen bee as well?' asked the little boy, who knew there was one among real bees.

'Why, yes!' said Granny. 'She flies in the thickest of the swarm! She's the biggest of them all, and never stops still on the ground but flies up into the black cloud again. Many a winter night she flies through the streets and peeps in at the windows, and then they freeze up ever so strangely, just like flowers.'

'Yes, I've seen it!' cried the two children, knowing then that it was true.

'Can the Snow Queen come inside?' asked the little girl.

'Just let her come,' said the boy, 'and I'll put her on the hot stove and make her melt.'

But Granny smoothed his hair and told them other stories.

In the evening, when little Kay was back home and half undressed, he climbed on to the chairs by the window and peeped out of the little hole. A few snowflakes were falling outside, and one of these—the biggest—came to rest on the edge of one of the window-boxes. The snowflake went on growing and growing until in the end it was a woman, dressed in the finest white gauze, which seemed to be made up of millions of starry flakes. She herself was so pretty and so delicate, and yet was made of ice—glittering, dazzling ice—although she was alive. Her eyes gazed like two bright stars, but were never still or resting. She nodded to the window and waved her hand. The little boy was frightened and jumped down from the chair; and at that moment a big bird seemed to fly past outside the window.

The next day was clear and frosty; and then it thawed, and then spring came. The sun shone, plants began to spring up, the swallows built their nests, the windows were opened, and the little children again sat in their tiny garden in the gutter high up on top of the houses.

The roses that summer bloomed so wondrously. The little girl had learnt a hymn and in it there was something about roses, and these roses made her think of her own. And she sang it to the little boy, and he joined in:

> 'Then seek your Saviour down below;
> For roses in the valleys grow!'

And the little ones held each other by the hand, kissed the roses, and looked into God's bright sunshine, talking to it as though the infant Jesus were there. What lovely summer days these were, and how delightful it was to be outside by the fresh-green rose-trees, which seemed as though they would never stop blooming!

Kay and Gerda were looking at their picture-book of animals and birds when—exactly as the clock in the big church tower struck five—Kay said: 'Ooh, something pricked me in the heart! And now I've got something in my eye!'

The little girl put her arms round his neck, and he blinked his eyes; but no, there was nothing to be seen.

'I think it's gone!' he said. But it hadn't. It was one of those very bits of glass that had flown from the looking-glass, the magic mirror that we remember; the horrid glass which made everything big and good that was reflected in it become little and nasty, while the bad and wicked came out very very clearly and every fault in anything was plain at once. Poor Kay! He'd got another bit right in his heart. Soon it would be like a lump of ice. It had stopped hurting now, but it was there.

'What are you crying for?' he asked. 'It makes you look ugly! There's nothing the matter with me. Ugh!' he cried all at once. 'That rose's worm-eaten! And look, its all lop-sided! What nasty roses they all are! They're like the boxes they're growing in.' And with that he gave the boxes a good kick and snatched off two of the roses.

'Kay, what are you doing?' cried the little girl. And seeing her frightened, he pulled off another rose and ran in through his window, away from dear little Gerda.

When she brought the picture-book afterwards he said that it was babyish; and whenever Granny told stories he would always find fault with them. If he got the chance he would walk up behind her, put glasses on, and take her off. It was Granny to the life, and people used to laugh at him. He was soon able to take off everybody in the whole street. Anything odd or not very nice about them Kay would take off, and people used to say: 'He's certainly got brains, that boy!' But it was the glass he'd got in his eye, and the glass that had stuck in his heart. That was why he even used to tease little Gerda, who loved him with all her heart.

His games were now quite different from what they used to be; they were so studious. One winter's day, as the snowflakes drifted in the wind, he brought a large burning-glass, and holding out his blue coat-tail allowed the snowflakes to fall on to it.

'Just look in the glass, Gerda!' he said. And when she did each snowflake grew much bigger and looked like a beautiful flower or a ten-sided star. It was lovely to look at.

'Isn't it peculiar,' said Kay. 'It's a lot more interesting than those real flowers. And there isn't a single fault in them; they're perfectly accurate so long as they don't melt.'

Soon after, Kay came wearing big gloves and carrying his sledge on his back. He shouted into Gerda's ear: 'I've been told I can sledge on the big square where the others are playing!' And with that he was off.

Over on the square the boldest boys would often tie their sledges to the farmer's cart, and then would get a good pull behind. This was grand fun. They were playing there when along came a big sleigh. It was painted white all over, and the person sitting in it was wrapped in a white fur cloak and wore a white fur cap. The sleigh drove twice round the square, and it wasn't long before Kay had tied his sledge to it and was being pulled along by it. Faster and faster it went and then it made straight for the next street, the driver turning round and giving Kay a friendly nod as though they had known each other. Whenever Kay tried to untie his sledge the driver would nod again, and Kay would sit still. They drove straight out through the city gates. And then the snow began falling so fast that the little boy couldn't see a hand in front of him, as they tore along. Suddenly he let go of the rope in order to get loose from the sleigh, but it was of no use; his little carriage was tied fast and travelling like the wind. He then gave a loud shout; but no one heard him and the sleigh went racing on. From time to time it would give a jump, and he would feel as though he was going over ditches and dikes. He was dreadfully frightened, and he would have said his prayers, only all he could remember was his tables.

The snowflakes grew bigger and bigger till in the end they were like big white hens. Then all at once they sprang to one side, the sleigh stopped, and the driver got up, The fur cloak and cap were all of snow, and the person who wore them was a lady, a lady so tall and straight and all gleaming white. It was the Snow Queen.

'We've made good headway!' she said. 'Why, but you're not cold? Wrap yourself in my bearskin cloak!' And seating him next to her in the sleigh, she put her cloak round him; it felt like sinking into a snowdrift.

'Do you still feel cold?' she asked, giving him a kiss on the forehead. Ugh! It was colder than ice and went straight to his heart, which already was half ice. He had a feeling that he was going to die; but only for a second, then he felt better for it and never noticed the cold after that.

'My sledge! Don't forget my sledge!' He remembered it first; and it was tied on to one of the white hens, which flew along behind, with the sledge on its back. The Snow Queen kissed Kay once more, and by this time he had forgotten little Gerda and Granny and everyone at home.

'That's the last kiss you'll get!' she said. 'Or I'll kiss you to death!'

Kay looked at her; she was so beautiful. A wiser and lovelier face he couldn't imagine. She didn't seem to be of ice now, as when she had sat outside the window, waving to him. To his mind she was perfect, and he didn't feel a bit afraid, but told her he could do mental arithmetic even with fractions, and that he knew the areas and populations of different countries, while all the time she smiled. It then seemed to him that all he knew wasn't enough, and he gazed up into the great big sky above, and she flew on with him, flew right up on to the black cloud, while the storm raged and roared, as if it were singing old, old songs. They flew over woods and lakes, over seas and lands. The cold wind whistled down below, and the wolves howled, and the snow glittered; over it flew black, screeching crows, while up above the moon shone out bright and clear and Kay watched it all the long, long winter's night. During the day he slept at the Snow Queen's feet.

Third Story. The Flower Garden of the Woman who could work Magic

But how did little Gerda get on when Kay didn't come back? Where could he be? No one knew, and no one could tell. The boys could only say that they had seen him tie his sledge to a splendid big sleigh, which had driven off down the street and out of the city gates. No one knew where he was and many tears were shed for him; little Gerda nearly cried her eyes out. And then they said that he must be dead; that he had fallen into the river which flowed past the town. What long, dark winter days these were!

Spring came round at last, bringing warmer sunshine.

'Kay's dead and gone!' said little Gerda.

'I don't think so,' said the sunshine.

'He's dead and gone!' she said to the swallows.

'I don't think so,' they all said. And in the end little Gerda didn't think so, either.

'I'm going to put on my new red shoes,' she said one morning; 'the ones Kay has never seen. And then I'll go down to the river and ask it.'

This was early one morning. Kissing her old Granny, who was asleep, she put on the red shoes and went all by herself through the gate and down to the river.

'Is it true that you've taken my little playmate? I'll give you my red shoes if you'll return him to me!'

And the waves seemed to nod so strangely to her that she took off her red shoes, the dearest of all she had, and threw them both into the river. But they fell close to the shore, and the ripples carried them straight back to her on the bank; it was as though the river didn't want to take the dearest of all she had, as it hadn't got little Kay. But she thought that she hadn't

thrown the shoes far enough out, and so, climbing into a boat which lay among the rushes and going right out to the far end of it, she threw the shoes out there. The boat wasn't tied up, and the movement she started made it float away from the bank. Feeling it move, she made haste to get back again, but before she could do so the boat was more than a yard out and floating faster and faster away.

This made little Gerda quite frightened, and she started to cry. But no one heard her except the sparrows, and they couldn't carry her ashore, though they flew along the bank, singing as though to comfort her: 'See, here we come! See, here we come!' The boat was drifting with the current, and little Gerda sat perfectly still in her stockinged feet. Her little red shoes floated after her, but couldn't reach the boat, which went faster and faster.

It was beautiful on both sides, with lovely flowers, old trees, and sheep and cows on the banks, but not a single person to be seen.

'Perhaps the river will carry me to little Kay!' thought Gerda; and cheered by this she stood up and gazed for hour after hour at the beautiful green banks. In time she came to a big cherry orchard, where there was a little house with curious red-and-blue windows, a thatched roof, and, standing outside, two wooden soldiers who shouldered their arms for those who sailed past.

Gerda called out to them, thinking that they were alive, but of course they didn't answer. She got quite close to them, as the river carried the boat right in towards the shore.

Gerda called out louder still, and an old, old woman came out of the house, leaning on a crooked stick. She was wearing a big sun hat, on which the loveliest of flowers were painted.

'You poor little child!' said the old woman. 'However did you get on to the big, flowing stream, drifting away into the wide, wide world?' And the old woman went right out into the river and, hooking her crooked stick on to the boat, pulled it ashore and lifted little Gerda out.

And Gerda was glad to get on to dry land, though a little bit afraid of the strange old woman.

'Now come and tell me who you are, and how you've got here,' she said.

So Gerda told her everything; and the old woman shook her head and said: 'H'm, h'm!' And when Gerda had finished telling her story she asked her if she had seen little Kay, and the woman said that he hadn't passed by but that he was sure to come: she should stop being so miserable, and should taste her cherries, and see her flowers which were finer than any picture-book—each one of them had quite a story to tell. Then she took Gerda by the hand and they went into the little house, the old woman locking the door after them.

The windows were right up at the top and the panes were red, blue and yellow. The daylight shone so curiously inside the house with all these colours, but on the table were some of the loveliest cherries, and Gerda ate as many of them as she liked, as she was allowed to. And while she was eating the old woman combed her hair with a golden comb; and the hair curled and shone so beautifully and golden round her friendly little face, which was so round and rosy.

'How I've longed for a nice little girl like you!' said the old woman. 'Now just you see how well we two are going to get on.' And as she combed her hair little Gerda forgot her playmate Kay more and more; for the old woman could work magic, though she wasn't a wicked witch: she just did a little wizardry for her own amusement, and now she wished to keep little Gerda. And so she went into the garden and pointed her crooked stick at all the rose-trees; and no matter how beautifully they were blooming, they all sank down into the black earth and it was impossible to see where they had been growing. The old woman was afraid that when Gerda saw the roses she would be reminded of her own and then, remembering little Kay, would run away.

She then took Gerda into the flower garden. What a lovely sight and smell there was! Every imaginable flower, belonging to every season, was in full and splendid bloom; no picture-book could have been more colourful and beautiful. Gerda skipped for joy and played till the sun went down behind the tall cherry-trees. And then she was given a lovely bed with red silk eiderdowns, which were stuffed with blue violets; and she slept there and dreamt as beautifully as a queen on her wedding day.

The next day she was again allowed to play with the flowers in the warm sunshine—and so on for many days. Gerda knew every flower; but for all there were so many, one seemed to be missing, though which she couldn't tell. But then one day she sat looking at the old woman's sun hat with the flowers painted on it—and the most beautiful of them all was a rose. The old woman had forgotten to take this off her hat when she had charmed the others into the ground. That's what comes of being forgetful! 'What!' said Gerda. 'Are there no roses?' And running in among the beds she searched and searched, but there wasn't one to be found; and she sat down and cried. But her hot tears happened to fall just where a rose-tree had sunk down, and as they moistened the soil the tree sprang up at once, as full of blooms as when it had sunk. And Gerda put her arms around it, and kissing the roses thought of the lovely roses at home, and with them of little Kay.

'Oh, how I've been delayed!' said the little girl. 'I set out to find Kay. Don't you know where he is?' she asked the roses. 'Do you think he's dead and gone?'

'He isn't dead!' said the roses. 'We've been in the ground. That's where all the dead are, but Kay wasn't there.'

'Thank you!' said little Gerda; and going to the other flowers, she looked into their cups and asked: 'Don't you know where little Kay is?'

But every flower stood dreaming in the sun its own fairy tale or story. Little Gerda was told lots and lots of these, but not one of them knew anything about Kay.

And then what was it the tiger-lily said?

'Do you hear the drum? Rum-tum! It has only two notes—always rum-tum! Hear the women's lament! Hear the cry of the priests! The Hindu woman stands in her long scarlet mantle on the bonfire, the flames leaping up around her and around her dead husband. But the Hindu woman's thoughts are on the living person who stands there in the crowd, the man whose eyes burn hotter than the flames which soon will burn her body to ashes. Can the heart's flame burn in the flames of the bonfire?'

'I don't understand you a bit,' said little Gerda,

'That's my fairy tale!' said the tiger-lily.

What says the convolvulus?

'Overlooking the narrow mountain road is an old castle. Thick evergreens are growing over the old red walls, twining leaf by leaf round the balcony where, leaning over the balustrade, looking down the road, stands a lovely young woman. No rose hangs more freshly on its sprays than does she; no apple blossom wafted from the tree by the breeze floats more lightly than she. How softly her silken robe rustles! "Will he never come?" she says.'

'Is it Kay you mean?' asked little Gerda.

'I speak only of my fairy tale, of my dream,' answered the convolvulus.

What says the little snowdrop?

'Hanging by the ropes between the trees is a long board, a swing. Two pretty little girls, their dresses as white as snow and with long green silk ribbons fluttering from their hats, sit there swinging. Their brother, who is bigger than they are, is standing on the swing; he has his arm round the rope to hold on, as in one hand he has a little bowl and in the other a clay pipe—he's blowing soap bubbles. The swing swings and the bubbles float away in lovely changing colours; the last is still clinging to the pipe-stem, bending in the wind, while the swing goes. The little black dog, as light as the bubbles, stands up on its hind legs, wanting to get on to the swing. It flies up, and the dog flops down, barking angrily. They make fun of it. The bubbles burst. A swinging board, a picture of bursting foam, is my song!'

'What you tell may be beautiful, but you tell it so sadly and say nothing about Kay. What do the hyacinths say?'

'There were three lovely sisters, all so light and delicate. The dress of one of them was red, that of the second blue, and that of the third perfectly white. Hand in hand they would dance by the silent lake in the clear moonlight. They were not fairies: they were human children. The air was sweetly scented, and as the girls vanished into the wood the scent grew stronger . . . Three coffins, the three lovely girls inside them, floated from the thickets of the wood across the lake, and fireflies flew glistening around like little floating candles. Are the dancing girls asleep, or are they dead? The scent of flowers tells that they are dead, and now the bells are ringing for them!'

'You're making me quite sad!' said little Gerda. 'You smell so strongly, I can't help thinking of the dead girls. Can little Kay really be dead? The roses have been under the ground, and they say No!'

'Ding, dong!' rang the hyacinth bells. 'We're not ringing for little Kay; we don't know him. We're only singing our song; the only one we know!'

And so Gerda went to the buttercup, which shone out from among its glistening leaves.

'You're a bright little sun!' said Gerda. 'Tell me if you know where I'm to find my playmate.'

And shining so prettily the buttercup looked at Gerda again. What song could the buttercup sing? But it had nothing to do with Kay, either.

'In a little yard Our Lord's sun shone warmly on the first day of spring. Its beams slid down the neighbour's white walls, and growing close by were the first yellow flowers, gleaming gold in the warm sunshine. Granny sat outside in her chair; her granddaughter, the poor but pretty servant girl, had come home for a short visit, and she kissed her grandmother. There was gold, heart's gold, in that warming kiss. Golden heart and golden kiss; golden sun and golden bliss! There, that's my little story!' said the buttercup.

'My poor old grandmother!' sighed Gerda. 'Yes, I expect she's longing for me and is sad because of me, as she was because of little Kay. But I shall soon be going home again, and then I shall take Kay with me. It's no use asking the flowers; they only know their own songs and don't tell me anything.' As she said this she tucked up her little dress so as to be able to run faster. But the narcissus as she sprang over it tapped her on the leg; and stopping, she looked at the tall flower and said: 'Perhaps you know something?' And then she stooped down to it. And what did it say?

'I can see myself! I can see myself!' said the narcissus. 'Oh, oh, how I smell! . . . Up in the little attic, half dressed, stands a little dancing-girl. She stands first on one leg and then on two, and she kicks out at everything and everybody, but she's only an illusion. She pours water from the teapot on to a piece of cloth she's holding—that's her bodice. Cleanliness is next to godliness. Her white dress is hanging on the peg, and it, too, has been washed in the teapot and dried on the roof. She puts it on, and with the saffron-yellow scarf round her neck the dress gleams whiter. Leg up! See how she holds herself on one stalk. I can see myself! I can see myself!'

'I'm not a bit interested,' said Gerda. 'That's no story for me!' And with that she ran to the edge of the garden.

The door was shut, but she shook the rusty latch till it came loose and the door sprang open. And then little Gerda ran in her bare feet into the wide world. Three times she looked back, but there was nobody following her. At last she couldn't run any longer and sat down on a big stone; and when she looked round she found that summer had gone and it was late autumn. You couldn't tell in the lovely garden, where the sun always shone and there were every season's flowers.

'Oh dear, how I've wasted my time!' said little Gerda. 'Why, it's autumn! Now I daren't rest.' And she got up to go.

Oh, how tired and sore her little feet were, while all round her it seemed cold and raw. The long willow leaves were all yellow and dripping wet in the mist, leaf falling after leaf. Only the sloe bore fruit; fruit so sour that it set one's teeth on edge. Oh, how grey and gloomy it was in the wide world!

Fourth Story. Prince and Princess

Gerda was forced to rest again; and while she was doing so, something hopped on the snow and there, right in front of her, was a big crow. It had sat looking at her, wagging its head, for quite a while, and now it said: 'Caw! Caw! 'Lo! 'Lo!' That was the best it could say, but it meant the little girl well, and asked

HEATH
ROBINSON

her where she was going to all by herself in the wide world. Gerda perfectly well understood 'all by herself' and what the words meant, and she told the crow her whole story and asked if it had seen Kay.

And nodding very thoughtfully the crow said: 'I may have done! I may have done!'

'What? Have you?' cried the little girl, nearly squeezing the crow to death as she kissed it.

'Go easy! Go easy!' said the crow. 'I think it may be little Kay. But I rather think he's forgotten you now for the princess.'

'Does he live with a princess?' asked Gerda.

'Why, yes!' said the crow. 'But it's such hard work talking your language. If you can understand crow's jabber I'll be able to tell you.'

'No, I've never learnt it,' said Gerda. 'My Granny could, and she knew the language. I only wish I'd learnt.'

'Doesn't matter!' said the crow. 'I'll tell you as well as I can, but it's bound to be bad.' And it told her what it knew.

'In the kingdom where we are now lives a princess who's tremendously clever, but then she's read all the newspapers in the world—and forgotten them again, she's so clever. She was sitting on the throne the other day (and they say there isn't much fun in that) when she happened to hum a song, the one that goes: "Why shouldn't I get married?" "I say, there's something in that!" she said, and so she decided she would get married. But she wanted a husband who knew how to answer when spoken to; one who wouldn't just stand looking genteel, because that's such a bore. She had all the ladies in waiting called together, and when they heard what she wanted they were thoroughly delighted. "Now, that's what I like," and "I was thinking so only the other day," they said. It's true, every word I say!' said the crow. 'I have a tame sweetheart who's free to walk about the palace, and she told me.'

Of course, his sweetheart was another crow, for birds of a feather flock together, and crows will be crows.

'The newspapers at once came out with an edging of hearts and the princess's monogram. They said that any good-looking young man was at liberty to come to the palace and talk to the princess, and the one who talked as though he was at home there, and talked best, would be chosen by the princess for husband.' 'Oh yes!' said the crow. 'You can take it from me; it's as true as I'm standing here. People flocked to the palace, and you never saw such a crowd and a commotion. But nobody succeeded either the first day or the second. They all knew how to talk, while they were in the street, but when they entered the palace gates and saw the Guard in silver and footmen standing all the way up the stairs in gold, and the big lighted halls, they were bewildered; and standing in front of the throne where the princess sat, all they could say was the last word she had said, and she had no wish to hear that again. In there it was as though people had swallowed snuff and fallen into a trance, till they got into the street again—they could talk then, all right. There was a queue stretching right from the city gates to the palace. I went in to have a look,' said the crow. 'They grew both hungry and thirsty, but nobody at the palace gave them as much as a glass of warm water. Some of the wisest, to be sure, had taken sandwiches with them, but they didn't share them with their neighbours; they thought to themselves: "Let him look hungry, and then the princess won't have him!"'

'But Kay, little Kay?' asked Gerda. 'When did he come? Was he among the crowd?'

'Hold hard! Hold hard! We're coming to him! It was on the third day that a little person, without horse or carriage, came cheerfully marching straight up to the palace. His eyes were shining like yours and he had lovely long hair, but poor clothes.'

'That was Kay!' cried Gerda, delighted. 'Oh, so now I've found him!' And she clapped her hands.

'He had a little satchel on his back,' said the crow.

'No, that would be his sledge,' said Gerda. 'He went off with his sledge.'

'You may be right!' said the crow. 'I didn't take so much notice. But I do know, from my tame sweetheart, that when he entered the palace gates and saw the Life Guards in silver and the footmen standing on the stairs in gold, he wasn't a bit down-hearted, but nodded and said to them: "It must be boring standing on the stairs; I'm going inside!" The halls were brightly lit; privy councillors and excellencies were walking about barefooted carrying golden dishes—it was enough to make anyone feel solemn! His boots creaked ever so loudly, but he didn't get frightened, not he.'

'That's Kay all right!' said Gerda. 'I know he had new boots; I've heard them creak in Granny's parlour.'

'Well, they certainly creaked!' said the crow. 'And as cheerful as anything he made straight for the princess, who sat on a pearl as big as a spinning-wheel. And all the ladies in waiting with their maids and maids' maids, and all the gentlemen in waiting with their servants and servants' servants (who keep pages), were drawn up all round, looking prouder and prouder the nearer they were to the door. The servants' servants' pages, who always wear slippers, will hardly bear looking at, they stand so proudly in the doorway.'

'That must be dreadful!' said little Gerda. 'And yet Kay won the princess?'

'If I hadn't been a crow I'd have had her, engaged or not engaged. He talked as well as I talk when I jabber crow-talk, so my tame sweetheart said. He was bright and cheerful; he hadn't come to propose, only to hear the princess's wisdom; and he thought it good, while she in turn thought him good.'

'Why, of course it was Kay!' said Gerda. 'He was so clever; he could do mental arithmetic with fractions. Oh, please will you take me to the palace?'

'It's easy to talk!' said the crow. 'But how do we do it? I'll speak to my tame sweetheart about it; I dare say she can advise us. I may as well tell you that a little girl like you will never be properly admitted.'

'Oh yes, I will!' said Gerda. 'When Kay hears I'm there, he'll come straight out and fetch me.'

'Wait for me at that stile!' said the crow; and wagging its head it flew off.

It had grown dark by the time the crow returned. "Rah! 'Rah!' it said. 'She sends you all her love! And here's a small loaf for you. She took it in the kitchen; there's plenty of bread, and I expect you're hungry. There's no chance of you getting into the palace; you're in bare feet. The Guard in silver and the footmen in gold wouldn't allow it. But don't cry; you'll get there. My sweetheart knows a little back staircase which leads to the bed-chamber, and she knows where to get the key!'

And so they went into the garden, along the big avenue where leaf fell after leaf; and when the palace lights went out, one by one, the crow took little Gerda to a back door which stood ajar.

Oh, how Gerda's heart throbbed with fear and longing! It was as though she was about to do something wrong, while all she wanted to know was whether it was little Kay. Why, it must be; she could clearly see his wise eyes, and his long hair. She could really see him smile, as he had done when they had sat at home under the roses. He would surely be glad to see her and hear what a long way she had walked for his sake, and learn how sad they had all been at home when he hadn't returned. Oh, how fearful and joyful she was!

Now they were on the stairs. A little lamp was burning on a cupboard. In the middle of the floor stood the tame crow, turning its head in all directions and looking at Gerda, who curtsied as Granny had taught her.

'My fiancé has spoken so nicely about you, my little lady!' said the tame crow. 'Your *vita*, as it is called, is very touching. If you will take the lamp, I'll lead the way. We'll go the straight way, then we shan't meet anyone.'

'I think there's somebody following us!' said Gerda; and something swished past. It was like shadows along the wall: horses with flowing manes and thin legs, hunting boys, ladies and gentlemen on horseback.

'That's only the dreams!' said the crow. 'They come and fetch the noble people's thoughts out hunting; that's a good thing, for then they're able to see them in bed. But if you find grace and favour, let me see you show a thankful heart!'

'There's no call to talk about that!' said the crow from the wood.

They now came into the first hall, which was hung with rose-coloured satin on which were artificial flowers. Here dreams were already sweeping past them; but so fast did they go that Gerda never caught sight of the noble people. Each room was more gorgeous than the one before: it was enough to astonish anyone—and now at last they were in the bedchamber. The ceiling there resembled a large palm with leaves of glass, precious glass; and hanging from a thick stem of gold in the middle of the floor were two beds which looked like lilies. One of them was white, and in this lay the princess. The other was red, and this was where she expected to find Kay. Bending aside one of the red leaves, she saw a brown neck. Yes, it was Kay! She called his name out aloud and held the lamp towards him: the dreams came sweeping back on their horses; he woke, turned his head, and—it wasn't little Kay.

The prince resembled him only in the neck, but was young and handsome. And looking out from the white lily bed, the princess asked what was the matter. And little Gerda wept, and told her whole story and what the crows had done for her.

'You poor thing!' said the prince and the princess. And they praised the crows, saying they were not at all angry, though they weren't to go on doing that sort of thing. But they should have a reward.

'Would you like to fly away?' asked the princess. 'Or would you like to have permanent appointments as Court crows, with anything that comes your way in the kitchen?'

And both crows curtsied and asked for permanent appointments; for they thought of their old age, and said that it was a good thing to have something 'for a rainy day', as they put it.

And the prince got up from his bed and allowed Gerda to sleep in it; it was the most he could do. Folding her little hands, she thought: 'How good they are, human beings and animals.' Then she closed her eyes and slept deliciously. All the dreams came flying back again, looking like the angels of God and pulling a little sledge on which sat Kay, nodding. But it was only dreams, and so it had all gone again the moment she woke up.

The next day she was dressed from top to toe in silk and velvet. She was given the chance of staying at the palace and having a good time, but all she asked for was a small carriage with a horse to draw it and a pair of little boots, so that she could drive off into the wide world and find Kay.

She was given both boots and a muff. She was now beautifully dressed, and when she was ready to leave a new coach of pure gold stood waiting at the door. The coat of arms of the

prince and princess glistened on it like a star; coachman, footmen, and postilions—for postilions there were as well—all wore gold crowns. The prince and princess themselves helped her into the coach and wished her good luck. The wild crow, which had now got married, went with her the first twelve miles, sitting beside her because it couldn't bear to travel with its back to the horses. The other crow stood in the gateway, flapping its wings; it didn't go with them as it suffered from headache, now that it had a permanent appointment and too much to eat. The coach was lined with sugar biscuits, and under the seat were fruit and ginger-nuts.

'Goodbye! Goodbye!' cried the prince and princess, and little Gerda cried, and the crow cried—and so they passed the first few miles. Then the crow also said goodbye, and this was the hardest parting of all! Flying up into a tree, it flapped its black wings for as long as the coach, which gleamed in the bright sunshine, was in sight.

Fifth Story. The Little Robber Girl

They drove through the dark forest, but the coach shone like a blaze of fire and hurt the robbers' eyes, so that they couldn't stand it.

'It's gold! It's gold!' they cried; and, rushing forward, they seized hold of the horses, killed the little jockeys, the coachman, and the footmen, and then pulled little Gerda out of the coach.

'She's plump, she's delicious, she's been fattened on nut kernels!' said the old robber woman, who had a long straight beard and eyebrows hanging down over her eyes. 'She's as good as a fat little lamb. Y'm, she'll taste nice!' And she drew out her polished knife, which glittered really dreadfully.

'Ooh!' cried the old woman all at once. She had been bitten

in the ear by her own little daughter, who clung to her back and was as wild and mischievous as anything. 'You horrid brat!' said the mother, missing her chance to slaughter Gerda.

'She shall play with me,' said the little robber girl. 'She shall give me her muff and her pretty dress, and sleep in my bed with me!' And she gave another bite, making the old robber woman jump into the air and twist about, and all the robbers laugh and say: 'See the way she dances with her youngster!'

'I want to go in the coach!' said the little robber girl. And she had to be given her own way, she was so spoilt and self-willed. She and Gerda got inside, and away they drove over stubble and bramble deeper into the forest. The little robber girl was the same size as Gerda, but stronger, more broad-shouldered, and dark-skinned. Her eyes were quite black and looked almost sad. Putting her arm round little Gerda's waist, she said: 'They shan't slaughter you as long as I don't get cross with you. I suppose you're a princess?' 'No,' said little Gerda; and she told her all her adventures and of how fond she was of little Kay.

The little robber girl looked quite seriously at her, gave a little nod of her head, and said: 'They shan't slaughter you, even though I do get cross with you; I'll see that I do it myself!' And drying Gerda's eyes, she put both her hands into the fine muff, which was so soft and so warm.

All at once the coach came to a stop; they were in the courtyard of a robbers' castle. It was cracked from top to bottom, and crows and ravens were flying out of the gaps, while big bulldogs, each looking as if it could have swallowed a man, were jumping into the air, though without barking, for that was forbidden.

In the big, old, grimy hall, on the stone floor in the middle, burnt a large fire. The smoke drifted up along the ceiling, finding its own way out. Soup was simmering in a big copper, and hares and rabbits were turning on spits.

'You shall sleep here tonight with me and all my little pets,' said the robber girl. They had something to eat and drink, and then went into a corner, where there were blankets and straw. Up above on sticks and perches were nearly a hundred pigeons, which all seemed to be asleep, though they turned slightly when the little girls arrived.

'They're all mine,' said the little robber girl, seizing one of the nearest and holding it by the legs and shaking it as it flapped its wings. 'Kiss it!' she cried, slapping Gerda in the face with it. 'There are the wood rascals,' she went on, pointing behind a number of bars which had been put up across a hole in the wall above. 'They're wood rascals, those two. They fly off at once unless you keep them properly locked up. And this is my old sweetheart Baa-baa!' And she tugged at the horn of a reindeer, which had a polished copper ring round its neck and was tied up. 'He's another one we have to hold on to, or he'll be off. Every night I tickle his neck with this sharp knife of mine; that frightens him!' And drawing a long knife out of a crack in the wall, the little girl ran it over the reindeer's neck. The poor creature lashed out with its legs, and the robber girl laughed and pulled Gerda into bed with her.

'Are you taking the knife to bed?' asked Gerda, looking at it rather nervously.

'I always sleep with a knife!' said the little robber girl. 'You never know what may happen. But tell me again what you told me about little Kay, and why you've come into the wide world.' So Gerda told her all over again; and the wood-pigeons went on cooing in their cage above, while the other pigeons slept. The little robber girl put her arm round Gerda's neck, and, holding the knife in her other hand, fell into a loud sleep. But Gerda couldn't get a wink of sleep, not knowing whether she was going

to live or die. The robbers sat round the fire, singing and drinking, and the old robber woman turned somersaults. Really, it was a dreadful sight for the little girl!

Then all at once the wood-pigeons said: 'Coo! Coo! We've seen little Kay. A white hen was carrying his sledge, and he was sitting in the Snow Queen's carriage, which travelled low over the wood while we lay in the nest. She blew at us young ones, and all but two of us died. Coo! Coo!'

'What's that you say?' cried Gerda. 'Where did the Snow Queen go? Do you know?'

'She'd go to Lapland, for there there's always snow and ice. Ask the reindeer that's tied up by that rope.'

'That's the place for ice and snow, and it's grand to be there!' said the reindeer. 'You can run about to your heart's content in those big, glistening valleys! The Snow Queen has her summer tent there, but the place which is her home is up near the North Pole, on the island called Spitsbergen.'

'Oh, Kay, little Kay!' sighed Gerda.

'Lie still there!' said the robber girl. 'Or you'll get the knife in your tummy!'

In the morning Gerda told her everything the wood-pigeons had said, and the little robber girl looked very serious, but then nodded and said: 'Never mind! Never mind! . . . Do you know where Lapland is?' she asked the reindeer.

'Who else should know if I don't?' said the animal, its eyes sparkling. 'I was born and bred there, and have romped in the snow-field there,'

'Look here!' the robber girl said to Gerda. 'As you see, all our menfolk are away, though Ma's still here and is going to stay here. But during the morning she'll have a drink out of that big bottle and then a little nap. I'll do something for you then.' She then jumped out of bed and, rushing over to her mother, flung her arms round her neck and tugged at her whiskers, saying: 'Good morning, mother nanny-goat!' And her mother clipped her on the nose, making it go all red and blue, though only out of pure loving-kindness.

Now, when her mother had had a drink out of her bottle and was having a nap, the robber girl went to the reindeer and said: 'I'd love to tickle you a lot more with that sharp knife of mine, because then you're funny. But never mind! I'm going to undo your rope and let you out, so you can run to Lapland. You've got to get a move on and take this little girl for me to the Snow Queen's palace, where her playmate is. I expect you heard what she said; she talked loud enough and you've got big ears!'

The reindeer leapt for joy. The robber girl lifted little Gerda up, and was careful to tie her fast and even give her a little cushion to sit on. 'You'll be all right,' she said. 'There are your furry boots, for it's going to be cold. But I'm keeping the muff; it's far too nice! Still, you won't be cold. Here are my mother's big mittens; they'll reach right up to your elbows. Hands in! Now your hands look exactly like my ugly mother's!'

And Gerda wept for joy.

'Now I don't like this snivelling!' said the little robber girl. 'You should be cheerful now! And here are two loaves and a ham for you; they'll keep you from going hungry.' Both were tied on to the reindeer's back. Then the little robber girl opened the door, coaxed in all the big dogs, and, cutting the rope with her knife, said to the reindeer: 'Off you go! But look after the little girl!'

Stretching out her hands in the big mittens to the robber girl, Gerda said goodbye, and the reindeer flew off over bushes and briers, through the big forest, and over swamps and plains, for all it was worth. The wolves howled and the ravens squawked. 'Puff! Puff!' sounded from the sky. It seemed to sneeze red.

'That's my old Northern Lights!' said the reindeer. 'See how they flash!' And faster and faster it ran, day and night. The loaves were eaten and so was the ham—and they were in Lapland.

Sixth Story. The Lapp Woman and the Finn Woman

They came to a stop at a little house. It was such a miserable one: the roof reached down to the ground, and the door was so low that the family were forced to crawl on their stomachs when going in or out. There was nobody in except an old Lapp woman, who was frying fish at an oil-lamp. And the reindeer told her Gerda's whole story (after telling its own, which it thought much more important), as Gerda, being so freezing cold, couldn't speak.

'Oh, you poor things!' said the Lapp woman. 'You've a long way to go yet! You'll have to go hundreds of miles into Finmark, where the Snow Queen's in the country, burning Bengal lights every night. I'll write a few words on a piece of dried cod—I've no paper. I'll give it to you to take to the Finn woman up there. She'll give you more information than I can.'

And so when Gerda had got warmed up and had had something to eat and drink, the Lapp woman wrote a few words on a piece of dried cod, and, telling Gerda to look after it, tied her on to the reindeer again, and off it sprang. 'Puff! Puff!' said the sky again; the loveliest blue Northern Lights burnt all night long. And so they came to Finmark, where they knocked at the Finn woman's chimney, for she didn't even have a door.

Inside, it was so sweltering hot that the Finn woman herself was almost naked; she was a little woman, and rather grubby. She at once undid little Gerda's clothes, took off her mittens and boots (she'd have been too hot if she hadn't), put a lump of ice on the reindeer's head, and read the message that was written on the dried cod. She read it three times and then, knowing it by heart, put the fish in the cooking-pot, for it was good to eat and she never wasted anything.

The reindeer then told first its own story and next little Gerda's, the Finn woman blinking her wise eyes but never saying anything.

'You're so wise,' said the reindeer. 'I know you can tie all the winds of the world in sewing-thread, so that when the captain undoes one knot he gets a fair wind, while if he undoes the second a rough wind rises, and if he undoes the third and fourth it blows a gale and flattens the forest. Won't you give the little girl a drink, so she'll have the strength of twelve men and will overcome the Snow Queen?'

'The strength of twelve men,' said the Finn woman. 'Well, that should do it!' And, going to a shelf, she took a large roll of skin which she opened out. Strange letters were written on it, and the Finn woman read till the sweat poured from her forehead.

But the reindeer begged so hard for little Gerda, and little Gerda looked so pleadingly at the Finn woman, with her eyes full of tears, that the woman began blinking her eyes again and drew the reindeer into a corner, where she whispered to it, while putting fresh ice on its head: 'Little Kay is with the Snow Queen sure enough, and there he finds everything to his heart's content and thinks it the best place in the world. But that's because he's got a splinter of glass in his heart and a bit of glass in his eye. They'll first have to come out, or he'll never be human again and the Snow Queen will have him in her power.'

'But can't you give little Gerda something to take, so that she will have power over things?'

'I can't give her any greater power than she already has. Don't you see how great it is? Don't you see how human beings and animals are forced to serve her, and how well she has got on in the world, in her bare feet? She hasn't to learn of her power from us; it's in her heart, in her heart! She's a sweet and innocent child. If she can't find her own way to the Snow Queen and get the glass out of little Kay, then we can't help her. Ten miles from here is the beginning of the Snow Queen's garden; you can carry the little girl there. Put her off by the big bush which stands bearing red berries in the snow; don't stand gossiping, but hurry back here!' And so saying the Finn woman lifted little Gerda on to the reindeer, which ran off as fast as its legs would carry it.

'Oh, I didn't get my boots! I didn't get my mittens!' cried little Gerda. In the biting cold she could feel that she hadn't. But, not daring to stop, the reindeer ran on till it came to the big bush with the red berries. There it put Gerda off and kissed her on the lips, while big, glistening tears rolled down the creature's cheeks. Then it ran as fast as its legs would carry it back again. And there stood poor Gerda, without shoes, without gloves, in the middle of dreadful, icy-cold Finmark.

She ran on as fast as she could, and soon met a whole regiment of snowflakes; but they didn't fall from the sky—that was perfectly clear, and was gleaming with the Northern Lights. The snowflakes were running along the ground, and the nearer they came the bigger they grew. Gerda remembered how big and strange they had looked the time she had seen them through the burning-glass. But here they were far, far bigger and more frightening: they were alive—they were the Snow Queen's sentries. They had the strangest of shapes: some looked like ugly black hedgehogs, others like masses of writhing snakes all sticking out their heads, and others again like fat little bears with bristly hair, all shining white, all live snowflakes.

And now Gerda said her prayers; and the cold was so fierce that she could see her own breath. It rose from her mouth like a cloud of smoke; denser and denser it grew, until it took the form of bright little angels that went on growing when they reached the ground. Every one of them wore a helmet on his head and carried a sword and a shield in his hands. More and more of them came, and by the time Gerda had finished her prayers she was surrounded by a whole army of them. And they set about the dreadful snowflakes with their spears and broke them into a hundred pieces, allowing little Gerda to walk safely and happily on. The angels stroked her feet and hands, so that she didn't feel the cold so much, as she walked briskly forward to the Snow Queen's palace.

But before we go any further we must see how Kay is getting on. He certainly wasn't thinking of little Gerda: least of all that she stood outside the palace.

Seventh Story. What took place in the Snow Queen's palace, and what happened after

The palace walls were of drifting snow, the windows and doors of cutting winds. There were over a hundred halls, according to the way the snow drifted. The biggest stretched for many miles. All were lit up by the fierce Northern Lights, and were so large, so empty, so icy-cold, and so dazzling. Never here was there any fun, not even so much as a little bear-dance when the storm would blow up and polar bears walk on their hind legs and give themselves airs; never a little party with games such as muzzle-slapping and tap-a-paw; never a little get-together by the white young lady foxes: bare, big, and cold it was in the halls of the Snow Queen. The Northern Lights flashed so regularly that you could tell by counting when they were at their highest point and when they were at their lowest. In the middle of that empty, endless hall of snow was a frozen lake. It had cracked into a thousand pieces, but each piece was so exactly like the next that it was quite a work of art. And in the middle of the lake, when she was at home, would sit the Snow Queen; and she would say that she sat on the Mirror of Reason, and that this of all things was the best in the world.

Little Kay was quite blue with cold, indeed nearly black; though he never felt it, as she had kissed away his shivers and his heart was as a lump of ice. He was busy dragging about some sharp, flat pieces of ice, laying them in all manner of ways, bent on getting something out of it all; just as in games we arrange

small wooden pieces to form a pattern. Kay, too, was forming patterns, the most curious of patterns; for this was the game of icy cold reason. To his eyes the patterns were very good ones and of the greatest importance; that was because of the glass splinter in his eye! He made patterns which spelt out a word, but could never find the one for the word that he really wanted, the word 'eternity', the Snow Queen having said: 'If you can form that pattern for me you shall be your own master, and I'll make you a present of the whole world and a pair of new skates.' But he couldn't.

'I'm off to the warm countries now,' said the Snow Queen. 'I want to take a peep into the black pots!' She meant the volcanoes, Etna and Vesuvius, as we call them. 'I'm going to touch them up with white! They need it. It does them good on top of lemons and grapes!' And the Snow Queen flew off, while Kay

sat by himself in the bare hall of ice many miles long, gazing at the pieces of ice and thinking and thinking till his brain creaked. Stiff and silent he sat; you would have thought he had frozen to death.

It was then that little Gerda entered the palace, through the big gates of biting winds. But she had said an evening prayer, and the winds had dropped as though they were going to sleep and she had stepped into the big, bare, and cold halls. There she saw Kay. She knew him at once and flung her arms round his neck, holding him tight and crying: 'Kay! Dear little Kay! So now I've found you!'

But he sat perfectly still, and stiff and cold. Seeing this, little Gerda shed hot tears, and they fell on his breast and went through to his heart, where they melted the lump of ice and swallowed up the glass splinter. He looked at her, and she sang the hymn:

> 'Then seek your Saviour down below'
> For roses in the valleys grow!'

Then Kay burst into tears; and wept till the bit of glass fell out of his eye, when he knew her again and cried for joy: 'Gerda! Dear little Gerda! Where have you been all this long time? And where have I been?' Then, looking around him, he said: 'How cold it is! How big and bare it is here!' And he held Gerda tight, while she cried and laughed for joy. So happy were they that even the pieces of ice danced for joy around them; and when they were tired and lay down they formed the very letters which the Snow Queen had said he was to find, so that he should be his own master and she would give him the whole world and a pair of new skates.

Then Gerda kissed his cheeks and they became rosy; she kissed his eyes and they shone like hers; she kissed his hands and feet and he was well and strong. The Snow Queen could come home if she liked; his release was written there in letters of glistening ice.

And taking each other by the hand they walked out of the big hall. They talked of Granny and of the roses on the roof; and wherever they went the winds dropped and the sun broke through. And when they got to the bush with the red berries, there, waiting for them, was the reindeer; it had with it another, young reindeer whose udder was full, and it gave the little ones warm milk and kissed them on the lips. Then they carried Kay and Gerda first to the Finn woman's, where they warmed themselves in the hot room and were given instructions about their homeward journey, and then to the Lapp woman, who had made new clothes for them and got ready her sledge.

And the old reindeer and the young reindeer ran alongside as

HEATH
ROBINSON

far as the country's border; there, where the first green things peeped up from the ground, they took leave of the reindeer and the Lapp woman. 'Goodbye!' they all said. And the first little birds began to twitter, the wood was in green bud, and riding out of it on a splendid horse which Gerda knew (it had been harnessed to the gold coach) came a young girl with a gleaming red cap on her head and pistols in front. It was the little robber girl, who, being tired of staying at home, wanted to go first north and then somewhere else if she didn't like it. She knew Gerda at once, and Gerda knew her; they were delighted.

'You're a fine one for roaming around!' she said to little Kay. 'I wonder whether you deserve to have people running to the ends of the earth for your sake!'

But Gerda patted her on the cheek and asked after the prince and princess.

'They've gone away to foreign countries!' said the robber girl.

'And the crow?' asked little Gerda.

'Why, the crow's dead!' she replied. 'The tame sweetheart's a widow now, and wears a piece of black wool round her leg. She complains miserably; nonsense, that's what it is! Now tell me how you've got on, and how you managed to find him.'

And Gerda and Kay both told her.

'Snip-snap-snorum! Hey, cockalorum!' said the robber girl; and taking them both by the hands, she promised that if ever she passed through their town she would call and see them. And with that she rode off into the wide world. But Kay and Gerda went hand in hand, and as they walked it was lovely spring, with flowers and everything green. The church bells were ringing, and they knew the tall towers and the big town: it was the one they lived in. And they walked into it and went to Granny's door and into the room upstairs, where everything stood where it had stood before and the clock said 'Tick! Tick!' as the hands went round. But as they walked in at the door they felt that they had become grown-up people. The roses from the gutter were blooming inside the open windows, and there stood the little stools; and Kay and Gerda sat down on their own and held each other by the hand. Like a bad dream, they had forgotten the cold, empty splendour at the Snow Queen's. Granny sat in God's bright sunshine, reading aloud from the Bible: 'Except ye become as little children, ye shall not enter into the Kingdom of Heaven!'

And looking into each other's eyes, Kay and Gerda at once understood the old hymn:

'Then seek your Saviour down below;
For roses in the valleys grow!'

So there they both sat, grown up and yet children, children at heart; and it was summer—warm and blessed summer.

THE DARNING-NEEDLE

ONCE upon a time there was a darning-needle, and she was so fine in her ways that she fancied herself a sewing-needle.

'Now, you mind who you're holding!' said the darning-needle to the fingers that picked her up. 'Don't drop me! If I fall on the floor I can get lost, I'm so fine!'

'Fine to medium!' said the fingers, holding her tightly round the waist.

'There now! I'm bringing my suite!' said the darning-needle, drawing a long thread after her—only it hadn't got a knot in it.

The fingers pointed the needle straight at Cook's slipper, the upper of which had split and was about to be sewn together again.

'This is common work!' said the darning-needle. 'I'll never go through, I'll break! I'll break!' And she broke. 'I told you so!' said the darning-needle. 'I'm too fine!'

'She's no use at all now!' thought the fingers, but they had to hold on to her while Cook dropped sealing-wax on and pinned her to her scarf.

'Aha, now I'm a brooch!' said the darning-needle. 'I knew I'd come into my own; when you're somebody you're bound to become something!' And she laughed to herself; for you will never see a darning-needle laugh to anybody else. And there she sat as proud as proud, as though driving in her coach, looking round in all directions.

'May I make so bold as to inquire if you are of gold?' she

asked the pin who was her neighbour. 'You have such good looks and it's your own head, though rather a small one! You must see about getting it to grow, for it isn't everybody that can be stuck up with sealing-wax.' And so saying the darning-needle drew herself up so proudly that she fell out of the scarf and into the sink, just as Cook was rinsing it out.

'Ho! Ho! for a journey!' said the darning-needle. 'So long as I don't get lost!' But that's what she did.

'I'm too fine for this world,' she said, as she lay in the gutter. 'I have my self-respect, though, and that's always something!' And so the darning-needle held herself erect and never lost heart.

All sorts of things went sailing over her—sticks, straws, pieces of newspaper. 'See how they go!' said the darning-needle. 'They don't see the point of me at all. I'm sticking where I am. Now just look at that twig! She hasn't got a thought in her head except for "twig", and that's herself! There goes a straw! Look at the way she swaggers! See how she throws herself about! You want to think less of yourself, before you go bumping into the pavement. Now there's a newspaper! It's all forgotten, everything in her; yet she has to go throwing her weight about. I sit quietly and patiently here! I know what I am and I'll stay as I am!'

One day there was something which shone so beautifully close by her that the darning-needle took it for a diamond, only it was a broken bottle. And, as it sparkled, the darning-needle spoke to it, introducing herself as a brooch. 'I suppose you are a diamond?' 'Well, something of the sort!' And so each thought the other was very precious, and they fell to talking about how proud the world was.

'You know, I used to live in a box belonging to a lady,' said the darning-needle. 'And the lady was a cook. On each of her hands she had five fingers, and for conceit I've never seen the like of those five fingers! Yet they were only there for holding me and taking me out of the box and putting me back again.'

'Did they sparkle at all?' asked the broken bottle.

'Sparkle?' said the darning-needle. 'No, but they were high and mighty! They were five brothers, all of the Finger family, and they all stuck together, though they weren't all the same length. The outside one, Thumbkins, was short and fat. He marched outside the ranks and he had only one bend in his back—he could only bow once. But he used to say that if he were chopped off a man, the whole of that man would be spoilt for active service. Lickpan used to poke his nose into things and point at the sun and the moon, and he did the squeezing when they were writing. Longfellow was head and shoulders above the rest; Ringman wore a gold belt round his middle; and little Peterkin did nothing at all and was very proud of it. Brag in the morning and brag at night—and so I took to the sink!'

'And so we sit here and sparkle!' said the broken bottle. All at once some more water came pouring into the gutter, and it overflowed its banks and carried the glass bottle away with it.

'There, now he's been promoted!' said the darning-needle. 'I'm going to stay here; I'm too fine, but that's my pride and I'm entitled to respect for it.' And there she sat, proud and erect and full of her own importance.

'I'm inclined to think I must have been born from a ray of sunshine, I'm so fine! And the sun always seems to be looking for me, under the water. Oh dear, I'm so fine that my own mother can't find me! If I still had my old eye that broke, I think I could cry! Though I wouldn't do it—fine ladies never cry.'

One day some street-boys came along and started grubbing in the gutter, looking for old nails, lost coins, and such-like. It was a dirty thing to do, but then that was *their* idea of fun,

'Ooh!' cried one of them, as he pricked himself on the needle. 'Just look at this fellow!'

'I'm not a fellow, I'm a lady!' said the darning-needle; only nobody heard her. She had lost her sealing-wax and she was black all over, but then black is slimming and so she fancied that she was finer than ever.

'Look, here comes an egg-shell!' cried the boys; and they took the darning-needle and stuck her into the shell.

'White walls to go with my black!' said the darning-needle. 'That's very becoming! Now I *shall* be seen. So long as I don't get seasick; because if I do I shall cast up and break.' But she wasn't seasick and she didn't break.

'It's a good remedy for seasickness to have a stomach of steel, and never to forget that one is a little more than human. Now mine has passed off. The finer one is, the more one can stand.'

'Crunch!' said the egg-shell, as a horse and cart passed over it. 'Ooh, I'm squashing!' said the darning-needle. 'This time I really will be seasick. It's coming! It's coming!' But it didn't; and she didn't break, even though a horse and cart had passed over her. She lay there all her length—and there we can leave her!

THE BELL

IN THE narrow streets of the big city, in the evening when the sun was setting and the clouds glistened like gold up among the chimneys, first one person and then another would hear a strange sound, like the peal of a church bell. But it would be heard only for a moment, as there would be such a rumbling of carriages and such a noise of people, and that is disturbing. 'The evening bell is tolling!' they would say. 'The sun is setting!'

Those who went outside the city, where the houses stood farther apart and there were gardens and small fields, saw the evening sky more beautiful still and heard the bell peal more loudly. It was as if the sound came from a church deep in the silent, sweet-smelling woods; and people would look there and grow quite solemn . . .

As time passed, one person would say to another: 'I wonder if there's a church in those woods? That bell has such a strange and lovely tone; let's go and have a look.' And the rich people would take to their carriages and the poor people to their legs. But it would seem such a strangely long way to them; and when they came to a lot of willow-trees growing at the edge of the wood, they would sit down and look into the long branches and think that now they were really in the country. The town confectioner came out and pitched a tent; and then came another confectioner who hung up a bell outside his tent, a bell which had been tarred so as to stand the rain and which had no clapper. And then when people went back home they would say it had been most romantic, which is really saying something. Three persons declared they had penetrated the wood as far as it ended and had kept hearing the strange pealing; but to them it seemed to come from inside the city. One of them wrote quite a song about it, saying that the bell had the sound of a mother speaking to a beloved and intelligent child; there was no melody more lovely than the pealing of the bell.

News of the bell also reached the emperor, who promised that whoever found out where the sound came from should receive the title of World Bell-ringer, even if it proved not to be a bell.

By now many people went to the woods to get a living there; but there was only one who came back with any sort of explanation. No one had been far enough, not even he; yet he said that the pealing came from a very big owl in a hollow tree. It was such a wise old owl and it continually beat its head against the tree; but whether the pealing came from its head or from the hollow trunk he couldn't say for certain. And so he was made World Bell-ringer and every year wrote a short paper about the owl; though no one was any the wiser.

Now it was confirmation day and the vicar had spoken beautifully and feelingly. The young people had been so greatly moved. This was an important day for them; from children they had suddenly become grown up, their childish minds turning, as it were, to wiser thoughts. It was the loveliest of sunny days. The young people went out of the city; and from the woods came, wonderfully loud, the pealing of the big, unknown bell. Hearing it they felt a great urge to find it; all except three. One of these had to go home to try on her party dress; for it was on account of this very dress and the party that she had this time been confirmed, or she would never have been there. The second was a poor boy who had borrowed his confirmation suit and shoes from the landlord's son, and had to return them by a certain time. The third said that he never went to any strange place without his parents, and that he had always been a good boy and would go on being one now he had been confirmed; and that's not a thing to make fun of, though they did.

And so three of them went no further, while the rest trudged along. The sun was shining and the birds singing, and the young people joined in the singing, holding one another by the hand; for they had yet to be given jobs, and were newly confirmed in the presence of our Lord.

Soon, however, two of the smallest of them grew tired, and so these two turned back towards the city. Two little girls sat down and made daisy-chains; and they, too, got no further. And when the rest of them reached the willow-trees where the confectioner lived they said: 'Well, here we are! There's no such thing as a bell; it's all imagination.'

Then all at once, deep inside the wood, the bell pealed out so sweetly and so solemnly that four or five decided after all to go further into the wood. It was so dense, so leafy, that it was hard work making headway. Woodruff and anemones grew almost too tall; flowering convolvuluses and brambles hung in long festoons from tree to tree, and there the nightingale sang and the sunbeams played. Oh, it was wonderful! But it was no place for girls; they would have got their dresses torn. Big boulders lay there, overgrown with mosses of every colour, and the fresh spring-water bubbled up, making a strange 'cluck-clucking' sound.

'Could this be the bell?' said one of the young people, lying down and listening. 'We must look into this!' And so he stayed behind, leaving the others to go on.

They came to a house made from bark and branches. A big crab-apple tree overhung it, as though to shake all its blessings off on to the roof, which was covered in roses. The long branches were clinging to the gable, and from this hung a small bell. Would this be the one they had all heard? Yes; they all agreed that it was—all except one. He said that this bell was too small and delicate to be heard at the distance they had heard it, and that they were quite different tones which had stirred them. The one who said this was a prince, and so the others said: 'A fellow like him always knows best.'

And so they left him to go by himself; and as he went his breast became fuller and fuller with the solitude of the wood. Yet still he heard the little bell which had so pleased the others, and now and then could also hear, as the wind blew from the confectioner's, the singing of people who were having tea. But the peals of the deep bell sounded even louder; it was as though an organ played with it. The sound came from the left, the side where the heart is.

All at once there was a rustle in the bushes and standing in front of the prince was a little boy, a boy wearing clogs and a jacket which was so short that you could easily see his long wrists. They knew each other. The boy was the very one who had been unable to go on because he had had to go home and return the suit and shoes to the landlord's son. He had done so, and now, in his clogs and his poor clothes, had started off alone; for the pealing of the bell had been so loud that he had had to come.

'Why, then we can walk along together!' said the prince. But the poor boy in the clogs was very shy; and tugging at the short sleeves of his jacket he said that he was afraid he couldn't walk so fast. Besides, he thought that the bell would be found on the right, where everything great and grand was to be found.

'Why, then we shall never meet!' said the prince; and he nodded to the poor boy, who went into the darkest and densest part of the wood, where the thorns tore his poor clothes and scratched his face, hands, and feet. The prince, too, got some nice scratches; but the sun shone on his path and he is the one we will follow, for he was a smart lad.

'I *will* find the bell!' he said. 'If I have to go to the ends of the earth for it!'

Horrid monkeys sat up in the trees, grinning and baring their teeth. 'Let's pelt him!' they said. 'Let's pelt him; he's a prince!'

But he walked steadily on, deeper and deeper into the wood, to where the most wonderful flowers were growing. There were starry white lilies with blood-red stamens, sky-blue tulips which sparkled in the breeze, and apple-trees on which the apples looked for all the world like big shining soap bubbles. Think how these trees must have glistened in the sunshine! All round the loveliest green meadows, where stags and hinds were frolicking in the grass, grew splendid oaks and beeches; and where a tree had split its bark there would be grass and long creepers growing in the crack. There were also big glades with peaceful lakes where white swans swam about, flapping their wings. The prince would often stand still and listen, thinking that it was from one of these deep lakes that the bell pealed up to him. But then he would find that it wasn't from there that the bell tolled, but from still deeper in the wood.

And now the sun went down. The sky glowed a fiery red; it grew so silent, so very silent, in the wood, and he fell upon his knees, sang his evening hymn, and said: 'Never shall I find what I seek! The sun is setting and then will come the night, the dark night. Yet even now I may see the round red sun once more before it sinks quite down behind the earth. I'll climb the rocks over there; they rise to the height of the tallest trees.'

And seizing hold of brambles and creepers, he climbed up the wet boulders where there were wriggling snakes and the toad almost barked at him. But up he got, before the sun had quite set as seen from that height. Oh, what grandeur! The sea, the great glorious sea beating its long waves against the shore, lay outstretched before him, and the sun stood out like a great shining altar at the meeting-point of sea and sky. Everything was fused in glowing colours; the woods sang and the sea sang, and his heart sang with them. All Nature was a great and holy temple, of which trees and floating clouds were the pillars, flowers and grass the woven velvet carpet, the sky itself the great dome. Up there the red colours went out as the sun disappeared, but millions of stars were lit and then millions of diamond lamps shone out. And the prince stretched his arms towards the sky, towards the sea and the woods—and at that very moment, along the right-hand path, came the poor boy with the short sleeves and the clogs. He had arrived there just as quickly; arrived by his own way. And they ran forward to meet each other, and clasped each other by the hand in the great temple of Nature and poetry; and over their heads pealed the invisible holy bell, while blessed spirits danced airily around them to the sound of a jubilant hallelujah.

THE RED SHOES

THERE was once a little girl—so sweet and pretty she was. Only in summer she always had to go barefoot because she was poor, and in winter she wore big clogs which made her little instep all red—ever so horribly.

In the middle of the village lived the old cobbler woman. She sat making, as well as she could, out of some strips of old red cloth, a pair of little shoes. Rather clumsy they were, yet well meant; they were for the little girl. The little girl was called Karen.

On the very day of her mother's funeral she was given the red shoes and wore them for the first time. Of course they were not the sort of thing for mourning; but then she hadn't any others, and so she walked in these in her bare legs behind the poor straw coffin.

As she did so a big old carriage came up in which sat a big old lady. She looked at the little girl and was sorry for her; and so she said to the clergyman: 'I say, give me that little girl, and I'll look after her!'

And Karen thought that it was all because of the red shoes; but the old woman said they were horrible, and they were burnt, while Karen was given clean and smart clothes to wear. She had to learn to read and sew. And people said that she was very pretty, while her mirror said: 'You are much more than pretty; you're really lovely!'

Now one day the queen travelled through the country, taking with her her little daughter, who was a princess. And people

flocked to the palace, Karen, of course, among them. And the little princess stood in her white robes at a window, letting herself be seen. She was wearing neither a train nor a gold crown but had lovely red morocco shoes. Of course they were smarter altogether than the ones the cobbler woman had made for little Karen. Nothing in the world could compare with red shoes!

Now Karen grew old enough to be confirmed; she got new clothes and was to have new shoes as well. The rich shoemaker in the town measured her little foot; it was in his own home and there were big glass cases full of charming shoes and polished boots. It looked so very fine; but the old lady had poor eyesight and so it was wasted on her. In the midst of all the other shoes was a pair of red ones, just like the shoes the princess had worn. How beautiful they were! The shoemaker told them that they had been made for an earl's daughter, but hadn't fitted.

'What fine leather!' said the old lady. 'Don't they shine!'

'Yes, don't they!' said Karen. And they fitted her and were bought. But the old lady did not realize they were red. She would never have allowed Karen to be confirmed in red shoes, but that's what she did now.

Everybody looked at her feet; and as she walked up the aisle to the chancel she felt that even the old pictures on the tombs, the portraits of clergymen and clergymen's wives in stiff collars and long black robes, fixed their eyes on her red shoes, and all her thoughts were of these when the clergyman laid his hands on her head and spoke of holy baptism, of the covenant with God, and of how she was now to be a great Christian. And the organ played such solemn music, beautiful children's voices sang, and the old choirmaster sang; while Karen thought only of the red shoes.

In the afternoon the old lady heard from everyone that the shoes had been red; and she said that it was horrid and it

wasn't proper, and that whenever Karen went to church from then on she was always to wear black shoes, even if they were old ones.

Next Sunday was Communion. And Karen looked at the black shoes, and looked at the red ones—and then she looked at the red ones again, and put the red ones on.

It was a lovely sunny day. Karen and the old lady took the path through the cornfield, where it was a little dusty.

Standing at the church door was an old soldier with a crutch-handled stick, and a funny long beard which was more red than white—in fact it was red. And stooping down to the ground he asked the old lady if he might wipe her shoes. And Karen stretched out her own little foot. 'My word, what lovely dancing shoes!' said the soldier. 'Sit fast when you dance!' And he tapped the soles with his hand.

And giving the soldier a copper, the old lady went with Karen into the church.

And everyone inside looked at Karen's red shoes, and all the portraits looked at them. And when Karen knelt before the altar and raised the golden chalice to her lips, she thought of nothing but the red shoes and they seemed to be swimming in the chalice in front of her. And she forgot to sing her hymn; forgot to say her Lord's Prayer.

Then everyone left the church and the old lady got into her carriage. Karen was lifting her foot to get in after her when the old soldier, who was standing near by, said: 'Look what lovely dancing shoes!' And Karen couldn't help herself but had to do a few dance steps; and once she had begun her legs went on dancing. The shoes seemed to have gained control of them. She went dancing round the church corner; she couldn't help herself. The coachman had to run after and catch hold of her, and lifted her into the carriage; but her feet kept on dancing, and she gave the good old lady some dreadful kicks. In the end they got the shoes off and her legs came to rest.

At home the shoes were put away in a cupboard, but Karen couldn't help looking at them.

One day the old lady fell ill and they said that she wouldn't live. She had to be nursed and cared for, and no one was more fitted for it than Karen, But over in the town there was a big ball and Karen had been invited. She looked at the old lady, who wouldn't live anyway, and she looked at the red shoes and thought there was no sin in that. She put on the red shoes, as of course she could. But then she went to the ball, and she began to dance.

But when she wanted to turn right, the shoes danced to the left; and when she wanted to go up the room the shoes danced down the room, down the stairs, through the street, and out of the town gate. Dance she did and dance she had to—right out into the dark woods.

There something shone out among the tree-tops and she thought that it was the moon. And a face it was, only it was the

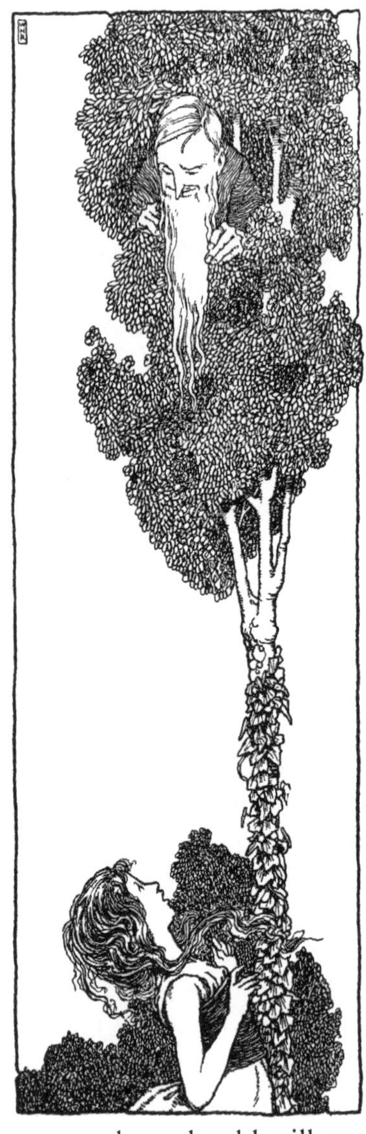

old soldier with the red beard. He sat nodding and saying: 'Look what lovely dancing shoes.'

This frightened her and she tried to pull the red shoes off; but they stuck fast and she tore her stockings, as the shoes had grown fast to her feet. And dance she did, and dance she had to; over field and meadow, in rain and sunshine, by night and by day. But the night was the most awful.

She went dancing into the open churchyard. But the dead there, they didn't dance; they had something a good deal better to do than dance. She would have sat down on the poor man's grave where the bitter tansy grew, but she found neither rest nor peace; and as she danced towards the open church door she saw there an angel in long white robes, with wings which reached from his shoulders down to the ground. His face was stern and serious, and in his hand he held a sword, so very broad and shining.

'Dance you shall!' he said. 'Dance in your red shoes till you grow pale and cold, till your skin shrinks up like a skeleton! Dance you shall, from door to door; and where there are proud and vain children you shall knock so that they will hear you and fear you! Dance you shall, dance——'

'Pity!' cried Karen. But she never heard what the angel replied, for the shoes carried her through the gate into the field, over roads and over paths; and always she had to dance.

One morning she danced past a door that she knew well. The sound of hymn-singing came from inside and they carried out a coffin decorated with flowers. Then she knew that the old lady was dead, and she thought that now she had been forsaken by all and cursed by God's angel.

Dance she did, and dance she had to; dance in the dark night. The shoes carried her off over brier and stubble and she scratched herself till she bled; and she went dancing on across the heath to a little, lonely cottage. She knew that this was where the headsman lived, and she tapped on the window with her finger and said:

'Come out! Come out! I can't come in, as I'm dancing!'

And the headsman said: 'You won't know who I am! I cut off the heads of wicked people, and I can feel my axe quivering!'

'Don't cut off my head!' said Karen. 'For then I should be unable to repent my sin! But cut off my feet with the red shoes!'

And then she confessed her sin, and the headsman cut off her feet with the red shoes. And the shoes danced with the little feet across the field and into the deep wood.

And he carved wooden legs and crutches for her, and taught her a hymn, the one which sinners always sing. And kissing the hand which had wielded the axe, she went off across the heath.

'Now I have suffered enough for the red shoes!' she said. 'Now I'll go to church to let them see me.' And she walked boldly up to the church door. But when she got there the red shoes danced in front of her, and she was frightened and turned back.

All that week she was sad and wept many a heavy tear; but when Sunday came round she said: 'There! Now I've suffered and struggled enough! I dare say I'm as good as many of those who sit there swaggering in church.' And she went off as boldly as ever. But she had got no farther than the gate when she saw the red shoes dancing ahead of her; and she was frightened, and she turned back and truly repented her sin.

And going to the vicarage she asked to be taken into service, promising to work hard and do anything in her power; the wages didn't matter, so long as she had a roof over her head and was among kindly people. And the clergyman's wife was sorry for her and took her in service. And she was hard-working and thoughtful. In the evening when the clergyman read aloud from the Bible, she would sit quietly listening. All the little children were very fond of her; but whenever they talked of dress and show and of being as lovely as a queen, she would shake her head.

The following Sunday they were all going to church, and they asked her if she would go with them. But she looked so sadly at her crutches, with tears in her eyes; and so the others went off to hear the word of God, while she stayed in her little room by herself. It was just big enough to hold a bed and a chair, and she sat down there with her prayer-book. And as she devoutly read it the wind carried the strains of the organ to her from the church, and she lifted her face in tears and said: 'O God, help me!'

At this the sun shone so very clearly, and just in front of her stood the angel of God in white robes, the one she had seen in the church door that night. Only now he was no longer holding the sharp sword, but a lovely green branch full of roses. And with it he touched the ceiling and it rose so very high up, and where he had touched it there glistened a white star. And he touched the walls and they opened out; and she saw the organ playing, and the old pictures of clergymen and clergymen's wives. The congregation were sitting in decorated pews, singing from their hymn-books; for the church had come home to the poor girl in her little room—either that or she had gone there. She sat in the pew with the rest of the clergyman's household; and when they had finished the hymn and looked up, they nodded and said: 'How right of you to come, Karen!'

'That was pity!' she said.

And the organ pealed, and the voices of the children in the choir sounded so very soft and lovely. The clear sunlight streamed so warmly in at the window to the pew where Karen sat. Her heart was so filled with sunshine, with peace and with joy, that it broke; her soul had flown on sunshine up to God, and no one asked any questions about the red shoes.

THE HIGH JUMPERS

THE FLEA, the grasshopper, and the skipjack decided to see which of them could jump highest, and they invited all the world, and anybody else who wanted, to come and see the match. And three whopping big jumpers they were when they got together.

'I shall give my daughter to the one who jumps highest,' said the king; 'for it would be rather mean to let these people jump for nothing!'

The flea was the first to come forward. He had such nice manners and bowed to everyone present, for he had gentle blood in his veins and never kept company with anybody but people—and that does make a difference.

Next came the grasshopper. He, to be sure, was very much stouter, yet he was rather well bred and he was wearing a uniform he had been born to, while he said that he had very old connections in the land of Egypt and was highly respected at home. He had been taken straight from the field and put into a house of cards which had three storeys, all of court cards facing inwards: in it there were both doors and windows, cut from life out of the Queen of Hearts. 'I'm such a singer,' he said, 'that sixteen born crickets, who have chirped since childhood without ever getting a house of cards, on hearing me have fretted themselves even thinner than they were to start with!'

And so the two of them, the flea and the grasshopper, made out a good case to show who they were, and why they thought themselves fit to marry a princess.

W HEATH ROBINSON

The skipjack never spoke a word, but of him it was said that he thought all the harder, and the Court dog, after taking a sniff at him, answered for the fact that the skipjack came of good family. The old counsellor, who had been given three decorations for holding his tongue, maintained that the skipjack had the gift of magic: you could tell from his back whether the winter would be a mild or a hard one, and nobody can tell that from the back of the man who writes the weather forecasts.

'Well, I'm saying nothing,' said the old king. 'But that's because I always believe in keeping my own counsel!'

By now it was time for the jumping. The flea jumped so high

that nobody could see him and so they declared that he hadn't jumped at all, and that now was mean.

The grasshopper only jumped half as high, but he jumped straight into the king's face, and that was nasty, said the king.

The skipjack stood a long time thinking it over, so that in the end everyone thought that he couldn't jump.

'I hope he isn't feeling unwell,' said the Court dog, taking another sniff at him. Swish! With a little sideward skip he had jumped into the princess's lap as she sat on a little golden footstool.

At this the king said: 'The highest jump is the jump up to my daughter, for that's the point of it all. But to do that you need a head, and the skipjack has shown that he's got a head. His legs are in his head!'

And he won the princess.

'I jumped the highest!' said the flea. 'But it's all the same to me! She can have the old drumstick—skin and grease and all! I jumped the highest, but to make your mark in this world you want body!'

And the flea went abroad on active service, where they say he was killed.

The grasshopper settled in the ditch and reflected on the ups and downs of this life; and he, too, said: 'Body's what you want! Body's what you want!' And so he sang his melancholy song; and it's from there that we have taken the story, though it could easily be untrue, even were it to be printed.

THE SHEPHERDESS AND THE CHIMNEY-SWEEP

HAVE you ever seen a really old, old cupboard, all black with age and with scrolls and foliage carved all over it? There was just such a cupboard standing in a drawing-room; it had been handed down from great-grandmother and there were roses and tulips carved on it from top to bottom. It had the quaintest of flourishes on it, and, in between, little stags popped out their heads full of antlers. But in the middle of the cupboard was carved the figure of a man—really, he was comical to look at! And grin—for you couldn't call that laughing! He had billy-goat legs, little horns in his forehead, and a long beard. The children of the house called him Billy-goat-legs-Lieutenant-and-Major-General-Commander-in-Chief-Sergeant, because it's a hard name to say and there aren't many who get that title. Fancy the idea of carving him on it! Still, there he was. His eyes were always fixed on the table under the mirror, for there stood a charming little shepherdess of porcelain. Her shoes were gilded, her frock was fastened up with a red rose, and she had a golden hat and a shepherd's crook—she was lovely! Close by her stood a little chimney-sweep, as black as coal but also made of porcelain. He was as clean and nice as anybody; a chimney-sweep was only something he was supposed to be and the porcelain-maker could easily have made a prince of him—it was the same to him.

He stood there so nicely with his ladder, and his cheeks were as fresh and rosy as a girl's, though that was really a mistake—he might have been made just a little bit black. He stood quite close to the shepherdess; they had both been placed where they stood, and being so placed they had become engaged. They made a good match: they were young people, they were of the same porcelain, and equally breakable.

Close by them stood another figure three times as large; this was an old Chinaman who could nod. He too was of porcelain and he said he was the little shepherdess's grandfather, though he certainly couldn't prove it. He claimed that he had authority over her, and so he had nodded to the Billy-goat-legs-Lieutenant-and-Major-General-Commander-in-Chief-Sergeant, who was offering to marry the little shepherdess.

'You'll get a man there,' said the old Chinaman; 'a man I almost think is of mahogany! He can make you Lady Billy-goat-legs-Lieutenant-and-Major-General-Commander-in-Chief-Sergeant. He has his whole cupboard full of silver, beside what he's got in his bottom drawer.'

'I don't want to go into that dark cupboard!' said the little shepherdess. 'I've heard tell that he has eleven porcelain wives in there already.'

'Then you can make the twelfth!' said the Chinaman. 'Tonight, as soon as the old cupboard there starts to creak, you two are going to be married—as sure as I'm a Chinaman!' And so saying he nodded off to sleep.

But the little shepherdess cried and gazed at her own true love, the porcelain chimney-sweep.

'I do so wish,' she said, 'that you would go away with me into the wide, wide world; for this is no place for us.'

'I'll do anything that you will!' said the little chimney-sweep. 'Let's go at once; I dare say I can support you at my trade.'

'I wish we were well off this table!' she said. 'I shan't be happy till we are away in the wide, wide world!'

And he comforted her, and showed her where to set her little foot on the carved corners and the gilt scrolls of the table-leg. He also made use of his ladder, and before long they had reached the floor. But when they looked across at the old cupboard there was such a commotion! All the carved stags were popping their heads out farther than ever, and were raising their antlers and twisting their necks! Billy-goat-legs-Lieutenant-and-Major-General-Commander-in-Chief-Sergeant was jumping into the air and shouting to the old Chinaman: 'They're running away! They're running away!'

This made them rather frightened and they lost no time in jumping into a drawer. In there were three packs of cards, which weren't complete, and a little toy theatre that had been set up as well as could be. There was a play going on, and all the queens—the queens of diamonds and hearts and of clubs and spades—sat in the front row, fanning themselves with their tulips. And behind them stood all the jacks showing they had heads on top and down below, the way that playing-cards have. The play was about two sweethearts who weren't allowed to have one another, and it made the shepherdess cry, it was so like her own story.

'I simply can't bear it!' she said. 'I must get out of here!' But when they got down to the floor and looked across at the table, they found that the old Chinaman had woken up and was rocking his whole body—down below he was a solid lump.

'Here's the old Chinaman coming!' screamed the little shepherdess. And she fell on her little porcelain knees, she was so miserable.

W·H·R

'I have an idea,' said the chimney-sweep. 'Let's creep into the big pot-pourri jar, in the corner there! We could lie there on a bed of roses and lavender and throw salt in his eyes when he comes near.'

'It won't be much good!' she said. 'Besides, I know that the old Chinaman and the pot-pourri jar have been sweethearts, and you'll always have a soft spot in your heart for someone you've been sweet on. No, there's nothing else for it but to go out into the wide, wide world.'

'Have you really the heart to go with me into the wide, wide world?' asked the chimney-sweep. 'Have you stopped to think how big it is, and that we should never be able to come back again?'

'Yes, I have!' she said.

And the chimney-sweep looked steadily at her, and said: 'My path lies through the chimney. Have you really the heart to creep with me into the fireplace and on through the grate? For then we shall get into the chimney, and once up there I know my way about. We'll climb so high that they'll never reach us, and up at the top there's a hole leading into the wide, wide world!'

And he led her to the fireplace.

'How black it looks!' she said. But she went in with him, into the fireplace and into the grate, where it was pitch-black night.

'Here we are in the chimney,' he said. 'And look! Look! There's the loveliest star shining up above us!'

And it was indeed a star, shining straight down to them from the sky as if to show them the way. And they clambered and they climbed, such a dreadful way: so high! so high! But he lifted her and he levered her, and he held her and he showed her the best places to put her little porcelain feet; and so they came to the very top of the chimney. And there they sat down, for they were so tired, as well they might be.

The sky with all its stars was overhead, and all the city roofs lay outstretched beneath them; they could see so far, so far into the world. The poor little shepherdess had never imagined it to be like this; and laying her little head against her chimney-sweep, she cried so that all the gilt was washed off her sash.

'It's too much for me!' she said. 'I just can't bear it! The world is much too big! Oh, if only I were back on the little table under the mirror! I'll never be happy till I'm back there again! I've come with you into the wide, wide world; now please take me home again, if you care for me at all!'

And the chimney-sweep talked sensibly to her and reminded her of the old Chinaman and of Billy-goat-legs-Lieutenant-and-Major-General-Commander-in-Chief-Sergeant; but she sobbed so pitifully and kissed her little chimney-sweep so, that in the end he had to give way to her, though he knew it was a mistake.

And so back they clambered with great difficulty through the chimney, and crept their way back into the grate—it wasn't a bit nice. So there they stood in the dark fireplace, and they listened quietly to find out what was going on in the room. It was perfectly still. Then they peeped out—oh! There, in the middle of the floor, lay the old Chinaman. He had fallen off the table in trying to follow them, and lay broken in three pieces. His back had come off in one lump, and his head had rolled into a corner. Billy-goat-legs-Lieutenant-and-Major-General-Commander-in-Chief-Sergeant stood where he had always stood, thinking things over.

'How dreadful!' said the little shepherdess. 'Poor old Grandfather's broken in pieces, and it's all our fault! This is too much for me!' And she stood there wringing her tiny hands.

'He can be mended,' said the chimney-sweep. 'He can be mended all right. Now, don't be so upset! When they've cemented him up the back and put a good rivet in his neck he'll be as good as new again, and as disagreeable to us as ever!'

'Do you think so?' she said. And they crept back again to their old place on the table.

'Back where we started from,' said the chimney-sweep. 'We could have saved ourselves all that trouble!'

'I only wish Grandfather was mended again!' said the little shepherdess. 'Will it be very expensive?'

He was mended all right. The family had him cemented up the back and he was given a good rivet in his neck. He was as good as new, but would never nod again.

'You've got rather stuck up since you were broken,' said Billy-goat-legs-Lieutenant-and-Major-General-Commander-in-Chief-Sergeant. 'But I don't see that it's anything to be proud of! Is she to be mine, or isn't she to be mine?'

And the chimney-sweep and the little shepherdess looked so pathetically at the old Chinaman; they were so afraid he would nod. But he couldn't nod, and it was disagreeable to have to tell people that he always wore a rivet in his neck. And so the porcelain people were left to themselves; and they thanked goodness for Grandfather's rivet, and loved one another till they broke.

THE LITTLE MATCH GIRL

IT WAS so dreadfully cold. It was snowing, and the evening was beginning to grow dark. It was also the last evening of the year—New Year's Eve. In this cold and in this darkness a poor little girl was walking in the street, bareheaded and barefooted. True enough, she had been wearing slippers when she had left home, but what was the good of that? They had been very big slippers; her mother had worn them last, so big were they. And these the little girl had lost in hurrying across the street when two carriages had passed by at dreadful speed. One of the slippers was nowhere to be found, and a boy had run off with the other. He had said he would be able to use it for a cradle when he got children of his own.

And so there walked the little girl in her little bare feet that were so red and blue with cold. In an old apron she held a lot of matches, and she had one bundle in her hand. No one had bought any from her all that day; no one had given her a copper. Hungry and frozen she went, looking so very, very sad, the poor little thing! The snowflakes fell on her long golden hair which curled so beautifully round her neck, though it was a sight which she certainly never thought about. Lights shone out from all the windows and in the street there was a lovely smell of roast goose. It was New Year's Eve; she did think of that.

In a corner between two houses, one of which jutted a little farther out into the street than the other, she stopped and crouched down. She drew her little legs up under her but only froze the more, and she dared not go home. She hadn't sold any matches and hadn't got a single copper. Her father would beat her, and even at home it was cold. They had no more than the roof over their heads and the wind whistled through that, stuffed though it was with straw and rags in the biggest cracks. Her little hands were very nearly dead with cold. Oh, a little match might do some good! If only she dared to pull one out of the bundle, strike it against the wall, and warm her fingers. She pulled one out. Ss! How it spluttered, how it flared up! It was a warm, clear flame, just like a little candle when she held her hand round it. It was a wonderful candle. The little girl seemed to be sitting in front of a big iron stove with polished brass knobs and a brass drum. The fire burnt so beautifully, and was so warming. I say, what was that? The little girl was stretching out her feet in order to warm them as well—when the flame went out. The stove vanished, and she sat with a little stump of the burnt-out match in her hand.

A new one was struck. It burnt, it shone; and where the glow fell on the wall it became transparent as gauze. She saw right into the room, where the table was laid with a glistening white table-cloth, with fine china, and with a lovely, steaming roast goose stuffed with prunes and apples. And, even grander still, the goose jumped off the dish, and waddled along the floor with a knife and fork in its back. Right up to the poor little girl it came. Then the match went out, and all that could be seen was the thick, cold wall.

She struck a fresh one. And now she was sitting under the loveliest of Christmas-trees. It was even bigger and more prettily decorated than the one she had seen through the glass door of the rich merchant the Christmas before. Thousands of candles were alight on the green branches, and brightly coloured pictures such as decorated the shop windows looked down towards her. The little girl stretched both her hands into the air—and then the match went out. The Christmas candles all went higher and higher, and she saw that they were the bright stars. One of them fell, leaving a long, fiery strip in the sky.

'Someone's dying!' said the little girl; for old Granny, the only person who had been good to her, but who was dead, had said that when a star falls a soul rises up to God.

She struck another match against the wall. It shone brightly round about, and in its glow stood her old granny: so clear, so shining, so gentle, and so loving.

'Granny!' cried the little girl. 'Please take me with you! I know you'll be gone when the match goes out: gone like the warm stove, the lovely roast goose, and the gorgeous big Christmas-tree!' And hurriedly she struck all the matches left in the bundle; she wanted so much to keep her granny. And the matches shone with such splendour that it was brighter than the light of day. Granny had never before been so beautiful and so big. Lifting the little girl on to her arm, she flew with her in radiance and glory so high, so very, very high. And there was no cold, no hunger, no fear: they were with God.

But there, in the corner by the house in the cold early morning, sat the little girl with rosy cheeks and a smile on her lips—dead, frozen to death on the last evening of the old year. The morning of the New Year rose on that little body sitting with the matches, one bundle of which was almost burnt. She had wanted to warm herself, they said. No one knew what beauty she had seen, or in what radiance she had gone with her old granny into the glad New Year.

THE SHADOW

IN THE hot countries the sun's a real scorcher! People are turned the colour of mahogany; and in the hottest countries of all they get scorched into Negroes. Well now, to the hot countries had come a scholar from the cold ones; and there he thought he could run about the way he did at home. Well, he was soon cured of that. He and every other sensible person had to stay indoors. Shutters and doors were closed all day long; it looked as though the whole house were asleep or there was nobody in. The narrow street with the tall houses where he lived, indeed, had been built so that the sun was sure to be on them from morning to night. It was simply unbearable! The scholar from the cold countries (he was a young man and a wise one) felt as if he were sitting in a red-hot oven. It wore him down and he grew quite thin. Even his shadow shrank and became a good deal smaller than at home—the sun wore that down too. They only livened up in the evening, when the sun had gone down.

It was great fun to watch. As soon as the candle was brought in the shadow would stretch itself right up the wall and even along the ceiling, so long did it grow. It had to stretch itself to pick up strength. The scholar would go out on the balcony to stretch himself there; and as the stars came out in the beautiful clean air he would feel that he was coming to life again. On every balcony in the street—and in the hot countries every window has a balcony—people would appear; for you must have air even if you are used to be being mahogany-coloured. It would grow so lively up and down the street. Cobblers and tailors—everyone—would move into the street. Tables and chairs would come out and lights would be lit. Yes indeed, over a thousand lights would be lit! And one would talk and another would sing, and people would stroll along, carriages would drive past, and donkeys go walking by saying 'ting-a-ling-a-ling' (for they had bells on). There would be funerals and hymn-singing, and street-boys letting off jumping crackers, and church bells ringing—yes, the street would be lively. Only in one house, which was just opposite the one where the stranger-scholar lived, would it be quite still; yet somebody lived there, for standing on the balcony there were flowers. They grew so beautifully in the heat of the sun, and they couldn't have done that without being watered, and somebody would have to water them; there must be somebody there. The door to the balcony over there did open, in fact, towards evening; but it was dark inside, at least in the nearest room. From further in came the sound of music. The stranger-scholar thought that it was marvellous; but then that may only have been his imagination, for he found everything marvellous in the hot countries, as long as the sun didn't shine. The stranger's landlord said that he didn't know who had rented the house opposite; one never saw anybody, and as for music, it seemed dreadfully dull to him. 'It's like somebody practising a piece he can't do; always the same piece. "I'll get it!" he seems to say. But he never will get it, no matter how long he plays.'

One night the stranger woke up. He slept with the balcony door open and the curtain in front of it was being lifted by the wind. And a wonderful radiance seemed to come from the opposite balcony. All the flowers glowed like flames, in the loveliest of colours, and among the flowers stood a slender and graceful young woman; she, too, seemed to glow. His eyes were quite dazzled. He opened them as widely as ever he could and was awake at once. At one bound he was on the floor, and silently he got behind the curtain. But the young woman was gone; the radiance was gone. The flowers no longer glowed, but stood very much as they had always done. The door was ajar, and from deep inside the room the music played so very softly and beautifully; it was easy to fall into sweet meditation at the sound of it. It was like some sort of magic. And who lived there? Where was the actual entrance? Shop after shop filled the ground floor, and people couldn't always be running through there.

One evening the stranger was sitting on his balcony. The candle was burning in the room behind him, and so it was perfectly natural that his shadow should cross over to the opposite neighbour's wall. Yes, there it was, straight across among the flowers on the balcony; and when the stranger moved the shadow moved too, as it will.

'I think my shadow is the only living thing there is over there!' said the scholar. 'See how nicely it sits among the flowers. The door's half open; my shadow should just nip inside, have a look round, and then come and tell me what it's seen. Yes, make yourself useful!' he said in jest. 'Please go inside. Well? Are you going?' And he nodded to the shadow, and the shadow nodded back. 'All right then, go! But don't get lost!' And the stranger got up, and his shadow across on the opposite balcony also got up. And the stranger turned and the shadow turned also; indeed, if anyone had been there to notice it, they would have clearly seen the shadow walk in at the half-open door of the opposite balcony just as the stranger went into his own room, dropping the long curtain behind him.

Next morning the scholar went out to get his breakfast and read the newspapers. 'What's this?' he said, as he came out into the sunshine. 'Why, I've no shadow! Then it did go last night, and it hasn't returned. This is just too bad!'

And he was annoyed at this; though not so much because the shadow was missing as because he knew of another story about a man who hadn't a shadow. It was known to everybody at home in the cold countries; and if the scholar were to go home and tell his, they would say he was copying, and there was no need for him to do that. And so he decided to say nothing about it; and that was a sensible idea.

That evening he went out on his balcony again. He had very properly placed the candle behind him, well knowing that a shadow always wants its master to screen it. But he couldn't coax it out. He made himself small and he made himself big; but there was no shadow, and none came. 'H'm! H'm!' he said; but that did no good.

It was an annoying thing; but in the hot countries everything grows so very quickly, and in a week's time he noticed, to his great delight, a new shadow growing out of his legs when he went into the sun; the root must have been left behind. In three weeks he had quite a passable shadow, which, when he set off for home in the northern countries, grew more and more as he travelled, so that in the end it was too long and too big by half.

And so the scholar returned home and wrote books about what was true in the world, and what was good and what was beautiful. And days passed and years passed: many years passed.

He was sitting one evening in his room when there came a quiet knock at the door.

'Come in!' he said. But no one came. So he opened the door, and there, standing facing him, was such an extraordinarily thin person that it made him feel quite strange. At the same time the person was extremely well dressed, and must have been a man of rank.

'Whom have I the honour to meet?' asked the scholar.

'There,' said the fine gentleman. 'I thought you didn't know me! I've grown so solid; I'm well provided with flesh and clothes. You'll never have expected to see me looking so prosperous. Don't you know your old shadow? Well, I dare say you thought I'd never come back. Things have gone pretty well with me since I was last with you. I've become in every respect a man of property. If I decide to buy myself out of your service, I can!' And he rattled a whole bunch of precious seals which hung by his watch-chain, and thrust his hand into the thick gold chain he wore round his neck. My goodness, how all his fingers glittered with diamond rings! And all the things were real ones.

'Why, I can't make this out at all!' said the scholar. 'What on earth does it mean?'

'Well, you wouldn't call it common!' said the shadow. 'But then you're not one of the common sort, either; and I, you know, have followed in your footsteps since childhood. As soon as you found me ripe enough to go out into the world alone, I went my own way. I'm on the full tide of fortune. But a sort of longing came over me to see you some time before you die—you will die! I also wished to revisit these lands, for a man always feels affection for his native country. I know you have got another shadow in my place. Do I owe it anything? Please let me know if I do.'

'I say, is it really you?' said the scholar. 'Why, this is most remarkable! I'd never have believed that one's old shadow could return a human being!'

'Tell me how much I owe,' said the shadow. 'For I should hate to be in any sort of debt!'

'How can you say such things?' said the scholar. 'What debt is there to talk about? Speak as freely as you wish! I am delighted to hear of your good fortune. Sit down, old fellow, and tell me how it all came about, and what you saw at the opposite neighbour's there in the hot countries!'

'Very well then, I'll tell you,' said the shadow, sitting down. 'But you must promise me this: never, no matter where you may meet me, tell anyone that I was your shadow! I mean to get engaged; I could keep more than one family.'

'Rest assured!' said the scholar. 'I shall tell no one who you really are. There's my hand! I promise; and I'm a man of my word.'

'I'm a shadow of my word,' said the shadow; for that, of course, was the way it had to speak.

Otherwise it was really quite remarkable how human it was. Dressed all in black, it had the finest of black coats, patent-leather boots, and a hat that could be let down flat, leaving only crown and brim—to say nothing of what we already know: the seals, the gold chain round its neck, and the diamond rings. Yes, the shadow was immensely well dressed; and it was just that which made it so very human,

'Now just listen to me!' said the shadow; and with that it placed its feet in the patent-leather boots as hard as it could on the sleeve of the scholar's new shadow, which lay like a poodle-dog near his legs—either from arrogance or perhaps to get it to stick. And the shadow on the floor kept perfectly still and quiet so as to be able to listen. It was anxious to know how a shadow could get loose like this and become its own master.

'Do you know who lived in the house opposite?' said the shadow. 'It was the loveliest of all things—it was poetry! I was there for three weeks, and it was just like living for three thousand years and reading everything that has ever been written. I'm telling you, and it's the truth. I've seen everything, and I know everything!'

'Poetry!' cried the scholar. 'Why yes, she's often an outcast in big cities! Poetry! Yes, I saw her for one brief moment, but I was sleepy. She stood on the balcony, gleaming like the northern lights. Go on, go on! You were on the balcony, you entered the door, and then . . . ?'

'I was in the ante-room,' said the shadow. 'You always sat looking across at the ante-room. There was no light, only a sort of twilight. But one door was open to the next in a long row of rooms and halls. And it was all lit up; I would have been struck dead by the light if I'd gone straight in to the young woman. But I was cool-headed; I gave myself time, as of course one should!'

'And what did you see then?' asked the scholar.

'I saw everything, and I shall tell you about it. But—this isn't pride on my part, only, being free and having the knowledge that I have, to say nothing of my excellent position and my admirable resources—I wish that you would address me as "Sir".'

'I beg pardon!' said the scholar. 'Old habits die hard. You are perfectly right, sir! And I shall remember. But now tell me everything that you saw.'

'Everything!' said the shadow. 'For I saw everything, and I know everything.'

'What did it look like in the inner halls?' asked the scholar. 'Was it like a fresh wood? Was it like a holy temple? Were the halls like the starry sky when you stand on top of mountains?'

'Everything was there!' said the shadow. 'Of course I didn't go right in; I stayed in the outer room, in the twilight. But I had a specially good place there; I saw everything, and I know everything! I have been at the Court of Poetry—in the ante-room.'

'But what did you see? Did all the ancient gods walk the great halls? Were the heroes of old fighting there? Were there sweet children, playing and telling their dreams?'

'I tell you I was there, and believe me I saw everything there was to be seen. Had *you* gone across you wouldn't have become human; but I did! And I also got to know my inner self, my native quality; the relationship I had to poetry. Now, when I was with you I never thought of it; but always, you know, when the sun rose and the sun set I grew so very big. By moonlight I would be almost plainer to see than you yourself. Then I never understood my nature; in the ante-room I realized it. I became a man! I came out mature, but you were no longer in the warm countries. As a man I was ashamed to go about as I was: I needed boots, clothes, all the human veneer that makes a man recognizable. I took the path—I can safely tell it to you, you won't publish it—I took the path to the old woman's petticoats, where I hid myself. She had no idea how much she was hiding. I only went out at night. I ran about the streets by moonlight. I flattened myself against the wall—it gives you a lovely tickling feeling in the back! I ran up and I ran down, looking in at the top windows, into the hall and on the roof. I looked where no one could see, and I saw what no one else saw; what no one was meant to see! When all's said and done, it's a mean world. I'd never want to be human, but for the fact that it's the thing to be. I saw the most unimaginable things in wives, in husbands, in parents, and in the dear, wonderful children. I saw,' went on the shadow, 'what no one was supposed to know, but what everyone was so eager to know—ill of their neighbour. Had I been writing a newspaper, it would have been read! But I wrote direct to the person himself, and there was great alarm in every town I visited. They were so afraid of me that they grew very fond of me. The professors made me a professor, the tailors gave me new clothes (I'm well rigged out), the mint-master minted money for me, and the women said I was so handsome! And so I became the man I am. And now I'll say goodbye. Here's my card; I live on the sunny side and am always at home when it's wet.' And so saying the shadow was gone.

'How very strange!' said the scholar.

Time passed by, and one day the shadow returned.

'How are things going?' it asked.

'Alas,' said the scholar, 'I write of truth, of goodness, and of beauty, but nobody cares to hear about them. I'm full of despair, for I take it so much to heart!'

'Ah, but I don't!' said the shadow. 'I'm getting fat, and that's the thing to do. You, now, you're no judge of the world. You're making yourself ill. You should travel. I shall be going on a journey next summer. Will you go with me? I could do with a companion! Will you come as my shadow? I'll be delighted to have you with me, and I'll pay the travelling expenses!'

'That's going a bit far!' said the scholar.

'As you care to take it!' said the shadow. 'It'll do you a world of good to go away. Be my shadow and you shall have everything on the journey paid for.'

'This is the limit!' said the scholar.

'Ah, but it's the way of the world!' said the shadow. 'And it isn't going to change.' And the shadow was gone.

The scholar was in a bad way, dogged by grief and trouble; and what he had to say about truth, goodness, and beauty was to most people like offering roses to a cow! In the end he was really ill.

'You look just like a shadow!' people told him; and the very thought of it made the scholar shudder.

'You should go to a health resort!' said the shadow, who called to see him. 'That's all there is for it. I'll go with you for the sake of old times. I'll pay for the journey and you can write the description and provide me with a little entertainment on the way. I'm going to a health resort; my whiskers aren't growing as they should, and you've got to grow whiskers! Now be sensible and take what I offer; we shall be travelling as old friends.'

And so they set off. The shadow was master now, and the master was the shadow. They drove together and they rode and walked together, side by side, before and behind, the way the sun turned. The shadow always managed to keep on the master's side, the scholar never giving the matter a thought. He was a good-hearted man, very kind and very friendly; and one day he said to the shadow: 'Now that we've become travelling companions, you and I, and moreover have grown up from childhood together, let's call each other by our Christian names. It's more friendly!'

'What's that you say?' said the shadow, now, of course, the real master. 'That was very frank and well meant of you; I'll be equally frank and well-meaning with you. You who are a scholar must know the strangeness of human nature. Some people cannot touch grey paper without feeling ill; others get the shudders if a nail is rubbed against a window-pane. It gives me the same sort of feeling when you're familiar with me: I feel flattened out as in my first job with you. It's only a feeling, you understand; it isn't pride. I can't allow you to use my Christian name, but I'm quite willing to use yours. That'll be something!'

And so the shadow called its former master by his Christian name.

'It's really the limit,' he thought, 'that I should have to be so polite, while he's so familiar with me!' Yet he had to put up with it.

And so they came to a health resort, where there were many visitors; and among them there was a lovely princess who had the failing that she saw only too well, and a very alarming failing it was.

She saw at once that the newcomer was an altogether different person from all the rest. 'He's here to grow whiskers, they say, but I see the real reason: he can't cast a shadow.'

Her curiosity had been aroused; and so she at once opened a conversation with the strange gentleman while out walking. As a princess she didn't have to stand on ceremony, and so she said: 'Your complaint is that you can't cast a shadow.'

'Your royal highness must be getting a lot better,' said the shadow. 'I know that your trouble is that you see only too well, but that's gone over: you are cured. As it happens, I have a rather unusual shadow. Do you see the person who always goes about with me? Other people have an ordinary shadow, but I don't care for ordinary things. One gives one's servant finer livery than the clothes one wears oneself, and so I've had my shadow polished up and made human; indeed, you will see that I have even given him a shadow. It's very costly, but I like to have something of my very own!'

'What?' said the princess. 'Can I really have recovered? This resort is the best in the world! The water nowadays has rather marvellous powers. But I shall not leave, for now it's getting interesting here. I have an extremely high opinion of this stranger. So long as his whiskers don't grow, because then he'll leave!'

In the big ball-room that evening the princess and the shadow danced together. She was light, but he was even lighter; such a dancer she had never seen. She told him the country where she came from, and he knew it: he had been there, though she had been away at the time. He said he had looked in at the windows upstairs and downstairs and seen this, that, and the other; and he knew how to answer the princess and throw out hints, a thing which quite surprised her. He must be the wisest man on earth, she thought. She developed such a respect for what he knew; and when they had another dance together she fell in love, as the shadow could tell, because she pretty well looked straight through him. Then they had yet another dance, and she was just about to tell him; only she was careful and thought of her country and her kingdom, and all the many people she would reign over. 'He's a wise man all right,' she said to herself. 'That's a good point. And he's a lovely dancer; that's another good point. But I wonder whether he has any real knowledge; that's just as important! He must be examined.' And so little by little she began to ask him some of the most difficult things that she couldn't have answered herself. And the shadow made a very strange face.

'You don't know the answer to that!' said the princess.

'I learnt it as a child,' said the shadow. 'I even think my shadow, over there by the door, will know the answer.'

'Your shadow!' said the princess. That *would* be remarkable!'

'Well, I don't say for certain that he will,' said the shadow. 'But I should think so; he's followed me about, now, for so many years, listening to me—I should think he will! But allow me to point out to your royal highness that he takes such pride in passing for human that if he's to be in the proper humour (and to give the right answers he must be) he must be treated as human.'

'I like that!' said the princess.

And so she crossed over to the scholar by the door, and talked to him about the sun and the moon and about man inside and out; and he answered wisely and well.

'What a man that must be, to have such a wise shadow!' she thought. 'It would be a real blessing to my people and my kingdom if I were to choose him as my husband. I will!'

And they were soon agreed, the princess and the shadow. Only no one was to know before she returned home to her own kingdom.

'No one, not even my shadow!' said the shadow. And he had his own reasons for that . . .

And so they came to the country where the princess reigned when she was at home.

'I say, old fellow!' said the shadow to the scholar. 'I'm as successful and as powerful now as anyone. Now I'm going to do something extra-special for you! You shall always live at the palace with me, drive with me in my royal carriage, and have five thousand pounds a year. In return you must allow everyone to call you shadow, you must never tell anyone that you were ever human, and once a year, when I sit in the sunshine on the balcony showing myself off, you must lie at my feet as a shadow should. I may tell you that I'm marrying the princess; the wedding will take place tonight.'

'Well, this is really the limit!' said the scholar. 'I won't; I'm not going to. It's cheating the whole country, and the princess into the bargain. I'll tell everything: that I'm human and you're the shadow, that you're only dressed up!'

'Nobody will believe it,' said the shadow. 'Now be sensible, or I'll call in the watch!'

'I'm going straight to the princess!' said the scholar. 'But I'm going first,' said the shadow. 'And you're going to get locked up!' And he was; for the sentries obeyed the one whom the princess was to marry, as they knew the princess would wish them to do.

'You're trembling!' said the princess, when the shadow went to her. 'Has anything happened? You mustn't fall ill tonight, the night of our wedding.'

'I've had the most awful experience one could ever have,' said the shadow. 'Just fancy—it doesn't take much to upset the miserable mind of a shadow! Just fancy! My shadow has gone mad. He thinks he's human and that I—just fancy!—that I'm his shadow!'

'How dreadful!' said the princess. 'Surely he's been locked up?'

'He has! I'm afraid he'll never be himself again.'

'Poor shadow!' said the princess. 'How wretched he is! It would be a happy release to rid him of what little life he has. And come to think of it, I think we shall have to do away with him quietly.'

'It's a hard thing!' said the shadow. 'He was a good servant!' And he gave what seemed like a sigh.

'You have a noble character!' said the princess.

That evening the whole city was illuminated, the cannon went 'Boom! Boom!' and the soldiers presented arms. It *was* a wedding! The princess and the shadow went out on to the balcony to show themselves and got another cheer.

The scholar heard nothing of all this; for they had done away with him . . .

THE OLD HOUSE

JUST UP the street there was an old, old house. It was nearly three hundred years old. This you could read on the beam, where the date was carved along with tulips and hop-bines. There were whole verses, spelt as in olden days, and cut in the beam over every window was a head which made faces. One storey hung a good way out over the other, and just below the roof was a lead gutter with a dragon's head on it. The rain was supposed to run out of its jaws, but it ran out of its stomach as there was a hole in the gutter.

All the other houses in the street were so very new and smart, with large windows and smooth walls. It was easy to see that they would have nothing to do with the old house. They would be thinking: 'How long is that monstrosity going to clutter up the street? First the bow window sticks out so much that nobody can see from our windows what goes on over there; and then the steps are wide enough for a palace and high enough for a church tower. The balustrade looks for all the world like an entrance to an old burial vault, and has even got brass knobs on. What an object!'

The houses across the street were also new and smart, and they had the same idea as the rest. But sitting at a window there was a little boy with fresh red cheeks and clear bright eyes, and he certainly liked the old house best, both in sunshine and by moonlight. And looking across at the wall where the plaster had come off, he would sit and make out the strangest of pictures, seeing the street exactly as it had used to look, with its steps, its bow windows, and its pointed gables. He would see soldiers with pikes, and gutters which ran about like dragons and serpents. It was a house to look at, indeed! And in it there lived an old man who wore velveteen trousers, a frock-coat with brass buttons on it, and a wig which anyone could see was a proper wig. Every morning an old manservant came to the house to tidy up for him and run errands; otherwise the old man in the velveteens was all alone in the old house. From time to time he would come to the window and look out; and the little boy would nod to him and the old man would nod back, and so they got to know each other and were friends, though they had never spoken to one another. But that made no difference to them.

The little boy heard his parents say: 'The old man over there is quite well off, but he's so terribly lonely!'

The Sunday after that the little boy took something which he wrapped in a piece of paper, and, going to the gate, he said to the man who went errands as he passed by: 'I say, will you take this to the old man there from me? I've got two tin soldiers and this is one of them. It's for him, as I know he's so terribly lonely.'

And looking very pleased, the old man nodded and took the tin soldier across to the old house. Later on there came a message to ask whether the little boy would like to call at the house himself. His parents said that he might, and so across he went to the old house.

And the brass knobs on the balustrade shone even brighter than ever, so that anyone would have thought that they had been polished up specially for the visit. And the carved trumpeters—for carved in the tulips on the door were some trumpeters—seemed to be blowing away with all their might: their cheeks looked so much fatter than they had done before. Yes, they played 'Ta-ra-ta-ra-tah! The little boy's coming! Ta-ra-ta-ra-tah!' And then the door opened. The hall was hung with old portraits of knights in armour and ladies in silk dresses, and their armour rattled and their silk dresses rustled. And then there was a staircase. It went a long way up and a short way down, and you were on a balcony: a very frail one, to be sure, with big gaps and long cracks in it. Growing out of all these were grass and plants; for the whole balcony outside the house-wall was overgrown with so much greenery that it looked like a garden, though it was no more than a balcony. Standing on it were old plant-pots with faces and dogs' ears on them. The flowers were growing just anyhow. One pot was overflowing with pinks; that is to say with the foliage, shoot by shoot. And it said as plainly as anything: 'The air has stroked me and the sun has kissed me and promised me a little flower on Sunday, a little flower on Sunday!'

And from there they entered a room where the walls were covered in pigskin on which were printed gilt flowers.

'Gilding's soon gone;
But pigskin lives on!'

said the walls.

And there were armchairs with such high backs and such carving on them, and with arms on both sides. 'Sit down! Sit down!' they said. 'Ugh, how my joints crack! I'm in for rheumatics like the old cupboard. Rheumatics in my back—ugh!'

And the little boy was in the room where the bow window was and the old man used to sit.

'Thank you for the tin soldier, my little friend,' said the old man. 'And thanks for coming across to see me.'

'Thanks! Thanks!'—or 'Crack! Crack!'—came from every piece of furniture. There were so many of them that they almost fell over one another trying to see the little boy.

And in the middle of the wall hung a picture of a lovely lady: so young and so happy, yet dressed in the clothes of olden days, with powdered hair and stiff skirts. She didn't say either 'Thanks' or 'Crack', but gazed at the little boy with her gentle eyes, so that he at once asked the old man: 'Where did you get her?'

'At the second-hand dealer's!' said the old man. 'There are so many pictures there. Nobody knows them or cares anything about them. But in days gone by I used to know her. And now she's been dead and gone these fifty years!'

And underneath the picture, framed in glass, hung a bunch of withered flowers; they, too, must have been fifty years old, so old did they look. And the pendulum of the big clock swung to and fro, and the pointer turned, and everything in the room went on growing older, though none of them noticed it.

'They say at home,' said the little boy, 'that you are so terribly lonely!'

'Oh,' he said. 'Old memories, and what goes with them, come to visit me. And now you have come! I'm all right!'

And from the shelf he took down a book of pictures. There were pictures showing big long processions, with the most wonderful coaches such as you never see nowadays, and soldiers like the jack of clubs, and citizens carrying waving banners. The flags carried by the tailors had a pair of scissors on them, held by two lions, while the shoemakers' had, not a boot, but an eagle which had two heads: for shoemakers must always be able to say 'It's a pair!' Yes, this *was* a picture-book!

And then the old man went into the next room to get some sweets and apples and nuts. Indeed, it was heavenly in the old house.

'I can't bear it!' said the tin soldier, who stood on the chest of drawers. 'It's so lonely here, and so dreary. No, when you've known a home life, you can never get used to this. I can't bear it! The days are so long and the evenings longer still. It isn't a bit like being at your house, where your father and mother talked so cheerfully and all you nice children made such a lovely noise. Oh, how lonely the old man is! Do you think he gets kissed? Do you think he gets nice looks, or a Christmas-tree? He'll get nothing—only a funeral. I can't bear it!'

'You shouldn't take it so seriously!' said the little boy. 'I think it's so lovely here. And then all the old memories, and what goes with them, come to visit the house!'

'Oh, those! I never see them, and don't know them,' said the tin soldier. 'I can't bear it!'

'You'll have to!' said the little boy.

And then the old man came in with the happiest of faces and the loveliest of sweets and apples and nuts. And the little boy thought no more of the tin soldier.

The little boy went home happy and delighted. And the days passed and the weeks passed, and nods passed to the old house and from the old house. And then one day the little boy went there again.

And the carved trumpets played 'Ta-ra-ta-ra-tah! Here's the little boy! Ta-ra-ta-ra-tah!' And swords and armour rattled in the pictures of the knights, and the silk dresses rustled, the pigskin talked, and the old chairs had rheumatics in the back. 'Ooh!' It was exactly like the first time; for over there every day, every hour, was like the last.

'I can't bear it!' said the tin soldier. 'I've wept tears of tin! It's all so miserable here! You might as well send me to the war, to lose my arms and legs! At least it would be a change. I can't bear it! Now I know what it's like to be visited by old memories and what they bring with them. Mine have visited me; and you take my word for it, it's no pleasure in the long run. In the end I was nearly ready to jump off this chest of drawers. I saw you all from the house over there as plainly as if you had been here. It was that Sunday morning again, you know! You children all stood up at table singing your hymns, just as you sing them every morning. You stood with your hands reverently folded, and Father and Mother were just as solemn. And then the door opened, and your little sister Maria, who's less than two years old, and who always dances whenever she hears music or singing, no matter what sort, was let in. She shouldn't have been. And she began to dance, but couldn't get in step as the notes were so long; and first she stood on one leg and tilted her head forward, and then she stood on the other leg and tilted her head forward, but still it wouldn't do. You all stood very serious, though it must have been hard. But I laughed to myself; and so I fell off the table and got a bump which I still have, because it wasn't proper of me to laugh. But now it's all come right back to me, along with everything else I've been through. That must be old memories and what goes with them. Tell me, do you still sing on Sundays? Tell me something about little Maria! And how's my old comrade, the other tin soldier? Ah yes, he's happy enough!—I can't bear it!'

'You've been given away!' said the little boy. 'You'll have to stay. Can't you see that?'

And the old man brought a tray with a lot of things to see: pencil-cases, scent-boxes, and old cards of such size and fine gilding as we never see now. And big drawers were opened and the piano was opened. It had a landscape on the inside of the lid, and was so hoarse when the old man played it. And then he hummed a song.

'Yes, she could sing that!' he said, and he nodded to the portrait which he had brought at the second-hand dealer's. And the old man's eyes shone very brightly.

'I want to go to war! I want to go to war!' cried the tin soldier, as loud as he could. And he toppled down on to the floor.

Well now, where had he got to? The old man searched and the little boy searched; but he was lost, and he remained lost. 'I'll find him!' said the old man. But he never did find him. The floor was too open and cracked. The tin soldier had fallen through a gap; and there he lay, in an open grave.

And that day passed and the little boy went home; and the week passed, and several weeks passed. The windows were quite frozen. The little boy had to sit breathing on them to make himself a peep-hole across to the old house. There the snow had drifted into all the scrolls and inscriptions, and it lay right up over the steps. And there was nobody in: the old man was dead.

That evening a carriage stopped outside, and they carried him into it in his coffin; he was to be taken into the country to be buried. That's where he went now. But no one went with him, for all his friends were dead. And the little boy threw a kiss to the coffin as it drove off.

A few days later there was an auction at the old house, and from his window the little boy watched them take away the old knights and the old ladies, the plant-pots with the long ears, the old chairs and the old cupboards. Some went one way, some the other. The portrait of the lady that had been found at the second-hand dealer's went back to the second-hand dealer's; and there it stayed, for no one knew her any more and no one cared for the old picture.

In the spring they pulled down the house itself; for it was a monstrosity, people said. You could see from the street straight into the room with the pigskin wall-covering, which was slashed and torn. And the greenery round the balcony hung desolately from the falling beams . . . And then they cleared up.

'That helped!' said the neighbouring houses . . .

And then they built a lovely house with big windows and smooth white walls. But in front, on the very spot where the old house had stood, they planted a small garden, and wild vines grew from it up the neighbour's walls. In front of the garden they put up a big iron fence with an iron gate. It looked grand. People would stand still and look in. And sparrows by the score clung to the vines, chattering away all at once as best they could. Only it wasn't about the old house, for they couldn't remember that. So many years had gone by that the little boy had grown into a man: and a clever man, whom his parents were proud of. He had just got married and with his young wife had moved into the house by the garden. And he stood beside her one day while she planted a wild flower which she had thought so pretty. She planted it with her tiny hand and patted the ground with her fingers . . . Oh! What was that? She had pricked herself. Something pointed was sticking out of the soft earth.

It was—just fancy, it was the tin soldier! The one that had got lost in the old man's house, and had been hustled and jostled about among timber and gravel and finally had been buried for many years in the earth.

And the young wife wiped the soldier, first with a green leaf, and then with her handkerchief. It had such a lovely smell! The tin soldier felt himself waking up after a deep sleep.

'Let me see him!' said the young man, laughing as he shook his head. 'Well, it can't be the same one, but he reminds me of a tin soldier I had when I was a little boy.' And he told his wife about the old house and the old man, and about the tin soldier he had sent across to him because he had been so dreadfully lonely. And he told it all so exactly as it had happened that his young wife had tears in her eyes as she heard of the old house and the old man.

'It might very well be the same soldier!' she said. 'I'll keep it and remember all that you have told me. But you must show me the old man's grave!'

'Why, I don't know it!' he said. 'And nobody knows it. All his friends were dead. Nobody looked after it, and I was only a little boy.'

'How dreadfully lonely he must have been!' she said.

'Dreadfully lonely!' said the tin soldier. 'And yet how lovely it is not to be forgotten.'

'Lovely!' cried something close by. But only the tin soldier saw that it was a scrap of the pigskin wall-covering. It had lost all its gilt and it looked like wet earth. But it had an opinion; and it said:

'Gilding's soon gone;
But pigskin lives on.'

Only, the tin soldier didn't believe it.

THE DROP OF WATER

YOU will know what a magnifying-glass is: a sort of round spectacle glass which makes everything seem a hundred times bigger than it is. If you hold it in front of your eye and look through it at a drop of pond water, you see thousands of funny little creatures which you don't usually see in water; though they're there, and that's a fact. They look very much like a plateful of shrimps, all hopping about together. And they're so ferocious, they tear one another limb from limb and into little bits and pieces. And yet they're happy and contented in their way.

Now, once upon a time there was an old man whom everyone called Creepy-Crawly, for that was his name. He always liked to get the best out of anything, and when nothing else would do he used to get it by magic.

Now, he was sitting one day, holding his magnifying-glass to his eye and looking at a drop of water taken from a puddle in the ditch. I say, what a creeping and a crawling there was! The thousands of tiny creatures were hopping and jumping about, tugging at one another and eating one another.

'Why, but this is atrocious!' said old Creepy-Crawly. 'Can't we make them live in peace and quietness, going about their own business?' And he pondered and he pondered, though all to no use. And so he had to try magic. 'I must give them some colour, so they're easier to see,' he said. And so he poured into the drop of water what looked like a drop of red wine, only it was witch's blood—the very best you can get for twopence. And then all the funny little creatures turned rosy-red all over their bodies. It looked like a town full of naked savages.

'What have you got there?' asked another old magician who had no name—which was the great thing about him.

'Well, if you can guess what it is,' said Creepy-Crawly, 'I'll make you a present of it. But it isn't easy to tell when you don't know!'

And so the magician who had no name looked through the magnifying-glass. It did indeed look like a town, with all the people in it running about without any clothes on! It was horrible! But it was even more horrible to see the way one pummelled and pounded another, and how they pinched and nipped and bit and tugged at one another. The ones at the bottom had to get to the top, and the ones on top had to get to the bottom. 'Look! Look! His leg's longer than mine! Biff! Off with him! There's somebody with a pimple behind his ear! A harmless little pimple; but it troubles him, and it's going to trouble him more!' And they hacked at him and they heaved at him, and they ate him for the sake of that little pimple. Another was sitting as quietly as any little lady, wanting nothing more than to be left alone in peace. And so they went for her; and they tugged at her and they tore at her, and they ate her!

'How very fascinating!' said the magician.

'Yes, but what do you think it is?' asked Creepy-Crawly. 'Can you make it out?'

'It's plain enough to see,' said the other. 'Of course it's Copenhagen, or another city. They're all alike! Anyway, it's a city!'

'It's ditch-water!' said Creepy-Crawly.

THE HAPPY FAMILY

THE biggest green leaf we have in this country is surely that of the butterbur. If you hold it in front of your tummy it makes quite a little apron, and if you put it on your head, then when it rains it's almost as good as an umbrella, for it's really enormous. One butterbur never grows by itself: where there's one there are sure to be more. It makes a splendid show, and all this splendour is food for snails, the large white snails which fashionable people in olden days used to make into a stew and then eat and say 'H'm, tastes good!' (because they thought they were lovely). These snails lived on butterbur leaves, and that's why the butterburs were grown.

Now, there was an old country mansion where they no longer ate snails, and they had died out. But the butterburs hadn't died out: they had spread and spread over all the paths and all the beds and had got quite out of hand—it was a whole forest of butterburs. Here and there grew an apple- or a plum-tree, and but for these you would never have taken it for a garden at all—everything was butterburs. And in there lived the last two ever-so-old snails.

They themselves had no idea how old they were; but they could remember that there had been many more of them, that they belonged to a family from foreign parts, and that it was for them and theirs that the forest had been planted. They had never been outside it, but they knew that there was another part of the world called the manor house and that there you were cooked, and then you turned black and were laid on a silver dish. But what happened after that they didn't know. And what it was like to be cooked and lie on a silver dish they couldn't tell, though it was supposed to be delicious as well as extremely fashionable. Neither the cockchafer, the toad, nor the worm whom they inquired of could give them any information: none of them had ever been cooked, or lain on a silver dish.

That the old white snails were the most fashionable in the world they did know; the forest was for their sake, and the manor house was there for them to be cooked and laid on a silver dish.

They now lived happily all by themselves, and having no children of their own, had adopted a little ordinary snail, which they were bringing up as theirs; only the little one wouldn't grow, being an ordinary snail. Still, the old people, and especially Mother—Mother Snail—thought they could see *some* growth in him. And she told Father, if he couldn't see it, to take a feel at the little shell; and he felt and agreed that Mother was right.

One day it was raining heavily.

'Listen to it rum-tum-tumming on the butterburs!' said Father Snail.

'And it's raining in!' said Mother Snail. 'It's coming straight down the stalks. Take my word for it, it's going to be wet! I'm thankful for these good shells of ours, and for our little one's. We've certainly had a lot more done for us than any other creatures have had; anybody can see we're the gentlefolk of this world! We have a house from birth, and the butterbur forest was sown all for our sake . . . I wonder how far it goes, and what's beyond it?'

'There's nothing beyond it,' said Father Snail. 'There couldn't be a better place than this, and I wish for nothing else!'

'Well,' said Mother Snail, 'for my part I'd like to go to the manor house, and be cooked and laid on a silver dish. All our forefathers have been, and you may be sure there's something special about it!'

'The manor house may have fallen in,' said Father Snail. 'Or the butterbur forest may have overgrown it all, so the people are unable to get out. And anyway, why all this rush? You always have to be in such a desperate hurry; and now the youngster's starting. The way he's climbed up that stalk these last three days, it makes me giddy to see him!'

'Now don't upset yourself!' said Mother Snail. 'He's very careful about the way he climbs; he's going to be a great comfort to us, and we two old snails have nothing but him to live for. But have you given any thought to the question of where we're going to find him a wife? Don't you think that, deep inside the butterbur forest, there should be some of our own kind?'

'Slugs! I think there are some of those,' said Father. 'Black slugs, without a shell to their backs. But they're so common, and have such big ideas! However, we could commission the ants to find one. They go running to and fro, looking very busy; I dare say they would know of a wife for our little snail.'

'We know of a really lovely one!' said the ants. 'But we're afraid it's no use, as she's a queen.'

'That's all right!' said the old snail. 'Has she got a house?'

'She has a palace!' said the ants. 'The loveliest ant palace, with seven hundred passages!'

'No, thanks!' said Mother Snail. 'Our son's going into no ant-hill! If that's the best you can do we'll commission the midges. They fly about a good deal, in rain and in sunshine; and they know the butterbur forest inside out.'

'We have a wife for him,' said the midges. 'Sitting on a gooseberry bush a hundred man's paces from here is a little snail with a house of her own. She's rather lonely, and of marrying age. Only a hundred man's paces away!'

'All right, then let her come to him,' said the snail. 'He has a butterbur forest; she has only a bush!'

And so they went and fetched the little lady snail. It was a week before she got there, but that was all in her favour, for it showed that she was of the right stock.

And so they were married. Six glow-worms shone for all they were worth; but apart from that it all went off very quietly, as the old snail folk couldn't stand a lot of feasting and merry-making. But a nice speech was made by Mother Snail; Father couldn't, he was so moved. And they left to them the whole butterbur forest, saying what they had always said, that it was the best place in the world, and that if they lived decently and honestly and increased and multiplied, then they and their children would one day go to the manor house and be cooked black and laid on a silver dish.

And after the speech was made the old folk went into their shells and never came out again; they had fallen asleep. The young snail couple reigned in the forest and had a large family, but they were never cooked and they never got laid on a silver dish. From this they concluded that the manor house had fallen in, and that all the people in the world had died out; and as nobody contradicted them, then of course it was true. And the rain played rum-tum-tum on the butterbur leaves for their sake, and the sun shone to give colour to the butterbur forest for their sake, and they were very happy: the whole family were happy, indeed they were.

THE STORY OF A MOTHER

A MOTHER sat with her little child. She was so very sad, so afraid he was going to die. He was so pale, his little eyes had closed, and he was breathing so very softly, with now and then a deep breath as though he were sighing. And then the mother would gaze even more sorrowfully at the little soul.

All at once there was a knock at the door, and in came a poor old man, wrapped up in what looked like a big horse-blanket. It was warming, and he needed warming, as it was a cold winter. Everything outside was covered in ice and snow, and the wind was blowing fit to cut anyone's face.

And as the old man was shivering with cold and the little child for a moment was asleep, the mother went and put a small potful of beer in the oven to warm for him. And the old man sat and rocked, and the mother sat down on the chair beside him, watching her sick child, who was breathing deeply, and holding his little hand.

'Don't you think I shall be allowed to keep him?' she said. 'Our Lord won't take him from me!'

And the old man, who was none other than Death himself, nodded so strangely that it could just as well have meant No as Yes. And the mother looked down into her lap, the tears running down her cheeks. Her head grew so heavy. For three days and nights she hadn't closed her eyes, and so now she fell asleep. But only for a moment, then she started up, shivering with cold. 'What is it?' she cried, looking around her. But the old man was gone and her little child was gone; he had taken the child with him. And over in the corner the old clock went whirring away and the big lead weight fell with a bump to the floor; then the clock itself stood still.

The poor mother ran out of the house, calling for her child.

Sitting in the snow out there was a woman in long black clothes, and she said: 'Death was in your house. I saw him hurrying off with your little child. He is faster than the wind, and never returns what he has taken!'

'Only tell me which way he went!' said the mother. 'Tell me the way, and I shall find him!'

'I know it,' said the woman in the black clothes. 'But before I tell it, you must sing to me all the songs you used to sing for your child. I like them; I've heard them before. I am Night. I saw your tears as you sang them.'

'I'll sing them all—all!' said the mother. 'Only don't stop me from overtaking him and finding my child!'

But Night sat silent and still. And so the mother, wringing her hands, sang and wept. And there were many songs, but many more tears. And then Night said: 'Go to the left, into the dark pine forest. I saw Death take that way with your little child.'

Deep in the wood the paths crossed, and she no longer knew the way to go. Growing there was a hawthorn bush. There was neither blossom nor leaves on it; of course, it was the depth of winter and ice was hanging from the branches.

'Did you see Death go by with my little child?'

'Yes!' said the hawthorn. 'But I won't tell you which way he went unless you warm me up at your heart first. I'm freezing cold; I'll soon be all ice.'

And she clasped the hawthorn tightly to her breast so as to warm it thoroughly; and the thorns went right into her flesh and her blood flowed in big drops. But the hawthorn put forth fresh green leaves, and flowers grew on it in the cold wintry night; so warm it was by a sorrowing mother's heart. And the hawthorn told her the way to go.

She then came to a big lake where there was neither ship nor boat. The lake wasn't frozen hard enough to bear her, nor was it open and shallow enough for her to wade through; but cross it she must, if she was to find her child. And so she lay down in order to drink up the lake, though of course this was too much for any person. But the sorrowing mother thought that a miracle might happen.

'No, that will never do!' said the lake. 'Better let us two agree to something. I like to collect pearls, and your eyes are the two clearest I have ever seen. Cry them out for me and I'll carry you across to the great glass-house where Death lives and cares for flowers and trees, each one of them a human life.'

'Oh, what would I not give to get to my child!' said the weeping mother. And she wept all the more, till her eyes sank down to the bottom and became two precious pearls. But then the lake lifted her up as on a swing and at one swing she flew across to the opposite shore, where there was a strange house that was a mile wide. There was no telling whether it was a mountain with forests and caves, or whether it was really a building, for the poor mother was unable to see it, as of course she had cried her eyes out.

'Where am I to find Death, who carried off my little child?' she said.

'He hasn't come yet,' said the old woman who had to look after Death's big glass-house. 'How did you find your way here? And who helped you?'

'Our Lord helped me!' she said. 'He is merciful, and so will you be! Where am I to find my little child?'

'Well, I don't know him,' said the woman, 'and you can't see. Many flowers and trees have withered in the night, and Death will soon come and replant them. You surely know that every person has his tree or flower of life, all according to the way each is made. They look like other plants, but they have heart-beats. Children's hearts can beat too! Follow that and you may tell your child's. But what will you give me for telling you what more to do?'

'I have nothing to give,' said the sorrowing mother. 'But I'll go to the ends of the earth for you.'

'Why, I've nothing to do there,' said the woman. 'But you can give me your long black hair. You yourself know that it is beautiful, and I like it! You shall have my white hair in exchange. That's always something!'

'If that's all you ask,' she said, 'I'll give it to you with pleasure!' And she gave her her beautiful black hair and got the old woman's snow-white hair in exchange.

And then they went into Death's big glass-house, where flowers and trees grew strangely mixed up together. There were fine hyacinths under cloches, and there were big bouncing peonies. There were water plants growing there, a few fresh and others half sick. Water snakes were lying on them and black crabs were nipping their stalks. There were lovely palm-trees, and oaks and plane-trees. There was parsley and there was flowering thyme. Every tree and every flower had its name, each was a human life and the person was still alive: one in China, one in Greenland, some all round the world. There were big trees in small pots, looking all squeezed in and ready to burst them. In many places, too, there was a dull little flower in rich soil with moss all round it, nursed and coddled. The sorrowing mother stooped down over all the tiniest plants and listened inside where the human heart was beating, and among millions of others she recognized her own child's.

'Here it is!' she cried, stretching out her hand over a little blue crocus that was drooping and looked quite ill.

'Don't touch the flower!' said the old woman. 'But stand here, and when Death comes (and he'll come when I least expect him) see that he doesn't pull the plant up. If you threaten to do the same to the other flowers, he'll be frightened. He has to answer for them to our Lord. None of them may be pulled up till He gives permission.'

All at once there was a whistling of an icy cold wind, and the blind mother could feel that Death had come.

'How did you find your way here?' he asked. 'How could you get here sooner than I?'

'I am a mother,' she said.

And Death stretched out his long hand towards the delicate little flower. But she held her hands firmly round it; very closely, and yet afraid of touching one of the petals. Then Death blew on her hands, and it felt colder to her than the cold wind, and her hands fell weakly down.

'You see, you can do nothing against me!' said Death.

'But our Lord can!' she said.

'I only do as He wills!' said Death. 'I am His gardener. I take all His flowers and trees and plant them out in the great Garden of Paradise, in the unknown country. But how they grow there, and what it is like there, I can't tell you.'

'Give me back my child!' said the mother, and she wept and pleaded. Then all at once she seized in her hands two beautiful flowers that grew nearby, crying to Death as she did so: 'I'll tear off all your flowers, for I am desperate!'

'Don't touch them!' said Death. 'You say that you are unhappy, and now you'd make another mother as unhappy as yourself.'

'Another mother?' said the poor woman, letting go of the flowers.

'There are your eyes!' said Death. 'I fished them up in the lake, where they shone so brightly. I didn't know they were yours. Take them back; they are clearer now than ever. Now look down into the deep well by your side. I'll tell you the names of the two flowers you were going to pull up, and you'll see their whole future; see what you were going to destroy.'

And she looked into the well. And it was a delight to see how one of them brought happiness into the world, and how much joy and pleasure was spread around it. And then she saw the other's life and it was grief and trouble, unhappiness and misery.

'Both are the will of God,' said Death.

'Which is the flower of unhappiness, which of happiness?' she asked.

'I shall not tell you,' said Death. 'But this much I will say: one of the flowers was your own child's. It was your child's fate, your own child's future that you saw.'

At this the mother cried out in fear: 'Which of them was my child? Tell me! Save the innocent one! Take him away instead! Take him into the kingdom of God! Forget my tears. Forget my prayers, and everything I have said and done!'

'I do not understand you,' said Death. 'Do you wish for your child back again? Or shall I take him with me to the place you do not know?'

Hearing this the mother wrung her hands and, falling on to her knees, prayed to our Lord. 'Do not hear me when I pray against Thy will, which is for the best! Do not hear me! Do not hear me!'

And she bowed down her head into her bosom.

And Death went off with her child into the unknown land.

THE COLLAR

THERE was once a grand cavalier whose whole outfit was a bootjack and a comb; but he had the handsomest collar in the world, and it's the collar that our story is about.

Now, the collar was old enough to think abut getting married, and as it happened, he arrived in the wash along with a garter.

'My word!' said the collar. 'Why, I've never seen anyone so slim and so smart, so soft and so adorable! Might I ask your name?'

'I'm not telling,' said the garter.

'Where do you belong?' asked the collar.

But the garter was very bashful and thought this rather a strange question to answer.

'I expect you're a girdle!' said the collar. 'One of those underneath girdles! I can see you're useful as well as ornamental, madam!'

'You're not to speak to me!' said the garter. 'I don't think I've given you any occasion to!'

'Well, when a lady's as pretty as you are,' said the collar, 'that's occasion enough!'

'Please keep away from me!' said the garter. 'You're too much like a man!'

'Yes, and I'm a grand cavalier!' said the collar. 'I have a bootjack and a comb.' Now of course that wasn't true; it was his master who had them, but he was boasting.

'Don't come near me!' said the garter. 'I'm not used to it!'

'Prim and proper!' said the collar.

And then he was taken out of the wash. He was starched, hung over a chair in the sun, and then laid on the ironing-board; and along came the hot iron.

'Madam!' said the collar. 'My dear madam! I'm getting all hot! I'm being done brown! I'm losing my creases! You're burning a hole in me! Ooh! . . . Will you marry me?'

'Rag-tag!' said the iron, riding proudly over the collar. For she fancied she was a steam-engine, going on the railway to pull carriages.

'Rag-tag!' she said.

The collar frayed a bit at the edges; and out came the scissors to clip the frayed edges off.

'Oh!' said the collar. 'I expect you're the leading dancer! You're good at stretching a leg! It's the prettiest I've ever seen. You're quite without an equal.'

'I know that!' said the scissors.

'You deserve to be a countess!' said the collar. 'I have nothing but a grand cavalier, a bootjack, and a comb. I wish I had a country seat!'

'Are you proposing?' said the scissors. And she was so cross she gave him a whacking big clip—and he was turned down.

'I suppose I shall have to propose to the comb now,' said the collar. 'It's remarkable the way you keep all your teeth, ma'am. Did you never think of becoming engaged?'

'Well, I should have thought you would have known,' said the comb. 'I'm engaged to the bootjack!'

'Turned down again!' said the collar. And so, as there were no more to propose to, he had no more use for proposing.

Time passed, and the collar found himself in a box at the paper-mill. The rags were holding a party, the finer ones for themselves, the common ones for themselves, just as it should be. They all had a lot to tell, but none more than the collar—he was a proper boaster.

'I've had an awful lot of sweethearts,' said the collar. 'They never left me in peace! Ah, but then I was a grand cavalier—well starched. I had both a bootjack and a comb, which I never used. You should have seen me then, seen me when I lay on my side. I'll never forget my first love! She was a girdle—so delicate, so soft, and so pretty! She threw herself in a wash-tub for my sake. Then there was a widow-woman who got all hot for me, but I left her to go black. There was the leading dancer; she gave me the gash I still bear, she was so passionate! My own comb was in love with me, and lost all her teeth of a broken heart. Yes, I've seen plenty of that! But I feel most sorry for the garter—I mean the girdle—that jumped in the wash-tub. I have a lot on my conscience, and it's time I was made into white paper.'

And he was: all the rags were turned into white paper, the collar becoming the very piece of white paper that we have here, and on which this story was printed. And that was because it boasted so dreadfully about what it had never been. So let us bear this in mind, that we don't go behaving in the same way; for we can never be really sure if we do that we won't also land up in the rag box and get made into white paper and have our whole history printed on us, every secret bit of it, and have to go about telling it like the collar.

IT'S PERFECTLY TRUE

'IT'S A dreadful affair!' said a hen, over in a part of the town where the affair didn't take place. 'It's a dreadful affair, this in the hen-house. I daren't sleep alone tonight! It's a good thing there are a lot of us on the roost together.' And she told a tale that made the other hens' feathers stand on end and the cock's comb fall down flat. It's perfectly true!

But we were going to begin at the beginning, and that was in a hen-house in another part of the town. The sun went down and the hens flew up to their perch. One of them—she had white feathers and short legs—used to lay her regulation eggs and, as hens go, was in every way respectable. As she settled on the perch she preened herself with her beak, and a little feather fell out.

'There now!' she said. 'The more I preen myself, the better-looking I shall be.' Now this, you know, was said in fun, for she was the bright bird of the flock, and otherwise, as I have said, very respectable. And then she fell asleep.

Darkness lay all around. Hen sat beside hen, and the one that sat next to her wasn't asleep. She heard and she didn't hear, as in this world you have to if you want to live your life in peace. Still she felt that she had to tell her other neighbour. 'Did you hear what she said?' she whispered. 'I mention no names, but there's a hen who means to pluck herself so as to look attractive. If I were a cock I'd despise her!'

And just above the hens sat the owl with her husband owl

and their owlet children. They had sharp ears in that family. They heard every word the neighbour hen spoke, and they rolled their eyes, and Mother Owl fanned herself with her wings and said: 'Don't listen, but I expect you all heard what she said? I heard it with my own ears—and it takes a lot to make them drop off! One of the hens has so far forgotten what is proper in a hen that she's plucking off all her feathers and letting the cock watch her.'

'*Prenez garde aux enfants!*' said Father Owl. That's no talk for children to hear!'

'All the same, I'm going to tell neighbour Owl! She's such a respectable owl, she is.' And away she flew.

'Hoo-hoo! To-whoo!' they both hooted down to the pigeons in the neighbour's dovecot. 'Have you heard? Have you heard? Hoo-hoo! There's a hen who's plucked all her feathers out for the cock's sake! She'll freeze to death—if she hasn't already! Hoo-hoo!'

'Where? Where?' cooed the pigeons.

'In the neighbour's yard! I as good as saw it myself! It's hardly a fit story to tell. But it's perfectly true!'

'Coo! coo! How very true!' said the pigeons, as they went cooing down to their own poultry yard. 'There's a hen—well, some say there are two—who's plucked all her feathers out so as to look different from the rest and catch the eye of the cock. It's a risky game. You can catch your death of cold—and they're dead, the two of them!'

'Wake up! Wake up!' crowed the cock, flying on to the fence. He was still a little sleepy about the eyes, yet he crowed: 'Three hens have died of love for a cock; they plucked all their feathers out. It's a nasty business; I'm not keeping it to my-self—pass it on!'

'Pass it on!' squeaked the bats. And the hens clucked and the cocks crowed: 'Pass it on! Pass it on!' And so the story sped from hen-house to hen-house and back in the end to the place where it had started from.

'Five hens,' they said, 'all plucked their feathers out to show which of them had grown thinnest in their love for the cock; and then they pecked one another till the blood flowed; and fell down dead—to the shame and disgrace of their families and the great loss of their owner.'

And the hen that had lost the loose little feather of course didn't know her own story again; and being a respectable hen, she said: 'I despise those hens! But there are more of that sort. These things shouldn't be hushed up, and I'll do my bit to see that the story gets into the paper; then it'll be all over the country. The hens have deserved it—and their families as well!'

And it got to the paper and was printed there, and it's perfectly true: One little feather can grow into five hens.

THE GOBLIN AT THE GROCER'S

THERE was a proper student; he lived in the attic and owned nothing. There was a proper grocer; he lived on the ground floor and owned the whole house. And the goblin kept well in with him because every Christmas Eve he was given a dish of porridge with a big lump of butter in it—the grocer could afford it. And the goblin stayed in the shop and found it very rewarding.

One evening the student came in by the back door to buy himself some candles and cheese; having no one to send, he had come himself. He got what he asked for and paid for it; and he got a nod and a 'Good evening' from the grocer and the grocer's wife. This was a woman who could do more than nod; in fact, she had the gift of the gab! The student nodded back, and then stood still, busily reading the sheet of paper that had been wrapped round the cheese. It was a page torn from an old book which should never have been torn up, an old book full of poetry.

'There's some more of that,' said the grocer. 'I gave an old woman some coffee for it. If you like to give me a copper or two, the rest's yours.'

'Thanks,' said the student, 'I'll have it instead of the cheese. I can eat plain bread and butter. It would be a great shame if the whole of this book got torn up. You're a fine fellow and a good business man, but you know as much about poetry as that bin.'

Now that was a rude thing to say, especially about the bin;

but the grocer laughed and the student laughed, for of course it was said sort of jokingly. But the goblin was shocked that anybody could dare to say things like that to a grocer, and one who was a landlord and sold the best butter.

When night fell, and the shop was shut and everybody in bed except for the student, the goblin went in and took the woman's 'gab'—she didn't use it when she was asleep. And whatever object in the room he put it on to at once found its tongue and was able to express its thoughts and feelings just like the woman, though only one could have it on at once—which was just as well, for otherwise they wouldn't have been able to hear one another speak.

And the goblin put the 'gab' on the bin where the old newspapers were kept. 'Is it a fact,' he asked, 'that you don't know what poetry is?'

'Why, of course I know,' said the bin. 'It's the sort of stuff that's at the tail-end of the papers and gets cut out; I fancy I've got more of it in me than the student, and I'm only a little bin compared to the grocer.'

And the goblin put the 'gab' on the coffee-grinder. Dear me, how it wagged! And he put it on the butter cask and on the till. Every one of them had the same opinion as the bin; and what the majority are agreed upon you have to respect.

'Now for the student!' said the goblin; and he crept quietly up the backstairs to the attic where the student lived. A light was burning there, and the goblin peeped through the keyhole and saw the student reading the tattered book from downstairs. But how bright it was in there! From the book came a ray of light which grew into the stem of a great tree that raised itself aloft and spread its branches over the student's head. Every leaf was so very fresh and every flower the head of a lovely girl, some with dark and sparkling eyes and others with eyes that were blue and wonderfully clear. Every fruit was a shining star, and the air was full of marvellous music and singing.

No, the little goblin had never dreamt of splendour such as this, let alone seen or heard it. And he stood there on tiptoe, peeping and peeping till the light went out. The student must have blown out his lamp and gone to bed, but the little goblin stayed where he was, for the music played on softly and sweetly, making a delightful lullaby for the student as he lay down to rest.

'This is wonderful!' said the little goblin. 'I never expected this. I think I'll stay with the student.' But thinking it over, and being sensible, he said with a sigh: 'The student hasn't any porridge!' And so he went—yes, he went downstairs again to the grocer. And a good thing it was that he did, because the bin had used up nearly all the woman's 'gab' in telling, on one side, what a lot he had in him, and he was just going to tell it all again on the other side when the goblin came and gave the 'gab' back to the woman. But from then on the whole shop, from the till to the firewood, took its opinions from the bin; and so great was their respect for it and their belief in it that whenever the grocer read out the 'art and theatre reviews' from the paper, the evening one, they used to think it all came from the bin.

But the little goblin no longer sat listening quietly to all the wisdom and common sense downstairs: as soon as the light shone out from the attic the rays seemed to pull him like strong anchor cables upstairs, and he would have to go and peep through the keyhole. And then there would come surging towards him a grandeur like that which we feel in the rolling ocean when God has passed over it in a storm, and he would burst into tears. Why he cried he had no idea, but they would be tears of unhappiness. How very wonderful it would be to sit with the student under that tree; but it couldn't be, though he was glad of the keyhole. He went on standing there in the cold passage even when the autumn wind blew down from the trap-door in the loft and it was so very, very cold. But the little fellow never felt it: not till the light in the attic was put out and the music had died down in the wind. Then, ugh! he would shiver and creep downstairs again to his warm corner where it was so snug and cosy. And then when Christmas came with its big lump of butter in the porridge—why, then the grocer was favourite.

Now, in the middle of the night the goblin was awakened by a terrible banging on the shutters; somebody was banging away on them outside, while the watchman was blowing his whistle. There was a big fire, and the whole street was aglow with it. Was it in this house, or was it at the neighbour's? Where? It was terrifying! The grocer's wife was in such a state that she took her gold ear-rings off and put them into her pocket, so as to save at least something. The grocer ran to get his bonds and the servant her silk mantilla—she could afford one. Everybody was bent on saving his treasures, and so was the little goblin; in a couple of bounds he was upstairs and in the attic, where the student stood at the open window, calmly watching the fire, which was in the opposite house. Seizing the wonderful book on the table, the little goblin stuffed it into his red cap and held on to it with both hands; the best treasure in the house had been saved! Then off he dashed, up on to the roof and right up on the chimney, where, lit up by the glow from the burning house opposite, he sat down, holding on to his red cap and the treasure inside it with both hands. Now he did know where his heart lay and to whom he really belonged.

But when the fire had been put out and he thought the matter over, well, then he said: 'I'll divide my time between them!

I can't drop the grocer altogether, because of the porridge!'

And that was perfectly human of him! We too go to the grocer—for the porridge.

THOUSANDS OF YEARS FROM NOW

YES, thousands of years from now they will come flying on wings of steam through the air and over the ocean! The young inhabitants of America will come visiting old Europe. They will come to our ancient monuments and our crumbling ruins just as today we travel to the mouldering glories of southern Asia.

Thousands of years from now they will come!

The Thames, the Danube, the Rhine will go rolling on; Mont Blanc will be capped with snow; the northern lights will shine over the northern lands. But generation upon generation will be as dust, successions of the mighty of their day forgotten like those who sleep in the mound where the wealthy flour-merchant, who owns the land, erects a seat on which to sit and look out across the level waving cornfield.

'To Europe!' cry the young people of America. 'To the land of our fathers, the splendid land of memory and romance, Europe!'

The airship comes. It is packed with travellers, for the speed is faster than by sea. The electro-magnetic wire under the ocean has telegraphed the size of the aerial caravan. Europe is already in sight; it is the coast of Ireland, but the passengers are still asleep as they were not to be called until they were over England. Here they set foot on the soil of Europe in the land of Shakespeare, as the learned call it: the land of Parliament, the land of machinery, others say.

A whole day they stop here: so much time have these busy people for great England and Scotland.

Off they speed under the Channel Tunnel to France, the land of Charlemagne and Napoleon. Molière's name is mentioned; the learned talk of a Classical and a Romantic school in the ancient past, and rejoice in heroes, poets, and scientists whom our day never knew but who were to be born on Europe's crater—Paris.

The air-steamer flies on over the land where Columbus sailed from, where Cortez was born, and where Calderon sang dramas in billowing verse. Lovely black-eyed women still live there in the flourishing valleys, and ancient songs tell of the Cid and the Alhambra.

Through the air and over the sea to Italy, to the place where ancient, eternal Rome once stood. Every trace of it has vanished and the Campagna is a desert. Of St Peter's Church a solitary ruined wall is shown, but its genuineness is doubted.

To Greece, in order to spend a night at the rich hotel on the top of Mount Olympus, to say they have been there. And so on to the Bosporus, to get a few hours' rest and see the site of Byzantium. Poor fishermen are spreading their nets where legend says there was the harem garden in the time of the Turks.

Remains of mighty cities by the swift-flowing Danube, cities our time never knew, are crossed in flight; but here and there at historic places—places still to come, places yet unborn—here and there the aerial caravan alights and once again takes off.

Down there lies Germany, once engirdled in the closest network of railways and canals: the land where Luther spoke and Goethe sang, and where Mozart wielded in his day the sceptre of music. Great names shine out in science and art, names we never knew. One day's stop for Germany and one day for Scandinavia, the homelands of Oersted and Linnaeus and of ancient heroes and young Norwegians. Iceland is seen on the way home: the Geysir has stopped boiling and Hekla has gone out, but like the imperishable records of the Sagas the island rock stands firm in the foaming sea.

'There's a lot to see in Europe,' said the young American 'and we saw it in a week! And it's possible to do it, as the great traveller' (mentioning a contemporary name) 'has shown in his celebrated work, *Europe Seen in Eight Days*.'

THE PIG BANK

THERE were such a lot of toys in the nursery, and standing on top of the cupboard was a money-box which was made of earthenware in the shape of a pig. It had a natural slot in its back which had been made bigger with a knife so that half-crowns would go into it, and in fact two of these had already gone in, besides a lot of smaller coins. The pig bank was stuffed so full that he couldn't rattle any more, and that is the very height of a pig bank's ambitions. So there he stood, up on top of the shelf, looking down on everything in the room and knowing that with what he had inside him he could buy up the whole lot, and that's something.

And that, too, was what the rest of them thought, only they didn't say so, they had other things to talk about. The drawer was standing half-way open and a big doll inside it got up: rather old, she was, and with a rivet in her neck. And looking up she said: 'Let's all play at being people; that'll always be something!' And what a commotion there was then! The very pictures on the wall turned round, showing they had backs to them, though not for the sake of contradicting.

It was the middle of the night and the moon shone in at the window, giving a light for nothing. The game was about to begin and everyone had been invited, including even the perambulator, though that was one of the commoner playthings. 'We're all good in our way!' it said. 'You can't all belong to the gentry. Some people have to make themselves useful, as the saying goes.'

The pig bank was the only one to get a written invitation, being too high up, they thought, to be got at by word of mouth; and he never replied to say if he was coming because he wouldn't come. If he was to be in at it, he would have to enjoy it from home; they would have to make the best of that, and so they did.

The little puppet theatre was set up at once in such a way that he could look straight into it; they were going to begin with a play, to be followed by tea and intelligent talk, only they started off straight away on this, with the rocking-horse talking of training and thoroughbreds and the perambulator of railways and steam power—all, of course, a part of their trade and things which they could talk about. The clock talked of politic-tick! tick!-s and knew what time of day it was, though they did say that it was backward. The walking-stick bragged of its ferrule and silver knob, being well off both at the top and the bottom; and on the sofa lay two embroidered cushions that were pretty and foolish. And so it was time for the play to start.

Everybody sat watching it and they had all been asked to bang and thump and smack as they felt inclined. But the riding-whip said that he never cracked for old people and only for those not engaged to be married. 'I bang for everything!' cried the bombshell. 'You have to be somewhere!' thought the spit-toon. That was what they were all thinking as they watched the play. The piece was no good though it was well performed, with all the actors showing their painted sides; you could only look at them on one side and not from the back. And so they all played very well, right up at the front of the theatre; their strings were too long for them, but then that made them all the easier to see. The doll with the rivet in her was so fascinated that her rivet came loose, and the pig was so fascinated in his own way that he decided to do something for one of them and include him in his will as the one to lie beside him in his open grave when the time came.

It was such a treat that they gave up the idea of having tea and stuck to the intelligent talk, which was what they called playing at being people: and there was no malice meant, because they were only playing. And they all thought of themselves and of what the pig bank was thinking, and the pig bank thought the longest because he was thinking of his will and funeral and when that would be—always it was before you expected . . . Crack! There lay the one from on top of the cupboard, down on the floor in little bits and pieces, while the coins went skipping and dancing, the little ones spinning round and the big ones rolling—especially the half-crown, which was intent on getting into the world. And that's what he did, and that's what they all did, while the broken bits of the pig bank went into the dustbin. But on the cupboard the next day stood a new pig bank of earthenware. So far there were no coins in it and so it couldn't rattle either, in which it resembled the other one. That was always a beginning—and with that we will end!

CLOD-POLL

Away in the country there was an old manor, and in it lived an old squire who had two sons; and they were so witty they were too clever by half. They were going to propose to the king's daughter; and there was no reason why they shouldn't because she had announced that she would marry the man who could give the best account of himself.

Now the two of them spent a week in getting ready; this was all the time they had for it, but it was time enough since they'd had some previous education, and that's so useful. One of them knew the whole Latin dictionary and the local paper for the last three years off by heart, reading both from the front and from the back. The other had learnt up all the company by-laws and what every alderman ought to know; this enabled him to discuss State affairs, he thought, and besides he knew how to embroider braces, because he was so clever with his fingers.

'I'm going to win the princess!' they both said. And so their father gave them each a splendid horse, the one who knew the dictionary and the newspapers getting a coal-black horse, and the one who was as clever as an alderman and could embroider getting a milk-white one. And the next thing they did was to oil the corners of their mouths with cod-liver oil to make them work easier. All the servants were in the courtyard to see them mount their horses, when along came the third brother—for there were three, only nobody counted him as a brother because he wasn't such a scholar as the other two, and they never called him anything but Clod-poll.

'Where are you two off to, dressed up in your Sunday best?' he asked.

'To Court, to talk ourselves into a princess! Haven't you heard the proclamation that's been read out all over the country?' And they told him all about it.

'Oh, I say! I'd better come with you!' said Clod-poll. The brothers, however, only laughed at him and rode on their way.

'Father, let me have a horse!' cried Clod-poll. 'I'm just in the mood for getting married! If she'll have me, she'll have me. And if she won't have me, I'll have her all the same.'

'Stuff and nonsense!' said his father. 'I'm not giving you a horse. You've got nothing to say for yourself. Now, your brothers—well, they're gentlemen!'

'If I'm not to have a horse,' said Clod-poll, 'I'll take the billy-goat. That's my own, and it can carry me.' And so he got astride the billy-goat, dug his heels into its sides, and made off along the road. Phew! What a speed! 'Here I come!' cried Clod-poll; and he sang out till the air echoed with it.

But his brothers rode on ahead in silence, never saying a word; they were busy thinking out all the clever sayings they were going to make, because it all had to be well worked out.

'Tally-ho!' shouted Clod-poll. 'Here I come! Look what I found on the road!' And he showed them a dead crow he had picked up.

'Clod!' they said. 'What are you going to do with that?'

'I'm going to present it to the princess!'

'All right, you do!' they said, laughing and riding on.

'Tally-ho! Here I come! Look what I've found now! You don't find this on the road every day.'

And the brothers turned round again to see what it was. 'Clod!' they said. 'Why it's only an old clog with the upper missing. Is the princess to have that as well?'

'Of course she is!' said Clod-poll. And the brothers laughed, and rode on and got well ahead.

'Tally-ho! Here I am!' shouted Clod-poll. 'I say, but it's getting worse and worse. Tally-ho! It's wonderful!'

'What have you found now?' said his brothers.

'Oh!' said Clod-poll. 'There's no telling! Won't she be delighted, the princess!'

'Ugh!' said the brothers. 'Why, it's mud you've got straight from the ditch.'

'You're quite right!' said Clod-poll. 'And it's the finest sort; you can't hold it.' And he filled his pocket with it.

But his brothers rode off as hard as they could go, and by the time they reached the city gate they were a whole hour ahead. All the suitors were being given numbers as they arrived, and were placed in rows, six by six, and so close together that they couldn't stir; which was just as well, because otherwise they would have knifed one another in the back, just because one was standing in front of the other.

The rest of the country's inhabitants were gathered round the palace, right up to the windows, to see the princess receive the suitors; and the moment one of them entered the room he would lose his tongue.

'No good!' the princess would say. 'Off with you!'

Then along came the brother who knew the dictionary, but he had clean forgotten it while waiting his turn in the queue; and the floor creaked, and the ceiling was of looking-glass, which made him see himself upside down. And then, standing at every window were three reporters and an alderman, all taking down everything that was said, so that it could go straight into the paper and be sold for twopence at the corner. It was dreadful; and what's more, they'd made up such a fire the stove was red hot.

'It's pretty hot in here,' said the suitor.

'That's because my father's roasting cockerels today,' said the princess.

Ooh! There he stood; and the talk wasn't a bit like what he'd expected. Not a word could he find to say, for he had meant to say something funny. Ooh!

'No good!' said the princess. 'Off with you!' And off he had to go. It was the other brother's turn now.

'It's awfully hot in here,' he said.

'Yes, we're roasting cockerels today,' said the princess.

'What—what's that?' he said. And all the reporters wrote down: 'What—what's that?'

'No good!' said the princess. 'Off with you!'

It was Clod-poll's turn now. He came riding his billy-goat straight into the room. 'It's as hot as blazes in here!' he said.

'That's because I'm roasting cockerels!' said the princess.

'This is a bit of luck!' said Clod-poll. 'Then I suppose I can have a crow roasted?'

'Yes, you can if you like,' said the princess. 'But have you anything to roast it in? Because I've neither pot nor pan.'

'Oh, but I have,' said Clod-poll. 'Here's a cooker with a tin handle!' And he pulled out the old clog and put the crow in the middle of it.

'There's quite a meal there,' said the princess. 'But where do we get the gravy?'

'I've got that in my pocket,' said Clod-poll. 'I've more than enough here.' And he turned a little of the mud out of his pocket.

'Now I like that!' said the princess. 'You always have an answer. And you can give a good account of yourself, so I'll have you for my husband. But do you know that every word we've been saying has been taken down and will be in the paper tomorrow? Look, at every window there are three reporters and an old alderman, and the alderman's the worst of the lot because he doesn't understand a thing!' Now, this she said only to frighten him. And all the reporters sniggered and made a blot on the carpet.

'They'll be the gentry,' said Clod-poll. 'Well then, here's one of the best for the alderman!' And he turned out his pockets and gave him the mud full in the face.

'Well done!' said the princess. 'It's more than I could have done. But I shall learn!'

And so Clod-poll became king, winning a wife of his own and a crown and a throne. And we have this straight from the alderman's newspaper—which isn't to be trusted!

THE BOTTLE NECK

STANDING in a narrow, crooked street along with other poor houses was a house, very narrow and very tall, which was built of timber frames that had sagged in all directions. Poor people lived there; and the poorest part of all was the attic, where, in the sunshine outside the little window, hung an old and battered bird-cage which didn't even have a proper bird-bath but only an upturned bottle neck, corked in the bottom and filled with water. Standing at the window was an old maid. She had just put some chickweed in the cage, in which a little linnet was hopping from perch to perch, singing away merrily.

'Yes, *you* can sing!' said the bottle neck. Well now, it didn't say it exactly as we might say it, for a bottle can't speak; but it sort of thought it to itself, as we human beings talk to ourselves.

'Yes, *you* can sing! You, who are sound in every limb. You ought to try losing your furbelows the way I have, and having only a neck and a mouth like me, and corked at that; then you wouldn't sing. Still, it's nice that somebody's pleased! I've no reason to sing, and couldn't if I tried! I used to be able to when I was a whole bottle and they rubbed me with a cork. They called me a real warbler—the great warbler! And as for the day when I went with the furriers on a picnic and the daughter got engaged—I remember that as if it had been yesterday. I've seen a lot in my time, come to think of it. I've been through fire and water, deep down in the black earth, and higher up than most. And now I'm hanging here outside the bird-cage in air and sunshine. I can tell a story worth listening to, but I shan't tell it aloud because I can't!'

And so deep down inside it it told (or it thought) the story of itself, which indeed was a strange one; while the little bird sang merrily on and people walked and drove in the street below, all full of their own thoughts or of no thoughts at all—the bottle neck certainly full of its own thoughts.

It remembered the blazing furnace at the factory where it had been blown into life. It could still remember that it had been very hot and that it had gazed into the roaring furnace, its original home, feeling a great desire to jump straight back into it, but then little by little, as it had cooled off, feeling fairly well where it was. It had stood in a row along with a whole regiment of brothers and sisters all from the same furnace, though some had been blown into champagne bottles and others into beer bottles, and that makes a difference! In the world later on, to be sure, a beer bottle may have in it the most priceless Lachryma Christi, while a champagne bottle may be filled with black-lead; but what you were born to is shown on the label, and the gentry are gentry even with black-lead in them.

All the bottles were soon packed, and with them our bottle. At the time it never thought that it would end up a bottle neck, working its way up to be a bird-bath, which is an honest life—at least you are something! It didn't see the light of day again until, along with its companions, it was unpacked in the wine-merchant's cellar and given its first rinse. It was a curious feeling. It was now empty and corkless and feeling sadly at a loss, missing something but not knowing what it missed. But then it was corked and sealed and labelled Premier Crus. It was like gaining top marks. But then the wine was good and so was the bottle. To be young is to be a poet! It trilled and carolled away about all the things it knew nothing about; about the green and sunlit mountains where the lime grows and where merry maids and jolly youths sing and kiss one another. Yes, it's grand to be alive! Of all this the bottle trilled and carolled away to itself just like the young poets, who often know nothing about these things either.

One morning it was bought. The furrier's boy had been sent for a bottle of the best wine, and it was put into the lunch basket along with ham, cheese, and sausage, where also there was the nicest butter and the finest bread. The furrier's daughter had packed it all herself. She was so young and so pretty; and she had laughing brown eyes and a smile on her lips which spoke as much as her eyes, and delicate soft hands which were so white, though not so white as her neck and breast. You could see at once that she was one of the prettiest girls in the town, and yet she wasn't engaged.

And the lunch basket rested on her lap as the family drove into the woods. The bottle neck was sticking out between the corners of the white cloth; there was a red seal on the cork and it looked straight into the girl's face. It also looked at the young ship's mate who was sitting beside her. He was a friend of her childhood, the son of a portrait painter; and by honest hard work he had just got his mate's certificate and was leaving in his ship for far-away lands the next day. There had been a good deal of talk about this during the packing, and, as they had talked, there had been little fun in the eyes and on the lips of the furrier's pretty daughter.

The two young people walked in the green wood, talking together. What was it they talked about? Well, the bottle didn't hear that; it was in the lunch basket. It was a strangely long time before it got brought out; but then, when it did, delightful things had taken place. There was laughter in every eye and the furrier's daughter was laughing too, but she had less to say and her cheeks blushed like red roses.

Father took out the full bottle and the corkscrew. What a strange feeling it is the first time you are uncorked! The bottle had never forgotten that solemn moment; when the cork was drawn it had given a regular 'plop' inside it and had said 'cluck!' when the wine flowed into the glasses.

'To the engaged couple!' said Father. And each glass was drained to the bottom, and the young mate kissed his pretty bride-to-be.

'Good luck and happiness!' said the two old people. And filling their glasses once more the young man cried: 'Home-coming and wedding a year today!' And when the glasses had been drained he took the bottle and, raising it into the air, cried: 'You were present on the happiest day of my life; you shan't serve anybody any longer!' And he threw it high into the air.

As he did so the furrier's daughter thought, least of all, that she would ever see it fly again, though she was to. It came to rest in the thick rushes which grew by a small lake. The bottle neck remembered as clearly as anything the way it had lain there thinking to itself: 'I gave them wine and they gave me pond water, though it was well meant.' The engaged couple and the happy parents were no longer in sight, but for a long time it heard their singing and merrymaking. Then along came two small country boys and, looking among the rushes, they saw the bottle and picked it up. It was taken care of.

To the cottage which was their home their eldest brother, who was a sailor, had come on the day before to say goodbye before going away on one of his voyages, and Mother was busily packing some odds and ends which Father was to take in to town that evening when seeing his son off on his journey and giving him his love and his mother's. A small bottle of some spiced cordial had already been packed when the boys came in with the bigger and better bottle which they had found; it would hold more than the small bottle, and the drink was such a good one for the stomach as it contained St John's wort. And so it was no longer red wine which went into the bottle but a bitter drink, though a good one too—for the stomach. It had been decided that the new bottle was to go instead of the smaller one, and so off the bottle went on its new journey, on board Peter Jensen's ship. And it happened to be the very ship where the young mate served; but he never saw the bottle, nor would he have known it again or even guessed that it could be the same from which they had drunk to his engagement and homecoming.

If there was no longer any wine in it, there was something just as good; and whenever Peter Jensen brought it out his shipmates used to call it the 'chemist's shop', for it contained such good medicine for the stomach and did good for as long as there was a drop left. It was a happy time, and when they stroked it with a cork the bottle used to sing. And so it came to be known as the 'great warbler', and 'Peter Jensen's warbler'.

A long time passed and it stood in a corner empty; and then one day—something happened. Whether they were outward bound or bound for home the bottle could never really say, as it had never been ashore, but one day a storm arose; big seas rolled black and heavy, lifting and tossing the ship this way and that. The mast broke, a wave smashed in a plank, the pumps could no longer keep out the water; it was pitch-black night; the ship sank. But in the last minute the young mate managed to write on a piece of paper: 'In the name of Jesus, we are foundering!' Then, adding the name of his bride-to-be, his own name, and that of his ship, he put the note into an empty bottle which he found, pressed the cork on firmly, and threw the bottle into the raging sea. He had no idea that it was the bottle from which they had drunk the toast of joy and hope for him and for her; now it was rocking on the waves, bringing a message of death.

The ship sank and the crew sank, while the bottle flew like a bird, having a heart, a love-letter, inside it. And the sun rose and the sun set, looking like the glowing red furnace of the bottle's earlier days, to which it longed to fly back. It passed through calm sea and fresh storms, never striking a rock and never getting swallowed by a shark; for days and years it drifted about, now going north, now south, where the currents took it. Apart from this it was its own master, although you can grow tired of that too.

The written message, the last farewell from bridegroom-to-be to his sweetheart, could only bring grief should it get into the right hands. But where were those hands; the ones that had shone so white as they had spread the cloth on the fresh grass in the green wood, that day of the engagement? Where was the furrier's daughter? Indeed, where was the country? And what was the nearest country? The bottle had no idea. It drifted and it drifted, and in the end got quite tired of drifting; it was never meant for that. Yet still it went on drifting until, at long last, it reached land, a foreign land. It couldn't understand a word of what was said there; this wasn't the language it had heard spoken before, and there's a lot you miss when you don't understand the language.

The bottle was picked up and studied; the note inside it was seen, taken out, turned over and over, but nobody could understand the words written on it. They could see that the bottle had been thrown overboard and that there was something about this on the paper, but what did it say? That was the strange part about it. And so the message was put back into the bottle and the bottle was placed in a big cupboard, in a big room in a big house.

Every time visitors came the note was taken out and twisted and turned over, so that the writing, which was only in pencil, became more and more indistinct, and in the end nobody could any longer see that there was any writing. The bottle stood in the cupboard for another year, and then it was put away in the loft, where it got covered up in dust and cobwebs. And it would think of its better days when it had served out red wine in the fresh woods and had rocked on the waves bearing a secret: a letter, a farewell sigh.

And so it stood in the loft for twenty years; it might have stood there longer, only the house was to be rebuilt. The roof was pulled off, and the bottle was seen and talked about; but it couldn't understand the language; that's not the sort of thing one learns by standing in the loft, even in twenty years. 'Had I stayed in the parlour,' it thought to itself, 'I should have learnt it!'

And then it was given a wash and a rinse, which it could really do with; it felt now that it was perfectly clear and transparent, and had grown young again in its old age. But the message it had carried had gone down the drain.

And now the bottle was filled with seed; of what kind it could not tell. Then it was corked and well wrapped up, so it could see neither lamp nor candle, let alone sun or moon; and you ought to see something on a journey, thought the bottle. But it didn't see a thing; only, it did what was most important—it travelled and it arrived where it was meant to arrive, and there it was unpacked.

'What a lot of trouble they've taken abroad!' they said. 'And then it's well cracked!' Though it wasn't. The bottle understood every word that was said; the language was the one it had heard at the furnace and at the wine-merchant's, and in the woods and on the ship; the only really good old language, the one you can understand. The bottle had come where it belonged, and was being welcomed! It nearly jumped out of their hands for very joy, and scarcely noticed that its cork had been drawn and that it had been shaken out and put in the cellar, to be left there and forgotten. Home is best, even in the cellar! It never occurred to it to think how long it lay down there; it lay there comfortably and for years. And then one day somebody came and took the bottles away, this one with the rest.

In the garden outside there were great celebrations; burning lamps hung in festoons and paper lanterns glowed like big transparent tulips. And it was a lovely evening too; the weather was calm and clear, the stars were shining brightly, and the new moon was lit. You could really see the round full moon, like a blue-grey globe half edged with gold. It was a grand sight.

In the side paths there was some illumination too; at least enough for anyone to see where they were going. Between the hedges there was a row of bottles, each with a candle stuck in it, and among them was our bottle, the one which in time was to end up a bottle neck, used as a bird-bath. At this moment it was finding everything so very lovely; once more at a picnic, present once again at feasting and merrymaking, hearing the singing and the music, listening to the bustle and murmur of many people coming especially from the part of the garden where the lamps were burning and the paper lanterns glowed in many colours. If itself it stood in an out-of-the-way path, that very fact gave it food for thought; for it stood holding a candle and was there both for usefulness and pleasure, which is the right sort of thing. At such a time twenty years in the attic is forgotten—and it's good to forget.

Walking just by it went a young couple, arm in arm like the engaged couple in the woods, the mate and the furrier's daughter; the bottle seemed to live all that over again. Guests walked about the garden, as well as some people who had been allowed to watch them and the show, and among these was an old maid, lonely but not alone; she was thinking of exactly the same thing as the bottle, thinking of the green woods and of the young engaged couple who were very dear to her. She herself was one of them, half the couple; it had been her happiest hour, and that is a thing you never forget, however old an old maid you may grow. But she didn't know the bottle again, and the bottle didn't know her. That's how in this world we pass one another by—till we meet again as these two did, for they had settled in the same town.

The bottle went from the garden to the wine-merchant's, was filled once more with wine, and sold to a balloonist who was going up in his balloon the following Sunday. A crowd of people gathered to watch him, and there was a regimental band, and all sorts of preparations. The bottle saw it all from a basket, in which there was a live rabbit that was very frightened, knowing that it was going up in order to go down by parachute. The bottle knew neither what was up nor what was down; it saw the balloon swell and swell and, when it couldn't swell any longer, rise higher and higher up and get very restless. The ropes which held it were cut, and up it soared with the balloonist, the basket, the bottle, and the rabbit, while the band played and the crowd cheered.

'How curious to go up into the air like this!' thought the bottle. 'This is a new way to sail; at least you can't bump into anything up here.'

And many thousands of people stood watching the balloon, the old maid watching with the rest; she stood at her open window in the attic, where the cage hung with the little linnet which then had no bird-bath but had to make do with a cup. On the windowsill itself stood a myrtle-tree, which had been moved to one side so as not to get pushed out when the old maid leant forward to watch. As she did so she clearly saw the balloonist drop the rabbit by parachute, drink a toast to the crowd, and then throw the bottle up into the air; but little did she think that she had seen that very same bottle fly into the air for herself and her friend on that happy day in the green woods, in the time of her youth.

The bottle had no time to think, it found itself so suddenly and unexpectedly at the height of its career. Roof-tops and towers lay far away below and the people looked so very tiny.

And then it began to fall, but at an altogether different speed from the rabbit, turning somersaults in the air and feeling so young and so mad with joy: it was half full of wine, though not for very long. What a journey! The sun shone on the bottle and all the people were watching it; the balloon was gone—and soon the bottle was gone too. It had fallen on to one of the roofs and had been smashed. But there was so much kick in the bits that they wouldn't lie down but skipped and danced till they got down to the yard and lay in even smaller bits. Only the bottle neck held together, looking just as if it had been cut with a diamond.

'It would do for a bird-bath!' said the cellar-man. But he himself had neither bird nor cage and it would have been too much to get himself these because he happened to have found the bottle neck that could be used as a bath; it would come in for the old maid in the attic, he thought. And so the bottle neck went up there, got a cork in it, was turned upside-down in the way things often happen when changes are made, was filled with fresh water, and was hung up in front of the cage for the little bird, which sang away for very joy.

'Yes, *you* can sing!' was what the bottle neck said. And the bottle neck was a strange thing, because it had been up in a balloon. Nothing else was known of its history. And now it hung there as a bird-bath, where it could hear people clattering and pattering in the street below and the old maid talking in the room within. There happened just then to be a visitor, a lady friend of her own age, and they were talking not of the bottle neck but of the myrtle that stood in the window.

'You certainly shouldn't give five shillings for a wedding bouquet for your daughter,' the old maid was saying; 'you shall have a nice little one from me, quite full of blossom! Look how beautifully it grows. You know, it was a cutting from the myrtle which you gave me the day after my engagement, the one that I was to make my own wedding bouquet from at the end of the year. Only the day never came! The eyes that were to have brightened my life in gladness and joy were closed. He sleeps peacefully on the ocean bed, my angel dear. The plant grew into an old plant, but I grew older still; and when it withered away I took the last fresh branch and planted it in the ground; and now the branch has grown into a really big plant and is going to a wedding after all, as a wedding bouquet for your daughter.'

And there were tears in the old maid's eyes as she spoke of the friend of her youth and the engagement in the woods, and thought of the toast that had been drunk and of the first kiss; only she said nothing of all this, as she was an old maid. She thought of so many things, but she never thought that just outside her window there was another memory of that time: the neck of the bottle that had said 'plop' when the cork had flown off before the toast. But neither did the bottle neck know her; for it never listened to what she was saying—partly, and mainly, because it was thinking only of itself.

PEN AND INK-POT

THE WORDS were spoken in a poet's study, by someone seeing his ink-pot which stood on the desk. 'It's strange,' he said, 'the things that will come out of that ink-pot. Now, whatever will it be next? Yes, it's strange.'

'It is,' said the ink-pot. 'It's a mystery! That's what I always say.' (It spoke to the quill pen and to anything else on the desk able to hear it.) 'It is strange, the things that can come out of me! Yes, you can hardly believe it! And I don't really know myself what the next thing will be when the person starts drawing from me. One drop of me, that's enough for half a page; and what won't that hold? I am rather remarkable! All the poet's works come from me. Those living persons that people think they know; those deep feelings; that excellent humour; those charming descriptions of nature! I just can't make it out, because I myself know nothing about nature; but there it is, it's in me. This host of graceful, charming maidens and these bold knights on their snorting steeds all came—and come—from me! No, I don't know of them myself. I assure you that I never give them a thought.'

'How right you are!' said the quill pen. 'You never think at all. Because, if you did, you'd know you only give liquid. You give moisture for me to express and put on to paper the things I have in me, the things I write down. It's the pen that writes! No human being is in any doubt about that; and most human beings, I'm sure, know just as much about poetry as an old ink-pot.'

'You haven't much experience!' said the ink-pot. 'You've hardly been in service a week, and already you're half worn out. Are you making out that you're the poet? You're only a servant, and I've had many of your sort before you came—both members of the goose family and the best English make. I know both quill pens and steel pens! I've had many of them in my service, and shall have many more when he, the human being who makes the movements for me, comes and writes down what he gets from inside me. I wonder what next he'll bring out of me!'

'Ink-tub!' said the pen.

Late in the evening the poet came home; he had been to a concert where he had heard an excellent violinist, and was thrilled and fascinated by his marvellous playing. It had been an astonishing flood of harmony that he had got out of that instrument; now like tinkling drops of water, pearl upon pearl, now like twittering birds in chorus; sweeping like a storm through a pine forest. He had imagined that he had heard the crying of his own heart, but to the melody one can hear in the lovely voice of a woman. It was as though not only the strings of the violin had played, but the bridge of the instrument and even the pegs and the sounding board. It was extraordinary! And though it had been difficult it had looked like child's-play, as if the bow were just running to and fro over the strings; you would have thought that anyone could have done it. The violin sang of itself, the bow played of itself; these two seemed to be doing everything, and the master who guided them and who gave life and soul to them was forgotten. The Master was forgotten! But it was of Him that the poet thought, of Him he wrote, as he set down his thoughts.

'How foolish it would be,' he wrote, 'for the bow and the violin to be boastful of their actions! And yet that is what we human beings—the poet, the artist, the scientific inventor, the general—so often are. All of us glory in our deeds; and yet all of us are but instruments played by the Lord. All glory be to Him! We have nothing to glory over.'

Yes, that is what the poet wrote; he wrote it as a parable, and called it *The Master and the Instruments*.

'That was one for you, my lady!' said the pen to the ink-pot, when they were once more alone. 'I suppose you heard him read out what I had written down.'

'Yes, what I gave you to write,' said the ink-pot. 'That was a little dig at you for your boastfulness. To think that you don't even know when you're being made a fool of! I gave you a tip straight from my heart. I know my own spite when I hear it.'

'Ink-crock!' said the pen,

'Scribble-spill!' said the ink-pot.

And they both had a feeling of having given a good answer; and it's a very nice feeling to know you've given a good answer, you can sleep on it. And they did sleep on it. But the poet didn't sleep; his thoughts gushed forth like the music from the violin, trickling like pearls, sweeping like a storm through the forest; he had heard there the beating of his own heart and had caught a glimpse of the eternal Master.

All glory be to Him!

THE FARMYARD COCK AND THE WEATHERCOCK

THERE were two cocks, one on the dunghill and one on the roof-top; vainglorious both of them. But which achieved most? Give us your opinion—we'll still stick to our own.

A fence separated the hen-run from another farm, in which there was a dunghill; and on this grew a big cucumber that was conscious of being a hot-bed growth.

'You're born to that!' it said to itself. 'Not everybody can be born a cucumber; there have to be other breeds as well. The hens, the ducks, and the whole stock of the neighbouring farm are creatures too. The farmyard cock on the fence is one I look up to; he's very superior to the weathercock, who's been put so high up and can't even creak, let alone crow! He hasn't any hens or chickens, and he only thinks of himself and sweats verdigris. No, the farmyard cock, there's a cock! See him step out; there's dancing for you! Hear him crow; that's music for you! Wherever he goes you can hear what a trumpeter he is! Supposing he were to come in here; supposing he were to eat me up, leaf, stalk, and all; suppose I became a part of his body, what a blissful death it would be!' said the cucumber.

Late that night there was a dreadful storm; hens, chickens, the cock as well, all ran for shelter. The fence between the farms blew down with a terrible crash. The tiles fell off. But the weathercock stood firm, and never even turned. It couldn't; for all it was young and newly cast it was sober and sedate; it had been born too old, and wasn't a bit like the birds, the sparrows and swallows, which fluttered in the air, and which it despised, calling them 'dicky-birds of small size and small account'. The pigeons were big and smooth and shiny, like mother-of-pearl, and looked a sort of weathercock; but they were fat and stupid and thought of nothing but stuffing their crops, said the weathercock; they made dull company. The birds of passage had also called, and had told tales of foreign lands and flying caravans, and exaggerated stories of birds of prey. All but the weathercock knew that afterwards they repeated themselves and it was always the same, and that's a bore! They were boring, and everything else was boring. Nobody was any company; they were all dull and flat.

'The world's no use!' it said. 'Rubbish, the lot!'

The weathercock was what you would call puffed up, which should definitely have made him interesting to the cucumber, had she but known. But she only looked up to the farmyard cock, and now that was down with her in the yard.

The fence had blown down; but the thunder and lightning were over.

'What say you of that cock-crowing?' said the farmyard cock to the hens and chickens. 'It was rather coarse and lacking in elegance.' And the hens and chickens stepped on to the dunghill, with the cock swaggering after.

'Garden growth!' he said to the cucumber; and in that one phrase she perceived his extensive refinement, while forgetting that he was pecking at her and eating her.

'Blissful death!'

And the hens came along and the chickens came along, for when one comes they all come; and they clucked and they cheeped, and they looked at the cock, all proud of him because he was one of their breed.

'Cock-a-doodle-doo!' he crowed. 'The chickens grow straight into big hens when I say the word in the world hen-run.'

And the hens and chickens clucked and cheeped behind him.

And the cock announced some great news.

'A cock can lay an egg! And do you know what's in that egg? There's a basilisk! Nobody can stand the sight of it. Human beings know that, and now you know it; you know what's in me, and what a high cockalorum I am!'

And so saying the farmyard cock flapped its wings, raised its comb, and gave another crow; and all the hens and all the little chickens gave a shudder, though they were proud to think that one of theirs was such a high cockalorum; and they clucked and they cheeped, so that the weathercock couldn't help but hear it, and did hear it, though he wasn't moved by it.

'Rubbish, the lot!' said the weathercock to itself. 'The farmyard cock will never lay eggs, and I can't be bothered. I'd lay a wind-egg if I wanted to! But the world isn't worth a wind-egg! Rubbish, the lot! I can't be bothered to go on sitting any longer!'

And with that the weathercock snapped off, but without killing the farmyard cock, 'though that was actually the idea!' as the hens said. And what says the moral?

'It's better to crow than to be puffed up and snap off.'

THE DUNG-BEETLE

THE EMPEROR'S horse was given shoes of gold, a gold shoe on either foot. Why was he given shoes of gold?

He was the loveliest of beasts, with slender legs, eyes so very intelligent, and a mane which hung down his neck like a veil of silk. He had borne his master through shot and shell and heard the singing and whistling of bullets; he had bitten and he had kicked and he had fought back when the enemy had pressed forward; with his emperor had cleared the fallen foe's horse at a bound, saving his emperor's crown of purest gold, and saving his master's life that was worth more than the purest gold. And that was why the emperor's horse was given shoes of gold, a gold shoe on either foot.

Then out crawled the dung-beetle.

'First the big and then the small,' it said. 'Though it isn't the size that matters.' And so saying it stretched out its spindly legs.

'What do you want?' asked the blacksmith.

'Gold shoes!' replied the dung-beetle.

'You can't be all there!' said the blacksmith. 'You mean to say you want gold shoes?'

'Shoes of gold!' said the dung-beetle. 'Surely I'm as good as that big beast which has to be waited on and groomed and kept, and fed and watered? Don't I belong to the emperor's stable as well?'

'But *why* is the emperor's horse getting gold shoes?' asked the blacksmith. 'Don't you see why?'

'See? I see it's a slight on me,' said the dung-beetle. 'It's an insult! And so now I'm going off into the wide world.'

'Buzz off!' said the blacksmith.

'Coarse fellow!' said the dung-beetle. And going outside it flew off and was soon in a nice little flower-garden, where there was a smell of roses and lavender.

'Isn't it lovely here?' said one of the little ladybirds flying around there, with black spots on their armour-plated wings. 'How sweet it smells, and how pretty it is!'

'I'm used to something better,' said the dung-beetle. 'Do you call this pretty? Why, there isn't even a dung-heap here.'

And so away it went again, into the shade of a big stock; and on this crawled a caterpillar.

'What a grand world it is!' said the caterpillar. 'The sun is so warm! Everything is so delightful! And when some time I fall asleep and die, as they call it, I shall wake up and be a butterfly.'

'You've got big ideas!' said the dung-beetle. 'I fly about like a butterfly now. I'm from the emperor's stable, but nobody there, not even the emperor's parade horse, though it may wear my cast-off shoes, has such big ideas. Get wings! Fly! Well, here we fly!' And away flew the dung-beetle. 'I'm not going to work myself up—though I do work myself up.'

Next it flopped down on to a large patch of grass; and here for a while it lay till it fell asleep.

Dear me, what a downpour came on! The dung-beetle was awakened by the splashing, and would have gone straight down into the ground only it couldn't. It toppled over and it swam about on its stomach and on its back; flying was out of the question, and it felt that it would never escape from that place alive. It lay where it had lain, and lay still.

When it began to clear up and the dung-beetle had blinked the water out of its eyes, it caught sight of something white; it was linen, which had been laid out to bleach. And crawling towards it, it crept under a fold of the wet cloth. Of course it wasn't to be compared with lying in the warm dung of the stable; but there was nothing there any better, and so there it stopped for a whole day and a whole night, while the rain didn't stop. The dung-beetle came out the next morning, and was very much annoyed at the climate.

Two frogs sat there on the linen, and their bright eyes shone for very joy. 'Oh, what glorious weather!' said one of them. 'How refreshing it is! And how beautifully the linen holds the water! There's a tickling in my back legs as though I was going to swim.'

'I wonder,' said the other, 'if the swallow, who's such a big flyer, has ever on all its foreign travels found a climate better than ours. Such a splashing and such a soaking! It's just like being in a wet ditch. Whoever doesn't like it has got no real love for his own country.'

'And so you've never been in the emperor's stables?' asked the dung-beetle. 'The wet there is both warm and spicy! That's what I'm used to, that's my climate; only you can't take it with you. Isn't there a hot-bed in the garden, where persons of quality like me can go inside and feel at home?'

But the frogs didn't understand him; or wouldn't understand him.

'I never ask my questions twice,' said the dung-beetle, when it had asked three times without getting a reply.

Further on it came to a broken pot, which shouldn't have lain there, but where it lay it gave shelter. In it lived several families of earwigs, who don't ask for much house-room but only company. The females are especially gifted with mother-love, and for this reason the children of each of them were the prettiest and the cleverest.

'Our son has got engaged,' said one mother. 'The pretty innocent! His greatest ambition is to be able some time to crawl into the ear of a parson. He's so delightfully childish, and being engaged keeps him out of mischief; it's such a happy thing for a mother.'

'Our son,' said another mother, 'was no sooner out of the egg that he was up to his tricks. He's full of them. It's such a joy for a mother! Don't you think so, Mr Dung-beetle?' They could tell the stranger from his uniform.

'You're both right,' said the dung-beetle; and at this it was invited inside, as far under the broken pot as it could get.

'Now you must have a look at *my* little earwig,' said a third, and then a fourth mother. 'He's the most lovable little thing, and ever so funny! He's never naughty except when he has a pain in his stomach, but then you get that so easily at their age.'

And so each mother talked about her children and the children talked as well, using the little nippers which they have in their tails to pull the dung-beetle's whiskers.

'They do think of some tricks, the little rascals!' said their mothers, oozing with mother-love. But all this bored the dung-beetle, and so it asked how far it was to the hot-bed.

'It's right out in the world, on the other side of the ditch,' said the earwig. 'None of my children will ever go as far, I hope; I'd die if they did.'

'I'm going to try and get as far, though,' said the dung-beetle, going off without saying goodbye, in the most gentlemanly way.

By the ditch it met several of its relations, all of them dung-beetles.

'Here's where we live!' they said. 'We've a cosy little spot. May we invite you down into our wallow? Your journey seems to have tired you!'

'It has,' said the dung-beetle. 'I've been lying on linen in the rain, and nothing takes it out of me like cleanliness. And on top of that I've got rheumatism in my wing-joint from standing in a draught under a broken pot. It's a real treat to be back among your own people again.'

'You come from the hot-bed, perhaps?' asked the eldest.

'Higher up than that!' said the dung-beetle. 'I come from the emperor's stable, where I was born with gold shoes on. I'm travelling on a secret errand about which you mustn't ask questions, because I won't answer them.'

And with this the dung-beetle got down into the rich mud, where there sat three young female dung-beetles, who giggled because they didn't know what to say.

'They aren't engaged yet,' said their mother; and at this they giggled again, though from bashfulness.

'I haven't seen any more beautiful in the emperor's stable,' said the travelling dung-beetle.

'Now, don't spoil my girls for me! And don't talk to them unless your intentions are honourable! But I see they are, and so I give you my blessing.'

'Hurrah!' cried all the others; and the dung-beetle was engaged. First engagement, then wedding; there was no point in waiting.

The next day passed off very well, and the next jogged along; but on the third day it was time to be thinking of something to eat for the wife and perhaps little ones.

'I let them take me by surprise,' it said. 'I dare say I can surprise them in turn . . .'

And it did. It was gone; gone all day and gone all night—and the wife was a widow. The other dung-beetles said that it was a proper vagabond they had taken into the family; the wife was left a burden to them.

'And here we have her unmarried again,' said the mother. 'My child! Shame on the dirty beetle for leaving her!'

Meanwhile he had started off and had sailed on a cabbage-leaf across the ditch. During the morning two people came along and, seeing the dung-beetle, picked it up and turned it this way and that in their hands, both looking very learned, especially the boy. 'Allah sees the black beetle in the black rock in the black mountain; isn't that what it says in the Koran?' he asked. And he translated the dung-beetle's name into Latin and described its family and its characteristics. The elder scholar voted against taking it home, as they had, he said, specimens that were just as good. This, thought the dung-beetle, was not a polite thing to say, and so it flew out of his hand and a long way off. Its wings had grown dry now, and so it came to the green-house, where, as there was an open window, it easily slipped inside and burrowed down into the fresh manure.

'This is delicious,' it said.

Soon it had fallen asleep and was dreaming that the emperor's horse had fallen and that Mr Dung-beetle had been given its golden shoes and the promise of two more. This was all very nice; and when the dung-beetle woke up it crawled out and had a look round. How grand it was in the greenhouse! Big fan-palms rose up aloft; the sun made them transparent, and below them grew a profusion of green leaves, and flowers which gleamed red like fire, yellow like amber, and white like fresh-fallen snow.

'What a gorgeous mass of plants! Won't it taste good when it starts to rot!' said the dung-beetle. 'This is a good larder; I suppose people of quality live here. I'll go in search of them, and see if there's anybody I can mix with. Proud I am, and that's my pride!' And so off it went, while thinking of its dream about the dead horse and the gift of golden shoes.

Then all at once a hand seized hold of the dung-beetle, and it was squeezed and turned this way and that.

The gardener's little son and a playmate were in the greenhouse, and they had seen the dung-beetle and meant to have some fun with it. It was put, wrapped up in a grape leaf, into a warm trouser pocket, where it tickled and prickled till it got a squeeze from the hand of the boy, as he hurried with it to the big lake at the bottom of the garden, where the dung-beetle was put into a broken old clog from which the arch was missing. A stick was fixed to it as a mast, and to this the dung-beetle was tied with a piece of woollen thread; it was a ship's captain now, going off for a sail.

It was a very big lake which to the dung-beetle seemed like an ocean, and it was so astonished that it fell sprawling on its back with its legs in the air.

The clog sailed off and there was a current flowing; but if the vessel got too far out, one of the boys would roll up his trousers and go out and fetch it. But as the clog was drifting out once more the boys were called—called strictly—and hurried away, clog or no clog. This drifted further and further out, further and further from land. It was dreadful for the dung-beetle; it couldn't fly, as it had been tied fast to the mast.

It was visited by a fly.

'Lovely weather we're having!' said the fly. 'I can rest here and bask in the sun. You're very comfortable!'

'You sound very sure of yourself! Don't you see I'm tied?'

'I'm not tied,' said the fly; and off it flew.

'Now I know the world,' said the dung-beetle. 'It's a mean world, and I'm the only respectable creature in it! First they refuse me gold shoes, then I have to lie on wet linen and stand in a draught, and on top of that they palm a wife on to me. When I take a quick trip into the world and see how things might be, along comes a human pup and puts me tied up on the wild ocean. And meanwhile the emperor's horse is wearing shoes of gold! That's what makes me most sick; but you can't expect sympathy in this world! My career is very interesting, but what's the good of that when nobody knows anything about it? And the world doesn't deserve to know of it, or it would have given me gold shoes in the emperor's stable when the parade horse was shod as it reached out its legs. If I'd been given gold shoes, I'd have been a credit to the stable; now it has lost me, and the world has lost me. It's all over!'

But it wasn't all over yet; for along came a boat in which were some young girls.

'There's a floating clog!' said one of them.

'There's a little creature tied up in it,' said another.

They were right alongside the clog, and they got it out; and one of the girls took a pair of scissors and, without hurting the dung-beetle, cut the woollen thread. And when they went ashore she put it down on the grass.

'Crawl, crawl! Fly, fly, if you can!' she said. 'Freedom is a glorious thing!'

And the dung-beetle flew straight in through the open window of a large building, where, tired out, it sank down in the delicate, soft, long mane of the emperor's war-horse, which stood in the stable where it and the dung-beetle belonged. Clinging tightly to the mane, it sat for a while as it regained its strength. 'Here I sit on the emperor's war-horse, sit like a horseman! What was that I said? Why, now I see it all! It's a good idea, and a right one. Why was the emperor's horse given shoes of gold? That's what he, the blacksmith, asked me. Now I see why! The horse was given gold shoes for my sake.'

And so now the dung-beetle was in a good humour.

'Travelling clears the head!' it said.

The sun was shining in on it, and shining very beautifully. 'The world isn't so bad after all,' said the dung-beetle. 'You've only to know how to take it!' The world was fine; for the emperor's war-horse had been given gold shoes because the dung-beetle was to be its rider.

'I'll crawl down now to the other beetles and tell them how much has been done for me. I'll tell them about all the pleasant things I've enjoyed on my foreign travels, and say that I'm going to stay at home now till the horse has worn out its gold shoes.'

PA ALWAYS DOES THE RIGHT THING

Now, I'll tell you a story I heard when I was a boy, and which whenever I've thought of it since seems to have grown ever so much nicer; for it's with stories as with many people, they grow nicer and nicer with age—and isn't that delightful!

You'll have been in the country. You'll have seen an old, old cottage with a thatched roof. Mosses and plants will grow on it of their own accord; there'll be a stork's nest on the ridge (we can't do without a stork!); the walls will be crooked; the windows will be low and only one of them will open; the chimney-piece will jut out like a fat little tummy; and the elder-bush will overhang the fence, where there'll be a little pond with a duck or some ducklings on it, underneath the knotted willow-tree. Yes, and then there'll be a watch-dog which barks at every passer-by.

Well, in the country there was a cottage just like this, and in it there lived two people, a farmer and his wife. Little though they had, there was one thing they could have done without, and that was a horse which used to graze by the roadside. Father would ride into town on it and the neighbours would borrow it, giving something in return; yet they thought they would get a greater return from selling the horse or exchanging it for something more useful to them. But what was that to be?

'You, Pa, will know what to do for the best!' said the wife. 'There's a fair on in town; ride there and sell the horse or make a good exchange. You always do the right thing. Ride off to the fair!'

So she tied his muffler (for she was better at that than he was), tying it in a double bow so that he looked really spruce; and then she wiped his hat with the palm of her hand and kissed him on his warm lips, and off he rode on the horse that was to be sold or exchanged. Oh yes, Pa knew all about it!

The sun was scorching; there wasn't a cloud in the sky. And the road was dusty with people going to the fair, some in carts and on horseback, others just walking. It was a baking hot day, and there wasn't a bit of shade anywhere on the way.

Along came a man driving a cow: as nice a cow as ever you could wish for. 'She'll give lovely milk!' thought the farmer. 'That might be a good swap!' 'I say, you with the cow,' he said, 'let's talk things over a bit! A horse is pretty certain to cost more than a cow. Still, never mind that; a cow's of more use to me! Shall we swap?'

'All right!' said the man with the cow. And so they swapped.

Well, that was that, and the farmer could now have turned back, having done what he had set out to do. But he had made up his mind to go to the fair, and to the fair he meant to go, just for the sake of seeing it. So off he went with his cow. He walked briskly along and the cow walked briskly along, and so they had soon overtaken a man driving a sheep. It was a good sheep with lots of meat on it and lots of wool.

'I wish that was mine!' thought the farmer. 'It would never be short of grazing at our roadside, and in the winter we could bring it indoors. In fact, we'd do better to keep a sheep than a cow!'

'Shall we swap?' he said.

The man with the sheep being willing enough, the exchange was made and the farmer went on his way with the sheep.

Coming to a stile, he saw a man with a big goose under his arm.

'That's a big fellow you've got!' said the farmer. 'There's flesh and feathers on that. It would look well tied up near our pond. It's just the thing for Mother to gather peelings for. She's often said "If only we had a goose!" Now she can have one—and she shall have one! Will you swap? I'll swap the sheep for the goose, and welcome!'

The other being quite willing, they swapped, and the farmer got the goose. He was near to the town now and the road was getting more and more crowded, packed with men and beasts walking along the road and the roadside right up onto the gate-keeper's potato patch, where his hen was tied up so that it wouldn't be frightened away and get lost. It was a bobtailed hen which blinked with one eye and seemed to be a good one. 'Cluck! Cluck!' she said. What she meant by that I have no idea, but the farmer when he saw her thought to himself: 'She's the prettiest hen I've ever seen; prettier than the parson's sitting-hen. I wish she was mine! A hen's never short of a grain of corn; she'll almost keep herself. To get that in exchange for the goose would be a good bargain, I think! . . . Shall we swap?' he asked. 'Swap?' said the other. 'Why, that's not such a bad idea!' And so they swapped; the gate-keeper got the goose and the farmer got the hen.

He had managed to do quite a lot of business on that journey to town, and as it was hot and he was tired, he felt that he could do with a drink and a bite to eat. He had reached an inn and was just going inside when the innkeeper's man happened to be coming out, and he met him in the doorway carrying a bag crammed full of something.

'What's that you've got?' asked the farmer.

'Rotten apples!' answered the man. 'A whole sackful for the pigs.'

'You've got a real good lot there! I only wish Mother could see it! Why, last year we only had one apple on our old tree by the peat-shed! That apple had to be kept, and it stood on the chest till it burst. "A little's always something!" Mother said. She'd be seeing something here, all right! Yes, if only she could!'

'What'll you give for them?' asked the man.

'Give? I'll swap you my hen for them.' And so he gave him the hen in exchange for them, entered the inn, and walked up to the counter. His sack of apples he laid beside the fire-place, where the fire was lit, though he never gave that a thought. In the room there were many strangers: horse-dealers, cattle-dealers, and two Englishmen. These are so rich that their pockets bulge with sovereigns, and they are fond of betting. Now, listen what happened!

'Hiss! Hiss!' Whatever was that noise by the fire-place? The apples were beginning to roast.

'What's that?' people asked. And it wasn't long before they had learnt the whole story about the horse that had been exchanged for the cow, and so on down to the rotten apples.

'H'm! You'll catch it when you get home!' said the Englishmen. 'There's trouble brewing for you!'

'It won't be trouble, it'll be kisses,' said the farmer. 'Mother'll say: "Pa always does the right thing!"'

'What'll you bet?' they said. 'A barrelful of sovereigns! A hundred pounds to a penny!'

'A bushel will do!' said the farmer. 'I can only lay my bushel of apples, with me and Mother thrown in. But that'd be more than full measure!'

'Done! Done!' they said; and the bet was made. And so out came the innkeeper's cart and on got the Englishmen, and the farmer got on and the rotten apples got on, and in time they all got to the farmer's cottage.

'Hello there, Mother!'

'Hello, Pa!'

'I've done a swap!'

'You know the way to do it, all right!' said the wife, putting her arm round his waist and forgetting both the bag and the strangers.

'I swapped the horse for a cow!'

'Thank Heaven for that milk!' said the wife. 'Now we can have milk puddings and butter and cheese on the table. You made a good swap!'

'Yes, but I swapped the cow for a sheep!'

'Why, that's even better!' said the woman. 'You always think of everything; we've plenty of grazing for a sheep. Now we can have sheep's milk and sheep's cheese, and woollen stockings and even woollen night things! The cow wouldn't have given all that; she loses her hair! You really do think of everything!'

'But I swapped the sheep for a goose!'

'You don't mean to say we've to have a Christmas goose this year, Pa dear? You always think of something to please me! Now that was thoughtful of you. The goose can be kept tied up and fattened for Christmas!'

'But I swapped the goose for a hen!' said the man.

'Hen! That's a good swap!' said the woman. 'The hen'll lay eggs, and then she'll hatch them and we'll have chickens—we'll have a poultry farm! That's just the very thing I've been wanting!'

'Yes, but I swapped the hen for a bag of rotten apples!'

'Well, now I must give you a kiss!' said the woman. 'Thank you, my dear husband! And now I've something to tell you. While you were away I thought I'd cook you a really nice meal—scrambled eggs and onions. I had the eggs, but no onions. So I went across to the schoolmaster's, where I know they have onions. But the wife's such a mean thing! I asked her to lend me some. "Lend you?" she said. "Nothing grows in our garden; not even a rotten apple! I couldn't lend you that!" Why, now I can lend her ten—a whole bagful! What a lark, Pa!' And she kissed him full on the lips.

'Now, that's what I like!' said the Englishmen. 'Always going down, but never down-hearted! It's worth every penny of our money!' And so they paid out their bushel of sovereigns to the farmer who got a kissing instead of a licking.

Ah yes, it pays a wife to know and admit that Pa's the wisest, and that he always does the right thing.

Now, there you have a story! I heard that when I was a boy, and now you've heard it as well—and know that Pa always does the right thing.

THE SNOWMAN

'I FEEL all of a crunch, it's so lovely and cold!' said the snowman. 'The wind can certainly nip life into one! And how that glarer there does glare!' (meaning the sun, which was just about to set). 'She won't get me to blink; I'm holding my ground!'

He had two big, three-cornered pieces of broken tile for eyes, and his mouth was part of an old rake, which gave him teeth.

He had been born to the sound of cheering boys and greeted by the tinkling bells and whip-cracking of sleighs.

The sun went down and the full moon rose up round and big, clear and lovely in the blue air.

'There she comes again from another side,' said the snowman, thinking it was the sun coming up again. 'I've stopped her from glaring! Let her hang there and show her light for me to see myself by. If only I knew how to get moving! I do wish I could move! I'd go sliding on the ice, if I could; the way I saw the boys doing. But I don't know how to run!'

'Off! Off!' barked the old watch-dog. (He was rather hoarse, and had been since his days as a house-dog, when he had lain under the stove.) 'The sun's going to teach you to run! I saw that with last year's fellow, and with the fellow before him. Off! Off! And off they all go!'

'I don't understand you, my friend!' said the snowman. 'Is that creature up there' (meaning the moon) 'going to teach me to run? She ran sure enough when I gave her a straight look the last time. She's sneaking back from the other side now.'

'You don't know a thing,' said the watch-dog. 'But then you've only just been thrown up! The one you see now is the moon. The one that went was the sun; she'll be back tomorrow. She'll teach you to run down the grate! We're in for a change of weather. I've a shooting pain in my left back leg; that means a change in the weather.'

'I don't understand him,' said the snowman. 'But I've a feeling it's something unpleasant he's saying. She that glared at me and then went down, the one he calls the sun, wasn't my friend either; I can feel that.'

'Off! Off!' barked the watch-dog; and after turning on his tail three times he went into his kennel to sleep.

There actually was a change in the weather. In the early hours a mist settled, thick and cold, over the whole neighbourhood. At daybreak a wind rose. It was icy cold and the frost nipped like anything. But what a gorgeous sight there was when the sun rose! All the trees and bushes were covered with hoar-frost. It was like a forest of white coral, as though all the branches were studded with silvery blossom. Countless numbers of delicate sprigs and sprays, the ones that in summer you can't see for the leaves, now stood out on every one. It was like lace, and as dazzling white as though a brilliant white light streamed from every branch. The silver birch stirred in the wind and seemed to be as much alive as trees in summertime. How very lovely it all was! And when the sun came, how everything sparkled. It was as though everything was powdered over with diamond dust, while big diamonds glistened on the snow-covered earth! You might even have thought that a myriad tiny candles were burning, whiter than the white snow itself.

'How very lovely!' cried a young woman, coming into the garden with a young man and stopping close to the snowman to look at the glistening trees. 'There is no lovelier sight in summer!' she said, her eyes sparkling.

'And no such fellow as this,' said the young man, pointing to the snowman. 'He's grand!'

The young woman laughed and, nodding to the snowman, went tripping off with her friend across the snow, which crunched under their feet as if they had been walking on starch.

'Who were those two?' said the snowman to the watch-dog. 'You've been here longer than I have. Do you know them?'

'Why, yes!' said the watch-dog. 'She's patted me, and he's given me a bone. I never bite them.'

'But who are they supposed to be?' asked the snowman.

'Sweethear-rr-ts!' growled the watch-dog. 'They're going to share a kennel and gnaw bones together. Off! Off!'

'Are those two as important as you and I?' asked the snowman.

'Why, they belong to the family!' said the watch-dog. 'It's precious little a fellow knows who was only born yesterday; that's plain to see! I have age and wisdom; I know everybody at this place. And I've known the time when I didn't stand here chained up in the cold. Off! Off!'

'The cold's lovely!' said the snowman. 'But tell me more about it! Only stop rattling that chain, or you'll upset my inside!'

'Off! Off!' barked the watch-dog. 'I was a puppy, a pretty little pet, they said. I used to lie on a velvet stool in those days, and in the lap of the master and the mistress; and I was kissed on the lips and had my paws wiped with an embroidered handkerchief. They used to call me "Nice doggie" and "Sweety pet". But then I grew too big for them and they gave me to the housekeeper. I came down in the world—into the basement! From where you are you can see it; you can look into the room where I made one of the family—that's what I was when I lived with the housekeeper. It may have been a poorer place than the one above, but it was cosier; and I wasn't cuddled and lugged about by children as I had been upstairs. My food was just as good, and there was more of it! I had a cushion of my own. And then there was the stove! At this time of the year that's the nicest thing in all the world. I would get right under it, out of everybody's way. Yes, I still dream of that stove! Off! Off!'

'Is a stove nice to look at?' asked the snowman. 'Is it like me?'

'It's the exact opposite of you! It's as black as soot, and has a long neck with a brass front. It eats wood till the fire comes out of its mouth. You have to keep near it, right up to it, underneath it; then it's as cosy as anything. If you look through the window from where you stand you should be able to see it!

And looking in, the snowman actually saw a polished black object with a brass front. The fire shone out from underneath it. And the snowman had a strange feeling inside him, a feeling he just couldn't make out. Something he had never known before had come over him, something known to everybody who isn't a snowman.

'And why did you leave her?' asked the snowman, thinking that it must be a she. 'Whatever made you leave such a place?'

'I couldn't help it,' said the watch-dog. 'They turned me out and chained me up here. I'd bitten the young master in the leg for kicking away the bone I was gnawing; and a leg-bone for a leg-bone, thought I. But it upset them, and I've been chained up ever since and have lost my voice. Hear how hoarse I am: Off! Off! And off I went!'

The snowman was no longer listening; he was still staring into the housekeeper's basement, into the room where the stove was standing on its four iron legs, looking about the size of the snowman himself.

'I've got such a crunching feeling,' he said. 'Am I never going to get inside? It's a harmless wish, and surely harmless wishes should be granted. It's my biggest wish, and my only wish; it would be rather unfair if I didn't get it. I must get in; I must lean my head against hers, if it means breaking the window.'

'You'll never get in there,' said the watch-dog. 'And if you did get to the stove, you'd be off! Off!'

'I'm as good as off now,' said the snowman. 'I'm breaking in two, I think.'

All day long the snowman stood gazing in at the window. At dusk the room seemed even more inviting; a gentle glow was coming from the stove such as never came from the sun or the moon, but such as only a stove can give out when there's something in it. Whenever the stove door was opened the flames would leap out in the way they had, shining bright red on the snowman's white face and throwing a red glow all over his chest.

'I can't bear it,' he said. 'How it suits her to put her tongue out!'

The night was very long, though not for the snowman, who stood there wrapped up in his own pleasant thoughts, which were all freezing hard.

In the morning the basement windows were frozen up. They had the loveliest frosty patterns that any snowman could wish for, but they hid the stove. The panes wouldn't thaw, and he couldn't see her. It crunched and it crackled; it was just the sort of frost that should please a snowman, and yet he wasn't pleased. He could have felt happy, and he ought to have felt happy, but he wasn't happy; he was pining for a stove.

'That's a bad complaint for a snowman,' said the watch-dog. 'I've been troubled with it myself, but I've got over it. Off! Off! There's a change in the weather.'

And there was a change in the weather; it changed to thaw.

The thaw went on and the snowman went off. He never said anything and he never complained, and that's a sure sign.

One morning he toppled over. What looked like a broomstick was left standing in the air where he had stood; the boys had set him up around this.

'Now I understand why he pined so,' said the watch-dog. 'The snowman had a stove-scraper inside him. That's what upset him. Well, it's all over now! Off! Off!'

And soon the winter, too, was over.

'Off! Off!' barked the watch-dog. But in the playground the little girls sang:

> 'Peep out, sweet primrose, proud and brave;
> Now, willow, your wool tassels wave!
> Come, cuckoo, soon, and skylark sing;
> For February spells the spring!
> Cuckoo! Tweet-tweet! I join your song!
> Come, welcome sun, shine all day long!'

And then no one ever thinks of the snowman any more.

THE BUTTERFLY

THE BUTTERFLY was wanting a sweetheart, and naturally he wanted a nice little flower. So he had a look at them. They all sat very quiet and sedate on their stalks, as young ladies who are not engaged should do; but there were so many to choose from, and it was so much trouble, that the butterfly couldn't be bothered and flew off to the dog-daisy. They call her Marguerite and she can tell fortunes, which she does when people pluck off her petals, saying of their sweethearts as they do so: 'He loves me! He loves me not! He loves me! He loves me not!' and so on. You can say it in any language. The butterfly, too, had come to ask its fortune; only he didn't pick off her petals but gave each one a kiss, believing that kindness gets you further.

'Sweet Marguerite Daisy!' he said. 'You are the wisest woman among all the flowers. You can tell fortunes. Tell me if I'm to marry this one or that! Tell me which one to marry! When I know, I can fly straight to her and propose!'

But Marguerite gave no answer at all. She didn't like him to call her a woman, for she was a lady, and a lady isn't a woman. He asked her twice and he asked her three times, and as he never got a single word out of her he couldn't be bothered to ask her any more but flew straight off to propose.

It was in the early spring and there were a lot of snowdrops and crocuses. 'They're very pretty!' said the butterfly. 'Sweet little things, but rather insipid!' Like all young men he was looking for older girls. He next flew to the anemones, but they were too sour for him; and the violets were too romantic, the tulips too showy, the narcissuses too respectable. The lime-blossom was too small and had so many relations; the apple-blossom, though it looked like a rose, blossomed only today and dropped tomorrow, just as the wind blew, and that would be too short a married life, thought he. The sweet-pea was of all the flowers the one that pleased him best: she was pink and white, she was fair and pretty, and was one of the domesticated girls who are both good-looking and can make themselves useful in the kitchen. He was on the very point of proposing to her when he saw, hanging close beside her, a pea-pod with a withered blossom at the end. 'Who's that?' he asked. 'My sister,' said the sweet-pea.

'So that's what you'll come to look like!' This so frightened the butterfly that off he flew.

Over the hedge hung the honeysuckle; lots of those young ladies who are so long in the face and sallow-complexioned. They were not the sort he liked. Well then, what did he like? Ask him!

Spring passed, summer passed, and autumn had come round; and he was no nearer. And the flowers put on their loveliest dresses; but what was the use of that, when the freshness and fragrance of youth were absent. Fragrance is exactly what the heart in old age requires, and there isn't very much fragrance in dahlias and hollyhocks. And so the butterfly came down to the mint.

'She has no flowers at all but is a flower all over, fragrant from tip to root, the fragrance of flowers in every leaf. I'll have her!'

And so at long last he proposed.

But the mint stood stiff and silent, and in the end she said: 'Friendship, but that's all! I'm old and you're old. We might well live for each other, but marry—no! Don't let us make fools of ourselves in our old age!'

And so the butterfly had no one. He had been looking too long, and one should never do that. The butterfly became, as they say, a crusty old bachelor.

It was late in the autumn, and raining and drizzling; the wind blew chill down the backs of the old willow-trees, making them creak. It wasn't the weather to be flying abut in one's summer dress, neither for love nor money, as the saying goes. But the butterfly wasn't flying about outside; he had happened to get inside, where there was a fire in the grate and it was as warm as in summer. He was able to live; only 'to live isn't enough!' he said. 'Sunshine, freedom, and a little flower are what you want!'

And flying towards the window he was seen, admired, and stuck on a pin in a box of curios. They couldn't do more for him.

'So now I'm on a stalk like the flowers!' said the butterfly. 'But it isn't what you'd call pleasant. I suppose it's like being married: you're a fixture!' And so he consoled himself with that.

'It's a poor consolation!' said the flowers on the pot-plants.

'But pot-plants aren't really to be believed,' thought the butterfly. 'They keep too much company with people.'

THE SNAIL AND THE ROSE-BUSH

SURROUNDING the garden was a hedge of hazel-bushes and outside it were fields and meadows with cows and sheep in them. But in the middle of the garden stood a rose-bush in bloom and under this sat a snail. He had a lot in him: he had himself.

'Wait till my time comes!' he said. 'I shall do something more than put forth roses and bear nuts; or give milk like cows and sheep.'

'I expect a tremendous lot from you,' said the rose-bush. 'May I ask when it will be?'

'I shall take my time,' said the snail. 'You, now, are in such a hurry! That doesn't raise hopes!'

The next year the snail sat in almost the same spot, in the sunshine under the rose-tree, which was budding and blooming: always fresh roses, always new ones. And crawling half way forward the snail stuck out his horns—and drew them in again.

'It all looks like last year! There's been no progress: the rose-tree keeps on with his roses and never gets any further!'

Summer passed, autumn passed. The rose-tree bloomed and budded right on till the snow fell and the weather turned raw and wet. Then the rose-tree bowed down towards the ground and the snail crawled into the ground.

Soon a new year began; and the roses came out and the snail came out.

'You're an old rose now,' he said. 'It's time you began to die. You've given the world all you had in you. Whether it mattered is a question I've never had time to consider. But it's plain to see that you haven't done a scrap for your inner development, or something else would have come out of you. Can you justify that? You'll soon be only a dried-up stick! Do you see what I mean?'

'You frighten me!' said the rose-bush. 'I never thought of that!'

'No, you'll never have gone in for much thinking! Have you ever accounted for yourself; for why you bloomed and how blooming came about? In what way, and why no other way?'

'No!' said the rose-bush. 'I bloomed for the joy of it, for I could do nothing else. The sun was so warm, the air so refreshing. I drank the clear dew and the heavy rain. I breathed; I lived! I drew strength from up above. I felt a blessing; always new, always great. And so I always had to bloom. It was my life; I could do nothing else!'

'You've led a very comfortable life,' said the snail.

'Certainly! Everything was given to me!' said the rose-bush. 'But even more was given to you! You are one of those thoughtful, deep-thinking natures; one of the highly gifted who will astonish the world!'

'I certainly don't intend to,' said the snail. 'The world doesn't concern me. What have I to do with the world? I have enough of myself, and enough in myself.'

'But shouldn't all of us here on earth give others of our best? Bring what we can? Well now, I've only given roses! But you? You who were given so much, what did you give to the world? What are you giving to it?'

'What did I give? What am I giving? I spit at it! It's of no use. It doesn't concern me. Put forth your roses; it's as far as you'll get. Let the hazel-bush bear nuts! Let cows and sheep give milk! They each have their public; and I have mine in myself.

I'm going in to myself, and there I shall stay. The world doesn't concern me.'

And the snail went into his shell and sealed it up.

'It's such a very great pity!' said the rose-tree. 'I can't for the life of me crawl in, but must always be springing out, springing into roses. The petals fall off and they blow away on the wind! Yet I saw one of the roses get put into the housewife's hymn-book; one of my roses was placed on the breast of a lovely young girl; and one was kissed by the lips of a child in very joy. That made me so happy; it was a true delight. That's my remembrance; my life!'

And the rose-tree bloomed innocently on, while the snail moped in his shell. The world didn't concern him.

And so the years rolled by.

The snail was dust of the dust and the rose-tree was dust of the dust; the rose of remembrance in the hymn-book had withered away. But in the garden new rose-bushes bloomed; in the garden grew new snails. They crawled into their shells and spat. The world didn't concern them.

Shall we read the story all over from the beginning? It won't be any different.

THE SILVER PENNY

THERE was a penny that had come bright from the mint, skipping and clinking. 'Hurrah!' it cried. 'I'm off into the wide world!' And it was.

The child held on to it tightly with warm hands and the miser with cold and clammy hands; old people turned it over and over many times while the young sent it rolling on at once. The penny was a silver one with just a little copper in it; and it had been a whole year in the world—that is to say, in the country where it had been minted—when, one day, it went on a journey abroad. It was the last of the country's coins that were left in the purse of its travelling master, and he had no idea that he had it till it got between his fingers.

'Why, I've still got a penny from home!' he said. 'It can travel along with me.' And the penny clinked and skipped for joy as he put it back into the purse. It lay there with foreign companions who came and went; one would make way for the next, but always the penny from home stayed behind. That was a distinction.

Several weeks had now gone by and the penny was far out in the world, without exactly knowing where; it heard from the other coins that they were French and Italian, and one would say that now they were in this town, and another would say that now they were in that; but of all this the penny could have no idea, for you don't see the world when you're always in a bag, which is where it was. But noticing one day that the purse wasn't shut, it crept to the opening in order to peep out. Now this it should never have done, but then it was inquisitive and you have to pay for that: it fell out into the trouser pocket, and when the purse was laid aside in the evening, the penny was left where it was and went with the clothes into the corridor; there it dropped straight on to the floor, and nobody heard it, nobody saw it.

In the morning the clothes were brought in and the gentleman put them on and went away. And the penny didn't go with him, but was found, put into service again, and went out with three other coins.

'Well, it's nice to see the world!' thought the penny. 'To know other people, other customs!'

'What sort of a penny's this?' somebody said all at once. 'This isn't our money! It's false! No good!'

And here begins the penny's story, as it afterwards told it.

'False! No good! It cut me,' said the penny. 'I knew I was of good silver and good ring, and of good mint. Surely they were mistaken and couldn't mean me! But they did mean me! It was me they were calling false! Me that was no good! "I'll have to pass this in the dark!" said the man who had me. And so I was passed in the dark and abused in broad daylight. "False! No good! We must get rid of this!"'

And the penny would tremble in the fingers every time it was to be secretly passed off as lawful coin.

'Miserable me!' said the penny. 'What was the use of my silver, my stamp, my mint, when they didn't mean anything? Your worth to the world is the value the world puts on you! How awful to have a guilty conscience and slink along paths of wickedness when I, though I was perfectly innocent, could feel as I did by only seeming to! Every time I was taken out I dreaded the eyes that would look at me, for I knew that I should be thrust back and flung on the counter, as if I were a cheat and a liar.

'Once I was passed to a poor penniless woman who got me in payment for her daily labour, and she was unable to get rid of me. Nobody would have me; I was a real trouble to her.

'"I can't help it, I shall have to cheat somebody with it," she said. "I can't afford to hold on to a bad penny. The rich baker shall have it; he can best afford it. But I shall still be doing wrong."

'"So now I'm going to trouble the woman's conscience!" I sighed. "Can I really have changed so very much in my old age?"

'And so the woman went to the rich baker's; but he knew, only too well, what coins were lawful. I didn't stay long where I was laid, but was flung in the woman's face; she got no bread for me, and I was made thoroughly miserable by having been thus minted for others' misfortune, I who in my younger days had been so cheerful and so confident, so conscious of my value and my goodness. I grew as melancholy as a poor penny can when nobody will have it. But taking me back home the woman looked at me very gently and with great kindness and friendliness. "No," she said, "I shan't cheat anybody with you! I'll punch a hole in you so everybody can see you're a bad one. And yet, come to think of it, you may be a lucky penny. Yes, I do believe! It's an idea! I'll punch a hole, thread a string through it, and then give the penny to the neighbour's little girl to hang round her neck for luck!"

'And so she punched a hole in me. It's never very nice to have a hole punched in you, but when the intention's good you can put up with a good deal. I was threaded and so became a sort of medal to be worn. I was hung round the little child's neck; and the child smiled at me and kissed me, and for a whole night I rested on her warm and innocent breast.

'In the morning her mother took me between her fingers and looked at me, thinking to herself as she did so, as I soon realized. Getting out a pair of scissors she cut the thread.

'"Lucky penny!" she said. "Well, we'll soon see!" And so saying she put me in acid and made me turn green; whereupon she sealed up the hole, rubbed me a little, and went off in the dark to the lottery agent for a lottery ticket that would bring good luck.

'How miserable I felt! I was so crushed that I could have snapped in two; I knew I should be called bad and flung back, and, what's more, in the sight of all those pennies and shillings with inscriptions and faces they could be proud of. But I escaped; there were so many people at the agent's, and he was so busy, that I fell clinking into the till with all the other coins. Whether the ticket ever won a prize I cannot say, but I do know that I was recognized as a bad penny the very next day, put on one side, and sent out to cheat, always cheat. It's unbearable when you're an honest character, as I declare I am.

'Year by year I thus passed from hand to hand and from house to house, always being abused and always looked down on; nobody believed in me, and I didn't even believe in myself or in the world. It was a hard time,

'Then one day a traveller came and, of course, I was made to cheat him, and he was innocent enough to take me for good money; but he was just about to spend me when once more I heard the cries of "No good! False!"

'"I took it for a good one," said the man, taking a closer look at me. Then all at once his face lit up, as no other face had ever done on giving me a closer look, as he said: "Why, what's this? If it isn't one of our own coins; a good honest penny from home with a hole punched in it, and they're calling it bad. Well, this *is* funny! I shall keep you and take you back home with me!"

'I was thrilled with joy: I had been called a good honest penny and was going back home where everybody would know me and tell that I was of good silver and true coin. I could have sparked for joy, only it isn't my nature to spark: that's for steel to do, not silver.

'I was wrapped up in fine white paper so that I shouldn't get mixed up with the other coins and be lost, and was only taken out on special occasions when fellow countrymen got together, and then was extremely well spoken of. They said I was interesting; and it's a pleasant thought that you can be interesting without saying a word.'

'And so I came home! My troubles were all over and my joys were beginning; for I was of good silver and I had the right stamp, and it didn't do the slightest harm having a hole punched in me for being bad, because it doesn't matter when you aren't. You have to hold out, for everything will come right in the end! Well, that's my belief!' said the penny.

THE TEAPOT

THERE was a proud teapot. It was proud of its china, proud of its long spout, proud of its wide handle. It had something before and behind, the spout before and the handle behind, and it used to talk of this. but it never talked of its lid: that had been broken and riveted; it was a fault and one never likes to talk of one's faults; other people are sure to do that. Cups and saucers, milk-jug, and sugar-bowl—the whole tea-service—would be certain to remember the lid's failing and talk about that rather than the good handle and the very good spout, as the teapot knew.

'I know them!' it said under its breath. 'And I know my own fault as well, and admit it; that's where I'm humble and modest. We all have our faults but we all have our good points. The cups were given handles and the sugar-bowl a lid; and, as for me, I was given both, and one thing in front that they'll never get, a spout, which makes me queen of the tea-table. The sugar-bowl and the milk-jug have been made servants of good taste, but I am the giver of it, the ruler. I dispense good cheer to thirsting humanity; in me Chinese leaves are brewed in boiling, tasteless water.'

All this the teapot said with youthful assurance. It stood on the laid-out table and was lifted by the most delicate hand. But the most delicate hand was clumsy: the teapot was dropped, the spout broke off, and the handle broke off. We will say no more of the lid; enough has been said about that already. The teapot lay swooning on the floor and the boiling water ran out.

It was a hard blow to the teapot, and the hardest thing of all was that they laughed; they laughed at the teapot and not at the clumsy hand.

'The experience is one that I shall never forget!' the teapot would say when afterwards it told itself the story of its own life. 'I was called a cripple, put away in a corner, and the next day given to a woman who had begged some dripping; I sank into poverty and was dumb inside and out. But it was as I stood there that my better life began; first you are one thing and then you become something else. I was filled up with soil, and to a teapot that is like being buried; but in the soil they planted a bulb. Who planted it, who gave it to me, I cannot tell, but it was in the place of the Chinese leaves and the boiling water, in place of the broken handle and spout. And the bulb lay in the soil, in me, and became my heart, my living heart; I had never had one like it before. There was life in me, there was energy and strength; my pulse beat and the bulb began to sprout, bursting with ideas and feelings, which then broke into flower. I saw it, I bore it, and forgot myself in its loveliness. How blessed it is to forget oneself in others! It never said "Thank you" to me, never even thought of me, as it was praised and admired. I was so glad because of this; so how much more glad it must have been! And then one day I heard them say that it deserved a better pot. I was broken in two; it hurt so dreadfully. But the flower was put into a better pot—and I was thrown into the yard and lie here an old broken pot. But I have the memory, and that I can never lose.'

HITTING ON AN IDEA

THERE was a young man studying to be a poet; he meant to be one by Easter, then get married and live on his poetry, and that, he knew, is a matter of hitting on an idea, only he couldn't hit on an idea. He had been born too late: every idea had been taken up before his time; every idea had been used and written about.

'How lucky the people born a thousand years ago!' he said. 'They could become immortal all right! Lucky the one born even a hundred years ago! There was still something to write about then. Now the world has been written up; what can I find to write down?'

He studied away till he made himself ill, the wretched fellow; no doctor could do anything for him, though the wise woman, he thought, might. She lived in a small cottage by a gate which she opened for drivers and riders; she could indeed open more than the gate, being wiser than the doctor who rides in his own carriage and pays surtax.

'I must go and see her!' said the young man.

It was a neat little cottage she lived in, though dull to look at, for there wasn't a tree and there wasn't a flower. There was a beehive near the door (very useful!), there was a small potato field (very useful!), and there was a hedge of sloes which had blossomed and bore fruit—the sort that set your teeth on edge if you taste them before the frost has touched them.

'The very image of our unpoetic times, I see!' thought the

young man. And that, anyway, was an idea; a pearl found at the wise woman's door.

'Make a note of it!' she said. 'Half a loaf's better than no bread. I know what you've come for; you can't hit on an idea and yet you want to be a poet by Easter!'

'They've all been written about!' he said. 'The olden days are over!'

'Yes!' said the wise woman. 'In olden days wise women were burnt and poets went about with empty stomachs and out at elbow. The times are good ones; they've never been better! But you haven't got the right way of looking at them; you haven't sharpened your hearing, and I dare say you never say your prayers at night. There are plenty of things to write and tell about when you know how to tell. You can unlock them from the plants and flowers of the earth, you can draw them from water running and standing; but you have to know how—know how to catch a sunbeam. Now, just try on my spectacles and put my trumpet to your ear; then pray to the Lord and stop thinking about yourself!'

The last, now, was very difficult. More than a wise woman can demand.

Taking the spectacles and the ear-trumpet, he was put into the middle of the potato field; here she placed a large potato in his hand, and it began to sing, singing a song with words, the story of potatoes, an interesting one—an everyday story in ten parts, ten lines being enough.

And what did the potato sing?

It sang about itself and its relations, of the coming of potatoes to Europe, and of the lack of appreciation they had suffered from before being recognized as a blessing greater than nuggets of gold.

'We were distributed by royal command at the town hall of

every city and proclamations were read about our great importance, but they weren't believed and nobody knew how to plant us. One man dug a hole and threw his bushel of potatoes in it; another stuck a potato in the ground here and another there and expected them to grow into trees he could shake potatoes off. Grow they did, and bore flowers and watery fruit, but then the whole plant died. Nobody gave a thought to what lay below; to the potatoes, the blessing. Yes, we've known trials and sufferings—or rather our forefathers have—they and us, it's all the same! What stories!'

'Now that will do!' said the woman. 'Look at the sloes!'

'We too,' said the sloes, 'have near relations in the land of the potatoes, further up north than they used to grow. From Norway there came some Norwegians, who, steering westward through fog and storms to an unknown land, found behind the ice and the snow green plants and bushes on which was the blue-black fruit of the vine. The sloes had frozen into ripe grapes, the way we do. And the country was called Wineland or Greenland, which is Sloe Land!'

'That's quite a romantic story!' said the young man.

'Now, come with me!' said the wise woman, as she led him to the bee-hive. He had a look inside. The life and the bustle there was! There were bees in all the passages, flapping their wings in order to create a healthy draught throughout their big factory, which was their job; and then from outside came other bees, born with baskets on their legs, who were bringing home pollen, which was shaken out, separated, and made into honey and wax. They came and they went. And the queen bee, too, wanted to fly; but then all the rest have to go with her, and it wasn't quite time. Fly, however, she would; and so they bit off her majesty's wings and she had to stay where she was.

'Now climb up on the bank!' said the wise woman. 'Come and look out over the road where there are people to be seen!'

'Why, what a swarm there is!' said the young man. 'Story upon story! Humming and buzzing! I'm in a whirl! I'm falling backwards!'

'No, go forward!' said the woman. 'Go right into the throng of people! Open your eyes to it; and your ears, and your heart as well! Then you'll soon hit on an idea! But before you go I want my spectacles and my ear-trumpet.' And she took them both back.

'Now I don't see a thing,' said the young man. 'I don't hear any more.'

'Then you'll never be a poet by Easter!' said the wise woman.

'Well then, when?' he asked.

'Neither by Easter nor by Whitsun! You'll never hit on any ideas!'

'Then what shall I do to get a living out of poetry?'

'You can do that by Shrovetide! Hit out at the poets! Hit out at their works; it's the same as hitting them. Don't be put off; let them have it good and hard, and you'll get all the cakes and ale you'll want, for yourself and your wife as well!'

'You've hit on the very idea!' said the young man. And he hit out at every other poet there was, now that he couldn't become one himself.

We got this from the old woman. She knows the idea.

THE FLEA AND THE PROFESSOR

THERE was a balloonist who came to grief: the balloon burst; the man tumbled down and dashed himself to pieces. Two minutes before this he had sent his boy down by parachute and for the boy it was a stroke of luck; he was unhurt and went about full of knowledge that would make him a balloonist, only he had no balloon and no means of getting one.

Live he must; and so he went in for conjuring tricks and for talking from the stomach; for ventriloquism, that is. He was a young man and good-looking, and when he had grown a moustache and dressed in good clothes anyone might have taken him for a young lord. The ladies thought him handsome; one young lady indeed took such a fancy to his elegance and conjuring that she accompanied him to foreign cities and countries, where he called himself professor—nothing less would do,

His constant idea was to get a balloon and go up with his little wife, but they still hadn't got the means.

'They'll come!' he said.

'If only they would!' she said.

'We're young yet! And now I'm a professor! Half a loaf's better than no bread.'

She was his loyal helper and would sit at the door selling tickets for the performance, which in winter was a cold pastime. She also helped in one of his tricks. He used to put her into a drawer, a big table drawer, and she would crawl into another drawer behind and was not to be seen in the front one; it was a vanishing trick.

But one evening when he pulled out the drawer she had vanished from him too. She was not in the front drawer, nor in the back drawer, nor in the whole house; nowhere in sight or in hearing. That was her conjuring trick. She never returned; she had grown sick of it. And he also grew sick, lost his good humour, and could no longer laugh and make fun, so that everyone stayed away. His earnings became poor and his clothes became poor; and all he possessed in the end was a big flea left to him by his wife, for which reason he was very fond of it. So he tamed it and taught it to perform tricks, such as presenting arms and firing a cannon—a small one.

The professor was proud of the flea and the flea was proud of itself, having learnt something and having human blood in its veins and been in the biggest cities and been seen by princes and princesses and won their great approval. It knew that it was a celebrity and could support a professor, indeed a whole family.

Proud it was and famous it was; and yet when it travelled with the professor they always went third class by rail, that being as fast as first. They had an unspoken agreement never to part and never to marry; the flea would remain a bachelor and the professor a widower. Fair's fair.

'Where you're most successful,' said the professor, 'you should never go twice!' He was a student of human nature, and there's knowledge in that.

In the end he had travelled every country except the land of the wild men; and so to the land of the wild men he meant to go. There indeed, as the professor knew, they eat Christian persons; but he wasn't a proper Christian and the flea wasn't a proper person, and so he thought they might safely go there and earn good money.

They travelled by steamship and by sailing-ship; the flea performed its tricks on the way and so they had free travel, and in time they got to the land of the wild men.

This was ruled by a little princess; only eight years old, but she ruled the roast. She had got the better of her father and mother, being self-willed and so very charming and mischievous.

The flea had no sooner presented arms and fired off the cannon that she took such a fancy to it that she said: 'Him or nobody!' She got absolutely wild with love; and wild, of course, she was to start with.

'My dear, sensible little child!' said her father. 'If only we could make a man of it first.'

'You leave that to me, old man!' she said; and it wasn't nice of a little princess to say that to her father, but then she was wild.

She placed the flea on her little hand.

'Now you're a man, ruling with me. But you must do as I tell you, or I'll kill you and eat the professor.'

The professor was given a large hall to live in. The walls were made of sugar-cane, which he could lick when he wanted to, though he hadn't got a sweet tooth. For sleeping in he had a hammock, and it felt like being in a balloon, the thing he had always wanted and that was his constant idea.

The flea stayed with the princess, sitting on her little hand and on her delicate neck. From her head she had taken a hair which the professor had to tie round the flea's leg, and she kept it tied to the large coral she wore in her ear.

What a lovely time it was for her and the flea, thought the princess. But the professor wasn't at all contented, for he was a traveller, who liked going from town to town and reading in the papers about his perseverance and skill in teaching a flea human behaviour. Day in and day out he would lie in his hammock, idling and getting well fed on fresh birds' eggs, elephants' eyes, and fried giraffe steaks; for cannibals don't live on human flesh alone—that's a delicacy. 'Shoulder of baby with sharp sauce is the nicest delicacy,' the princess's mother used to say.

The professor was bored, and anxious to get away from the land of the wild men; but the flea would have to go with him as that was his wonder and his livelihood. How was he to go about getting it? That wasn't so easy.

He strained every nerve of his brain, and then at last he said: 'I've got it!'

'Father of the princess,' he said, 'graciously allow me to do something! Permit me to teach the people of this country the art of presentation: what in the great countries of the world is called etiquette!'

'And what can you teach me?' asked the princess's father.

'My greatest art,' said the professor. 'To fire a cannon that will shake the earth and bring all the tastiest birds of the air roasted to the ground. It'll go with a bang!'

'Bring up the cannon!' said the princess's father.

But in all the land there was no cannon to be had, except the one brought by the flea, and that was too small.

'I'll cast a bigger one!' said the professor. 'Only give me the means! I want some fine silk material, a needle and thread, ropes and cords, and some sickness drops for balloons, which blow up light and airy and give the report in the cannon's stomach.'

He got everything he had asked for.

The whole country flocked to see the big cannon. The professor only called them when he had the balloon all ready to fill and ascend.

The flea sat watching on the princess's hand. The balloon was filled, swelled out, and could hardly be held, it was so wild.

'I shall have to get it in the air to cool off,' said the professor, stepping into the basket which hung below it. 'I shan't manage to steer it all by myself; I must have a skilled companion to help me. No one else here knows how to, except the flea!'

'I'm unwilling to allow it!' said the princess; but she passed the flea to the professor, who placed it on his hand.

'Let go the ropes and cords!' he cried. 'The balloon's going off.'

They thought he said 'cannon'!

And off went the balloon, higher and higher, up above the clouds, away from the land of the wild men.

The little princess, her father and mother, and all the people stood there waiting. They are waiting still; and if you don't believe it go to the land of the wild men, where every child talks of the flea and the professor and thinks they will come back again when the cannon has cooled off. But they won't come back again, for they are back home with us, back in their own country, travelling by rail, first class not third; earning big money with a large balloon. Nobody asks how they came to have the balloon or where they got it from; they are prosperous and respected people, the flea and the professor.

HANS CHRISTIAN ANDERSEN (1805–75) was born in Odense, Denmark, the son of a poor shoemaker, who nonetheless was a great reader, made a toy-theatre for his son and taught him to notice every natural wonder as they walked in the woods together on Sundays. His father died when he was eleven, and it wasn't until six years later that, with the help of a patron, he finally went to a state secondary school attended by much younger children. There he suffered at the hands of a cruel headmaster, but he acquired an education and was determined to be a writer. He published his first novel and his first fairy tales in 1835; thereafter he wrote over 150 more of these stories which have become classics in many languages.

A lonely man who never married, he was also an anxious man; he loved travelling, but would carry a coil of rope with him in case of fire in his hotel. Although he originally addressed his fairy tales to children (and some would maintain he had a streak of childhood in his nature) he insisted they were 'for all ages', and the gentleness and humour that are their characteristics are recognized by everyone.

William Heath Robinson (1872–1944) was the youngest of the three artist sons of a wood engraver. Born in Hornsey Rise, north London, he studied at Islington School of Art and briefly at the Royal Academy Schools. At first it seemed inevitable that his career as an illustrator would follow that of his brothers Thomas and Charles, but his unmistakable, humorous style showed itself in a story for children that he both wrote and illustrated, *Uncle Lubin*, published in 1902. He went on to develop this talent in comic cartoons for *The Strand Magazine* and other periodicals, devising in his drawings the weird contraptions that later gave his name to the English language for any mechanical device 'absurdly complicated in design and having a simple function'. At the Memorial Exhibition after his death, one of his few peers in humorous drawing, Nicolas Bentley, compared him to Leonardo da Vinci, claiming that Heath Robinson 'had the advantage of Leonardo, in that some of his inventions did at least *look* as if they might have worked'.

Heath Robinson illustrated three editions of the Andersen stories, the second in collaboration with his two brothers. It is the drawings for the third of these, first published in 1913, when he had become an established artist, that are reproduced here.